LIVING LIES

LIVING LIES

Jan Henley

Hodder & Stoughton

First published in Great Britain in 1996 by Hodder and Stoughton
A division of Hodder Headline PLC

10 9 8 7 6 5 4 3 2 1

A CIP Catalogue for this title is available from the British Library

ISBN 0 340 64716 7

Typeset by Avon Dataset Ltd, Bidford-on-Avon, Warks

Printed and bound in Great Britain by
Mackays of Chatham PLC, Chatham, Kent

Hodder and Stoughton
A division of Hodder Headline PLC
338 Euston Road
London NW1 3BH

For Keith

With apologies to my family for the many times they were denied my full attention, and grateful thanks to Keith, Mum and Dad, Juliet Weissberg, Wendy Tomlins, Pauline Bentley, Elizabeth Roy, and Carolyn Caughey at Hodder. And special thanks to Sheila and family who were responsible for my discovery of Purbeck.

'How Can I Lie To You' from *Just Give Me a Cool Drink of Water 'Fore I Diiie* by Maya Angelou is reprinted by kind permission of the publishers, Virago Press.

How Can I Lie to You

now thread my voice
with lies
of lightness
force within
my mirror eyes
the cold disguise
of sad and wise
decisions

Maya Angelou

('Just Give Me a Cool Drink of Water 'Fore I Diiie', p21.
Virago 1988.)

1

Christie Fifer gazed towards the ceiling. Part of her was up there, clinging to the Artex, looking down at the two bodies on the bed with a certain detachment. And part of her was indisputably here. Christie's husband Robin was doing his best to make love to her, and she wasn't enjoying it one bit.

It shouldn't be like this, she was thinking. It really shouldn't be like this.

Robin was up on his elbows, panting. 'You're beautiful . . . You're beautiful. God, you're beautiful.' As if such words could maintain what would soon be lost.

This was tearing her apart.

She arched slightly to accommodate him, wanting it to be over, not wanting him to even try. Because it was always the same. Night after night.

But what choice did she have? How else could she keep her marriage intact? And somehow she always half-hoped . . . maybe this time it would be different.

Sweat-beads glistened on Robin's dark face. But already he was wilting inside her. His eyes, deep-set and hooded, were distanced from the present, his thin lips mouthing the inevitable words of love. Poor Robin.

Love surely bore no relation to what was happening on this bed. She and Robin – the people they should have been – had become two animal bodies, one heaving, one passive. Christie was waiting, always waiting, it seemed. For something to change. For a feeling other than that of desperation.

She closed her eyes. Why did he have to go on? Where was the point of going on?

'I love you, Christie. God, I love you.' His voice was husky around the edges. It had attracted her once. Now it scratched on her surfaces, made her wince with irritation. And how she loathed that irritation, hated herself for doing this to him.

'Love you too,' she mumbled. Anything to make him stop. Yes, there was a place for lying. The guilt and regret might lurk like storm clouds above her. But there was always a place for lying, even for the honest.

Still he went on, going through the motions, hot, sticky and invasive inside her. She should search for the pleasure. She should nurture the excitement. But there *was* no excitement. How could there be, when her marriage was falling apart? Still, perversely, she allowed herself a brief flickering fantasy of oiled biceps on male bodies. But it was too exhausting to contemplate. It made her want to cry, not squirm. She was tired, so tired. Tired of having to pretend.

'Christie, Christie . . .' He seemed to need to say her name, over and over, as if it offered some security.

Should I leave, should I stay? Should I leave, should I stay? The words took on his rhythm as, ignoring his own limpness, he thrust a futile path onwards, out of her pleasure, out of her life, to that place he often went to – somewhere quite apart from her. She wasn't welcome there. Should I leave, should I stay?

There was no easy answer.

At last his pace faltered, and she felt him shrink still further inside her. Repulsed, needing to be free of the feel of him, unable to bear any more, she pulled away as he rolled towards the empty side of the bed. How could she treat him like this – the man she'd only ever wanted to love?

'What's the matter?' she heard her voice snapping. Cold, brittle, unwifely.

'I just can't.' His dark head bowed suddenly. Another brick in the wall.

This was the time. She should hold him close, reassure him that it didn't matter, that none of it mattered because she loved him. But she couldn't do it. She opened her mouth and the words wouldn't form. She had consoled him so many times – and still he wouldn't tell her what was wrong. Still he shut her out.

'Robin . . .'

'I don't want to talk about it.' His voice was unyielding, his face closed to her.

The anger swept over Christie, and she couldn't hide it. She'd hidden it too often before. Perhaps she'd come to the end of the line.

'Maybe you should see a doctor.' She paused. 'Since you won't talk to me.' She was his wife, wasn't she? And yet excluded from so much of him. 'They must be able to do something for . . .' She turned the knife. 'For impotence, mustn't they? There must be something you can do.'

You can do, not *we* can do. Had he noticed the unintentional slip?

Robin slammed a fist into the pillow. 'Jesus, Christie . . . Why do you have to keep *on*?'

'Because *I'm* frustrated too.' In one leap she was off the bed, grabbing a robe, running her fingers through spiky hair.

'Where are you going?' His words were muffled.

'To the bathroom.' Anywhere. She must leave the room before she started another row. It was like a madness in her, this compulsion to strike out, to damage. A madness that was a response to him, to the man she no longer knew.

'Don't go.' She knew he was demoralised and that it was probably her fault. Or didn't it even matter who was to blame?

'I have to get to work. It's after eight.' She almost ran from the room, away from the claustrophobia that seemed to lie, stagnant, between them. Resting her hands on the wash-basin, she took deep calming breaths. One, two, three. Should I go, or should I stay?

She blinked hard, suddenly scared, sure that it must show in her face. What was she doing to the man she'd married? What was he doing to her?

Frowning, Christie splashed water on her face, as if she could wash away the fear. She was twenty-four years old. As a child she had been accustomed to a secure, well-ordered life, shielded from worry. But now she was a married woman with her own gardening design business to run – a business she had fought for, a business that had given her an independence she cherished. This was 1990, when a woman had choices. And Christie had chosen her path. She must take responsibility in her stride, not drown in its muddy waters.

'Why do you have to work? I told you I was taking the morning off.' Robin had pulled on a shirt – perhaps not confident enough to be naked after this morning's fiasco – and the shirt-tails flapped around his lean thighs as he stood framed in the doorway.

Christie eyed him resentfully. He gave her no space. 'I know what you told me.' She buried her face in the towel. 'But I didn't say I could do the same. I've got too much work on. I really have.'

She looked up, registered the rare anger moving in his grey eyes.

'I assumed you'd take the time off too.' His voice was cold.

'Well, maybe you assumed wrong.' He hadn't asked, had he? Yet again, he'd implied that her work didn't matter. That she was playing at being a business woman.

She'd worked for it all right. But horticulture had always been both a pleasure and a passion, from the first walks she'd taken with Gramma in the Purbeck countryside as a child, learning about the wild flowers and vegetation scattered over cliffs, marshes and heathland. Gramma too had presented her with her own patch of garden, and carte blanche to grow whatever she pleased. Sunflowers, Christie remembered with a smile. Sunflowers that grew taller than she was, multi-coloured lupins that she guarded jealously from slugs and snails, and Wedgwood blue delphiniums – still her favourite flower. Yes, Gramma had encouraged her every step of the way, even helping her clear out the musty greenhouse one Sunday so that she could progress to Charentais melons and sweet cherry tomatoes. When the time came, Gramma had supported her through college too. Not financial support – that had come from her mother – Gramma had given a different kind of support. She had made Christie feel that she could do it. That she could set up her own business.

'Why not?' She remembered Gramma's laugh. 'You can do anything, Christie, if you're determined enough.'

'Do you think it will work?'

Gramma took her hands. 'You can make it work.'

Precious independence. Christie saw it in her grandmother's eyes and it had made her proud, knowing she felt it too. Yes, she'd thought, she could make it work.

It was early days, and yet already she *was* making it work.

Before they were married she had never expected Robin to be like this, to belittle her work at every opportunity.

'It wouldn't kill you to take some time off.'

Christie pushed past him, flinging off the robe and grabbing her clothes quickly as if Robin were likely to haul her naked protesting body down on the bed again.

'What have you got to do that can't wait?' He followed her back into the room, aggressive now, as he was never aggressive in bed.

There was an animal look about Robin, a kind of hooded tension in the way he held his narrow body, as if he too were waiting. But what could Robin be waiting for? She only knew that this hint of dark aggression had been part of the attraction for her throughout their whirlwind romance, part of an unspoken promise. A promise as yet unfulfilled.

'Some work for Gramma that's way overdue.' She dragged a faded, mauve T-shirt over her head.

He pulled a face. 'She's not a client.'

'She pays me.' Christie was defiant. She reached for the blue denim jeans that were standard attire for gardening. Without her business, they wouldn't have been able to afford the dishwasher, or last year's holiday in Greece. So Robin had no right to mock, no right to undermine her contribution.

'It's only one morning, Christie. We could relax, take it easy. Like we did in the old days . . .' His voice was persuasive. But had they really been together long enough to have old days? Two years two months was still the early days, wasn't it?

'It could be so-o-o nice,' Robin went on. 'Breakfast in bed, a couple of sleazy albums to listen to. Pretend there's nothing to get up for.'

For a moment she was drawn back, remembering when they'd first met, could have easy relaxed conversations, had nothing to prove, everything in their future.

But he moved closer, standing behind her, his hands on her shoulders, massaging tension, making tension, in their second contact of the morning. The first had been when he launched himself on top of her without preamble. Without preamble and yet with a strange reluctance that she often recognised now, as if sex was expected of him night after night, instead of being something he himself desired. He was wrong. It wasn't expected by Christie – she would rather avoid it completely than have to endure what they had both endured this morning.

'We could spend all morning in bed.' He grinned.

She pulled away, blinking hard. She mustn't cry now. A morning in bed wouldn't solve a thing. What they needed was to talk. 'How can I? I'm interviewing that chap at twelve for the labourer's position.'

Robin frowned. 'Where?'

'At Gramma's.' It had seemed important not to conduct her first proper interview in the small terraced house she shared with her husband in Ulwell. It seemed necessary to separate business from married life, and Gramma's was the obvious place. Only a bicycle ride away for Christie, it was a small cottage looking out over Studland Bay and backed by a yew grove. Old, old trees that flavoured the cottage itself and gave it a name. Yew Cottage was where Christie had spent a carefree childhood, and what's more, it still felt like home.

'How the hell can you justify employing someone?' Robin grumbled. 'You're not exactly making a fortune.'

'I need a man to take over some of the heavy work. I have to expand.' They had been through all this before and Christie was sick of it. It was the way forward. Businesses didn't stand still. If Purbeck Garden Designs was to succeed, it must grow. And Christie was determined that it would succeed. Advertising and word of mouth would spread her reputation. Because she was good at what she did – she knew it – and she wouldn't let Robin persuade her otherwise.

'Maybe you should forget expansion,' he suggested. 'Maybe you should consider something else . . .'

'Like being a housewife?' she shot at him.

Robin shrugged. 'I don't reckon this gardening lark is going to work out. That's all.'

'I like it. It's my work. It's what I do.' More than that, she loved it. She couldn't imagine doing anything else. Wouldn't imagine doing anything else.

'There are other jobs.'

She stared at him. His aggression was gone, but the pomposity replacing it was worse. It's no job for a woman, that's what he was telling her. No job for his wife. That's what her husband, the dedicated new man he'd always pretended to be, was telling her. He'd rather have her at home fetching him cups of coffee and dainty sandwiches every five minutes. Or working in an office somewhere, shut up in a tiny room tapping away at a word processor all day. Christie shuddered at the thought.

'It's how we met.'

'Aw, Christie . . .' He was about to apologise, say he hadn't meant it, she could tell. And she didn't want to hear those words. Sometimes she didn't even believe them. Wondered if Robin had always been too good to be true. If she'd misunderstood him right from the start.

'I'll make some tea.' She ran down the stairs, half-angry, half-sad. They should talk, really talk. She should insist they saw a doctor. *If I loved him.* The words stopped her in her tracks. What was the point of pretending? What was the point, if she didn't love him?

Should I leave or should I stay . . . ?

And yet there were times that still held hope. Times when Christie ignored that small elusive something that had always been missing from her life. That corner piece to make the rest of the image fall neatly into place. Wasn't it possible? To dismiss the vague dissatisfaction always lurking in every background to every day?

The steaming kettle shook her back to the present. She glanced at her watch, dropped in tea bags and hurriedly made two cups.

'There you go.' She put the cup down beside him and kissed the top of his dark head.

He was sitting gloomily in front of his computer – Robin had squeezed three PCs into their small house. In front of the little screen that Christie loathed, he came alive, bonded to the PC in a way that he had not managed with his wife. Could she possibly be jealous of a computer?

She sighed. 'I was mean to you. I'm sorry.'

'It doesn't matter.' His shoulders were hunched. Already he was launched into the safe and predictable PC world where emotions didn't exist and there would never be tears.

'It matters to me. We should talk about it. We really should. Maybe tonight . . .' As she spoke, Christie turned to straighten the duvet automatically, drawing back as her hands touched something wet and sticky. 'What on earth . . . ?'

He didn't even look round.

Christie stood upright, her mouth twisting with distaste. She moved behind him, put her face close to his. 'At least have the decency to clear up your own mess,' she hissed.

That made him take notice. He swung round, a blush creeping to his neck, as he swallowed the pain in her eyes. 'Sorry.'

She'd had enough. 'I'm going.' A few long strides and she was out of the marital bedroom. Marital bedroom, that was a laugh. He must have done it while the blank face of his computer looked on in admiration. He was more married to the voyeur in their bedroom than to his own wife. Nothing to fear from the PC. No emotion. No comment.

My God. Was it her then? Was it all her fault that her impotent husband was potent enough to have an orgasm when she wasn't there – in the few lonely minutes that it took for the kettle to boil?

She shuddered.

* * *

7

Minutes later, Christie was pedalling furiously along the road that led to Studland village. When she found the right man to help her with the backbreaking part of the landscaping business, she decided, he could drive the pick-up truck, and she would travel like this – in the way she relished. Wind streaking past her T-shirt and body-warmer, funnelling her spiky hair from her scalp like a demented blow-drier. Breath coming fast, heart pumping, legs working her up the hills, skeetering down the gentle slopes that made up the Purbeck countryside she loved.

The Isle of Purbeck was like a separate miniature of Britain itself. This part of Dorset had everything – heathland, beaches, cliffs and meadows. And Christie loved it. She wouldn't want to live anywhere else.

The winding road dipped into the village, past the inn cloaked in Virginia creeper and the path down to Old Harry Rock. She cycled on, beyond the lane leading up to the church on the hill, and then through to Yew Cottage.

A quick glance around showed her that Gramma's Landrover was absent, so instead of going into the cottage, Christie propped her bike against the grey Purbeck stone, and ran down the path to the yew grove beyond.

She sighed with pleasure as she leaned heavily against the twisted, aged bark. The sombre beauty of the yew grove always calmed her. It was her escape, her haven. The broad canopy of the spreading branches hid the world beyond – it was hard even to know what kind of weather lay above the dense, protecting arms of the old yews. And right now Christie didn't need to know. She closed her eyes. All she could think about was Robin.

Robin Fifer had been her second client and she was immediately impressed by him. It was refreshing that he hadn't expected a man to head 'Purbeck Garden Designs' – he hardly batted an eyelid when Christie appeared dressed in regulation jeans and T-shirt, armed only with an outsize sketch pad and a pencil.

'Hi.' He was a few years older than her, she guessed. And he had a lovely smile.

Most people eyed the small, slim figure doubtfully. *She's just a slip of a girl.* It was written in their eyes if not spoken. But Robin was different.

'I can't decide whether to re-design the garden or just clear the lot and have crazy paving,' he admitted.

She laughed. 'It could be an investment for the future. Nice gardens sell houses.' After all, wasn't it part of her job – encouraging people to see their gardens in a different light? And as for crazy paving . . . 'There are more interesting options,' Christie smiled.

'Such as?' His eyes were encouraging – and something else besides.

'I thought a meandering path, and curving beds here.' She pointed with her pencil on the rough plan. 'Curves are easy on the eye and they'll make the garden seem wider.'

'Hmm.' He bent closer, and she became aware of a woody fragrance that reminded her of the yew grove itself.

'And they lead the eye through to the main focal point.'

'Which is . . . ?' His gaze was questioning.

'The pond.' She indicated the spot. 'I can do a low-maintenance garden with lots of trees and shrubs. But it still needs a focal point. A pond with a maple here . . . it would be lovely.'

'I'm sure it would.' He folded his arms. 'And how much would this garden made in paradise actually cost me?'

Christie grinned once more, made some rapid mental calculations, and quoted a low price because she needed the work. The job was appealing – and so was the client, she had to confess.

He eyed her thoughtfully, another smile twitching at his mouth. 'You've convinced me. It's all yours.'

That July, Christie employed the temporary labour of a couple of students to help her get the garden into shape. She battled with the jungle of weeds and nettles that made up Robin's garden by day, and she battled with Barry's demands by night.

Barry was the kind of good-looking man who possessed the confidence and strength to draw her. But she wasn't sure how far she was willing to be drawn, and up till now she had resisted the undeniable physical attraction. Christie recognised her own sexual needs, but sex with Barry lacked long-term appeal. Her life would be all fight with Barry, one way or another, and Christie was beginning to realise that brute strength was not the kind of strength she was looking for.

Robin Fifer was different.

She and Robin had civilised conversations that metamorphosed into hot debates – almost every time he brought her out a cup of tea, which he did often. She began to listen for the click and slide of the patio door, to watch for his long, lean shadow. They talked so much that the work was in danger of never being completed. But Robin didn't seem to care, and neither did Christie. She was fascinated by him. He cared about the

9

environment, feminism and art. Yes, he was attractive, but he was clever too.

He did much of his computer programming work at home, and she watched him sometimes through the patio doors, a dark and intense figure, poring over his PC. The fingers that touched the keys were gentle, sensitive fingers. The eyes that surveyed the screen were calm and grey. But all that was on the outside. What was on the inside? Did the kindness go right through? Was she only imagining those hints that betrayed the intensity of the man? And the pure, unbridled passion – the sort of passion that was worth waiting for?

One day Barry insisted on picking her up for lunch. He sat astride his motorbike, all leathers and machismo, revving it up. Christie had always loved bikes, especially this kind, for the marvellous sense of freedom they provided. There was nothing quite like speeding on the back of a bike down a country lane, wind in your hair, your body alive with a kind of throbbing excitement, and the scent of leather deep deep in your nostrils. Perhaps that had been her undoing.

'C'mon, baby . . .' he yelled. 'Get a move on or there'll be no grub left.'

Christie winced with embarrassment. She saw Robin glance through the front window, his wave and smile stopping in mid-flow. This was a mistake.

And it got worse. The pub was full of tourists and Barry had to queue for beer. He blamed Christie.

'You're bloody rooted to that garden, you are.'

She shrugged, indifferent to his anger. Becoming indifferent to Barry now that she was getting to know him better. 'There's a lot to do.'

'As long as it's not him you're doing.' Barry too must have seen the wave and read the smile. He pointed a big, grease-stained finger, his dark eyebrows squeezing into a caterpillar of rage.

'What the hell do you mean?' Christie rose to her feet, face flushed in fury. But at the same time she realised what Barry had already instinctively realised. Yes, she found Robin attractive. Yes, the hands that brushed against her own as he brought her cups of tea in the garden, were tender hands. Sometimes she found herself closing her eyes to savour the spindles of electricity that charged through her as they pored over her design plans for his garden together. And there was more – much more – beyond the physical. Yes, she was moving on.

'You know damn well,' he growled.

'He's a client.' Her blue eyes glinted with cool arrogance, her only weapon against this man. Barry had good looks and a certain swaggering charm. But that was not enough. The man had no soul.

'He fancies his chances.'

Their eyes locked in battle. People were staring but Christie didn't care. She felt only a shaft of triumph that they were against each other rather than on the same side. So it was a victory, whether she won this particular battle or not.

'Are you taking me back to Ulwell?' She hated having to ask, but it was two miles to walk, and she was already late.

'Take a bloody hike.' He turned away from her, his fingers zipping his black leather jacket.

Christie grabbed her bag. 'My feelings entirely.' She swept out of the pub.

It was a great exit line, although not quite so satisfying when she was plodding back down the country lane towards Robin's house. But what the heck – at least she'd see no more of Barry.

'Everything okay?' Robin's grey eyes were curious as she slipped in by the garden gate. He'd been waiting for her, she realised.

She smiled, conscious of an odd shyness with him now that she was free. 'Men like Barry don't enjoy taking no for an answer,' she told him.

His nod was understanding. With this man, she realised, she wouldn't always have to spell it out. And after Barry's obsession with his ego, that was sweet relief indeed.

'Well, if you're free later, I'm cooking Chinese,' he said. 'And you're welcome to join me.'

She meant to say no, she really did. The last thing she intended was to leap from one man to another, however attractive she might find the world of Robin Fifer. She was independent. She was strong. Whatever was missing from her life she would provide it herself.

But as the early evening sun began touching the distant ridge of the Purbeck Hills with red and gold filaments of light, and as the assorted fragrances of sesame oil, chillies and black bean sauce wafted through the open kitchen window, she knew she couldn't resist. Christie loved good food. She tried to tell herself that was all it was, but of course she wasn't being honest. There was a warm excitement drumming through her veins that had nothing to do with food. This, she knew, was a man in a million.

For Christie, the evening was tense with unspoken sexuality. It was there in the intensity of Robin's expression as he watched her, in the brooding lines of his mouth as they talked. But he made no move towards her that night, and in a strange way, she was glad. Men took sex for granted in a casual manner that irritated her. This man was different.

Their romance was just that – a gradual blossoming that was poetry rather than passion. And it wasn't until Christie found herself choosing her own favourite clematis and fragrant white roses to climb the trellises and walls of Robin's garden, that she realised she was making it her own.

When the garden was finished, there was a sense of an era ending. Robin had hardly kissed her. A brush of the lips on the cheek goodnight wasn't enough to build a relationship on. She knew there would have to be more. Could she have been mistaken? Was this relationship doomed to remain one of friendship alone?

They stood on the tiny patio as dusk fell. It was a new-born garden they were looking at. Beyond the garden lay Swanage and the sea. Behind them was the ridge of Purbeck Hills.

'It's only a beginning,' she said. 'It'll take a few seasons for the plants to get established.'

Robin bent towards her. 'Will you marry me and watch it happen?'

She blinked furiously. Marry him? She hardly knew him. And yet she knew him a whole lot better than she'd ever know the Barrys of this world. She had talked to Robin more than she had talked with any other man. She was drawn to him in a way that was both bewildering and irresistible. And as for the passion – wouldn't she enjoy seeing that develop between them too?

'I know it's a bit sudden.' He was talking quickly, as if reluctant to hear her reply. 'You probably think I'm crazy. But . . .'

She flung her arms around his neck, flooded by that wild irresistible sense of freedom that might have been her undoing once before. 'Who cares if you're crazy? Let's both be crazy. Let's do it.'

His grey eyes locked on to hers, confused and caring. And then his lips were close, so close. A kiss crammed with promises. New-born garden. New-born love.

There seemed to be a faint whispering in the yew wood that snapped her away from memory. Nostalgia was a dangerous kind of comfort. And yet the macabre atmosphere that lay quiet and still in this small wood always pulled her back to the past. But what was the point of nostalgia, when her problems were here and now, in the present? With the Robin who was now her husband – not with the man she'd first known.

She had promised to love him for better for worse. But the fecundity of the garden she'd created for him only mocked them now. The white roses with the heady perfume that drifted heavy on the air on warm summer evenings, the virginal clematis, the water lilies glinting in the pond on hot days like sun-worshippers on leafy rafts.

She'd known nothing in those early days of his past, of whatever made it impossible to get through to Robin's other world. The world where he was, perhaps, the man that Christie could still love.

'Excuse me.'

Christie almost jumped out of her skin as a male voice jolted her forcefully back to the present.

'Who the hell are you?' She tensed, ready to run. He didn't look like a homicidal maniac. He was younger than she, with floppy blond hair and pale blue eyes. But he was a big man. She'd be powerless against him. And didn't they say that perverts always looked normal? She took a step backwards.

'Trevor Swift.' He held out his hand.

She stared at the huge hand for a moment without absorbing the name.

'You are from Purbeck Garden Designs? The woman in the house said I'd find you here.' He pointed back towards Yew Cottage, and it all fell into place for Christie. She'd completely lost track of time.

She sighed. 'I do apologise. I'm Christie Fifer.' Briskly, she shook his hand. But this wasn't exactly how she'd envisaged conducting her first interview.

'Have you had any experience?' She led the way down the path. The sooner she got him out of the wood, the happier she'd be.

His blue eyes met hers, questioning and amused.

'Gardening experience.' Her mouth pursed into a thin line. A joker – that's all she needed.

He shook his head. 'But I'm willing to learn.'

'Can you drive?' She rubbed clammy hands on her jeans. He appeared harmless enough but she still felt nervous of this young giant.

He nodded.

'Because I shall want you to drive the pick-up,' she explained.

He nodded again. He was certainly the strong, silent type.

She stared at the big hands swinging by his side. 'Are you married?'

'Is that relevant?' He looked her square in the face and she glanced away quickly, feeling the tell-tale flush stain her skin.

'No. No of course not.' She forced a smile. 'I was just curious.'

At last they emerged from the wood and Christie breathed a sigh of relief. She turned to him. 'I want someone to take over the heavy work. Digging. Lugging around wheelbarrows and paving stones. Do you think you'd be up to it?'

Before she knew what he was doing, he bent, grabbed her round the waist and lifted her high in the air. She was too startled to protest.

'What do you think?' he grinned.

Perhaps it had been a stupid question. She looked down into his face. He was tall, he was strong, and he was extremely good-looking. He didn't talk too much and he had a sense of humour.

God help her.

'I think you'd better put me down,' she said, attempting to summon some dignity.

He did so.

'And you'd better forget about pulling any more stunts like that one.' She ran her fingers lightly through her hair. 'If I'm going to be your boss.'

2

That afternoon, rain drove Christie from the garden into the workshop adjacent to Yew Cottage where her grandmother was doing some wood sculpture.

Isobel Vaughan looked up. She was a small vital woman who always wore overalls in her workshop, her long charcoal-coloured hair plaited to her waist.

On impulse, Christie ran to kiss her.

'Hello, my dear.' Isobel's brown eyes were vague. 'Have you finished already?'

Christie laughed. 'You know I haven't. I was stopped by the rain.' She ran a finger lightly through the sawdust on the workbench, tracing the pattern of a flower.

'Once upon a time I would have slapped your wrist and told you you'd get splinters.' Isobel Vaughan's fingers moved deftly over the smooth grain of the wood, her dark eyes darting constantly from the piece itself back to her preliminary sketches. Her eyes might be fading a little these days, but still at seventy-one, Gramma possessed an enthusiasm for life that never seemed to fade.

'An old softy like you?' Christie teased. 'You'd never have dared.'

'Maybe you weren't always under my feet in those days.' She shot her a sharp glance.

Christie wasn't fooled. She knew she was always welcome at Yew Cottage, and she also knew that this was her grandmother's way of making a point. It was true that she spent a lot of time here. Too much time, some might say, for a woman with a husband at home.

'That's not how I remember it.' Christie's voice was low. Being here in her grandmother's workshop, watching her sculpt – create wonderful living images from wood – was one of her most precious childhood memories. She had tried never to disturb her; it was enough to watch the absorption on Gramma's face, to follow the swift movement of her fingers wielding the tools, to savour the silent companionship.

'But you're not a child any more,' Isobel reminded her. 'The rain's set in. Why don't you go home?'

'Trying to get rid of me?' Restlessly, Christie wandered to the end of the workshop.

'You know me better than that, my dear.' Isobel paused. 'What's wrong?'

'Nothing.' The denial came automatically. It was tempting to confide in this woman who'd brought her up, whom she'd always felt so close to. But how could she, when she hadn't talked it out with Robin first?

Isobel shrugged. 'As you like.' She selected first a file and then a chisel to shape and mould the form she was searching for.

There was no malice in her. And yet Christie knew that Gramma had experienced more than her fair share of pain. Even now, she had her own brand of suffering to live with. Apart from his disabilities, life with Vincent Pascoe couldn't be easy. But she would come through. She always had before.

'Why is life so complicated for women?' Christie hardly expected an answer. But the interview with Trevor Swift had unnerved her more than she cared to admit.

Isobel looked up in surprise. 'It's a legacy.' She pared away some thin shavings of wood with the chisel, blowing them from the arching shape destined to be that of a dolphin. 'A legacy of our past.'

'Past subordination to men?' Christie grinned. They'd had this kind of conversation before. They might not be militant feminists, but they both believed there was room for change.

Isobel nodded. 'Perhaps. Male dominance. Patriarchy . . .'

'The delicate male ego . . .' Christie laughed. Lucky that Robin couldn't hear her now. The laughter caught in her throat, and once more her grandmother's eyes were upon her, as if searching for the truth.

'Is it bad?'

'I'm not sure.' Christie looked away, beyond her, into the rain battering at the workshop window. She felt stifled, trapped by her marriage in a way that she knew wasn't right. 'I can't think straight.' She pressed her fingertips into her temples.

'Stay here if you'd like to.'

'Really?' Christie's heart did a flick of a somersault. Relief, she realised. Relief at the prospect of not going home.

'Of course.' Isobel smiled. 'Yew Cottage is always your home – for as long as you need it.'

Home. Yes, it still was her home. In some ways she had never left Yew Cottage. It pulled her now as if the attachment had grown only stronger with marriage, with her leaving the home of her childhood where her sense of security had been disturbed only by visits from the remote beautiful lady she called Mother. The lady who told her strange haunting stories from another time and place. Who sang to her. Who seemed to belong on a different plane from the ordinary mortals who made up Christie's world. Home. It was too tempting to resist.

'I'll phone Robin.' She darted off.

From the study she could hear Vincent's reedy and plaintive voice as he talked into the microphone of his tape recorder. Poor Gramma. Poor Vincent. But the thought remained a fleeting one.

She dialled the number and told Robin quickly, before he could raise objections.

'But tomorrow's Saturday.'

'So?'

'So I thought we could do something . . . together.'

The silence lay heavy between them.

'I'm seeing Fran tomorrow lunch-time,' she said at last. 'We arranged it ages ago. I'm sorry.' She didn't feel sorry. She felt only relieved. The events of this morning had somehow built more of a barrier between them.

'What about later? The afternoon? The evening?'

'I don't know.' Christie paused. 'We may go and see a film or something.'

'You and Fran?' He sounded jealous.

'Well, why not?' It was an appealing thought. Fran could always cheer her up and help her regain perspective. 'You don't mind, do you?' After all, he usually spent Saturdays hunched over the PC.

No answer.

She sighed. 'Just because we're married we don't have to live in each other's pockets. We always said we'd never do that.'

'Are we still married?'

Christie gripped the receiver more tightly. 'What are you talking about?'

17

'It's beginning to sound like this is some sort of separation.' His voice rose.

'Of course it's not.' And yet . . . and yet . . . *Should I go, or should I stay?* The words resounded in her head as if they were making love again, as if he were flailing against her with some pretence of potency, on and on, his very desperation grinding her into nothing but body and no entry signs.

'Christie?'

'It's not a separation.' She took a deep breath. 'I need a bit of space, that's all.' She waited. 'Can I have it?'

Silence. And then, 'Of course.' His voice was clipped and cool.

She tried to imagine his dark head bowing low, his brooding eyes. 'I'll be back soon,' she told them both. 'I promise.'

'And then we'll talk.' His words rang decisively in her ears. But would they? Would they really?

'Yes. Then we'll talk.' She put down the phone.

Christie turned around and Gramma was there, familiar and comforting as always. 'Oh, Gramma . . .'

Isobel held out her arms.

Christie sank into them gratefully, buried her head in the warm breast. No need to explain to Gramma. She would offer comfort but she would never ask for anything in return.

Despite being six years her junior, Fran Cassidy had become a close friend over the past two years, ever since Christie had first found her sobbing her heart out in the church at Wareham. Christie had gone there to look at the remains of the mediaeval frescos in the church. And to think. She and Robin were newly married, Christie's life had changed in a way she hadn't really expected. And then she'd seen Fran.

'What is it?' She moved closer to the thin figure curled up on the pew, unable to just pretend she wasn't there. 'Is there anything . . . anything I can do?'

The red-haired teenager shook her head vehemently, but the sobbing subsided just a little.

'Do you want me to go away?' Christie sat down next to her, some inner voice telling her that the girl needed company.

Huge green eyes, wet with crying, peered through the splayed fingers. She sniffed, shook her head once more.

They sat in a silence punctured only by the sounds of tears, until two American tourists entered the church, their footsteps loud on the flagstones, their voices abrasive in the hushed sanctuary of the old stone building.

'Say, this is a real cute church,' the larger one brayed.

The girl winced, caught Christie's gaze and simultaneously they grinned.

'Let's get out of here,' Christie whispered.

Once in the churchyard, the girl whipped a pair of designer sunglasses out of her pocket and put them on. 'God save me from loud American tourists.'

Christie smiled, knowing she was acting tough. She was about sixteen, she guessed, tall, awkward and at odds with her own physique. Her red hair was tangled around her blotchy face, and yet there was a touch of class about her, in her manner and in the cut of the clothes she wore.

'Do you want to talk about it?'

The girl shrugged. 'My mother died.' She swung around and began walking among the gravestones, veering from the path.

'Your mother?' Christie was paralysed by her own tactlessness. 'I'm so sorry. I didn't realise.' Maybe she should have allowed this girl to grieve in peace.

The girl's thin body stiffened. 'But I hated her. God, I hated her.' She slammed her fist against a marble slab. 'Does that make me a prize bitch? What do you think – whoever you are?'

'Christie Fifer.' Christie thought of her own mother. She hardly knew her. And then she thought of Robin. She couldn't make love with him without wishing he were different. And she'd married him less than a month ago. Did that make her a prize bitch too?

'Nope.' She shook her head. 'I expect you've got your reasons.'

'They don't think so.'

'They?'

'The relatives. Fawning over my stepfather. Fawning over me. Refusing to tell me what's going on, treating me like a kid.' Her narrow breasts were heaving under the skintight sweater she wore.

'But you're not a kid.' Christie spoke softly. She thought of her mother's last visit to Purbeck. Whispering to Gramma. '*I won't tell her – not yet. She's just a child.*' Well, the child had grown. The child was a woman, a married woman. And her mother was still a stranger.

19

'You're right. I'm not.' The girl seemed to draw strength from this assertion.

Christie touched her arm. 'So who are you?'

'Francesca Cassidy. Fran. My mother was . . .'

'Amy Cassidy.' It was all becoming clearer to Christie now. She had read about it, of course – the most dramatic thing that had ever happened in Purbeck. The actress Amy Cassidy had committed suicide, leaving behind her second husband. And this girl.

She nodded. 'Just because I was crying back there . . .' She hesitated, rubbing her knuckles ruefully. ' . . . Doesn't mean I care.'

'No. No, of course not.' Christie felt inexplicably drawn to this motherless girl who was so determined to feel hatred rather than love.

She had come into this church today thinking of Robin. Robin's gentle hands, Robin's pale skin, the intensity of his eyes. The frisson of excitement that ran through her when skin touched skin. Still only a spark. Because the spark had never been truly ignited.

Robin held her every night. He held her and he kissed her, not with passion but with the strange detachment that was part of him, almost an other-worldliness, as if Robin, the man she'd married, wasn't part of this physical creature who came to her every night. He came to her, but he never claimed her as his own. He never reached that part of her that was waiting for him. Still waiting. And already she was thinking . . . would he ever? So much tenderness. Wasted, wasted tenderness.

But she left the church thinking of Fran Cassidy. Fran would distract her, already she seemed a friend. Already there was a bond between them, like a sisterhood. Us against those who would have us different, she thought. Us against those who would deny us the right to know the truth.

Since that time, their friendship had developed. In Fran, Christie found the light-hearted part of herself, the youth that she'd never really wallowed in. The part of her that could turn round and say: to hell with it. Devil-may-care rebellion. That's what she got from Fran, and what she gave in return she gave willingly. Fran had changed from the gangly sixteen-year-old who was fed up with being treated as a child, who was determined to be brave and tough at all costs. She seemed to have her life well under control. But Christie had seen her vulnerability. Maybe she knew better.

Since her mother's death, Fran had continued to live with her stepfather Dominic in the elegant modern house he had bought for Amy only a year before her death, on the outskirts of Wareham.

Her tall slender figure moved swiftly around the kitchen as she assembled salad, quiche and pâté on a tray to take outside.

She turned to face Christie, hands on hips. 'So what's he like, this new man?'

'New man?' Christie's mind was fixed on women's emancipation.

'The gardener.' Fran smoothed her skimpy, striped vest top over the curves of her breasts. 'It's a bit like Lady Chatterley, isn't it?' She giggled. 'His name isn't Mellors, by any chance?'

'No, it's not.' Christie laughed. 'And I'm not Lady Chatterley by any stretch of the imagination.'

'Oh, I don't know . . .' She grinned. 'Tell me all about him. Is he wickedly gorgeous, or just your average hunky cave man?' Standing in front of the mirror, Fran smoothed her sleek, auburn hair from her narrow face. She put it up with one hand and surveyed her reflection critically. 'And when can I meet him?'

'Whenever you like.' Christie watched her. 'But you wouldn't be interested.'

'Is he tall?'

Christie smiled. 'About six four.'

Fran raised one eyebrow. 'Is he good-looking?'

Christie shrugged. 'It depends on your point of view.'

'Married?'

'Nope. As his employer, I can now vouch for that.'

'Say no more, darling.' Fran spread her hands. 'I rest my case.'

'You're incorrigible.'

'So you've always told me.' Fran grabbed the tray and led the way through the conservatory, tastefully furnished with bamboo and wicker, and lush with huge palms and figs.

Christie followed her out on to the brick-paved patio. The thought of Trevor Swift wasn't an entirely comfortable one. She wasn't even sure that she should have employed him at all. Her marriage was too unsteady, she was too vulnerable.

'Now I know why you went into the gardening business.' Fran's light green eyes were cool and amused. 'Because of all those lovely muscle-bound men you can get to work for you. Lady Christie Chatterley lifts a finger and they run to do her every bidding.' She giggled.

Christie raised her eyebrows. 'Very funny.'

'What's up?' Fran's expression changed. 'Has he got to you, this gardener of yours?'

'No. It's not Trevor.' Christie sat down at the wooden table, took some French bread and buttered it thoughtfully.

'It must be Robin, then. It has to be a man. What else is there?' Fran sat down next to her. 'Come on – out with it.'

Christie fought back the sudden rush of emotion. The futility of a love that had never fulfilled its promises, even the decision she'd been wrestling with.

In seconds Fran's arms were round her shoulders. 'What is it? He hasn't been seeing someone else, has he?'

'Robin?' Christie's hysterical laughter was mixed with indignation. 'You're joking. Do you really imagine that Robin . . . ?' Words failed her. She stared at Fran in disbelief. Was that the impression that Robin gave? Was that how Fran saw him?

Fran's eyes narrowed in consideration. 'Well, why not? He's rather wonderful, that husband of yours.'

Christie shook her head. 'He's not the type.'

'Every man is the type, darling. Even I know that much.' She tossed back her hair.

'Not Robin.' That was one thing she was sure of, although Fran didn't look convinced.

'Does he know how much you appreciate his loyalty?' Her tone was dry.

Christie nodded, unable to repress a small smile. She did know his virtues – that was half the trouble. How could you leave someone when they hadn't put a foot wrong?

'What is it then?'

'We've been having some problems . . .' Christie was reluctant to elaborate. So many times she had been tempted to confide in Fran. She sensed that she would understand . . .

'Not the gardener?' Fran's eyebrows hit the ragged red fringe.

'No, not the gardener. Forget the blasted gardener.' Christie had to laugh. Fran was outrageous, but she also had a way of putting things into perspective. That was part of her charm. 'I'm not happy,' she confided at last. 'We're not happy.'

'In bed?' Fran bit hungrily into a thick slice of cucumber.

'And the rest.' Christie sat back to survey the view. She still didn't want to say too much. Fran had become a close friend, more like a sister in some ways. She benefited from her refusal to take life too seriously, but there were boundaries. To discuss Robin's sexual problems with Fran seemed a betrayal.

In the distance stood the high pines of Wareham Forest. And in front of the fencing, the sloping garden itself had been cleverly landscaped, and layered with the spring quilts of daffodils, narcissus and crocuses. The magnolias were still in flower, the patio was fringed with purple and white tulips, and camellias and forsythia climbed the walls and fences. To the right of where they were sitting, beyond a row of conifers, was a secluded area which Christie knew housed the pool and cabana.

She stretched her arms up towards the sky as if the warm spring sun might provide some clue. 'Sometimes there seems so little left between us,' she confessed. 'I don't know what makes him tick. He can't open up. He won't tell me what's wrong. I can't stop myself being mean to him. In fact, our entire marriage seems a bit of a farce.'

'You're bored.' Fran spread some pâté on to her bread. 'That's what it is. You're bored out of your mind.'

'No, I'm not.' But there was an element of truth in Fran's statement. Christie was unwilling to admit it, but the man who had seemed to be offering her so much had failed to deliver what she needed. All those head-to-head discussions of the early days had meant a lot. A man you could talk to about any subject in the world must be precious. And a man who understood was unique.

But in the end they were only words – and words didn't move her. The words, it seemed, had all been spoken. These days Robin talked more to his computers than he did to her. And what was the point of having a man who pretended to be liberated in every way, if he couldn't make your heart move? If there was no current of excitement between you? If he couldn't even let you love him?

No, it wasn't boredom. But yes, she needed something more.

'He's a great cook,' Fran commented.

Christie laughed. 'I know.' These days she left most of the cooking to Robin.

'And he's not a chauvinist.'

'Very true.' She wouldn't dispute the importance of that.

'He's supported your career.' Fran stretched out long legs encased in tight red leggings.

23

'Hmm.' Christie selected some grapes from the bowl on the side. She'd always thought so, but that was a little more dubious after yesterday morning's conversation.

'And he never even goes out drinking with the lads.'

'Are you counsel for the defence?' Christie sucked the blue-black globe of fruit with obvious pleasure.

Fran spread out her hands. 'Well, what more do you want?'

That was the big question. And Christie wasn't entirely sure of the answer. 'I know his good points,' she said at last. 'But it's not enough. We seem to be tearing each other to pieces, and I don't want that. If there's nothing left between us, isn't it just living out some sort of lie to stay together? Wouldn't it be better to split and be done with it?'

'Some people don't find it so easy,' Fran drawled lazily. 'My parents stayed together for five years of bickering – not to mention Father's womanising – before Mother finally met Dominic and swept him away.'

'Five years of bickering?' That was something she couldn't contemplate. Sometimes two years seemed like an eternity.

Christie got to her feet and wandered on to the pristine lawn. She herself had never even known the identity of her father, and it was hard to forgive her mother for that. Maybe there was a valid reason. Maybe the stranger-mother she hardly knew had had some reason for dumping Christie on Gramma all those years ago. But if she did, why hadn't she ever told her? Didn't she owe Christie at least that much?

She had been brought up by women. Gramma, most of the time, with bits of her mother thrown in for good measure. The odd visit when she could spare the time . . . The thought jarred painfully.

'It's different when children are involved.' Fran's voice became softer as she joined Christie by the bright forsythia. 'It's even harder to make the break.'

All the more reason for leaving now, while there were no children to complicate the decision. Or was she just looking for excuses? Christie had a business to run and children didn't come into the equation – at least not yet. But she sensed that Fran was thinking of her own past, and she didn't want to interrupt that. At least she herself had a mother and a grandmother. Fran's father never came near her, so both parents were lost to her now.

'Was your mother happy with Dominic?' she asked, thinking of Amy's suicide. What could drive you to that? Her own problems were insignificant in comparison.

24

Fran's laugh was cynical. 'You could put it like that. He was obsessed with her from the moment he laid eyes on her. He worshipped her. Sometimes I wonder if he still does.'

'Do you mind?' She would have thought it was some comfort to be living with a man who respected your mother's memory. And yet – hadn't Fran admitted to her that she hated her mother? A hatred born of resentment, no doubt, but hatred nevertheless. It did seem rather odd to Christie that they shared this house, now that Fran was eighteen, with enough money to be as independent as she chose.

'He's not here very much,' Fran told her. 'And when he is, he keeps himself to himself. He's got a flat above the office where he stays during the week.'

'Don't you get lonely?' Christie looked back at the white facade of the house behind them. It was a beautiful place, but impossible to imagine as a home. 'Rattling around here on your own?'

'Not on your life.' A sudden grin lit up Fran's sharp features. 'Don't say a word to a soul . . . But I'm thinking of making part of it into a refuge.'

Christie stared at her. Fran's stuttering enthusiasm for good causes was legendary, and Christie knew that she had recently done some counselling training, but she'd never gone this far before. 'A refuge? Who for?'

'Battered women. Single mothers with nowhere else to go. Whoever needs a place. It seems criminal to have all this space going begging when it could do so much good. The nearest centre is Poole, and I hear that it's overflowing with applicants.' Fran sounded sincere enough – and Christie couldn't doubt her intentions – yet there was another less easily identifiable expression on her face.

'Does Dominic know?' Christie knew this to be his house, not Fran's.

Her voice dropped to a whisper. 'I haven't told him yet.' The green eyes narrowed and Christie thought she could detect an unexpected streak of malice. 'But he won't say no.'

'How can you be so sure?' Christie followed her across the lawn towards the conifers. She had only met Dominic a few times, but despite what Fran had told her about his adulation of her mother, he struck her as a strong personality who would do exactly as he chose.

Fran shook back her head in a gesture of cool arrogance. 'Because he never does.' Beckoning Christie closer, she put a finger to her lips and carefully parted the branches of a conifer.

Christie's eyes widened.

In front of the pool, on the close-shorn square of grass edged by white paving, stood Dominic Redfern dressed all in black.

Instinctively, Christie withdrew. There was something separate, something exclusive about this man and whatever he was doing, that made her want to run. And yet she couldn't look away.

He was engaged in some sort of physical exercise. But it wasn't the usual physical jerks or press-ups. This was a smooth flow of movement that was more like a dance, and it had a mystic, Oriental feel to it. He was moving gracefully, effortlessly, shifting balance, his long legs bending back and forward, his arms and hands held out, away from his body, curving and swooping in a kind of rhythmic harmony.

'What's he doing?' she whispered.

Fran shrugged. 'Don't ask me. He says it calms him and allows his energies to circulate freely.' Her voice was mocking, but for once, Christie couldn't respond to the laughter in her eyes.

She stared, mesmerised, at the tall dark figure that seemed both balanced and still. There had always been something faintly mysterious about Dominic. Even something scary that had brought a shiver to her lips when she'd spoken to him. Yet there was a quiet confidence too, a sensation of inner peace. Was this how he achieved it?

Beginning to feel like some sort of voyeur, she took a step back. 'We shouldn't be watching.' She mouthed the words almost silently as she turned away. 'It's an intrusion on his privacy.'

But Fran's smile revealed a hint of cruelty once again. 'You have to admit it though, darling,' she murmured. 'He's one hell of an attractive man.'

Despite her misgivings, Christie peered once more over Fran's shoulder. He wasn't conventionally good-looking – the nose was too long, and the high cheekbones and features too angular. But he had masses of wild, curly dark hair, and she still remembered the fierceness of his hazel eyes, although he was too far away for her to see them now. The man was compelling, that's what he was. And what's more, there was a hunger about Dominic Redfern that made her curious.

Annoyed with herself, and annoyed with Fran, she pulled her away. 'He's your stepfather,' she reminded her. Fran's air of worldliness didn't convince her in the slightest. But still, sometimes she went too far.

'So? We're not blood-related, are we?' Fran lengthened her stride to match Christie's. 'And he was a lot younger than Mother.'

She didn't like this side of Fran. It was all very well to be outrageous, but Fran was beginning to sound incestuous into the bargain. Was she really suggesting that she fancied her late mother's husband? Or was her bitterness towards Dominic – the bitterness that Christie was unable to understand – the reason behind her strange behaviour?

'How old is he?' Christie couldn't rid herself of the memory of the enigmatic figure in black.

'Thirty-two.' Fran smirked. 'But hands off. I found him first.'

Christie couldn't help laughing. She was impossible. 'Your mother found him first,' she corrected.

As she cycled back to Yew Cottage, Christie remained disturbed, unable to shake his image from her mind. He was a solitary man. According to Fran he had few friends, preferring his own company. Was that because he was still mourning his wife? The woman who Fran said he still adored?

Whatever Fran might pretend to the contrary, Christie wondered how much tension existed between Dominic and his stepdaughter. It was a strange situation. And one thing she was sure of. She wouldn't like to live in the same house as a man like Dominic Redfern. No way.

3

'There's another chapter ready for typing.' Vincent Pascoe tossed the dictaphone on to Isobel's lap.

'All right.' It filled her with dread. These tiny tapes and the sound of his voice filled her with dread. Isobel felt a pang of longing for the workshop. For the feel of cold metal and smooth wood beneath her finger-tips.

But she had promised him a few hours of her time. It wasn't easy for him. Vincent had his longings too.

'Don't bother if you've got something better to do.' He jerked the wheelchair round so he had his back to her. A back bent with efforts and frustrations.

'Vincent . . .' She held out a hand, knowing he wouldn't take it. He didn't allow her to reach out for him these days. Too much bitterness in the way. 'I said I'd do it. I always do your typing.' Yes, she always had. She had lived with it for so long.

His thin claw of a hand moved to grab a notebook from the desk, but he mistimed the lunge and it fell to the floor. 'Shit.'

'I'll get it.' She rose to her feet.

'I don't want you to get it.' He spun the chair round once again, his eyes livid behind the thick glasses he wore, the wheels of the chair twisting and tearing the pages. 'I want to be able to get it myself.' The voice was tight with tension.

'I know you do.' Isobel sighed. What more did he want from her?

'But that's not possible, is it?' He headed for the door, staring straight ahead, his hand twitching spasmodically. 'I'm dependent on you, aren't I? I'm nothing but a bloody vegetable.'

'Vincent . . .'

But he was out of the door, somehow managing to slam it behind him, still fostering guilt, fostering control, as he had always fostered it.

Isobel stared out of the window of the small study, at the garden that her grand-daughter was re-designing for her. She must think of something else. She had to. She was shaking with the resentment she always had to repress. So she must think of something else. Of Christie.

It was early days, but it was beginning to look as if Christie had found her niche. And Isobel had no doubt that she would make a success of her business. She was a stubborn individual, was Christie, and Isobel was glad of it.

Maybe because she had brought her up here at Yew Cottage, Isobel felt a close affinity to her grand-daughter that was more than affection and family bonding. Christie reminded her so vividly of what she herself had been at that age. What she had felt was what Christie was feeling now. And knowing what she did made it all the harder for Isobel not to speak out. Not to shriek her own experience and pain from the rooftops, so that Christie might learn.

But it was against her principles to do so. Christie would learn by her own mistakes, as she herself had done. There was no other way.

She must get on. She flicked a switch and it started – Vincent's thin, tape-recorded voice.

Isobel's shoulders sagged. Her fingers, always a little dusty and splintered with wood, poised over the typewriter, and she began.

As if she were playing chords on a piano that had been in the family for generations. Always the same chords, over and over, until the dreadful monotony made her want to scream.

Vincent was writing his family's biography. He had gone back years to distant ancestors he'd never known. And although he began other projects many times, he always returned to this. He had been writing and re-writing it off and on since she'd known him. And she'd known him for fifty years, for heaven's sake.

Isobel put her head in her hands and wept, something she rarely did these days. The hot tears clung to the dry lines of her skin. And meanwhile Vincent's voice raved on, existing in a world of its own, where nothing mattered but the bitterness – the bitterness that had filled his life and now filled hers. Fifty years . . .

* * *

She'd been newly-married when she first met Vincent. Newly-married with a husband who'd been only too happy to charge off to war. Jack had been concerned with doing his bit for his country, whatever the cost.

Isobel's dark eyes grew dim with an old half-forgotten tenderness. You couldn't blame him. They were all like that then, all the young fresh-faced lads who stood so proud in their uniforms and talked about bravery rather than death. Of mother country rather than destruction.

Vincent wasn't like that though. She smiled. He was a few years older and, more importantly, he didn't have the option of going to war because his eyesight didn't meet the requirements. He advertised in the paper for a part-time typist, and Isobel rushed round there as soon as she could. Newly-married with no children, it seemed an ideal position. Until Jack came home, anyway.

'You're married, then.' Vincent Pascoe had glanced at the plain band on her finger. The pale green eyes behind thick lenses gave nothing away. There was not a flicker of emotion.

'You said that's what you wanted.' She'd wondered why, but even from the start, Vincent Pascoe wasn't the kind you asked many questions of. He was distinguished and aloof. Tall, well-educated and rather superior. No doubt he didn't want a silly young girl doing his typing for him.

'I'm a writer.' He tapped his gold pen on the desk in an important manner, and Isobel looked suitably impressed.

'That sounds interesting.'

'Probably not to you,' he corrected, smoothing fair hair from high forehead. 'But I don't need a critic. I need a typist. This is a serious subject. And I expect serious dedication. I expect commitment.'

Isobel was twenty years old. Her life, until her marriage to Jack, had consisted of outings with the crowd – to the pictures, to pubs, and to dances at Hammersmith Palais. Her most valued possession was her black net dress with royal blue sequins. Jack had become one of the crowd only six months ago. He was exciting – even a bit of a rogue – and he was a superb dancer. His quickstep had swept her off her feet and brought a flush of excitement to her cheeks that she'd never experienced before. No. Serious, dedication and commitment were not words in Isobel's vocabulary. But she needed this job.

They discussed terms.

'And your husband?' Vincent raised his sandy eyebrows. 'He's in the army, I take it?'

'He enlisted first chance he got.' Isobel's eyes were proud. Her Jack was no shirker. He would be fighting with the best of them.

'Another real man,' Vincent drawled in that arrogant way he had. 'Or should I say, another lamb to the slaughter?' His thin lips tightened with derision.

Isobel frowned. 'He's a brave man, yes. Of course he is.' She'd never had to defend Jack before, and it was a strange feeling. No-one had ever questioned his motives, any of their motives.

'And that's why you married him?' Vincent thrust his face close to hers. She could almost touch the starch-stiffness of his fair moustache, the bristles on his unshaven jaw.

Isobel drew back. 'Not entirely. He does have other qualities.' She paused. 'But with all due respect, I'm not sure they have much to do with you.'

His laughter took her by surprise. She had half-expected to be bawled out for rudeness. But when he replied, his tone remained harsh. 'At least you've got some backbone, girl. Stick up for him, why not? Where he's going, he needs all the help he can get, poor sod.'

Isobel blinked. 'You don't approve then . . .' She hesitated. 'Of war?'

'I'd like to bang their bloody heads together.' In seconds he was across the room. He grabbed a notebook from the desk. 'You'll see, when you read this. War did for my old man. War did for thousands of them.' His eyes were bloodshot and staring, his breath coming fast.

Isobel was both fascinated and repelled.

'But what do the top dogs do first chance they get?' His voice rose. 'Send another bloody lot out there to be butchered, that's what. It's nothing but hypocrisy, I tell you.'

She drew herself up to her full five feet two. 'They didn't have a choice. Hitler . . .'

'Hitler, my arse.' He sat down abruptly, as if all the breath had been knocked out of him. 'They're all as bad as each other. Egomaniacs, the lot of them. What do they care about all the little people? The people who they get to do their dirty work for them?'

Isobel tried to argue with him. She had tried to argue with him so many times. Asked him what alternatives there were, attempted to put the case for defending the country as she saw it, as Jack saw it, as everyone seemed to see it.

But as time went by, and she continued working for him, typing up his untidy scribbled notes and chapters, absorbing the bitterness of his father's death and what it had done to his family, to so many other families, Isobel became drawn to Vincent's kind of pacifism.

She had always thought as others around her had thought. For too long perhaps. She had never considered alternatives. She had never let her own voice develop, never seen that she didn't have to be like all the rest, that she could be different.

And so, as the war hit London, Isobel avoided the War Effort for as long as she could, working instead for Vincent, telling herself that she was doing something so much more worthwhile for her country. For the future. Helping to bring to people's attention the truth that it wasn't necessary to fight. That peace could bring its own solutions, and save lives.

But, unlike Vincent, Isobel wasn't quite brave enough to let her views be known. She wasn't in a position to. She had a life to live, away from Vincent and his manuscript. She had a husband away at war and a mother now living in Dorset. She had friends and neighbours who applauded the War Effort. So Isobel kept quiet.

Until it seemed that there was only one place where she could be herself – the flat that Vincent shared with his crone of a housekeeper. And there she ran whenever she could get away, not listening to the voices who began telling her how bad it looked – a woman with her husband away at war. A young woman, an attractive woman. A woman on her own.

But Isobel didn't care. It became the most important part of her life. With Jack away, it became a passion that filled the gap of his absence. A passion for pacifism swelled her heart so much more than the patriotic fervour of war. Pounding away at Vincent's typewriter, listening to his angry words – this was how she wanted to spend her days.

Now, she re-wound the tape. Chapter thirty. How many more times would she type chapter thirty? Re-type chapter thirty? How much more bitterness could she swallow?

Purbeck Garden Designs was due to begin a new contract the following Monday, and Christie felt the usual accompanying surge of excitement. This was what she loved most about her job, the anticipation. She had discussed the plans with the clients, amended her designs to suit their needs, organised her timetable and ordered the plants from the nursery. Now it was only a case of supervision, a lot of hard work and of waiting to see if the garden would take the precise shape she had envisaged.

It was also Trevor Swift's first day, and Christie had to admit to a sense of apprehension. She was still staying at Yew Cottage, taking the space that Robin had offered her, telling herself that this wasn't a separation.

She rose at six, gazed out of the window towards the dew-sodden, grassy path that led to the yew grove, flung on some clothes, and ran out there on impulse. There was a certain atmosphere in Yew Cottage that inspired such behaviour, made Christie do things she would never contemplate doing in the small terraced house she shared with Robin. Mind, there was nowhere there to run to at six in the morning. Or at any other time. No yew grove nestling behind her back garden where she might bump into squirrels or even roe deer.

And there was also Robin to consider. Here, she could please herself. Perhaps she had been wrong, believing she was ready to share her life. Perhaps she still needed too much solitude.

Outside the cottage, a cool morning mist clung to her skin, creeping through her thin denim jacket, coating her jeans with moisture. And as she entered the wood she felt that the trees were waiting for her, calling to her even, with their strange silence and beckoning arms. Closer. Closer.

The cobwebs between the branches were painted with silver, glistening from the mist that had penetrated the shroud of the yews. There was no sound – no bird song, no traffic, not even a whisper of a breeze. All was still. And that was what Christie wanted – the stillness, the peace.

She ran her fingers across the rough reddish-brown bark of one of the oldest yew trees, perhaps thirty feet in girth, although it was hard to tell their age since the stems writhed together, merging into one whole as they grew, defying all attempts to date them. She smiled, stroked the spiny needles, sniffed deeply of the musty pine perfume. These were atheist trees, twisted, knotted and confused, with no straight, guiding light to call them upwards, but sewn instead with wild, wriggling clematis and rose-briars.

The ground beneath her feet was soft and yielding humus. There was little growing under the yews. Little light, little food. But there was shelter. As much shelter as a girl could ask for.

Christie's feet were sodden as she made her way back to the cottage half an hour later. She put her hand to her short, spiky hair – it was wet to the touch.

As she neared the cottage she looked up. From an upstairs window,

Gramma stood watching, her long dark-grey hair loose and hanging around her shoulders. She was too far away for Christie to make out her expression. But she saw her smile.

She was at the top of the stairs as Christie came through the door.

'Whenever you want to talk . . .' was all Isobel said. She turned to walk away.

'Thanks, Gramma.' It was only a whisper.

Trevor arrived at eight. 'You don't live here, do you?' he asked, as they loaded equipment into the pick-up truck.

'I stay over sometimes.' Christie was abrupt, determined to keep her personal life strictly apart from business.

'I see.' He straightened, fixing her with an unexpectedly piercing gaze as if he really did see. Had he guessed that she was thinking of leaving her husband? Or did he imagine she was seeing someone else?

She flushed. 'I should make it clear . . .' She jumped out of the truck. 'That what I do in my own time is none of your damn business.'

He should have been offended, but clearly this man was as thick-skinned as they came. He only grinned. 'Fair enough. I didn't mean to overstep the mark . . . ma'am.' He touched an imaginary cap.

She laughed. 'No need to over-do it.'

But she couldn't complain about his work rate. They were clearing old paving slabs from the front garden, and Trevor made it look easy, so much so that she was allowing him to do the lion's share of the work, while she prepared the ground that lay underneath.

'Jesus, it's hot.' Without warning Trevor stood and pulled off his tattered shirt, the same shade of blue as his eyes.

Christie blinked. Brown skin. Brown skin and golden chest hair. Broad shoulders and narrow waist. A pathway of fine hair that led from his belly button down into denim jeans.

A jangle of excitement jabbed her in the ribs.

She looked away, digging her spade deep into the sandy earth, shovelling hard core from the path with renewed energy, as if she must keep moving, must stop thinking. There was no place for fantasy for a woman in her position.

In front of her, Trevor laboured on, seemingly oblivious. He bent over the slabs one by one, his long, brown back exposed to the hot sun, and to Christie's reluctant gaze. She couldn't seem to take her eyes off him.

He worked with an easy, relaxed rhythm. First, he methodically freed the slab. Then, taking a deep breath and bending his knees, he lifted, exhaling simultaneously, his muscles straining, his balance perfect.

She stood up and stretched as he passed her with the wheelbarrow. His fair hair was plastered to his forehead. They exchanged a sweaty glance. She pulled the peak of her baseball cap further over her eyes as if it might protect her from more than the sun.

They worked on in silence.

Each time he passed her, her senses became more attuned to his coming. His shadow blocked the sun, bringing welcome shade. He never touched her, but there was a brush of static as he passed, like a moment of contact between them, although they were inches apart.

His jeans were slung loosely around his narrow hips, held in place by a worn, brown leather belt. Beads of sweat glinted between his shoulder blades as he worked, clung to the damp hair of his powerful arms, glazed the muscular sinews of his shoulders and back.

Christie's thin, sleeveless T-shirt was soon damp and clinging to the curves of her breasts, her legs were hot under the denim cut-offs, her hair wet under the baseball cap. Her body was steaming, her head pounding. She was breathing heavily from the effort, her chest heaving, her lungs aching. How long could she go on before snapping from this tension, this heat?

'Christie?'

She swung round. 'Robin! What on earth . . . ?'

The road was obscured by a high fence, and she had been too absorbed to hear the sounds of a car stopping, or even footsteps. He must have crept through the front gate like a blasted cat burglar. She had been caught in the act. But what act? She hadn't done anything. Christie tore off her baseball cap and gardening gloves, angrily raking her fingers through her damp hair. 'What's up?'

He laughed – not a pleasant sound. And his critical eyes were absorbing the sight of her muscle-bound garden labourer, as Trevor straightened to cart another wheelbarrow load of rubble away to the skip out front. Christie knew exactly what Robin was thinking.

'I'm just paying you a visit.' He folded his arms. 'I didn't realise I had to make an appointment.' His gaze travelled from her damp, blonde hair and flushed face, down to the T-shirt clinging to her breasts.

'You don't.' Resolutely she turned her back on Trevor, and transferred the full force of her attention to her husband. But she was annoyed. He had broken the spell, and she felt cheated, as if she'd been given a narrow escape that was safer, but a hell of a lot less fun.

'That's all right then.' Robin stared back at her.

'But I am working. Couldn't it have waited?' She was unable to shake off the knowledge that he was checking up on her.

'If your wife won't come home, then you have to go looking for your wife.' His mouth was set in a stubborn line.

Christie sighed. 'It's only been a couple of days. I did tell you I needed some space. You agreed . . .'

'I didn't know it was this much.' He nodded darkly in Trevor's direction.

'What are you implying?' Christie sensed her own panic rising. 'I said space, and that's what I meant. I feel trapped. I need room to breathe.'

'You sound like your mother. Give me some space. My God. Can't you think of an original line?'

Robin could hardly have chosen anything to say that was guaranteed to irritate her more. Christie's mother had been a teenager in the 1960s, and sometimes it seemed that she'd never learned to take her responsibilities seriously. Especially the responsibilities of motherhood.

She glared at him. 'It's hardly in your interests to bring my mother into it,' she pointed out.

'Why's that?'

'Because I might be tempted to bring *your* mother into it.' She leaned closer towards him as Trevor strolled past. 'And you wouldn't want that, would you, Robin?'

She knew it was an unfair weapon. Robin's mother had died two years before they'd even met, but Christie had been quick to appreciate the influence she'd had on her son's life – and still had, even from the grave. She sounded a dominating harridan of a woman, who was doubtless responsible for her son's prowess in the kitchen. But was she at all responsible for what happened to Robin in the bedroom? Christie had often wondered. She guessed that there was more – much more – to Robin's relationship with his late mother, that she hadn't yet discovered.

He paled. 'At least she isn't around to witness this . . . this *behaviour* of yours.'

She hated the pomposity he invariably sought refuge in. 'And what behaviour might that be?'

'I don't need to spell it out for you, Christie. I've got eyes.'

37

They both glanced towards Trevor who was still lifting paving slabs as if the two of them weren't there, whispering in the far corner of the front garden.

'Maybe you need glasses,' Christie murmured. But Robin wasn't stupid. He must have read the frustration that she was hardly able to hide.

'I could have a dozen pairs of glasses but he'd still be a bloody Neanderthal, and you'd still be lusting after him.' He glared, challenging her to deny it.

Christie's anger rose. He had gone too far this time. 'How dare you come here and talk to me like this? What gives you the right? This is a new contract. It's important to me. You're jeopardising my reputation.'

'Looks like you're managing to do that yourself,' Robin jeered. 'Managing just fine.'

Christie fought for control. 'You're imagining things. These are my clients. And he . . .' She pointed at Trevor. ' . . . is my employee.'

'That's a new word for it.' There was no stopping him. Belatedly, Christie realised that he was trembling with anger. But by now, so was she.

'I hate jealousy, Robin.' She took a step closer. Their faces were only inches apart. 'It's destructive and it's dangerous.'

'So is adultery.' He didn't even blink.

'You're crazy.' At last she turned from him. There was no way he would believe her. And why should he? Even though it had only existed in her head, she knew how it must have looked.

'And you're crazy for some of that, aren't you, Christie?' He continued to goad her, his face livid, his eyes delirious.

She shook her head. 'No. You've got it all wrong.'

But Robin wasn't listening. 'Is that really what you want, Christie?' He grabbed her elbows. 'A stud like him? Is that what it's all about? And I thought you were worth so much more . . .'

'Get off me.' She struggled, her arms flailing. What was the matter with him? What had happened to the man who had always seemed kind and sensitive? The man so attuned to her needs? The man she'd married.

'Is everything all right, Mrs Fifer?' It was the first time Trevor had called her that. He stood in front of them, still naked from the waist up, radiating strength, his eyes calm and non-threatening. And he was waiting – for a sign, she guessed, that she needed help.

She shook her head. 'Mr Fifer . . .' She spoke pointedly. '. . . . is just leaving.' Her breath was coming fast.

Robin stared at her. 'See you tonight, Christie.'

It was a threat. She knew that it was a threat, and as such, it shocked her. Robin had always been such a gentle man. But he wasn't showing much evidence of it now.

She nodded, her eyes locked on to his, unable to refuse. 'See you tonight.'

Before she guessed his intentions, he bent forwards, his mouth pressing on to her lips, forcing them apart, demanding a response as he pulled her closer.

His touch was cold. It repulsed her – it wasn't right. This wasn't right. She was about to cry out, push him away, but already he had released her, so abruptly that she almost fell. He was staring over her shoulder, a strange expression of male arrogance in his eyes.

She twisted round. Trevor was still standing only feet away, watching, an ironic half-smile on his handsome face. Christie burned with humiliation.

Robin looked back at her in triumph, and she realised what that kiss had been all about. Possession. This is mine. This was her husband, the New Man. And he had the bloody nerve to talk about Neanderthals.

Without taking her eyes off him she wiped her mouth deliberately with the back of her hand, as if removing all trace of him. You bastard, her eyes were saying. He would know what she meant.

At last Robin looked away.

'Later, Robin,' she said. Hating men. Hating all of them. And not even knowing if her words were a threat or a promise.

4

The summer of 1990 was a sultry one, and much as she loved the outdoors, Christie found herself constantly longing for shade. She worked with Trevor in the gardens of their clients, and she wondered how long it could go on, this heat, this sense of the static, of nothing changing.

Despite her anger with Robin, Christie's guilt and desire to make her marriage work had brought her back to Ulwell. They never mentioned that afternoon. Their marriage could almost have been unchanged. Robin still spent most of his time with his computers, still cooked wonderful Chinese meals and they still pretended the nights and mornings away in bed. But he still wouldn't talk to her. So, how could they go on?

One night Christie went too far. He launched himself on top of her without thought, touch or tenderness. And she clenched her teeth and pretended to come. Oh God, it was shocking. She dragged him closer, squirming and gasping as if she could somehow compel him into orgasm.

'Please . . . Please.' It was too horrific of her to pretend like this. She wanted to scream. She did scream. What was she doing? How could she let this happen?

But Robin seemed barely to register her response. He went on – interminable minutes and motions of nothing – until exhaustion claimed him and saved her. Just at the moment when it seemed she could stand no more. Not one more touch, not one more stroke of desperate pity.

He closed his eyes and rolled away from her.

Christie kept her eyes wide open, staring at the Artex ceiling as she had stared so many times.

She could live with passionless, joyless, impotent sex. Other women got a worse deal. There would always be dissatisfactions. What made her so different – believing she had the right to expect so much more?

'I love you, Christie,' he said.

'I love you too.'

If only he wouldn't say it. If only she felt it.

The glimpse of the jealous, arrogant male that he'd given her that day in the garden when he kissed her in front of Trevor, had been dusted from existence. Her husband, the New Man, had returned. Once more, she could walk all over him. Once more she was powerless against him. He gave her much too much and nowhere near enough.

Before he went to sleep she broached another subject that had been bothering her.

'I need more help with the business,' she said. Work was pouring in. 'I'll have to get another man.'

'Another man,' he echoed. He turned from her, to sleep.

So Christie chose an older man this time, part-time only, with a definite stoop and not a whiff of animal attraction. She had learned her lesson.

She also bought another secondhand pick-up truck for Trevor's use. She never mentioned him to Robin, yet Trevor had been a find. His work-rate was high, he was trustworthy and reliable, and Christie was giving him more and more responsibility. Sometimes she wondered if the business could continue without Trevor Swift – he seemed so much a part of it. And business was booming. They had more work than they could handle.

But there had been no recurrence of the events of that first day. Christie made sure she kept her distance. And if there was any thread of unconsummated desire stretching between them, she ignored it. Just as she ignored the sight of his long, brown limbs and straining muscles. She was his employer. She was married. She must have been mad.

One Sunday she visited Yew Cottage as usual. It was as much her sanctuary as ever, and her grandmother rarely commented on her frequent visits. Today, Gramma was in her workshop, and Christie was surprised to see Vincent there too. Ever since she could remember, the workshop had been Gramma's particular lair, Vincent's his study.

'Hi.' She stood warily in the doorway, sensing a heated debate that her presence had halted. 'Am I interrupting something?'

Gramma and Vincent had always been separate in Christie's view, as if they'd never really belonged together, but had drifted there through circumstances beyond their control. She knew Vincent was not her grandfather. But she'd never analysed her own relationship with him –

she'd never needed to. Vincent had always been there, a background person. He was kind, in a gruff sort of way, and he didn't bother her. Gramma had brought her up, and Vincent had rarely interfered – almost as if he were just a lodger, tasting family life temporarily, before returning to some solitary existence somewhere.

Gramma shook her head. 'Of course not, my dear.'

'Don't know why it's such a big secret,' Vincent grumbled. He turned to propel his chair out of the door.

Christie dodged out of the way, just catching Gramma's surreptitious wink.

'There isn't any secret.' But even as she spoke, while his back was turned, Isobel deftly draped a black cloth over something standing on ground level.

Christie pulled a face at her. 'Can I help you, Vincent?'

'No, no. Out of the way. I've got work to do.' Vincent's chair careered down the slope to the ground at an alarming speed.

Christie knew better than to insist. She watched him heading for the house. 'So what was that all about?' She peered around the workshop, wondering what was under the mysterious black drape.

'Don't you start.' Isobel began to plane a piece of wood, a faint smile on her lips. 'Questions, questions . . .'

'I didn't know you could be so irritating.' Grinning, Christie went over to the table on which Gramma placed finished pieces before they were polished or burnished with oil. A female figure caught her eye and she picked it up curiously. Female and yet not quite female.

'I've hardly even started.' Isobel laughed. 'I irritate myself sometimes. Poor old Vincent.'

Christie turned the sculpture around in her hand. 'I've often wondered . . .' she began. 'Does Vincent mind?'

'Mind?'

'All this.' Christie's gesture encompassed the workshop, benches, lathe, saws, chisels and all the other tools of Gramma's trade. And the wood – all shapes, sizes and kinds, piled in untidy heaps on the floor.

'He doesn't have to, does he? It wasn't part of the deal. He has his private times, I have mine.'

Christie thought of Robin, of his resentment against her work, that he'd never seemed to feel before they were married. In fact, surely he'd been proud of her achievements before they were married?

'Did you ever work, Gramma?' she asked. 'When you were first married, I mean? To Grandfather Jack?'

Isobel Vaughan's dark eyes dimmed. 'I worked for Vincent.' She laughed. 'Doing his typing.'

Back then? Christie watched her with surprise. She rarely spoke of those days. 'Some things never change . . .' she murmured.

'And of course I worked in the war. Most women worked in the war.' Isobel went across to the coffee percolator she always kept bubbling. 'Coffee?'

Christie nodded. 'What did they do?'

'They worked in factories, drove ambulances – whatever there was, they did it. In the war, women took over. Who else was there?' There was a glimmer of reminiscence on Isobel's worn face as she poured the coffee. 'But when the men came home they took back the jobs. That's the way things were.'

'Even if a woman could do the job better?' Christie's eyes widened with disbelief.

Isobel laughed. 'Especially if they could do it better. Women had to be kept in the home, otherwise everything would fall apart. Or so they thought.'

'What would fall apart?' Christie took the mug offered to her.

Isobel watched her thoughtfully. 'Marriages, home life, society, men's power. It was a man's world, my love. You don't realise . . .'

'How lucky I am?' Christie sipped her coffee. She'd heard that one before.

Isobel smiled. 'I'll let you be the judge of that.'

'And when did you start sculpting?' Christie's gaze returned to the small female figure. Did this piece have a connection with what Gramma was now working on? Whatever it was under the black drape that she wanted to keep secret? That Christie longed to take a peek at.

'A type of Eve,' Isobel informed her. 'A sort of life symbol. Woman. Birth. Perhaps a Goddess. A bit of a universal female, I suppose.' She came closer. 'Do you like it?'

'Kind of.' Christie wasn't sure. There was something disquieting about the strange, androgynous figure.

Isobel straightened up with some difficulty. 'It's not supposed to be easy to like,' she commented. 'And it hasn't got the individual's personality yet. That comes later.'

So. It was a kind of portrait. But whose portrait would it be? 'Is it supposed to be disturbing?' Sometimes it was hard to define the emotions that Gramma managed to squeeze from her subjects.

'Disturbing . . . moving . . . whatever.'

'Then it's a success.' Christie finished the last of her coffee.

'Oh, this is only a rough.' Isobel wiped her hands on her blue apron. 'The real thing will be a lot bigger. It's a commission. And, as I said, it will have a personality by then.' She smiled mysteriously.

Christie was more intrigued than ever. 'And you're not going to tell me who it's for?'

Isobel adjusted the plane. 'You should know better than to ask.'

'What are you making it in? Are you allowed to tell me that?' Christie was teasing her now. She picked the sculpture up again.

'Yew wood.'

What else? She smiled. Yew. The life symbol. Its golden-brown markings and knots gave any piece a unique character that could be exploited by the sensitive sculptor. And Gramma was certainly that. 'Very special,' she said, replacing the female form carefully on the table.

'Very special,' Isobel agreed, her dark eyes inscrutable.

'Someone loves another someone very much.' Christie wondered if it was anyone she knew.

She left the workshop, humming softly, a melody that she remembered her mother singing. Over the years it had become strangely embedded in her mind, almost as if it were a song of love.

That evening, Fran phoned to invite Christie and Robin to a lunch and swimming party the following week-end.

'We'll have a barbecue,' she said. 'Bring a piece of steak or a sausage or something.'

Christie laughed. 'What are we celebrating?'

'Whatever you like. The end of the summer. The beginning of the Refuge. The end of an era.' Her voice changed.

'Dominic's agreed, then?' Christie was faintly surprised. She couldn't imagine anyone relishing being turned out of their house and home by a load of single mothers, no matter how worthy the cause. And especially not a man like Dominic.

There was a silence on the other end of the line. 'Kind of.' Fran forced a laugh. 'Can you imagine him being able to stop me?'

'Not really.' Fran was pretty good at getting her own way. Although Dominic . . . Christie thought of the lone, dark figure by the swimming-pool, and shivered.

'So will you come?'

Christie laughed. 'Just try and keep me away.' It might be just what she and Robin needed – a chance to relax together, socialise, have fun.

'Good girl.' She could imagine Fran consulting her list. 'You're guest of honour, you know. You might even meet some potential clients. I've told them all about you.'

Christie was smiling as she put down the phone. 'Fran's invited us to a party,' she told Robin.

He pulled a face. 'When?'

She told him. 'Let's go. We both need to unwind. Don't we?' she pleaded.

'How the hell can I unwind with your friend Fran around?' His voice rose. 'I don't like the woman. I never have and I never will.'

Christie groaned. He was twenty-four and beginning to act as if he were fifty, as if he didn't want to have a good time. 'You don't even try,' she complained. It scared her, how Robin seemed to be changing, how the distance was stretching between them until sometimes she couldn't even make him out any more.

'I don't want to try.' Robin picked up his newspaper, refusing to look at her, cue that a subject was due for closing. 'She's a silly kid. She's man mad and she's a tramp.'

Christie's face flushed with a hot anger. 'You've never really got to know her, Robin. It's all a front. She's not like that at all deep down. And she's been through such a lot.' She paused. 'She thinks you're wonderful. She told me.' Weren't all men supposed to be susceptible to flattery?

'I wear trousers, don't I?' he growled. 'The entire male population is wonderful to her. I don't care what she thinks. I'm not going.'

'Robin . . . she's my friend.' Christie felt the familiar frustration rising once more to the surface. 'Can't you make an effort – for me?'

'I've got too much work on. It's not my scene.'

'But there might be some potential new clients there – for the business. All the people Fran knows are rolling in it. She said she'd put in a word for the business . . .'

'The business, the business,' he jeered. 'I'm sick to death of bloody Purbeck Garden Designs. Why don't you go to the stupid party on your own if you feel that way about it?'

Robin knew she wouldn't go alone. If he'd had any doubts, he would never have used the bluff. Francesca Cassidy made him feel uncomfortable with her flashy house and easy attitude. He couldn't bear those pouting lips and come-on eyes of hers. She was a flirt, and Robin had no time for flirts. He wanted to keep his Christie away from women like that.

'All right.' She got to her feet. 'I will.'

Robin blinked at her. 'You'd really go without me?'

'If I have to.' She looked so proudly defiant standing there in front of him, so small and resolute, that he wanted to reach out and hold her. Envelop her in the kind of hug that she'd never escape from. He wanted those cornflower-blue eyes to be filled with love for him, not vague and unseeing as she mentally planned her day, her present contract, her new designs.

But he couldn't back down, not now. 'That's up to you.' He kept his voice cold, so that she'd know he wasn't pleased. But he'd never try and stop her – she was her own woman. Not his woman, unfortunately.

'Robin . . .' Her voice was pleading. She knelt at his feet and tugged at the newspaper like a small child might. Demanding attention.

He wanted to smile, but instead he frowned. 'What?'

'We should talk.' Her eyes were sad.

'What about?' Fear sliced through him. He knew what was coming next, and he dreaded it. Constantly tried to put it off, as if one day it might just disappear and let him breathe again.

'About us.' She was gentle. One hand rested on his knee. Gentle, female hands but stained with grass and earth. She was almost begging him. How could he refuse?

'There's nothing to talk about.' He looked past her, through the patio doors towards the garden she'd made for him. He had planned to do it himself until he'd seen her in her pick-up truck visiting a client. He had phoned the number painted in bold black on the side of the truck. Prayed that it wouldn't be a huge company. Prayed that it would be her who came to him. Because it seemed to Robin, from just one look at her, that she was the woman of his dreams.

And she had come, looking even more vulnerable than he'd expected. Vulnerable, yet strong. And right from the start he'd loved her so much that it hurt. But he was a patient man. He determined there and then to be exactly what she wanted. Nothing more, nothing less. Only it wasn't so easy, was it? There was always something getting in the way.

'You're wrong.' She was shaking her blonde head. 'There's so much to talk about. We've been married for two and a half years, Robin. Things aren't right between us. You know they're not.' All she wanted was an acknowledgement, he was aware of that. But he was unable to give it to her.

'Everything's fine as far as I'm concerned.' His voice tensed. 'You're letting your imagination run away with you again.' Hysterical woman. Emotional woman. Women always were too emotional, weren't they? Didn't they always analyse too much? Shut up, Christie. Shut up, Christie.

'What about sex?' The words sank into the vacuum between them. He could hardly believe she'd said those words. So stark and cruel.

He stared at her.

'Sex is important in a marriage, Robin. Especially if it's going wrong.' She stroked his arm, as if trying to soften the words. 'I think we should see someone. We could go together and . . .'

'We have sex.' He got to his feet abruptly, pulling away from her. 'We're always doing it, for Christ's sake. How much more do you want?' It was intended as the worst kind of criticism.

How come she was so experienced that she knew how it was meant to be? How many had there been before him? He put a hand to his head, remembered that oaf on the motor-bike. No, best not to think of it.

She took it squarely, spreading her hands. 'I don't want *more*. You know it's not that. But it's not right between us, is it?'

He couldn't reply. Why didn't she say the word? Impotency. She'd said it before.

'And that's not all . . .' She seemed determined to go on. 'We're not close. There's no . . .' She searched for the word. 'Intimacy between us, Robin.' A sigh escaped from her lips. 'There's no love between us – even when we make love. We stay miles apart. A marriage shouldn't be like that. Sex shouldn't be like that.'

'I didn't realise you were such an expert.' He couldn't bear her to talk like this. He couldn't be just one in a line. He didn't want to think about it, couldn't think about it. That's why he had never questioned her about her past. He couldn't admit that she had one.

He thought of the day when he'd seen her and that blasted labourer of hers, working up a sweat in the garden. He'd smelt the stench of sex in the air. How much had been in his head, and how much had been for real?

He'd believed Christie when she said that nothing had happened between them. And now? He was her husband. Didn't that count for anything?

'I'm not an expert.' Her eyes clouded. He felt her pain. Didn't she know that her pain hurt him so much more?

'You surprise me,' he drawled.

'But I do know that something's wrong.' She was trying to be patient, he knew that much. She hesitated. 'And unless you admit it, Robin . . .'

'What? What will you do?' he jeered. Hurting inside. Hurting so much inside. Couldn't she see?

'I'll leave you.' Her beautiful face closed up to him. 'I'll have to. I won't have a choice.' There were tears in her eyes.

It was his turn to beg. Where were the words that should be spoken? Don't leave me. I need you. They weren't far away, but still they stuck in his throat. Male pride took over. Didn't it always? 'Okay. Who's stopping you?' A challenge in his eyes. She had never asked for challenge.

Slowly, Christie turned away. 'If you feel like that, why didn't you say so before?'

He was losing her. Oh God, he was losing her.

'I don't,' he snapped. 'But I don't appreciate being thought of as some sort of stud, either.' He didn't understand. He really didn't understand why it mattered so much. Why wouldn't she see? He didn't want to cause her pain. He wanted her to stay pure, unhurt, undefiled. His woman.

His woman . . .

'Real ladies don't enjoy that sort of thing . . .' His mother's voice came back to him from the past. 'You'll find out soon enough.'

Real ladies – like Mother. She had never enjoyed it. He knew because he'd heard her scream it at the top of her voice. 'It's dirty. It's disgusting. Isn't one child enough for you? Haven't you and that son of yours put me through enough?'

'A man's got his needs.' His father's voice.

'Men and their needs.' She mocked him, cold and brittle, her voice snapping him in two. 'I've had enough of it. Had enough, I tell you.'

And he must have had enough too, because Father left them that day. Muttering under his breath, dragging the big black suitcase that they never used down the stairs. 'It's enough to drive a man to drink.' Those were his last words to her.

Mother stood, arms and lips folded, watching his reluctant escape.

After he left she bolted the door behind him. There were just two lonely tears channelling the lines of her face. 'It's you and me now,' she said. 'We don't need him. Just you and me.' She brushed the tears away, and as far as he was aware, she cried no more.

He knew what she wanted from him, he'd always known that. But it wasn't so easy when you were fifteen and growing up fast. He tried to find time alone, but she was always after him, forever watching him.

And at last she found what she'd always seemed to be waiting for. 'Just like him,' she muttered. 'You're just like him. Men are all the same.'

He knew that he had failed her. Failed her at fifteen and failed her on the day she died.

'I don't think of you like that, Robin.' Christie sounded tired. She'd given up again, he could tell. Thank God.

He took her in his arms. Held her close.

She let out a deep sigh. 'I don't think of you like that at all.'

The following Friday lunch-time, Christie and Trevor were parked in Wareham having a quick sandwich in the pick-up truck when Fran sashayed over.

'Hello, darling.' She spoke to Christie, but her cool green eyes took in the sight of Trevor, sitting in the driver's seat, and they glinted with approval. 'I can see why you've been hiding him,' she murmured.

Christie repressed a giggle. Fran always made her feel like an irresponsible teenager. 'I haven't been hiding a thing.' She widened her eyes in mock innocence. But she was hiding – hiding the fact that it was nearly impossible to be this close to Trevor without recalling the heat of that afternoon. A heat coming not just from working bodies and the sun. A shaft of suppressed desire streaked through her. Not for Trevor especially, but for the warmth of the physical, a warmth she longed for in her marriage. Intimacy.

Fran grinned. 'You are coming to the party tomorrow? You haven't forgotten?'

'Just try keeping me away.' Her voice remained light.

'And Robin?' Fran's eyes rested on Trevor's brown arms once more.

'Robin . . .' Christie lowered her voice, reluctant to talk with Trevor's curious eyes upon her. 'He won't be there.'

'Oh?' Fran leaned her arms on the open window and Christie caught a tantalising whiff of musky perfume.

'He's too busy.' She knew the heat was rising in her cheeks. She felt as if she were admitting to a rupture in her marriage. 'He would have liked to come. He's really sorry.'

'I bet he is.' Fran pouted prettily at Trevor. 'Never mind – we'll manage without him.' She bent lower and Christie could almost see her scheming away.

'Fran . . .' she warned.

'What about you, Trevor? Will you come to my little shindig? We're bound to be short of men.'

Trevor only grinned, looking from one to the other. Like a spectator at a blasted tennis match, Christie thought.

'Why on earth should Trevor want to come?' she said. 'He won't even know anyone.' And he works for me, she silently added. And work is supposed to be separate from social life, from the personal. And . . .

'He'll know *you*.' Fran's eyes glinted wickedly.

Christie heard her own forced laughter. What was Fran playing at? Sometimes it was difficult to recall the sad teenager she'd met in Wareham Church who had reached out to Christie in a way no-one had reached out before. The girl who had made her feel needed.

'He sees enough of me at work,' she muttered. 'He's bound to have plenty of better things to do.' Yes, and why didn't he say something? Why didn't he help her out?

'Have you got anything better to do?' Fran gazed in open appreciation at Trevor.

'Not a thing.' His grin was a lazy one. 'I wondered when you two were going to consult me about this.'

Christie eyed him warily. He was being perverse – she might have known it.

'So will you come?' Fran tapped red lacquered nails on the white paintwork of the truck. 'Pretty please?'

'Sure.' Trevor shrugged. 'Why not?'

Christie ignored Fran's grin of triumph, then tried to ignore the burning sensation that started in her neck and spread down. Down past her belly and into the warmth beyond.

'Good.' Fran's voice became brisk. 'Christie will give you the address. Won't you, darling?'

'Yes, *darling.*' She pulled a face. They were both staring at her as if she had two heads. If she didn't know better she'd swear they were collaborators. She was trapped. She had to go to the party – it had become a point of principle between her and Robin rather than just a party. And besides, there was the business to think of, and she'd promised Fran, But to go without Robin, when Trevor was there, was something else again. It was dangerous, she acknowledged.

Trevor and Fran were still smiling at each other in mutual admiration.

'Time to get back to work.' Christie tapped her watch, paying no attention to Trevor's glance of amusement. They were in his truck – the second of the fleet, as he called it.

'Right you are.' He turned the ignition key.

With a wave, Fran turned and was gone.

Christie watched her. 'You don't have to come to this party, Trevor.' Her voice was soft. She couldn't look at him. 'It may not be a very good idea.' She hoped he'd understand her meaning. She certainly wasn't going to spell it out.

'Don't you think so?' He indicated, and pulled away.

'No, I don't.' Her voice became firmer. She was the boss, after all. She must remember that. 'It won't be in the slightest bit interesting for you.'

'Oh, I don't know . . .' For a brief second his eyes left the road, flickered swiftly across her shoulders like a caress.

A slow shudder vibrated through her, and she realised she was gripping the door handle with tight fingers. Slowly, she loosened her hold, let it slip from her hand.

He laughed. 'I'm rather looking forward to it already.'

'You are?' She stared at him in alarm. There was an unmistakable determination in his pale blue eyes. Trevor had, quite clearly, already made up his mind.

5

Christie selected a simple blue halter-neck sundress for the party, and wore her black costume underneath. She loved swimming, but not sun-worshipping in a bikini. She would leave that to the Frans of this world.

And true to form, Fran looked stunning in a brief pale green two-piece, cut so high that her long, golden-brown legs seemed to go on for ever.

She came over to sit with Christie near the pool but beyond the conifers, where they had a good view of the big white house.

'I've been simply dying to know . . .' Frowning into the sun, she unclipped her dark glasses from her bikini. 'Have you decided what to do about Robin?'

'Not really.' Christie gazed towards the antiseptic blue of the pool. Young men and their women were laughing, talking, splashing, careless and carefree in a way that Christie would like to be. She was only twenty-four years old. Okay, so she had the responsibility of her own business to think of, but she didn't want to stop having fun. She wasn't ready for that at all.

'Why wouldn't he come to the party?' Fran's eyes were invisible behind her dark glasses. She grabbed Christie's sun-tan oil and began smoothing it on to slim thighs.

What could she tell her? That Robin disliked her? That Robin didn't want to socialise? That Robin seemed to have forgotten how to have fun?

'He's changed,' she said instead. But could she admit even to herself how much he'd changed? 'I don't know the way his mind works. We're drifting apart, Fran.'

She watched Trevor. His body swooped into a crawl as he glided effortlessly along the length of the clear blue pool. She couldn't imagine him drifting anywhere.

53

Fran followed the direction of her gaze. 'You never told me he was *that* good-looking.'

Christie laughed. 'Was that why you invited him to the party?'

'Perhaps it was.' Fran's expression became inscrutable. 'You know me, darling. I firmly believe that you can never have too many attractive men at a party.'

Christie giggled and sipped her wine. 'Maybe so, but you knew I didn't want him to come.'

Fran leaned forward, whispered in her ear. 'Ah, but you don't have to talk to him.'

Christie grunted. If only it were that easy.

'And he's not even married.' Fran nudged her playfully. 'I thought the best ones were already taken.'

'No, he's definitely not married. He's very young, though.' Christie leaned back. It was wonderful, just toasting in the sun, without a worry in the world, not having to think about gardens or Robin, or anything in the least important. Just listening to the laughter and splashing coming from the pool, sniffing the fragrance of barbecue sauce wafting towards them from the house, and having one of these ridiculously teenage conversations with Fran.

'Plenty of energy, mind you.' Fran smirked.

'Perhaps he has some dreadful vice that I don't know about,' Christie speculated.

'I could live with that.'

They both laughed.

'Especially if I got to look at that body every day.' Fran flopped on to her belly.

'You're all talk, you are.' Christie grinned. 'You'd be bored out of your mind if he had nothing to say for himself.'

'Oh, I wouldn't want him to *speak.*'

Christie's giggle ended in a shriek as the splash of cold water hit her bare thighs. She jerked upright, squinting in the sun at the tall, blond figure dripping on to the grass beside her. 'Get away from me – you're soaking!'

Lazily, Trevor draped himself down beside them. 'Isn't it time for a little exercise, ladies?'

Christie stared longingly at the pool. She had already done her bit, small-talking with the people Fran had introduced her to as 'my wonderful friend who creates simply glorious gardens from the most awful jungles'. And now the pool seemed to represent a care-free zone, a place where she could forget herself for a while. 'Shall we?' She glanced at Fran.

But Fran, despite what she'd been saying only a few moments before, wasn't even looking at Trevor. In fact, she was looking towards the house.

'Fran?'

'You go.' She jumped to her feet. 'I have to speak to Dominic.'

'But . . .'

'Go.' Fran bent back towards her. 'Don't worry about a thing. Just have a good time.' Her voice dropped to a whisper. 'Remember, darling. All work and no play makes Christie Fifer a dull girl.'

Christie hugged her knees, watching Fran as she made her way over to where Dominic Redfern stood by the barbecue, dressed in a black T-shirt and jeans, turning steaks and sausages and chatting to guests. He seemed friendly enough from a distance, and yet he remained solitary, despite the company. There was an aura of stillness around him that set him apart.

Fran had told her Dominic was raising difficulties about the refuge – insisting on involving Social Services, pointing out the legal pitfalls and responsibilities. She had seemed worried, as if something else was bothering her, even when she'd been larking about, teasing Christie about Trevor. It hadn't seemed quite real, as if even to Christie, she had to pretend.

'Seems like a nice girl.' Trevor, sitting with a towel slung loosely around his neck, was watching her too.

'She is.' Christie felt protective. 'She's not as tough as she makes herself out to be.' Her gaze returned to the man standing by the barbecue.

Dominic's long lean body stiffened as Fran approached, and he stepped back slightly from the people he was with, as if preparing a space for the tall slender girl with the sleek red hair and arrogant eyes, creating a tableau for them both.

Christie sensed the taut atmosphere between them as she read the body language. Fran leaned towards him, as if threatening his circle of space and stillness and Dominic seemed slowly drawn towards her. Fran stepped closer, slinging one arm in a loose caress around his neck. He seemed caught off-guard, his hands moving to her waist.

Christie stared. It looked for all the world as if he would kiss her. She remembered Fran's words on the day they'd watched him by the cabana. Surely there was nothing like that between them?

But even as Fran tried to wrap him nearer, he pushed her away from him, his face tight and unsmiling. She tossed her red hair carelessly back over her shoulder and made for the house.

'And how about you, Christie?'

She jerked her attention back to the disturbing male presence by her side. 'Me?'

'Are you as tough as you pretend to be?' He laughed.

She stared at him, wondering for a moment how she appeared to him. How did he see her? Then she responded to the humour in his eyes. 'I'm tough as old boots, I am.' She jumped to her feet and slipped out of her dress in one easy movement, observing his faint gasp of surprise with pleasure. 'Race you to the pool.'

Christie had a good start, but he was much faster, and as she ran, feeling the adrenalin rush, she sensed him gaining behind her. She half-screamed, half-laughed, then, before she knew what was happening, he lifted her as he had lifted her that day in the yew grove when she was supposed to be interviewing him, lifted her easily, holding her body close to his warm damp skin, drying now in the hot sun, only a few droplets of water still resting on his shoulders.

'Ready?' he whispered.

Her eyes widened in horror. She clung to his neck, conscious of the delicious male scent of him, the heat coming from his flesh, for just a second. And then he jumped, slicing through the water, still holding her, the cool liquid like a slap on a hot face.

Christie screamed with delighted laughter, let go of him, and plunged forwards into a slow, deep crawl, feeling the water playing gently around her face and hair, accustomed now to the change in temperature, the smooth movements clearing her head, freeing her body.

'How tough?' He was waiting for her at the deep end.

She laughed. 'What a way to treat your employer . . .'

'We're not at work now.' He smiled down at her as if he'd never heard her laugh before. And he certainly wasn't looking at her as if she were his employer either. He was looking at her as if she were only a woman today. Only a woman . . . Christie shivered, but this time not because of the cool water. She shivered because she was letting him get too close. And she was enjoying every minute of it.

They swam until her legs were weak. Everyone else had left the pool. They were all eating by the house or sprawled on the lawn. And still

Christie and Trevor stayed in the water. She turned over to float on her back, closing her eyes to the sun. This was heaven. Absolute heaven.

'I'll go and get us a drink.'

Something in his voice . . . She stared at him, through the glare of the sun. He waded closer until she lay in his shadow. His hands moved in the water towards her, resting around her waist, holding her. Not sexual. He was holding her. Christie could feel herself sinking. But he was holding her . . . holding her . . .

'Christie!' The sound of Fran's voice reached her.

She stood up in the pool, shielding her eyes.

'Christie! Phone!' Fran was calling from outside the house.

She waded to the edge, hoisting herself out, dripping on the white stone, her black costume clinging to her body, her skin glistening, her legs hardly supporting her own weight. 'Coming!' She grabbed a towel on the way, rubbing at her hair, reluctantly shaking herself back to reality.

Reality. She knew who it would be. Couldn't Robin leave her alone for five minutes? Did he always have to stay so close, treading on her toes, hemming her in?

She passed the luscious scents of lavender and honeysuckle, half-running through the exotic conservatory and into the house.

'Sorry . . .' Fran told her.

'It's okay.' If Fran hadn't fetched her, Robin would only wonder. She picked up the phone.

'Christie . . .' His voice was slurred.

'Robin? Is that you? What is it?' Her heart sank. It was impossible to escape into dream-land, wasn't it? She would always be pulled back.

'I want you to come home.'

The hand holding the receiver tightened imperceptibly. 'Why? What's wrong?'

'Nothing's wrong. But I want you here. With me.'

Christie frowned. There was a certain inflection that had lately crept into his voice, a tone she shrank from. She loathed being dictated to. And what right did Robin have to make demands? He could have come here with her, she'd begged him to come, hadn't she? 'Why?' She must stay calm. He was drunk, that's all.

'Because I miss you.'

She repressed a groan. Throwaway words like these were too easy. And she could hear the meanings behind them. She remembered his jealousy.

The look in his eyes. The need for possession. Jealousy and self-pity. Coating his voice. Scaring her half to death.

Christie took a deep breath. 'I'm not leaving yet.' She transferred the receiver to her other hand. 'I thought you had loads of work to do. That's why you didn't come, isn't it?'

'Damn the bloody work.' His voice rose.

She winced. 'You chose not to come, Robin.'

'I didn't imagine you'd go without me,' he challenged. As if she were unnatural. As if they were joined by invisible chains and couldn't move without one another's permission.

'I didn't want to come without you,' she reminded him. 'But I'd promised . . .'

'You were a long time coming to the phone. What were you doing?' His voice, bleak and accusing.

Christie held on to the banister rail beside her. 'Swimming.'

'I see.'

'Do you?' Didn't he realise he was driving her away? Didn't he know that he was making her want to hate him?

'I see more than you think.' He sounded nasty, very nasty.

She caught her breath. 'I'm going to put the phone down now, Robin,' she said clearly. 'You've been drinking. You're upset. Maybe you should make yourself some black coffee, and we'll talk about it when I get home.'

'Don't hang up on me, Christie,' he moaned. 'Come home now. Please?'

She hesitated. Maybe she should go home. Maybe she owed it to him. Maybe it was dangerous to stay. But if she gave in this time . . . 'I'll be home later, Robin.'

Her hand trembled as she replaced the receiver. She had tried so hard to love this man, maybe too hard. But how could she love him when he wouldn't even trust her enough to tell her what was wrong?

She moved from the phone, sensed a movement on the landing above her and jerked her head up.

Dominic Redfern was walking slowly down the stairs. 'I do apologise. I wasn't listening,' he said in his polite voice.

'Listening?' She stared at him. There was an unfathomable expression in the hazel eyes which weren't as fierce as she remembered.

He seemed about to take her arm, and then appeared to change his mind. 'To your conversation. Are you all right?' Christie registered the concern on his face. Why should he care? She hardly knew the man. 'I'm fine. Absolutely fine.' But she wasn't fine. She was angry, confused and hurting. She could see her marriage dissolving in front of her, and she seemed powerless to stop it.

His expression told her that he understood. 'Can I get you something to drink?'

Before she could reply, Trevor appeared in the doorway, a glass in each hand. 'Your wine.' He passed it to her. She took it with shaking fingers and looked up at him. Their hands touched.

Dominic stared at them both for a long moment. Then, with a curt nod, he turned and was gone.

'I've had enough of this party.' Christie sighed. Trevor was standing beside her, and she felt an urge to lean against him, to lean against something, anything. Have someone take the pressure from her head. It had been so good to forget her troubles, but that blissful hour had only made it doubly hard to return to them.

'How about a walk?' He was watching her carefully.

She stared back at him. He had put on his shirt and jeans but his hair was still damp. And he had brought her blue sundress for her, draped it over a chair.

'Oh, no. I should be getting back . . .'

'Already?' Trevor sipped his wine, his blue eyes alert over the rim of the glass.

Christie thought of Robin's distrusting voice squeezing away loyalty. His anger mocking her good intentions. Could she face her husband in his present mood?

She hesitated. A walk was appealing. A walk away from the crowds.

His hand brushed against her shoulder. 'There was something I wanted to say to you . . .'

The light compulsion of his touch seemed to sink into her. Christie was so tired. She realised that she didn't want to leave, not yet. She thought of Fran's words. *All work and no play . . .* And she nodded. 'Okay. Let's walk.' Her voice was soft. 'I know a place . . .'

The Sika trail lay at the back of Fran and Dominic's house, acres of pine wood and trails that made up a good part of Wareham Forest. The section near the car park – for the trails began by the road – was well-populated at this time of year. But the area where Christie took him, which backed on to Dominic's land and wasn't accessible by road, was deserted.

They walked without speaking for about half a mile, partly sheltered from the hot afternoon sun by the needles and branches of the tall, dense pines. The landscape was dry, the atmosphere sultry, and the scent of the pines burned in her nostrils.

But before long Christie was exhausted. She felt as if she were walking with a burden of lost promises. A tight wad of pent-up emotion she couldn't shake off was squatting on her shoulders, bringing her down.

Her pace slowed until she stopped completely, resting for a minute against a tall tree trunk that probably prevented her from falling. 'Let's sit.'

They found a shady place nearby, but away from the main trail, where two fallen logs formed a V-shape, and where the ground was soft, sandy and scattered with pine cones.

He leaned back against one of the logs, stretching out long legs in denim jeans. 'Feeling any better?'

She nodded. 'A bit.' For the first time since they'd been walking, she wondered what she was doing here with him in this remote forest. Was she absolutely mad? What would Robin say if he knew? If he could see her?

Oh, what the hell . . . Christie sat back against the tattered, broken bark of the other log and closed her eyes. She was quite safe. She would just rest for a minute, and then they should start back.

The sun was warm on her bare arms. Gradually, she began to feel more peaceful, the burden slipping from her shoulders, her head free of pressure. 'What was it you wanted to say to me?' she asked him lazily.

'I just wanted to tell you something.'

The tone of his voice made her eyes flick open.

He moved forwards, towards her, crouching, holding her gaze. His hair had dried now, and she wanted to touch it as it glinted golden in the sun. She wanted to smooth it from his face.

'What?' Her body tensed.

'That you look beautiful.' He smiled. 'That today, you look absolutely beautiful in that dress.'

Embarrassed, she looked down at the dress. He was used to seeing her in jeans. 'Hardly suitable for gardening work . . .' She tried to laugh.

Her throat was dry and constricted. Her limbs were aching.

'But very suitable for a walk in the woods.' He drew closer, a predator.

She stared at him. What was happening here? What had she done? There was a drumming in her head that wasn't due to the sun or the pressures and disappointments. It was a rhythm of longing, a pulse of life.

He reached out and touched her face. 'I want to kiss you.' His words hung in the stillness of the air around them. Everything was quiet and motionless, as if the whole world were waiting, hanging on this moment they shared.

Her lips parted as a streak of desire shot through her. An ache of pure wistfulness. Her shoulders tensed. She was holding back. But she knew he must see the longing in her eyes.

'I have to kiss you.' Now his mouth was only inches from hers.

She trembled, her eyes closing as a wave of emotion swept through her body. Limbs of liquid. Burning cheeks. Hot mouth. Hunger.

She had held back too often, denied passion for too long, ignored the sexuality that was urging her forwards, welcoming him, wanting him.

With a groan that meant both acceptance and defeat, Christie held out her arms, and in seconds his lips were on hers.

They fell back into the soft earth, their bodies entwined and aching. Lust and longing, joining them, transporting them both back to some sort of primal beginning.

He offered her a lift in the truck, but Christie had come to the party on her mountain bike and she chose to cycle home, fast and furious, free as the wind. She was elated, on a high, wanting to laugh, loud and strong, feeling pure liberation. Perhaps there should be guilt – anyone would say there should be guilt. But Christie felt only release from the problems that had been weighing her down, release from the dense sadness that had become such a part of her. She was twenty-four years old. Fran was right. All work and no play made Christie a dull girl. There had to be more to life than this. And she had found a taste of it.

Anyone watching her would think her quite mad. She rounded the proud ruins of Corfe Castle with a small whoop of appreciation, taking the road to Studland which wound its way through fields of sweet corn and rape, before she began to come down to earth. It wasn't any answer, was it? Of course it couldn't be. There were too many complications, and besides, she was married, for heaven's sake! But nothing could dim her secret smile, as she pedalled past the high hedges, grassy banks and tumbledown cottages. In the distance was the ridge of Purbeck Hills, always there, watching her, resting on her horizon.

Christie didn't care that it was a long ride. She needed the time. Her blue sundress swept out behind her, her short, blonde hair scraped from her scalp as she cycled on, up the hill, past the Studland heath of heather, gorse and chalky ridges.

Would Robin know that she was different? Would it be drawn on her face somehow? She hoped not. She wanted to clutch it to herself, inside her. Her own secret knowledge.

Christie had made love with Trevor Swift. She giggled, revelling in the unaccustomed wickedness, shocking herself. She had made love with Trevor Swift in the middle of Wareham Forest, and it had been glorious. An experience of a lifetime.

You're beautiful. She recalled his words, remembered clinging to every syllable.

A beautiful woman. His fingers had traced patterns of beauty on her face. As if she could only be beautiful because he believed she was.

Briefly she took one hand off the handlebars to touch that face. Did those lines of his show? Could a person make anyone feel beautiful that way?

And I want you. Abruptly her legs felt weak, too weak to pedal, her strength fading, quite gone as she re-played her passionate response. She went down two gears.

No words of love. If she'd heard words of love she would have been up and out of it. Because that wasn't always what it was about. She hadn't known it until today. Life had been very black and white, ordered and neat, crammed with words like faithfulness, trust and adultery. Words with strict, no-nonsense boundaries.

But that wasn't the end of the story, was it? Some kinds of love were also about sexual fulfilment and release. And that was what she had achieved. It was a matter of sexual chemistry. Simple, uncomplicated, wonderful. It was warmth, a physical warmth that she'd never known before. She had never dreamed that making love could be quite this good. She had only been half-living, she realised. There was so much more than she'd ever suspected.

Was that why there seemed to be no questions left? Or at least none that must be answered? Was that why there was no guilt? Or at least none that didn't seem to disappear with the wind like cobwebs in her hair?

She turned off towards the house they shared in Ulwell. Was that why she wasn't apprehensive of seeing Robin?

Could this possibly be an answer after all? Was this how she could stop her marriage dissolving in front of her very eyes? Why not take a lover? Other people did. And as for Robin . . . She felt a faint stab of guilt at last. She would be patient with Robin. This would give her the strength to help him work it out.

Christie swung easily from the bike, wheeled it up the drive into the garage to give herself a few moments for her flushed cheeks to cool. Because she didn't want to hurt Robin. That was the last thing she wanted. Was she living in cloud cuckoo land, believing that this experience could help her marriage? She couldn't justify what she'd done, but that didn't mean their marriage was shattered.

She didn't want to damage Robin. She wanted there to be hope for them still. She couldn't let go of those promises so easily. There were, after all, many different kinds of love. And there was marriage. Robin was right – there was much more to marriage than sex. There was friendship, shared interests, stimulating conversations. All the things that made the world go round. A tiny voice whispered in her ear – as long as you have the right kind of sex, a backdrop of the right colour, the right setting for everything else to exist as it should.

Christie put her key in the lock. Well, she did have that now. Maybe she could have it all. Why not? She would use this experience to get her marriage back into perspective. And as for Trevor, their relationship at work wouldn't change. He was her employee. She was his boss, and that was how it would stay.

The secret smile returned. But there would be other moments. She hoped there would be other moments.

Robin came into the hall.

'Hi.' He stared at her.

'Hi.' Was it written all over her face? Were there pine needles in her hair, soil-stains on her dress, a whiff of sexuality in her breath?

She took his hand with the old confidence. 'I'm sorry about earlier, Robin,' she began. 'I left the party, but I went for a walk in the forest. You see, I needed to think things through . . .' His eyes were blank, and she realised he was stone cold sober. 'There's someone to see you,' he said. 'In here.'

Christie walked into the living-room. Her expression froze when she saw the woman sitting there, drinking coffee and smoking a cigarette. 'Hello, Mother,' she said.

It had been a long time.

6

Christie advanced further into the room, drawn irresistibly towards the woman in the chair. She had always wanted to love her, but when had her mother stayed around long enough to let her? Was it significant that she was here, now, at this turning point in Christie's life?

'Darling!' Faith Vaughan jumped to her feet, her eyes lighting with a warmth Christie wanted to believe in. 'How are you?'

'I'm fine. What brings you to Dorset?' Christie was trying to keep cool, but it was there, the old resentment clinging to her words. How could she help it, when her mother had always seemed determined to keep a distance between them?

'Oh, Christie.' Faith's wide smile broke almost as soon as it began. 'I'm sorry. I know it's been much too long.'

One year, five months . . . and three days. Even at Christie and Robin's wedding, her mother had arrived an hour before the service and left half-way through the reception.

'I suppose you've been busy.' She wouldn't let her mother get close this time. She'd been let down by her too often, wanted her to stay too much, mourned her every time she left.

'It has been hectic.' Faith frowned. There were lines of worry on that face, but it remained lovely – huge olive eyes, fair skin, soft pouting lips.

Christie found herself wondering how many men had been in love with her. How many men had wanted to kiss her mother, like Trevor had kissed Christie in the forest? And what about her father – whoever he was? Had he loved Faith Vaughan?

'Don't give it another thought. You've got your life and I've got mine.' But if her words were true, then why did her life seem so intertwined with the life of this woman? It wasn't just that she was her mother, and that blood was supposed to be thicker than water. It was much more than that – had always been more than that.

'And how is your life?' Faith hesitated, looking around, but Robin had left the room. 'Robin was a bit upset when I arrived.'

'Drunk, you mean?' Christie couldn't be bothered to pretend.

'A bit of both.' Faith's voice remained gentle. Confide in me. Hypnotic and tantalising. 'Is there something wrong?'

Christie's eyes narrowed. Did she really think she could barge in here unannounced and expect to be told everyone's business, like some agony aunt on an occasional home visit? 'Nothing we can't handle.' She stood straighter, the blue dress remaining warm around her hips, her arms and legs still glowing from the sun.

'I don't blame you for being angry with me.' Faith Vaughan got to her feet and put her hands on her daughter's shoulders. 'But I do think it's about time we got to know each other a bit better.' With a deep sigh, she looked into the cornflower-blue eyes that would always be special. But not unique, because they were his eyes.

A deep sadness seemed to streak through her and settle on her heart. Christie had always meant so much to her, although she'd often tried to deny it. Felt she had to deny it. Because Christie was evidence of another memory, a painful memory that she'd fought for many years. It still hurt – seeing her daughter's face, recognising an echo of *his* face. And every time she saw her it became harder not to unlock her memories. But could she bear to, after everything that had gone before?

'You're never here, Mum.' But still, despite this small capitulation, Christie seemed to shrink from her touch. 'How can I get to know you when you're never around?'

'I want to change all that.'

'Yeah?'

Faith let her hands drop to her sides. Christie seemed so self-assured and confident. 'I suppose it's too late to make it up to you . . .' Her voice tailed off.

Perhaps she shouldn't have come here. Perhaps she should have stayed to cope with the relatively easy pressures of running 'The Basement' boutique in London. Travelling, buying, trying to forget. Determinedly making a success of business since her personal life had gone down the chute. She had made herself believe that she could never come back to

Dorset for good. She had stayed away. So many times she'd wanted to come, longed to hold her daughter in her arms . . . But always she'd been scared – scared to open herself up to that old pain. Even now, with the decision made, she still wasn't sure if she was ready.

Christie had grown up fast in the wilds of Dorset. She was no longer a child to be pacified with distant fables and sad songs. She was a woman, a married woman. Faith had worried for her when she'd met Robin, married Robin. There was something about him that she found disturbing, that had made her unable to stand by and watch her only daughter giving herself to him with such trust. And the Robin who had opened the door to her, drunk and belligerent, was even more worrying.

'How long will you be staying this time?' Christie's voice was a desolate whisper that cut into Faith's senses, laced her with guilt. She had failed as a woman, failed as a mother. 'An hour? An afternoon?'

Not trusting herself to speak, Faith shook her head and lit another cigarette. She took a deep drag. 'A lot longer than that if you'll let me. Maybe even lousy mothers can be half-reasonable friends.'

A smile twitched at Christie's lips. 'Why now?'

'I couldn't *not* come, after so long.' This seemed the only way to explain it. 'I needed to see you. See you properly.'

'Where will you stay?'

'At Yew Cottage to start with.' It would be a mistake to stay here. It was best for her relationship with her daughter to develop slowly, if it were to develop at all. Although Yew Cottage meant Vincent. 'But I'll move out as soon as I find a place to rent.'

Christie seemed bemused. 'I see.'

Faith couldn't tell what she was thinking. But then, she hardly knew her well enough for that, did she? She recalled the look of Christie when she'd first walked into the room. As if she were holding the silent threads of some secret close to her heart.

'What about Stuart and Lola? What about The Basement?'

Faith ground her cigarette out in the ashtray. She didn't want to think about Stuart and Lola. They had begun as her bosses, but Faith had become ambitious. She'd made herself invaluable to The Basement since its first days in the late sixties when it began as just another trendy boutique springing up in the King's Road, Chelsea. It had come a long way since then. They had all come a long way since then.

'Stuart and Lola have been having problems,' she told Christie. No need to add that they'd been having problems for two decades. No need to tell her that Stuart Denyer had been in love with her for too long. These things were her troubles, not Christie's concern. 'I'm going to branch out on my own. Every partnership has to end some time.'

Christie's eyes clouded as if with some private thought. 'Would you really leave The Basement? I thought that place was your baby.'

Faith stared at her. Surely Christie wasn't jealous of the business? Did she really imagine that a fashion boutique meant more to Faith than her own daughter? And yet, what reason had she given her to think otherwise?

'Oh, Christie . . .' She reached out to touch the soft, fair hair. 'You're the one who's always been my baby.'

It was an unexpected burst of affection – Faith so rarely allowed herself to care – and a kind of surprised silence sprang up between them. Mother and daughter. Was it really possible after all this time? Faith prayed that it could be. She didn't deserve it, she'd left it for far too long, unwilling to allow herself to care. But now . . . She would stop the downhill slide.

'You have no life of your own,' Stuart had said. 'Let me care for you.'

No-one to love, he had meant. He had intended only to be kind. But his words had cut through Faith's veneer of indifference. He was right. She had no-one to love. She had punished herself for too long.

But Christie's face was drawn with an old pain. 'Then why did you ever leave me?' she whispered.

Abruptly, Faith got to her feet. 'I had to.' When you start to care, you begin to feel pain. That was the truth. Now that she was here, she would have to tell Christie those things that she'd rather keep locked in her past for ever. She was still scared to let them see the light of day, still scared of their power to hurt, to destroy.

'I knew I couldn't look after you as well as your grandmother could,' she said at last. 'I was only nineteen when you were born. Practically a child myself. There are no excuses, so I won't give you any. Maybe I was wrong. But I did most of my growing up in Yew Cottage. And you seemed to belong there right from the start.'

Of course it had never been as simple as that.

She thought of the tiny baby cradled in her arms. Those long-ago evenings at Yew Cottage. Vincent stomping off to his room with the paper – because of course he wasn't confined to a wheelchair in those days – and Isobel sitting in her old rocker by the fire.

* * *

'You could always leave the baby with me.' Isobel, her mother, was offering an escape route, holding out her arms for the bundle wrapped in the same white crocheted shawl that Faith herself had once been wrapped in.

The blue, baby eyes blinked open and Faith handed her over, tears on her face, feeling the stab of betrayal that was so much a part of it all. She loved this baby – her little Christie – so, yet sometimes she could hardly bear to look at her. 'She's my child,' she said. Her fists were tight, as tight as the baby's instinctive fists when given a finger to hold.

'Of course.' Her mother seemed to give so much while taking everything away. 'And I'll make sure she never forgets it.' Crooning to her, already remembering the best lullabies to sing.

Faith felt her mother watching her, knowing her so well.

'Stay here whenever you can,' Isobel said. 'Have the baby whenever you can. And the rest of the time . . .' There was a moment of complicity between them. 'I'll take care of her until you're feeling better. For as long as you like.'

Faith rushed from the room, from the cottage, her footsteps ringing on the cold flagstones of the porch. Would she ever feel better? Would the pain of losing her lover ever disappear? Would she ever forgive herself for what she had done?

At first it hadn't been so bad. She found a bed-sit and a job in Poole selling cinema tickets. She lived a single life in the week, and returned to Yew Cottage and little Christie at the week-ends. If it had been only her mother and the baby, maybe she could even have stuck that sort of existence, found a better job, not let herself drift with the wrong sort of people into the wrong sort of life. A life that tried so hard to forget by beginning with a hangover and ending with the pub. Every day.

But it wasn't only her mother and the baby, was it? There was Vincent. For so long, there had been Vincent. Not a father. Not even a step-father. But always there.

'Vincent hates having me around,' she said to her mother on one of those week-ends. 'Why not admit it?'

Isobel's mild, brown eyes darkened. 'He does his best.'

'Not to hate me?' She'd seen it, lurking in his pale eyes behind those thick glasses of his. Loathing of Isobel's child. Of Jack's child.

Isobel shook her head. She wore a pained expression that Faith didn't understand. Why did her mother always defend Vincent? Why hadn't she felt like that about Dad? Why had she ever left Faith's father for Vincent?

'He doesn't hate you.' Isobel spoke slowly. 'He's never hated you. You don't understand . . .'

'What?' Faith glared at her. But she didn't want to understand, did she? Didn't want to know anything more about the man who had always made her life a misery.

Isobel's voice softened. 'He probably hates himself more than he hates anyone else. He's got too many problems of his own to spend energy on hating other people.'

Faith wasn't convinced. 'And what about the baby? Does he mind Christie being here?' She didn't want to talk about herself and Vincent. Didn't want to hear anything that might make her hate him less. As far as she was concerned he had tried to take her father's place, and she could never forgive him for that, whatever the circumstances.

'If I want to have her, then that's fine by Vincent.' Isobel managed to avoid the question. But the question remained in Faith's head.

Christie blossomed at Yew Cottage. Faith had always known she would – perhaps that was why she had brought her here. But Faith herself was losing control of her own life. And in the end – even for her baby – she couldn't stick it. She had left this cottage at sixteen because she couldn't stand living in the same house as Vincent, and it was just as intolerable now, even for week-ends.

He was *there*, always there in every room, his presence like a dismal shadow that spoiled everything. Tainted her world, touched her with madness. She hated the criticism in his carping voice that never softened into pleasure. She hated the way he snapped at Isobel as if he owned her. Never satisfied, always complaining, Vincent had no joy in his heart.

And she hated the way he expected her mother to go on typing his bloody memoirs when it was obvious they'd never be published. It was wasting her time, demeaning her time, demeaning her.

She shrank from the worn look of Isobel's skin and the sadness in her dark eyes. She blamed him for that. Faith knew he had imprisoned her mother, through guilt and through pity. And she hated him for that too.

There were no excuses for Vincent. She had lost her father because of Vincent. She had lost her family, her stability, the security she needed to be free.

So one day Faith packed her bags and left Dorset once more, this time heading for London.

'I'll get back to see the baby as often as I can,' she promised Isobel. 'Don't let her forget me.' There were tears in her voice, a gaping hollow of loneliness in her heart. But Christie was better off with her grandmother, Faith had no doubt about that. What could she – a single mother – hope to offer her?

Isobel nodded. 'And don't forget us.' There was resignation in her face. Perhaps she understood about need.

Faith gulped back the tears as she held her close. Planted one last kiss on Christie's soft, baby brow. She wouldn't forget.

'I belonged in Yew Cottage, and you belonged in London,' Christie said now. At least the resentment had gone from her voice – maybe there was time for her to understand after all.

Faith nodded. 'Something like that. I half-thought I'd be back when my money ran out.' She paused. 'But I'd only been there for a few days when I landed the job in the boutique. The Basement was just starting out. I was lucky.'

Christie nodded. Her face was solemn. Lucky for some, she might have been thinking.

'But now I'm planning to open one of my own.'

'A boutique?'

'A small store.' Faith laughed. 'That's what I meant about branching out.'

'Another basement,' Christie murmured.

'Faith's Basement.' She shrugged. 'Well, I might as well use my connections. After all, I helped to make it what it is. What do you think?'

Christie smiled. 'Why not? Where would it be?'

'Well . . .' Christie watched her mother's eyes brighten at this discussion of a new business scheme. Maybe that's where Christie's own career-mindedness had come from. Her mother was a business woman through and through. She might not have recognised it originally, but if she hadn't made it in London, building a successful enterprise out of a tiny cellar boutique in the 1960s, Christie was sure that Faith Vaughan would have made it somewhere. 'I was thinking of Wareham.'

Wareham. Christie smiled. A picture came from nowhere to sit in her mind. An image of Dominic Redfern in a dark, well-cut suit, behind a desk in his Wareham solicitor's practice, his wild, curly hair tamed and smoothed from his dark face, his hazel eyes intent and serious. The image seemed incongruous next to Faith's Basement.

'Wareham's a tourists' paradise,' she murmured, thinking of Fran and the loud American tourists. 'They come in droves to see the Church and Lawrence's statue.' So close, she would be so close.

'That's what I thought.' Faith's voice became brisk. 'So if I rented a shop and organised some secretarial help, would you be interested in sharing office space?'

'Office space?' Christie stared at her. Sharing an office – herself and her mother? That close?

Faith's wide mouth curved into a smile. 'Mother was telling me all about the success of your garden design company at lunch. And your slogan – from concept to creation. Brilliant.' She took Christie's hands in hers. 'I'm so pleased for you. That you've managed to use everything you did at college. That you've set it up yourself, and made a go of it. So pleased . . .' She hesitated. 'And proud.' The expression in her olive eyes seemed sincere. She drew Christie into a hug, surprising her once more.

So little and so much. It was a strange sensation, being the focus of her mother's pride. Would she be so proud if she'd seen her daughter a couple of hours ago in Wareham Forest? Christie suppressed a grin. What she did know was that it felt good to be this close to her again, to smell the faint fragrance of her Armani perfume mingling with the menthol cigarettes she smoked.

'But I don't need any office space.' She drew away from her, reluctantly. 'Robin takes the calls when he's at home, and I phone clients back later.'

Faith pulled a face. 'Doesn't he mind?'

'Sometimes.' Actually it was one of Robin's main gripes.

'It would be easy to have two lines. Probably take some of the worries from your shoulders too. And it's much more professional, to be honest.'

'Well . . .' It was appealing. Only one reservation stopped her – should it be this easy?

It was all happening too quickly for her to absorb. One minute she was with Trevor in Wareham Forest, feeling her whole world shifting from its regular axis of normality. And the next minute her mother arrived out of the blue with this new bombshell, making promises that Christie hardly dared believe in.

'You need to think about it. I wasn't going to mention it straight away.'

Faith moved from her side. 'There's plenty of time.' Plenty of time for us, she seemed to be saying.

Christie stared at her. She was only forty-two, and still a beautiful woman. Why had she never married? Had she and Stuart Denyer been involved for all these years? There was so much she longed to ask her. And yet something vulnerable in her mother's eyes always stopped her from asking, from making too many demands. As if Faith would be too easily hurt.

She sighed. And what about her father? Why would she never speak of him? Christie's lips tightened in determination. She stuck out her jaw. She had to think of herself too. Her mother owed her something. And she needed to know.

She took a step forwards, towards the sad eyes. 'There are things you have to tell me. Things I want to know . . .' she began.

She saw the understanding on her mother's face. On previous occasions when she'd tried to get through, Faith had veered from this subject, her shuttered expression refusing admission more effectively than words. But this time she seemed different.

'I realise that.' She nodded. 'Just give me a while longer, Christie. I'm getting there.' On her face was a silent plea. A while longer. With that, at least for now, Christie had to be content.

Christie was gentle with Robin that evening, finding it easy, even comforting, to care. Maybe she had been too busy staking her own independence to consider what Robin wanted from the relationship.

'I shouldn't have phoned you at the party,' he said. 'It was stupid. Irrational. I don't know why I did it.'

'It was just the booze.' As she smoothed on the cream to cleanse her face of the sparse make-up she wore, Christie waited for the guilt to come. There might have been a glimmer . . . if he knew. But he didn't know, and there were no regrets. She was surprising even herself.

'I'm sorry.' He hung his dark head.

'Don't.' She spoke more sharply than she'd intended. 'It really doesn't matter.' And it didn't matter now – that was the strange thing. She felt as if they had gone past that. That their relationship would be changed irretrievably, never the same again. And she wasn't being negative. They needed change. How could they have gone on as they were?

'I behaved like a right prat.' There was an expression of curiosity on his lean face. As if he knew she was different, but didn't understand why.

Christie went across to the bed where he was sitting up against the pillows. Gently she took his hand. His skin was cold to her touch. 'If I'd known it meant so much to you I wouldn't even have gone to the damn party.' For a brief moment that was almost true.

'Wouldn't you?' His grey eyes widened in surprise.

Christie shrugged. 'It doesn't seem so important now.'

She climbed into bed beside him and felt his narrow body tense. What had she done to this man? What had they done to each other in their frantic search for love? 'Let's have a cuddle,' she said.

He opened his arms for her and she rested her head on his chest. It felt comforting and warm.

But then his hand sidled towards her breasts, almost apologetically, as if it were expected of him.

'It's all right, Robin,' she whispered. 'Just hold me.'

She had thought it, but never been able to say it before, always felt that she had to give him that chance to prove himself just one more time. Never understood – till now – his deep-seated reluctance for sex. Now she sensed his answering tension being rapidly replaced by relief. How long had it been since they had held each other like this – wrapped in each other's arms, without the sex equation creeping into the proceedings, distorting their feelings for one another? Each secretly wondering how to avoid it or how to make it better?

Had Robin always been trying to prove himself to her? Constantly confirming his manhood . . . Was that what had gone wrong between them?

Now that she knew the truth, Christie was amazed she hadn't recognised it before. Robin didn't want sex with her very much at all. No wonder he couldn't let himself go. No wonder he was impotent. But he couldn't admit it to her. He'd be ashamed of what she might think. Worried that he wasn't living up to her expectations.

Christie sighed. She didn't want some sort of stud, but her sexuality still existed – Trevor had shown her that much. Trevor had opened her eyes as well as her body. She liked sex – it was impossible for her to deny it. And hopefully the days were long gone when women were forced to deny it. No matter how much she wanted to love Robin in all the ways he needed to be loved, she couldn't agree to deny such an important part of her. She wouldn't deny it.

His breath was moist and warm on her skin. He was breathing easily, almost asleep already. Calm and trusting.

That was what it was, then. Robin had denied his own sexual appetite. And he wanted to deny hers. Robin wanted her to be quite different.

Like his mother perhaps?

Christie shivered. If he began to trust her, would she learn what he was afraid of? Would she understand why the promises between them had never been fulfilled?

There still had to be hope for their marriage, didn't there? Her eyes began to close. There must be more between them. There had to be. She couldn't give up on their marriage so soon.

But that was in the future. In the meantime she wanted to sleep and re-live the day.

And so, once more, she turned to another. In those sweet moments of drifting, semi-sleep, the touch of Trevor Swift still burned on her skin. His hands undressed her, his voice slurred her senses into liquid heat. His eyes drank her in, wanting her, needing her, taking her. His lips hovered, tantalisingly close, then grazing her lips, entering her mouth, penetrating the part of her that she sometimes pretended didn't exist. Penetrating her and yet leaving her whole. Adding to her, not taking away as Robin did with his machinations of love. She thought of Trevor. He washed all over her. He smouldered in her night-time senses, and threatened all her dreams.

7

It was two weeks before Christmas. The hazy days of late summer and early autumn had long disappeared. Isobel Vaughan had cut so many sprigs of holly from the tree outside the workshop window, that as she sculpted she had a clear view of the Purbeck Garden Design pick-up truck when it came bumping up the drive towards Yew Cottage.

Isobel selected a different size gouge for making the hollow required in the hard laburnum wood she liked to use for small-figure carving. And she let out a deep sigh. She hesitated to interfere, had always believed passionately in people's right to make their own choices. But given the options, she would have chosen a very different path for her granddaughter.

Christie jumped down from the passenger side of the truck, a small figure clad in fleece jacket and figure-hugging jeans. She was rubbing her hands together with the cold, laughing like a child without a worry in the world.

And he followed, tall, blond and faintly disturbing, this man who had become Christie's lover. Trevor Swift. An action man. A bit of a cardboard cut-out of a lover, really, Isobel reflected.

'Ouch.' A splinter of wood dug into her thumb nail. Serve her right for not concentrating. Isobel laughed at herself, as she smoothed the rich, olive-brown wood with her fingers. Softer than skin. More rewarding than a lover. Easily moulded, too.

She couldn't imagine that Trevor Swift would be easily moulded despite his apparent easy-going attitude. That type found it less bother to be easy-going, so long as things were going their way . . .

But Christie had hardly chosen herself a man who was going to change her life. The best he could ever provide would be a quick romp in the woods. Soon done, even sooner forgotten.

She glanced out of the window once more.

Christie was looking around, checking they weren't being watched, but not checking very well since Isobel remained unobserved. She grabbed his hand and, giggling, they moved behind the van.

Isobel frowned. She wouldn't deny Christie her right to have a good time, and God knew she was no prude. But these two were flaunting their affair to the world. Didn't the silly girl know how dangerous that could be?

She knew almost exactly when this affair had started. She had recognised the bright pinpoints of excitement in Christie's cheeks and somewhat ruefully remembered the day when she'd done the same, when she and Vincent had first gone to bed together. A disaster. She clicked her tongue softly. It was always bound to be a disaster, for Vincent had never been a physical man, even in the early days. But it was illicit, and therefore thrilling, wicked and delightful all at the same time.

Christie and Trevor had been discreet at first. Isobel saw her behaving as she always had behaved with him, slightly arrogant and yet vulnerable too, and knew that it was still going on. There was no spark of conflict. That alone gave them away.

Now she could hear their voices outside, raised and laughing. At least he could make her laugh. It never would have been a one-off for a girl like Christie, married to that wet rag of a husband of hers. She needed fun, and Isobel guessed that fun was about the last thing Robin Fifer provided. You could see it in his dead eyes. And he was getting worse, old before his time, wrapped up in his computers. Whoever had killed his sense of fun, it was long-buried, long-gone. Isobel could recognise that much.

But in the past few weeks she'd watched the relationship between Trevor and Christie change. It worried her. Trevor had become braver, more assertive. And that was risky. Isobel knew nothing of his home background – Christie probably knew nothing of it either – but she guessed that Trevor had less to lose. Once, she had seen him pulling Christie towards the yew grove after work. And as for today, well . . . She peered out of the window. There they were, kissing in broad daylight, Christie's blonde head thrown back in abandonment, her body cleaving to his.

Isobel turned the wood lovingly between her fingers, and watched Christie wave him goodbye as Trevor took off in the truck Christie had provided him with. Bought for him more like, and there was a word for that. He was roaring down the drive too fast, needing to impress. In a moment Christie would grab her bike out of the other pick-up that she kept here most of the time, and be gone. And Isobel knew she must speak to her.

'Christie!' She waved from the window.

At least the girl had the grace to look shame-faced. But she'd recovered by the time she walked in the door.

'What are you up to, Gramma?' She helped herself to coffee, pulling off the fleece jacket, and perching on a stool at the workbench as she had sat and watched Isobel so often in her childhood. Her eyes flickered over the half-finished pieces on the work-bench, and came to rest on the black drape concealing the statuette in the corner.

To distract her, Isobel showed her the sculpture she was working on. It was going well – the backs and buttocks smoothed and rounded, the man and woman made from one piece of wood, bound together, the growth rings of the laburnum seeming to mark their flesh with limbs and muscle. 'The Lovers.' She held it out to Christie.

Christie blushed furiously. 'Are you trying to tell me something, Gramma?'

'Do you need me to?' Isobel retrieved the sculpture, and continued finishing the lines.

Christie shook her head. 'No. But d'you think it's terrible of me, Gramma? Do you think it's wrong?'

Isobel's heart went out to her. Despite her knowing air she was still such an innocent. Christie seemed so like Isobel herself that she dreaded the girl would have the same problems, the same pain. She was, after all, still learning about life and love, and Isobel felt almost responsible for her predicament.

'I'm not judging anyone,' she told her. Christie should know her well enough to realise that she wouldn't do that. Look at her own life, for heaven's sake. She had no right to judge.

'I don't love Trevor.' Christie's voice was stark. 'Not really. It's just . . .'

'I know.' Isobel smiled reassuringly. Did she think that made everything all right? Or did she think a lack of love made an affair inexcusable – that one should only go on with it if too infatuated to do otherwise? Nothing was that black or white, and at least Christie was truthful enough not to plead an emotion she didn't really feel.

Her fingers travelled swiftly over the laburnum. This piece had begun life as another Eve – first woman, first temptation, inevitable sin. Was that where human beings went wrong – believing that sex equalled sin? She smiled at Christie. 'But do you love your husband? That's the more important question.'

'I don't know. I suppose I can't, can I? Or this wouldn't be happening.' Her fists clenched. 'If I loved Robin I wouldn't be lonely. If I loved Robin I wouldn't need Trevor, would I?' Her clear, blue eyes were angry. Was she angry with herself? Or angry with what she perceived as her own weakness?

'Then why don't you leave him?' Isobel's voice was matter-of-fact. She had every sympathy in the world for Christie, but the girl had to be made to see the consequences of her own actions. How long did she think she could carry this off without someone finding out, without someone being hurt? Besides, Isobel was of the private opinion that the relationship between Christie and Trevor would founder immediately if she left her husband. It was built on nothing but dissatisfaction as far as she could see. The best sex in the world couldn't survive on such flimsy foundations.

'Just like that?' Christie stared at her as if she had suggested cold-blooded murder.

Isobel shrugged. 'A clean break is sometimes best, my dear. At least it's honest.'

Christie flinched as if from a blow. 'Was it that easy for you, Gramma?' Her voice was soft. 'Was that why you left Grandad Jack, all those years ago?'

'All those years ago,' Isobel murmured. No, it had never been easy.

By the time Jack returned from the war in 1945, Isobel had become a different person from the fun-loving girl he'd married. It wasn't just Vincent's influence, of course – they had all changed with war, even Jack, although strangely, perhaps he had changed least of all.

Isobel hadn't worked for Vincent through all the war years; she'd spent time with her mother in Dorset in the summer of 1942 when Poole was a target of Baedeker air raids, and she'd been compelled to join the War Effort when even married women were dragged into the fray. Not that she'd minded too much. Pacifism was all very well, but it was hard to stand by and watch everyone else do all the hard work.

But working in the auxiliary ambulance services – driving an ambulance, nursing in air-raid shelters and often as not being first on the scene to bomb-damaged houses – had only driven pacifism further into her heart. Like Vincent, she didn't want revenge, she only wanted to stop the killing. It seemed like a madness to her.

Different things became important to them all during the war. The material held less value for hearts that had to cope with the death of loved ones. Thrift was the fashion, in food, clothes, emotions. Because it was the only way to be. Mend and make do, avoid buying new. People grew close, others further apart. Once a pregnant woman went into labour in a shelter, and Isobel's brief training had never prepared her for that. There was little in the way of equipment. They drew a makeshift curtain around her, someone fetched water, someone else fetched gin, and they prayed.

It was a long, hard labour, but the woman was uncomplaining. 'I want a girl!' she shrieked as she pushed. 'For God's sake, let it be a girl!'

When the baby was born, someone found towels to wrap around it. It was all skin and bone, blue and shivering. And then it started to scream.

'Thank God,' Isobel sighed.

'Well?' The mother's voice was tinged with desperation.

'It's a boy.' The cheer rumbled around the rest of the shelter until it was drowned by the wailing siren.

The woman wept.

First chance she got, Isobel left the ambulance service. Men were coming home. She went back to her typing job, to Vincent.

'You won't be staying,' he told her. There was a sadness in the pale eyes behind the thick lenses he wore. Vincent understood so much about men and women. So much about life.

Over the war years she had become close to him, not just in identifying with his ideas, but in beginning to want something more than just a return to pre-war values. It wasn't only his pacifism that appealed to her. And it certainly wasn't Vincent himself – he'd never made the slightest move towards her, and he asked for no loyalty. But it was as if he had become her teacher, her mentor. He had shown Isobel that there was another way to live. That there were other options, other truths to strive for.

Jack said the same thing as Vincent had said, when he returned in 1945, a hero. 'You won't be staying there,' he told her. 'You won't be working, now I'm back.'

'But you haven't got a job.' She stared at him. She had been waiting so long for these first moments. The touch of his hand firm on her shoulders, the proud look in his eyes. But he seemed like a stranger. They'd have to get to know one another all over again.

'No problem. I'll get a job easy enough.' His eyes clouded. 'But even if I don't, you won't be staying there.'

Isobel didn't argue with him. She opened her mouth, but one look at his face and she thought better of it, realising she had no say in her own life any more. And she wondered – had he treated her that way before the war, or was it she who had changed? She, who now wanted her voice to be heard, who had only just learned that she had one?

Jack got a job very quickly. The building trade was crying out for strong, active men like him, and everyone wanted a hero. Jack lapped it up. He was the first to take off his shirt when the sun came out, the first to shout out to the women walking past in high heels and tightly-belted coats that emphasised the new waspish waist. The end of the war years. And Jack was a ladies' man. More than anything, Jack wanted to be admired. He even told Isobel that he'd enjoyed the fighting, the feeling of power it provided.

Isobel felt the sickness lurch in her stomach. 'Even when you've killed a man?' She gazed at the youth who had whisked away her heart at Hammersmith Palais, but the youth was gone. Instead, she saw a broad-shouldered man with a handsome face, deep blue eyes, and a jaw shadowed with darkness.

Jack nodded. 'It's him or me. That's what you say to yourself.'

'And afterwards? When you think about it afterwards?' Isobel was a realist. She only wanted one word of sorrow from him, one ounce of sensitivity.

He laughed. 'I never think about it afterwards.' Already his hands were around her waist, wanting what he seemed to want all the time. 'I thought about you afterwards though, baby. I thought about you, and it made me hot with wanting you.' His breath was warm in her ear, his voice cloying her senses. The passion rose inside her – one touch from this husband of hers, and she could feel herself melting for him. But she didn't like what he was telling her. He made it sound as if violence was part of sex. As if she had been part of the brutality. And she didn't want that; she couldn't admit it. It made her turn from the man she'd married.

She couldn't talk to Jack, but she could talk to Vincent. So she ran there, secretly, whenever she could, ostensibly to do his typing as she had done for so long, but more importantly to talk and be heard. Vincent knew she had a voice and he seemed to want to hear it. That was important. Vincent seemed to have lived so many more lives than she had. She longed for his knowledge, his experience. She drank it in thirstily, wanting more.

As if sensing that his passion was no longer enough for her, Jack slowly became a violent man. The violence had always been there, festering inside him, sometimes erupting in a quarrel with a workmate, or a smashed ladder, but the war had brought it to the surface. He was a bloodthirsty man and he needed to be satisfied, in bed and out of it. He needed to dominate, in bed and out of it. And he needed to be a hero when heroes were already becoming a thing of the past.

The first time he hit her was when his meal wasn't ready on time. Isobel had been at Vincent's. He'd been reciting poems by Wilfred Owen, and she had stayed too long, mesmerised by the words, and by the painful knowledge in his eyes.

'Sorry, Jack.' She was humming to herself as she got the casserole out of the oven. As if being late didn't matter, he must have thought.

He waited until she'd put it on the table, and then he slapped her. Hard.

She blinked up at him. The world seemed to slip into slow motion as she touched her cheek. 'What was that for?' She wanted to cry, but she was too shocked, too numb, for tears.

'That's what you get when my dinner isn't on the table.' He turned away quickly, as if to avoid her accusing eyes. He had cherished her once, until she had become his wife.

Isobel rushed from the room. How could he do that to her? And for so little. With no real reason at all.

Two days later she answered him back without thinking, as if she were with Vincent and had the right of free speech.

'Cheeky cow.' He cuffed her across the temple. 'Who do you think you are?'

It seemed that he had developed a taste for it. The romance was over, the real world remained. Could this be the man with the smooth voice and the magical quickstep?

Isobel told her friend Brenda, who lived a few doors along the street. But she was neither impressed nor shocked.

'It's the war,' she said philosophically. 'They get used to being rough.' She gazed at Isobel with speculation. Maybe she was thinking about Jack's sleepy blue eyes and easy charm. 'But he's a decent man, your Jack. I wouldn't worry about a couple of slaps here and there.'

Isobel gaped at her. Was that how it was for others? No matter how much she looked around, it was impossible to know what went on behind closed doors. Maybe they were all contented – these housewives with bright faces immersed in motherhood and happy families – now that disruption was over and the men had returned from war. Or maybe they just kept quiet.

'Perhaps that's what I need,' she whispered to herself. 'A child.' Perhaps then she would feel like part of a family again. But there were no signs, no indication that she could even become pregnant. And in a way she was relieved. To have Jack's child suggested that she was somehow bonded to him. And she wasn't, was she?

One day Jack was more than usually vicious, and Isobel's lip was badly swollen by the time she got to Vincent's.

'What's happened?' He stared at her. 'What's he done? Has he . . . ?'

'No. It's nothing.' She shook her head. Pushed past him.

'Nothing?' He grabbed her by the arm, held her so that she was forced to stare into the hall mirror. Blurred, frightened eyes blinked back at her. 'This isn't nothing. Just look at yourself.'

It did look bad. She shouldn't have come here, but she'd felt the need to talk, the need to get away. Her lip was cut and swollen into a red weal. There was a fat, dark bruise forming at the side of her mouth. She moved her jaw gingerly. Lucky no teeth were broken.

'Well?' He was staring at her and she couldn't lie to him.

'Jack gets these moods.'

'Moods?' He turned her so that she was facing him. 'You mean he knocks you around?'

She nodded.

'Regularly?' His eyes narrowed.

'Not very often.' She hesitated, hating to admit to it, feeling that she was the one at fault for letting it happen. 'It's just his way.' She felt ridiculous even saying the words.

'And that makes it acceptable?' His voice was dangerously low. 'You can live with that, can you?'

He didn't understand. He was a man, wasn't he, and men were in control. For the first time, Isobel flared into anger against him. 'What am I supposed to do?' Her eyes filled with tears of frustration. 'What choice do I have?'

84

'You could always leave.' He folded his arms and waited.

She turned her head away. He had no idea. 'How many divorcees do you know around here?'

He was silent.

'And if there were any, would anyone give them the time of day?'

Vincent straightened his shoulders. 'That's no reason, Isobel. Because it isn't the done thing. Because other women will put up with it.' He hesitated. 'Violent marriages are insupportable. Violence is insupportable. You know that. It shouldn't be tolerated. And surely, if it's the right thing – to leave . . .'

'Oh, the right thing!' She pulled away from him. 'What bloody use is the right thing if you've got nowhere to go?' Her voice shook. 'How could I live? I'd need more than a part-time typing job to keep me going. Who'd give me a job that paid enough, round here?'

He was watching her closely.

She sighed. 'And I'd have to leave the house. Where would I go?' She'd thought about it. God knows she had thought about it. Thought about the wagging tongues as well. Jack was the hero, wasn't he? What would she be called – the woman who rejected a hero? No . . . People would find out that she still came here to Vincent. They would call her much worse than that.

She stomped into the kitchen, began filling the kettle – more for something to do than because she needed a cup of tea. Over the years she had come to think of Vincent's house almost as her own. Her other life. The other side of her coin.

'Doesn't your mother live in Dorset? Couldn't you go there?' His voice behind her.

That was it, then. The tears came at last, mingling with the water from the tap which was still gushing out, overflowing the kettle, pouring over her hand, soaking her sleeve. Her shoulders were shaking uncontrollably. Couldn't he see? This was her life, here. How could she leave it all behind?

'Isobel.' Vincent reached out to turn off the tap. He prised the kettle from her grasp, dropped it in the sink, turned her around and put his hands gently on her shoulders. 'What is it? What is it really?'

She looked up at him, rubbing the tears from her eyes with her sodden sleeve. 'I wouldn't want to leave you.' There, it was said. Vincent had set her mind free. Vincent had helped her find a voice.

For a moment he looked almost surprised. Then his hand drifted to her hair, smoothing the thick dark strands from her brow. 'Ah, Isobel,' he said. 'Sweet, sweet Isobel.' His fingertips moved to her swollen lips – gently.

She winced.

He drew her, swiftly and easily, towards him. 'I love you, Isobel. I've loved you for a long time in my own way.' His hands were on her breasts. 'But you should be strong. You shouldn't stay with a man like that.'

It was a strange feeling. She had imagined his body once or twice when his solemn voice had been reciting poetry to her and she'd been able to close her eyes and lose the present. He had read of the suffering of war and yes, she had imagined his body, in a kind of detached way, as if it would never really matter.

But it felt quite, quite different from any expectation. Thin and bony, sharply angled. Alien after Jack's broad and bulky frame. Jack had taught her passion, and Vincent . . .

She was left with a sensation of afterthought and error. It hadn't seemed right, and yet perhaps it had been inevitable. Perhaps inevitable that she and Vincent would make love, that their relationship would change. In a strange kind of way, Vincent's love – from the head rather than the heart – joined her to Jack more than it pulled her away. It destroyed every chance of her leaving.

For seven years Isobel was the mistress of Vincent Pascoe for all but six months when she kept away. And for seven years she stayed with Jack, tied to his domination, before at last she found the strength to leave.

Isobel turned to Christie, who was watching her curiously.

'Was it easy to leave Grandad Jack?' she asked again. 'Did you leave him because of Vincent?'

She shook her head. 'No, it wasn't easy to leave him.' She hesitated. 'And no, it wasn't because of Vincent either. It was much harder for a woman to leave in those days.'

'I suppose most women stood dutifully by and didn't expect love to last for ever?'

Isobel laughed. 'Something like that, my dear. But it wasn't just a matter of duty. Divorce wasn't the done thing. You had to be very brave – you'd be a social outcast for a start. And you'd lose your respectability into the bargain. That was just about all some of us women had in the first place.'

'You were brave,' Christie murmured.

'Oh, no.' Isobel shook her head. 'I was a coward for seven years. I let myself become a victim.' The longer she stayed, the more she disliked herself. The more she lost everything that Vincent had given her.

'But you had Mum. No wonder it was difficult to leave. The thought of taking her away from her father, and all that.' For a moment Christie looked as if she would say more. But she put down her cup and grabbed her fleece jacket. 'Fran says it's different when there are children involved. It must be, surely.'

Isobel stared at her. Different when children are involved? You could say that again. 'Will you think about what I said?' She laid a hand on Christie's arm.

Christie nodded. 'I will, I promise.'

Isobel held her close for a short moment as her granddaughter kissed her cheek. She smelt so fresh, looked so young. And she *was* young – barely more than a child.

Yes. It had been different when she'd had Faith to consider. When she first had Faith – that's when she should have left Jack. But it had taken seven years. And seven years was a long, long time to carry on pretending.

8

In the new premises of 'Faith's Basement', Christie and her mother were painting the bare walls.

'Highland Mist.' Faith sniffed. 'Looks more like Highland Rain to me.'

Christie leaned back to survey their efforts. 'I like it. It's warm, but not gloomy.'

'I still think green would have been better.' Faith pulled a face. 'A soft jade. More earthy. More of a background for all this ethnic stuff.' She gestured towards the cardboard boxes stacked in the corner. During the past month, since finding the premises, she had been buying madly, throwing herself into her new project with an infectious enthusiasm.

'This isn't the sixties, Mum,' Christie teased.

'The sixties re-lived in the nineties, what's the difference?' Faith scratched her nose and added another streak of paint to her face. 'It's a pity we didn't manage to open sooner. At this rate we'll only just make Christmas.'

Christie poured thick paint into the roller tray. 'At least you'll be in time to compete with the January sales.'

'Very funny.' Faith frowned. 'And I've still got tons of stuff upstairs to unpack.'

'Go and do it then.' Christie shooed her away. 'Trevor will be here in a minute. He's promised to paint the ceiling.' Despite herself, Christie felt a judder of longing. They hadn't made love for almost a week. It was getting more difficult now that the weather had grown colder; some of their outdoor places weren't so much fun with a freezing breeze on your backside. The house in Ulwell was naturally out of the question; Trevor's mother was apparently housebound and wouldn't approve, and since

89

Gramma's 'lecture' even Yew Cottage was no longer an option. It was true that she didn't love Trevor. But she needed him. She wanted what he gave her, she couldn't resist the pull of it.

'Trying to get rid of me by any chance?'

Christie smiled. She knew how hard her mother was trying. Trying so hard for friendship, for mother-daughter love. And even she herself was beginning to believe that they could get there. If only her mother would open up and talk of her past . . . If only she would tell Christie what she most needed to know.

'Think yourself lucky we finished the winter digging yesterday,' Christie chided. 'No more work till after Christmas.'

'I'll pay you . . .' Faith disappeared up the stairs. 'So long as you get the job done – eventually.'

Trevor began undressing her practically as soon as he walked in the door.

'Stop it. My mother's upstairs.' But she giggled, feeling herself responding so rapidly, so eagerly to his kisses. And yet it was Robin she respected, Robin she loved. Why couldn't it be like this with Robin?

'Later, then.' Trevor pulled on the old boiler suit he'd brought.

'Where?' Christie's eyes were burning.

'Anywhere.' They laughed, only looking away from each other's faces as the shop bell jangled insistently.

Christie went to undo the catch. On the doorstep stood a tall thin mousey-looking girl.

'Yes?' Christie stared at her. 'We're not open yet, you know.'

'I wasn't sure where to . . .' She peered past her. 'Is Trevor here?'

'Trevor?' Still hot from his kisses, Christie pulled the door open wider, allowing her in, watching his face. Who on earth . . . ?

'What's up, Pam?' Unfazed, Trevor grabbed the pot of white paint and levered off the lid.

Pam? Christie blinked at her.

The girl stepped forwards uncertainly, not taking her eyes off Christie. 'Sorry to bother you at work . . .'

Christie shrugged. 'Bother away.' She resumed her place on the stepladder. They weren't exactly at work, were they? But who was she? And what was she doing here?

'It's your mum.' She wrung her thin hands together.

His mum? Was this girl some sort of carer perhaps?

'What about her?' For the first time Trevor seemed concerned. He moved closer towards her, the paint forgotten.

'She's had a bit of a fall. A loose paving-stone, they said.'

Paving stone? But she was *housebound*, wasn't she? A sense of foreboding drilled through her. Christie stiffened.

'Is she all right?' Trevor's voice changed.

Christie waited for the girl's reply.

'They've taken her down the hospital.' She took a deep breath. 'But they reckon she's just twisted her ankle.'

'No bones broken?' Christie asked.

The girl jumped, as if she'd forgotten she was there. 'I don't think so, er . . .'

'Mrs Fifer,' Trevor provided in a dry voice.

'And you are?' Christie had to know.

The girl looked at Trevor, as if for confirmation of her identity.

'My girlfriend, Pamela.' His blue eyes were unblinking.

Christie stared at him. Girlfriend? But he had let her assume he was free and single . . .

'I left a note on the pad at home,' the girl was telling him. 'In case I missed you.'

At home . . . Christie's mind whirled into confusion. Quite obviously they lived together. And as for living with the housebound mother, well that was blatantly untrue. The reason why they had never been able to go to Trevor's house to make love was becoming very clear indeed.

She couldn't look at him. Instead she smothered the roller with paint and slammed it against the wall. 'You'd better get down to the hospital, Trevor.' She spoke quickly, coldly, wanting them out of the way, the sooner the better.

'Are you sure?' His voice was a drawl, but already he was pulling off his boiler suit. And not in the circumstances she'd hoped. 'She did say she's all right. No bones broken.'

'Shaken up though,' Pamela reminded him.

'She'll obviously want to see you.' Christie was furious with him. He'd deceived her. Surely he'd pretended that this affair between them was more than a quick fling? And she was angry with herself. She was married. She had no right to mind the fact that he had a live-in girlfriend, that he was as good as married himself. And that made her mind all the more. 'Take as long as you need. I'll do the ceiling.'

For a moment he hesitated, but she flashed him a contemptuous glance and watched his expression harden. 'Not giving me the sack, are you . . . Mrs Fifer?' He brushed past the stepladder, and she caught a whiff of the scent of him, the male scent that never failed to turn her on.

Not this time. She shook her head, not trusting herself to speak, looking instead at the girl, Pam. Such an insignificant looking person, she found herself thinking, then chided herself for being a prize superior bitch.

'Thanks.' Pam had apparently recovered some poise. Maybe she'd expected to be bawled out for disturbing him at work. Only he hadn't minded, had he? And Christie had been in no position to mind.

'I'm sure she'll be fine,' Pam murmured. 'Still, better to be safe than sorry.'

'Of course.' Christie nodded. 'Better safe than sorry,' she echoed.

'Bye then.' As she moved away, Christie smelled the stench of stale cigarettes, clinging to the girl's scruffy coat and greasy hair. How old was she? Seventeen? Eighteen? A wave of sympathy for the unknown girl swept over her. An unexpected guilt.

She shoved the roller once more, hard against the wall, the pale pink/grey paint spattering her dungarees, her hands and face. She rolled, up and down, up and down with fierce energy, working out her frustration and anger, until Highland Mist was smooth and serene on the bare walls of Faith's Basement.

So this was Trevor's life. And she'd known nothing about it. They had rarely conversed, she realised. She had known nothing of his life at all.

'Robin. We should talk.' Christie crept up behind him as he sat at the PC, tapping out instructions, shifting the mouse deftly with finger and thumb.

'What about?' He didn't stop tapping. She was a sideline for him these days, an unwelcome distraction, like a linesman waving his flag when you were about to shoot at goal.

'You know what about. Although a conversation about anything would be nice.' Christie perched on the desk trying to look cheerful.

'But it's nearly Christmas.'

'Ye . . . es?' She failed to see the relevance.

'And you know how everything shuts down for a least a fortnight over Christmas.'

Christie frowned. She wished the blasted computer would shut down. 'So?'

'So there's too much on, for me to just flick a switch so that I can stop working and amuse my wife.'

She stared at him. His eyes were cold as stone.

'That's not what I wanted.' She jumped down, crossing to the cupboard, pulling out her fleecy jacket and black gloves. Why was she even bothering? 'I never asked to be amused.'

'Now where are you going?' Robin scraped back his chair, irritated, pushing his dark hair from his eyes. 'What have I said?'

'Nothing.' That was just the point. Nothing, nothing, nothing. Was Gramma right? Was a clean break the only way? Even though she no longer had Trevor. How could she have Trevor after yesterday? And yet without Trevor, her marriage seemed more unstable than ever.

And she shrank from the thought that he would never again hold her, never again kiss her lips, never run his tongue along her collar bone in the way he had, that drove her mad with desire for him . . .

'I asked you where you were going.' Robin stood beside her. Oh yes. She had his full attention now that she was leaving. But that wasn't any answer, was it?

'To Yew Cottage.' Reading his sad expression, the doleful tilt to his mouth, she relented. 'I'll be out of your way. You can fiddle with that damn computer to your heart's content.'

He grabbed her wrist. 'It's not a game, Christie. It's my job.'

'I know that.' She stared pointedly at his hand. Not like Trevor's hand – large, warm and brown, rough skin but such a gentle touch. She shook her head, cross with herself. Robin's hand was thin, white, sensitive. Robin's hand seemed to belong on the keyboard rather than on her skin.

'I won't be long.' She stood on tiptoe to kiss the side of his mouth. He didn't respond.

He returned to the PC, but as she glanced at him before shutting the door, his eyes weren't focused on the screen. He was staring blindly, straight ahead.

Christie ran down the path towards the pick-up truck she had taken to using more often since the weather had got colder. Automatically, she drove towards Yew Cottage. Her sanctuary.

The air in the yew grove was mild and damp. It had been raining, and the humus let out a hiss of welcome as she stepped under the first rusty branches. It was barely mid-afternoon but already the imminent darkness seemed to be loaded like a gun barrel on the horizon, ready to shoot down another winter evening that went on for ever. Heavy and dull, barely promising that the season would ever outgrow itself. Almost Christmas.

Her feet moved as if of their own accord through the trees and once she was well inside the wood, the earth became dry again, protected by the spiked umbrella of needles and twisted branches above.

There was no sound in the yew grove – not a whisper. Christie made her way on tip-toe, not wanting to disturb the voice of silence, to her favourite tree. She squatted down by its gnarled roots. At her feet were the small new saplings, self-seeded or grown from lower, fallen branches – strong, vertical shoots that seemed to spring from the life of the old tree. So . . . The yew tree needed only itself to survive. It would continue to produce new generations of trees under any conditions. Christie smiled. The yew tree was a survivor.

And she too would survive the loss of Trevor. Against her will, she thought back to the afternoon in late autumn when she had let Trevor drag her here. She should never have consented to that.

'Come on, Christie,' he urged. 'See those trees over there? Do you remember? That was one hell of a day.'

Oh, yes; she remembered the day in Wareham Forest. The first time she'd made love with Trevor Swift. She'd never forget it.

She shook her head. 'Not here. What about Gramma and Vincent – they might see us.'

'Where then?' His breath was hot and demanding on her cheek as he bent closer.

'You're crazy.' She felt her own breath catch in response.

'Crazy for you. Where then?'

'I don't know.' She tried to push him away but it was half-hearted. Besides, he was big, strong, and refusing to take no for an answer.

And however much she resented this macho spark in Trevor – the same easy chauvinism that she had found in Barry – there was a fire in his eyes that ignited the fire in hers. Every time. Every time, logic, reason and all the principles she believed in simply flew out of the window. Every time she didn't resist him, she thought she'd be lost for ever.

'You know you want to.' The insinuation in his voice was distasteful but he was right. What did she want? She wanted to run from him, but she wanted him to kiss her at the same time. She wanted to be free of him and she longed for his warm fingers on her cold skin. She wanted to drown in this desire that sometimes seemed more like a torment.

'Christie?' His hands around her waist. His mouth on her neck. The heat of his tongue moistening her flesh.

She felt the urge to giggle. 'It's not even private property, that wood. It doesn't belong to Yew Cottage. Anyone could go there.'

He took this as acceptance, which she supposed it was. 'We'll hide in the trees. Come on.' Tugging her hand. She followed him.

They ran until the trees were dense, leaving the path, his big feet thrashing into the delicate saplings. Would they survive his trampling?

'Here.' He stopped, a wildness in his eyes.

But the thrill that she always felt when his lips drew close, when his body clamped on hers, was suffocated. She felt unable to breathe. There was an unexpected competitor in the yew wood – the atmosphere of suspense that lived here.

'It's a bit spooky, isn't it?' Trevor frowned. He loosened his belt but she knew he didn't like it. And that made her glad.

'Not afraid of ghosts, are you?' She teased, her eyes challenging and free from caring for him.

'I'll exorcise them.' He grabbed her, ripping at buttons as if his life depended on it.

'Careful . . .' She smiled.

But all the time they made love – a brief coupling that lacked their usual desperate passion – she sensed him half-looking over his shoulder into the perpetual twilight of the yew wood. Trevor was nervous. He wasn't comfortable in here. He wasn't in control. She smiled once more, feeling as if she had claimed a small piece of herself back. The wood was still sacred then. They hadn't touched it, hadn't spoiled it. He still hadn't entered her life.

Now, Christie stretched out her legs, resting her back against the huge girth of rough, flaking bark.

Until yesterday afternoon she hadn't considered that Trevor Swift had a life apart from Purbeck Garden Design, apart from her and their illicit affair. It showed how little she really thought about him, she supposed. It was the times when they were together – the pure, physical presence of the man – that had some place in her life, not any lingering moments with the power to stay in her heart.

As she looked up into the dark tentacles of the tree above her, Christie became uncomfortably aware that she wasn't alone. Just above her head was a low, long branch stretching parallel with the ground. She sat on this sometimes, swinging her legs like a child, but now it acted as a camouflage, tucking her small form almost into the folds of the ancient tree itself. Cautiously, remaining still, moving only her eyes, she looked around her.

There was a slight movement to her left, some metres away, towards the thicket beyond the grove. She let out an involuntary gasp of surprise and pleasure. A roe deer stood poised under the protective branches of a yew, her coat merging with the sheen of the reddish-brown bark. She tensed, as if about to take flight.

Christie was mesmerised by the sight. She had always known there were deer in these woods, but had never seen one before – they were nervous creatures and rarely ventured so close to the house.

As she gazed at the dignified, quiet beauty of this shy animal, another distant rustle caught her attention. She blinked, saw the deer stiffen as she looked around her with wide startled eyes. Then she ran.

A minute passed. There was no further sound and Christie began to breathe more easily again.

'They come to eat the yew berries.'

She jumped. Dominic Redfern, dressed in a bottle-green waxed jacket, laced walking boots and woollen socks, was standing not ten feet away.

'I thought they were poisonous to livestock.' It was all she could think of to say. She stared at him. His face seemed darker and more weather-beaten today. But Fran was right – in his way, he was a very attractive man.

'To sheep and cattle, but not deer.' His hazel eyes were apologetic. 'I didn't mean to startle you.'

'It's okay.' Mind, he had a way of creeping around that did rather unnerve her. Supposing he had come across herself and Trevor in the yew wood that time they were making love? This thought brought a flush to her cheeks. She looked down at his boots. They were very muddy indeed.

'Where have you . . . ?'

'I suppose I should have stayed on the path . . .'

They spoke at the same time.

Dominic raked his unruly hair with his fingers, and smiled. 'I fancied a bit of a walk, so I left the car in Swanage.'

'I see.' Feeling at a disadvantage, Christie grabbed the low branch and pulled herself up into a standing position.

'Over Ballard Down,' he elaborated. 'I was on my way to the cottage.' He nodded towards it.

'Oh?' What on earth would Dominic Redfern want at Yew Cottage? For the first time, Christie wondered about his background. Was he a Dorset man born and bred? Hardly. His cool, polite voice betrayed no trace of an accent.

'I was going to see your grandmother,' he supplied, as the silence stretched between them. Was it the atmosphere of the yew wood that made the air seem charged – or was it something about the personality of this strange, enigmatic man?

But Gramma had few friends, and Christie would never have guessed Dominic Redfern to be one of them. 'I didn't realise you knew her.' She scuffed some fallen needles with the toe of her ankle boot.

'I've commissioned some work.'

'Really?' She wondered which piece. It wouldn't be The Lovers, would it? Dominic didn't seem the type to want something like that in his home. But then, she knew so little about him. He was closeted inside himself. He gave nothing away.

'I'm very impressed with what I've seen so far.' He rubbed at his unshaven chin. 'She's a talented lady.'

Christie smiled in appreciation of this compliment to her beloved grandmother, still intrigued, watching him as he stood, long, lean and brooding, against the background of a low-lying yew tree. This man was as still as the wood itself, his body poised in a way that reminded her of the rhythmic, Oriental dance that she'd witnessed beside the swimming pool that day. 'I should be going.' She turned abruptly, suddenly wanting to leave the sombre atmosphere of the yew grove behind her.

'I'll walk with you.' He moved to her side.

But she didn't know what else to say to him. 'How's Fran?' she heard herself asking. 'Still set on the idea of the Refuge?' Now why had she said that? It was bound to antagonise him.

'She does what she likes.' He frowned.

'But it's your house.' Christie felt perverse.

'As far as I'm concerned, the house is Fran's.' He became vehement. 'I don't even like the place. I never did.'

'Then why . . . ?' Christie hesitated. Shut up, shut up, she told herself.

She wanted to know why he still spent time there if he hated it, why he didn't sell it, why he had bought it in the first place. But she didn't dare ask.

'Why what?' He raised his eyebrows in quizzical interrogation.

'I'm sorry. I'm too nosy – or so I'm always being told.' She thought of her mother and Gramma. And that was about all she was being told. The rest was one big mystery.

He smiled, but didn't disagree. Neither did he offer any further explanations.

'And how's Faith's Basement coming along?' was what he did say after a minute or two of listening only to their footsteps sinking into soft earth.

Christie glanced at him in surprise. 'Do you know my mother, too?' She wasn't sure that she liked this idea.

'I've spoken to her a few times.' He paused. 'And I've seen the two of you going into the shop.'

Of course. His office was very close to Faith's Basement.

'It'll be opening any day now.' She wasn't entirely sure that it would work, this idea of sharing office space with Faith. Did she still resent the ease with which her mother had slotted back into her life?

'It must be nice for you, having her here in Dorset.' He was making polite conversation, but Christie sensed more, remaining unsaid. Was it nice for her? Hadn't she got on with her life just fine by herself?

'Perhaps,' she murmured.

They had reached the outskirts of the wood. Once again, the yew grove and its vague air of regret was behind them.

'Families can be difficult.' Dominic took a step closer towards her. 'The problem is that we're supposed to like them. Made to feel guilty if we don't.'

She nodded. 'I suppose so.'

But he continued speaking almost as if he were talking to himself. 'Sometimes we can't stand them and sometimes we love them too much.' His eyes misted – with some personal memory, perhaps.

Christie stared at the fine, narrow features of his face. The high cheekbones and Roman nose. The broad forehead, mass of curly dark hair and sad hazel eyes. Which was it for him?

Even as she watched, the shutters came down. 'I'm sorry I disturbed you in the wood.' He nodded, cool and distant once more. 'But I'm glad we had this chat.'

'So am I.' Her gaze followed him as he strode towards the workshop. It had been a strange encounter, uncomfortable and stilted, and yet somehow it pleased her. He pleased her in some way she couldn't define. 'See you, then.'

Dominic Redfern waved, kicked the mud from his boots, knocked lightly and walked in to Gramma's workshop. As if he'd been there before. She heard the sound of laughter.

Christie pulled the keys to the pick-up truck out of her jeans. She must get home. She had reached a conclusion in the yew grove today. She had decided what to do about Trevor, and she was going to sort this whole thing out, first chance she got.

9

Isobel Vaughan wiped her hands on her blue apron and returned his firm handshake. 'Hello, Dominic.'

'I'm sorry to disturb your week-end. Especially so near Christmas.' He smiled. His dark eyes became warm when he smiled.

'Nonsense. Christmas is another ballgame entirely when you don't have children to do it all for.' She paused. 'Besides, it was a good excuse to get away from the typewriter.'

They both laughed. She had already told him about Vincent's writing, trying not to sound disloyal.

'Not that I mind,' she added quickly. Wasn't it one of the few things that Vincent had left? It really wasn't much to ask.

'How is he?' The smile faded from Dominic's face.

'About the same.' Isobel's fingers fidgeted, as they often did when she had no wood to hold. 'They say he might not deteriorate any further. If he's lucky.'

'It's bad enough though, isn't it?' He patted her arm awkwardly, and Isobel was reminded once more of Dominic Redfern's kindness. He was a nice man. One of the few she genuinely respected. Now, if she were thirty years younger . . . she surprised herself by thinking. If she had met someone like him when she'd first moved to Purbeck, maybe she would have chosen a different path after all.

She watched him as he wandered around the workshop, picking up a piece of sculpture every now and then, immersed in contemplation. She liked that – it seemed to make her work worthwhile.

'Help yourself to coffee,' she told him.

A nice man. A gentle man. As so often happened – more and more as time took it further away from this, her present life – she felt herself slipping back into the world she'd known before Dorset. Jack's world. It was like an unwelcome hand on her shoulder that she couldn't ignore. A memory that could never be far away.

In the seven years before Isobel had moved here, she had become used to living Jack's way. Living with the violence. It might have begun as an isolated incident, but it had so quickly formed a part of her life.

Over those seven years it shocked her how easily she had become accustomed to it, how slyly she found ways to avoid it. Even how she used it against Jack when she had the chance. A lever of guilt, a key of submission.

'I don't know how you can stay with that man.' Vincent always took her apparent subservience as a slight against him.

'That's my business.' She was done with telling him she had no other choices. That had been in the early days, when she'd more or less begged him to love her. Now she was stronger, as if feeding from his strength of will and superior intellect. She found it easy to stand up to Vincent since he didn't try and dominate her with violence, only with words. Sometimes it seemed as if Vincent ruled her head and Jack her heart. While she struggled to be free of both of them.

'It's my business too, when I see the bruises.'

Oh, so easy to be self-righteous. She moved closer towards him. 'Yes, but you don't feel them, do you, Vincent?'

He turned away, as always embarrassed when she edged too close to the truth. The truth was that Vincent had not asked her to divorce Jack and be his wife. Neither had he asked her to move in with him. That was the truth as Isobel saw it. Vincent wanted her, but he wouldn't commit to her. He'd rather see her hurt first.

He clenched his right fist hard against his left palm, a gesture uncharacteristic for the mild-mannered Vincent. 'Vicious bastard. Picking on a woman. What sort of a man do you call that?' Unusual words for him too.

She touched his arm lightly. She was being unfair. It did cause Vincent pain to see her abused. She could see the shame of it in his pale eyes, even in the stoop of his shoulders when he saw what Jack had done to her. And if she were to ask . . . Then maybe he would agree to her living here, even agree to them going away together somewhere.

But another part of the truth was that Isobel didn't want to ask – she wanted the suggestion to come from him. So that he wouldn't be providing a favour. So that he was pleasing himself. So that it was a free choice, not something he'd been pushed into. She had half-wanted that from the beginning, and she'd waited a long time. Perhaps she'd stopped waiting now.

'If Jack were to really hurt me, Vincent . . .' she began.

'Yes?' He turned on her. 'Would you leave him then? Or would it be too late? Would you be lying at the bottom of the stairs, maybe?'

She moved away from him. 'If he really hurt me, then I'd be off. You can be sure of that.' But who could tell until it happened?

'It sounds as if you're waiting for it.' His voice was edged with cynicism.

She shrugged. 'I can avoid it most of the time. Most of the time, he's fine.' She knew that wasn't what he wanted to hear. Life wasn't all bad with Jack. Unbelievably, there were still times of passion. There were still times when he seemed closer to the young rogue who'd stolen her heart at Hammersmith Palais during that quickstep of a lifetime. 'And then there's Faith . . .' Jack was so good with Faith, she couldn't deny that.

'Ah yes. Faith.' Vincent shuffled some papers on his desk. That always shut him up.

Isobel knew only too well that children had no place in Vincent's life. She'd always known it. He had met Faith only a few times despite all Isobel's efforts, his indifference driving another wedge between them. Because she loved her daughter. Faith came first in her life and affections, before any man. What was good for Faith would be tolerated by Isobel. And Jack was good for Faith. Jack was a family man, when it suited him to be. So many reasons. Nothing was black and white, she reminded herself once more.

'You shouldn't allow children to dictate your life.' Vincent sounded disapproving, but he'd said it all before. 'They won't thank you for it.'

What do you know? she wanted to scream. Not everything written in a book was true. Some truths could only be learned by living them. Some lies too.

'You know they adore each other,' she told Vincent, wanting to turn the knife a little. Didn't he deserve it? Right from the start, she'd fought for his right to have a relationship with her daughter, but she couldn't fight alone. If he didn't want to know Faith, then what use was any of it? All this heartache and soul-searching would be worthless.

Would it have been different if she'd been more honest? No, surely not. Hadn't she given him every chance? All he would take into consideration were practicalities. He was not a man of affection or spontaneity – two of the qualities that she'd loved in Jack. All Vincent could worry over were the consequences of seeing Faith. Whether she was old enough to confide in her father about who she'd been with. Or what might happen to Isobel if Jack were to find out. Vincent wouldn't want to cause more trouble. Maybe he just didn't want to be involved. But not wanting to be involved was cowardice, wasn't it?

'You're making too much of it. Letting your imagination run away with you. She'd get over it in time.' Vincent never credited children with feelings. Couldn't he remember his own childhood or didn't he want to?

'Maybe she wouldn't, though.' Isobel sank heavily into the armchair. This was a possibility that plagued her. 'Maybe she'd never forgive me.'

She considered the way Jack was with Faith. A father that dreams were made of. He thought nothing of getting down on his hands and knees to give her a pretend pony ride; he gave her ice cream or sweets almost every time she asked, and his bedtime stories had a life of their own. Jack was big, strong and invincible. He was her protector. His bear hugs could dry her tears, and he called her Daddy's little girl in a way that brought a lump to Isobel's throat. When he was with Faith he reminded Isobel so vividly of her first dreams of romance. Jack had seemed such a perfect and exciting hero. Isobel would have given him the world, had he ever asked, and she knew that her daughter felt the same. But of course, she hadn't known him then. Hadn't known him at all.

'Come on now. You're her mother.' Vincent showed a rare willingness to offer comfort as he stood behind her, his thin fingers stroking the long dark hair that fell loosely around her shoulders. 'Of course she'd forgive you. And as she gets older . . .'

'As she gets older it'll be even harder.' Isobel turned, buried her face in his legs. Smelling the tweed and spice that were part of Vincent.

'As she gets older she'll see for herself what he's like,' he corrected, sinking to his knees so that their faces were level with each other. 'How can she miss it? She'd have to be blind. What do you think Faith will say about her precious father when she watches him beating shit out of her mother?'

'Vincent . . .' His words shocked her. But she knew she must protect

Faith from ever seeing Jack's violence. It wasn't fair. It would shatter all her illusions, carry on hurting her for the rest of her life.

Jack had never lifted a finger against Faith – she couldn't imagine that he ever would. And neither did he hit Isobel when Faith was around. No. Jack waited for the small, dark hours when others were sleeping. That's when he liked to practise his domination.

But in 1954, after seven years of violence with Jack, and seven years into her affair with Vincent Pascoe, two things happened that changed everything. Isobel's mother died, leaving her Yew Cottage in Purbeck – the place she'd bought after Isobel's father died, a few weeks after Isobel married Jack. And Jack Vaughan went too far.

After Beatrice's death, Isobel visited the cottage, finding, in this place that had meant so much to her mother, some solace for her grief.

She went to the yew grove, remembering how she had come here in the war years, before Jack had become a vicious hero and before Vincent had become her lover. Most of all she remembered the total darkness of the wood, the quilted black cover that surrounded and drowned everything even more effectively than the black-outs she was used to. In the yew grove even the moon couldn't seem to creep through the broad, layered branches.

Isobel returned to London only to collect Faith. There was still more to sort out in Purbeck – the cottage must be cleared of her mother's belongings, and papers had to be signed with Redferns, the solicitors. John Redfern's family had owned the cottage originally, and he was eager to buy it back, so that was one problem easily solved. It saddened her, that Beatrice's precious cottage could be lost again so quickly. But what choice did she have now?

When she got back to the house in London, Jack was standing at the top of the stairs, his shoulders heaving and his blue eyes burning.

'About bloody time too,' he hissed. 'What kept you?'

'Where's Faith?' Isobel stood at the bottom of the stairs gazing up at the tall menacing figure of the man she'd married, trying not to recognise the signs. What had got into him this time? Did he even need a reason, or was the very sight of her enough to spark him into violence?

'Next door. But you're her mother. You're the one who should be looking after the kid.'

She took off her coat, playing for time. 'There was a lot to do, a lot to sort out. There still is.' She spoke like an automaton, devoid of emotion, hardly knowing what she said.

'Get up here.'

Going up those stairs seemed the longest journey of her life. 'I'm tired, Jack.' That was the way. Play for his sympathy. It had worked before.

'And so am I.' He moved to let her pass. 'I'm bloody tired of you not being around when I want you.'

Her dark eyes met his. Unflinching. 'What did you want me for, Jack?'

'A bit of what you're best at, my love.' He grabbed her by the shoulders, ripping the buttons of her blouse as he tore it open. 'That's what.'

'Jack . . .' She struggled against him. The journey and her grief had exhausted her. All she wanted was a cup of tea and a lie down and she'd be fine. She knew she'd be fine. 'Please, not now. I can't . . .'

'Oh, yes you can.' He pulled her roughly towards him. His mouth was a gaping, grinning hole in the crater of his face. He seemed all mouth, and she didn't think she could stand it this time.

She shook her head, sure she would faint. 'Please . . .'

He pushed her down to his feet. 'Beg me, then.'

It was Isobel's worst humiliation so far. But she had to stop him somehow. 'Please . . . Not now,' she repeated.

'Not now?' His voice seemed to echo around the landing. 'Think you can dictate when a man has his needs, do you, my love?' His words slid over her, saturated her consciousness. Her head was swimming. She felt herself go limp.

'No, Jack . . .' As he pulled her to her feet once more, she pushed at him, hardly touching him really, but finding some last ounce of strength from desperation.

'I'll give you bloody, no . . .' He tore off the remainder of her blouse, ripped the bodice of her thin nylon slip, and grabbed her breasts from the white lace bra.

Isobel groaned. 'Jack . . .'

'I'll teach you who makes the decisions round here.' That huge, gaping mouth came closer and closer. His lips were red and wet. He tore at her mouth, forcing her lips apart, his tongue rasping at her teeth, until she thought she'd choke on him.

After an eternity he stopped for breath.

'Get off me!' She was fighting for survival now. She tried to run.

In seconds he was after her, pulling at her skirt, tearing at her stockings, her pants, anything his rough hands could get hold of. His fingers bruised her tender skin. His breath came in thick heaves of anger and excitement, his eyes a madman's eyes – dilated pupils and wave upon wave of distanced, torrid blue.

Still, she struggled against him. He yanked her towards the sweating bulk of his male body. Her thin wrists slipped from his grasp, her strength fading.

For a moment she teetered on the edge of the landing, her eyes wide and frightened, her hands groping out of the darkness. For balance. For sanity.

He reached out and slapped her hard. 'Bitch. Come here, bitch.'

The force of his blow stung her cheek, immobilised her limbs. She tried to move, lost her footing and fell down the stairs, her body thumping, her arms flailing, her scream a thin wail of terror. This is what Vincent predicted, was all she could think. Until the ceiling went black.

'Get up.' Jack was the new ceiling, standing above her, no trace of regret in his cold eyes. The fire had gone out.

She rose, like a child, obedient and beaten, aching and bruised, allowing him to lead her into the living room.

He took her on the couch, rising over her like some great warrior of death. And when he was done, he brought her the cup of tea she wanted, covered her with a blanket, said he was sorry.

Isobel felt the blood warm between her thighs, and she knew that she had lost her second child. She wept. She could never forgive him for this.

In the event it was easier to leave him than she'd ever expected. There was Yew Cottage empty and waiting, offering Isobel the new start that she knew she had to grab with both hands before her choices receded once more.

'If you go, I'll not take you back,' Jack said as she packed her case.

'I won't be coming back.' She kept Faith in the room with her, her protection against this man.

'You should have told me you were pregnant.' The words blurted into the space between them.

She stared at him in disbelief. He had abused her until she had become worthless to him. It didn't matter to Jack Vaughan that he could have killed his wife. But losing the child . . . that mattered to him. She would have been worth a little more if she'd been carrying his child.

She thought he might cry as Faith clung on to his neck. But he seemed made of stone. He showed no trace of emotion. She guessed that he would cut the memory of them both from his life. As for Faith, she couldn't understand what was going on. Isobel looked at her. Daddy's little girl. Would she ever forgive her mother for taking her away?

Saying goodbye to Vincent was harder, because Vincent had given her the strength to leave in the first place. He had taught her about freedom, but he was part of the old life, and she must leave him too.

'I'll come and see you,' he told her. His pale eyes were confused, as if some opportunity had slipped past him untaken.

She nodded. Perhaps he would visit, but she would almost prefer it if he stayed away. He too must become the past. He too had his own need to dominate, even if only with words. And she'd had more than her fill of domination. She was ready to stand alone.

10

'I saw your granddaughter in the yew grove.' Dominic's voice brought Isobel sharply back to the present.

'Oh?' She turned. 'What was she doing there?'

'Thinking, I should imagine.' His voice was dry. 'And I disturbed her, I'm afraid.'

Isobel watched his hazel eyes soften, and a thought occurred to her. She pushed it away. 'Christie's got a lot to think about,' she remarked obliquely. 'And she loves it in that wood.'

'I know how she feels.' They exchanged a glance of understanding.

'I wonder what it is about those old yews.' Isobel was thoughtful. 'Some people might find the place unbearably spooky.'

The lines of Dominic's mouth were grim. 'Most do. You wouldn't even catch me going there at night. The yew tree is a pagan tree if ever I saw one.'

'And yet you find them in so many churchyards.' Isobel smiled to herself. She knew he was itching to see the sculpture and yet he was far too polite to say.

'They were traditional for churchyards. People thought they absorbed the vapours of putrefaction.' Dominic laughed. 'Or so I read somewhere. There's a book in the library about trees and legends. I should dig it out for you.'

'You should dig it out for my granddaughter.' Isobel poured more coffee. 'Christie would be fascinated.'

'She was brought up here, wasn't she?' The dark eyes flickered with interest.

Isobel nodded. But she didn't want to go into that. Not now, and definitely not with Dominic. It was hard enough to even talk with her own family. So much had been closeted in darkness for so long.

'Did your uncle bring you to the yew grove when you were a child?' Isobel asked. She had learned about the Redfern family connection with Yew Cottage when Dominic first visited her a year ago. Perhaps she should have guessed – her mother's solicitor John Redfern had been eager enough to buy the place when her mother died. But there had been too many things going on in Isobel's life at that time – grief, violence and parting – to give it a second thought. They might even have heard talk in the village, but neither Vincent nor Isobel had much time for gossip.

Dominic shook his head. 'I was brought up in Sussex. Almost in the shadows of Kingley Vale. That's a yew grove ten times as big as this one.' His eyes became sad once more. 'I didn't come to Purbeck to live with Uncle John until I was thirteen.'

Knowing that it was the death of his parents in a car crash that had brought the teenage Dominic to this part of the world, Isobel laid a sympathetic hand on his arm. 'And that's when you found out how much this place meant to your uncle?'

He nodded. 'Dad never talked about it much. He only told me that some ancestor of his had built Yew Cottage out of Purbeck stone, and that he and his two brothers had grown up here.'

Isobel sighed. 'His father could never have intended that the family would lose the cottage, surely?'

Dominic shook his head. 'They assumed he forgot to change his will. He died quite suddenly, I believe.'

'So when he died the cottage went to the eldest son,' Isobel murmured.

'Rather than being divided among the three sons, Roland got the lot. That's right.' Dominic nodded.

'You'd think Roland would have given them a share,' Isobel suggested.

'He wasn't known for his loyalty or family feeling.' Dominic's tone betrayed a harsh resentment of the uncle he'd never known. 'He sold the place and emigrated, leaving Uncle John and my father with nowhere to live. Uncle John reckoned it was the first honest thing he'd seen Roland do in his life. He hated his family, so he sold what his family loved most.'

'Your father must have been very bitter about that,' Isobel said. Who wouldn't resent having their birthright taken away from them?

But Dominic shook his head. 'Maybe at first. But later he had my mother, and the farm. He wasn't the type to hold a grudge.'

'Whereas John . . .' she prodded.

'John stayed in Purbeck. He got his qualifications, and started up the practice. But he never married. He spent his time waiting. Waiting for the cottage to come back on the market, Dad always said.'

Isobel smoothed back a strand of dark hair that had escaped from the long plait she wore. Dominic seemed fairly philosophical about his family history. But she couldn't help wondering if it was all as clear-cut in his mind.

'Were you close to your uncle?' she asked. John Redfern must have thought his luck had changed in 1954 when Isobel came to sort out her mother's estate, telling him she wanted to sell the place. And the poor man must have been shattered when she changed her mind. She sighed softly to herself. No wonder he'd been so unfriendly whenever she'd passed him in the village.

Dominic perched himself on the stool where Christie usually sat, an incongruous figure in the place Isobel regarded as Christie's alone. 'We were very close,' he said. 'That's why after he died I felt I had to come and see you to explain. Over the years he became so bitter, you see.'

Isobel understood. Dominic was the sort of man who would always want to set the record straight. She sipped her coffee slowly. She too knew all about bitterness and hypocrisy. 'That's families for you,' she murmured. She was thinking of her daughter Faith and how she had lost her, but a glance at Dominic's inscrutable expression told her that he was thinking of something quite different.

'Did you mind me coming to see you that time?' Dominic asked. 'I never meant to make you feel bad. After all, it's over now. John's dead, Roland too, for all I know. Either that or he's an old man.'

Isobel smiled. 'Only because I feel the place still half belongs to you.'

'Not a bit of it.' Dominic seemed surprised. 'It's never been mine, and I'd never think of it that way.'

Isobel was satisfied he was telling her the truth. After all, since he'd come of age and inherited his mother's considerable legacy, Dominic Redfern could afford to buy several Yew Cottages of his own if he wanted to. But still, he had connections with this place. She could feel it, almost as if it were in his blood.

She watched him as he picked up the piece of sculpture she had named The Lovers. He turned it thoughtfully around in his hand. Poor Dominic. He had lost both his beloved uncle and the wife he worshipped. What's more, he had never recovered from the loss of Amy Cassidy. Isobel's mouth twisted. More fool him.

She decided to take pity on him at last. 'Don't forget to have a quick look at your statuette before you go,' she teased.

'How's it coming along?' His eyes were eager, searching the workshop openly now for a glimpse of it.

'I'll show you.' Walking to the corner she pulled off the black drape. 'I suppose I shouldn't really let you see it. It's not finished yet.'

He caught his breath, walking up to the female figure carved in yew. 'She's going to be beautiful.' He reached out a hand tentatively to touch, as he might once have reached out to touch Amy's skin.

Isobel flicked at a piece of rough wood. After what he'd said about pagan trees it rather surprised her that he'd chosen yew wood from the choices she'd given him. But there were other legends attached to yews – they were a symbol of life, for a start. Isobel's eyes darkened. Amy Cassidy was dead.

'So beautiful,' Dominic repeated.

'Not necessarily beautiful in the way you're expecting her to be, Dominic.' Isobel's voice remained gentle. But she was warning him. She hadn't done the face yet, and the face would tell its own story, as faces always did. As the artist, she could take command up to a certain point, but after that the sculpture had a way of taking over, of dictating its own destiny.

Isobel frowned. She had explained all this to Dominic when she first agreed to take on the commission.

'She'll be beautiful.' Dominic sounded confident enough. 'How could she not be?'

'A kind of eternal Eve.' Isobel watched him appraisingly. How did Dominic feel about sin and temptation?

There was a flicker of doubt in the hazel eyes and then it was gone. 'Amy would have loved it.' His mouth twitched as if at some private joke.

'Would she?' Isobel raised dark eyebrows. Maybe he was right. Or maybe Amy Cassidy would have taken it as an insult. Isobel did honest explorative sculpture; there was no other kind for her. 'Where will you put it?'

'I'm not sure.' Dominic picked up his mug to finish the last of his coffee. 'I'll give it some thought.'

'Tell me when you decide. We'll have to discuss the finishing. I might have to do some work in situ.' Isobel was about to replace the black drape, but he grabbed her hand to prevent her.

'I want this to be more than a memory of Amy, you see, Isobel.' His voice was rough with passion. 'I want to be reminded of everything. And I want the tangible – something I can touch.'

'I understand.' Isobel nodded. He wanted something that could almost be seen as still living. But sculpture wasn't about the living. There would be no flesh and blood in this statue.

A shudder seemed to run right through him. He raked long fingers through his wild dark hair. 'I'm not a religious man,' he whispered. 'I've never got a lot out of cold gravestones.'

'Of course.' She replaced the black drape. Dominic had cared too much. Apparently he still did.

Isobel had known the actress Amy Cassidy for a long time before she met Dominic. Amy had been in the habit of commissioning work from Isobel – more because a unique sculpture reflected her chosen self-image, than out of admiration for the actual work or form. Or so Isobel had always believed.

But Dominic had seemed to be easily ensnared. He had put her on a pedestal of her making, and it seemed that Amy Cassidy hadn't lived long enough with her second husband to be brought down to the land of the living where people were fallible and real. To be recognised by Dominic for what she really was.

To Isobel, Amy was a cold calculating bitch whose first husband had found someone younger, kinder and less demanding. At thirty-three, Amy seemed determined not to be outdone, marrying Dominic on the rebound – a man five years her junior with plenty of old family money to put at her disposal. Isobel didn't know why Amy had killed herself, but it wasn't for lack of money or adulation.

But it would be callous and cruel to say any of this to Dominic. And besides, it wasn't her concern. Perhaps he held himself somehow responsible for Amy's death. Isobel liked the man, but at times it was difficult to guess what lay behind the calm face that he presented to the world.

In Isobel's view, the Amy Cassidys of this life were no loss. But Dominic would never understand that. Dominic would probably grieve for her for ever.

* * *

On Monday morning, in Faith's Basement, Christie watched her mother as she collected her things together at high speed – bags, cheque book, credit cards, accounts, and a file of names and addresses. At the same time she was jotting down a list in a spiral note-pad and giving brief instructions to her young assistant Sarah.

'Tell him I'll take ten of these letter-racks to start with. But at *this* price.' Faith jabbed a finger. 'No more. And if he argues, no deal. I can pick this stuff up anywhere.'

Christie laughed. She was beginning to understand why her mother was such a successful organiser. It left Christie out of breath just watching.

'I'm late.' Faith glanced at the gold watch on her slender wrist. 'I'm going to miss the train. Where's that blasted taxi?' She stared out into the teeming rain, her olive eyes fretful, and lit another menthol cigarette.

'You should have let me drive you.' Christie tucked her hands into the pockets of her jeans. There was little work she could do in this weather, so she'd driven to Wareham to help in the shop while her mother went to London to wander around warehouses and order more stock. Although she couldn't imagine her wandering. It would doubtless be more of a twelve hour dash.

Christie examined the small shop, newly painted and now crammed to bursting. Keen to cash in on the new nineties ethnic market, Faith Vaughan had partially branched away from the clothes business she knew so well. Assorted mobiles and wind-chimes decorated the ceiling of the shop, while scented candles, fragrant oils and incense sticks were stacked on the shelves, with multi-coloured rugs, patchwork bags, enamelled mirrors, and assorted jewellery. And today, Faith was concentrating on building up the clothes stock, using her contacts from the city. She wanted Indian dresses and skirts, flowing kaftans and silk blouses to adorn the clothes rails of Faith's Basement, as well as the embroidered waistcoats that were becoming so popular.

'No need, darling.' A horn blared outside. 'I'm on my way.' Faith grabbed her bag and ground the cigarette into a blue glass ashtray. 'If you need anything from the flat, the key's above the till.'

They embraced, her mother kissed her cheek, and Christie felt a vague desolation as she swept out into the rain, leaving behind only a faint fragrance of Armani. It hadn't taken them long to establish an easygoing friendship. But Christie was still waiting. Her mother had half-promised more than that. She had promised to provide Christie with her past. And only when she did that would Christie be able to love her mother in the way she longed to.

She braced her shoulders and smiled at Sarah, who looked very young and overwhelmed. 'Fancy some tea?'

As the kettle boiled, her thoughts turned to Trevor. He hadn't been in touch, so she had no idea if he intended working today. His mother may have had only a slight fall, but Christie had told him – hadn't she? – to take as much time off work as he needed.

She drummed her fingernails on the Formica work surface. He should have phoned. She wanted to talk to him, now that her decision was made. It struck her – and not for the first time – that Trevor was behaving less like an employee and more like a boss. And whose fault was that?

She threw the tea bags in the pot, poured on water, and wandered back out to the shop. Perhaps she should phone him at home? That way she could find out what was going on, let him know where she was, maybe even indulge her curiosity. No harm in that.

Sarah was chatting to an early customer, so Christie grabbed the key, and went up the stairs to her mother's flat. She needed privacy for this call.

She punched out the numbers, looking around the sleek modern interior of the flat – all black and white and chrome, giving away nothing of her mother's personality, and worlds apart from the basement downstairs. Which was the real thing? Who *was* Faith Vaughan? Would she ever find out for sure?

The phone rang and rang. No answer. At last she slammed it down, irrationally irritated. 'Where the hell are you, Trevor?' she said.

'Right here.'

She spun around. Trevor was lounging in the doorway, all long legs and blue jeans. His blond hair was wet and plastered to his tanned face, his brown leather jacket clung to the broad shoulders.

She stared at him, self-conscious and defensive. 'I didn't know if you were working today or not . . .' Her voice tailed off.

'I'm working.' He stood quite still, watching her. 'If you want me.'

If you want me . . . Her head was spinning. Against her will she was remembering what he had done for her – the way he'd shown her what love could be like, how it could satisfy, how it could leave you hungry for more.

'How did you know where I was?' she asked.

'Your husband told me.' His voice gave nothing away.

115

'Robin?' Christie shot him a glance of concern. 'Was he . . . Does he . . . ?'

'He was fine.'

Relief swam into embarrassment at being alone with him in this flat. 'And how's your mother?' she asked at last. 'Has she recovered from her fall?' That was the way. Distant and polite. Keep to safe subjects. Return to the roles they'd started with.

He shrugged. 'No harm done. She'll be fine in a day or two.' But the blue eyes met hers and she knew they were both remembering the last time they'd been together, when his girlfriend had turned up out of the blue in the shop downstairs. Only last Friday . . . Christie desperately wanted to bring up the subject, but how could she do it in an appropriately casual way? Trevor would know immediately how she felt. And she didn't want him to know how much she minded.

'This is a nice flat.' He was looking around with some interest.

'My mother has good taste.' Christie didn't want him here. She didn't want to be alone with him, not yet. She didn't want to be reminded. She made a move towards the door, but he stayed loitering in the doorway, watching her. She couldn't exactly squeeze past him. That would be much too close for comfort.

A sly smile crept into his eyes, curved the corners of his mouth. 'Where is she now?' His voice dropped to a whisper.

'On her way to London.' Ridiculously, she heard herself whispering back.

Trevor's smile broadened. 'And where's the bedroom?'

He had some nerve. Christie suppressed the giggle of hysteria that rose in her throat. All of her authority had gone, cancelled out by love. Sex had given him the touch of her body, the intimacy that elevated him to equal status, maybe even superior status, according to the arrogant smile on his face. How come it didn't work that way for women when they had an affair with their boss? Christie's anger returned. 'And how's your girlfriend?' Her voice was crisp, her eyes unblinking.

'Okay.' He laughed. 'How's your husband?'

'That's hardly the point, Trevor.' She walked over to the window, looking out at the main road of Wareham, with its mosaic of old shops and houses. The rain was still teeming down on to the flint and cobbles.

'Then what is the point?' He followed her to the window, standing behind her. Too close.

She wouldn't turn round and face him. 'The point is that you deliberately withheld from me the fact that you lived with someone.' God, she sounded pompous. She hated it when she sounded that way.

He laughed again. 'What does it matter?'

Christie loathed his casual indifference. 'It always matters,' she snapped. '*Do* you live with her?'

'Of course.' His eyes gleamed. 'Why do you think I couldn't take you home?'

'You said you lived with a disapproving mother who was housebound.' Even as she spoke she felt a fool. For believing him. For acting like a silly teenager. For not being the responsible adult she was supposed to be.

He grinned. 'I didn't expect you to fall for it.'

Ah, but she had, hadn't she? What was the matter with her? Was honest deception the only kind she understood?

'Would it have changed anything?' His voice was soft and sensual, the very tone taking her back to Wareham Forest and all the other occasions they'd made love. 'If I'd come right out and told you?'

She closed her eyes. 'Maybe.' Probably not. It had been good between them. Too good. Too much sexual chemistry – maybe it had been inevitable.

'Oh, I don't think so.' Without warning, his hands were on her waist, sliding down to her hips. His lips nuzzled into the soft skin of her neck. 'Do you?'

Christie shivered as the delicious licking desire streaked along its familiar path. He was a compelling lover. Despite her resolution it would be so easy to fall back against him and let him do whatever he wanted, whatever she wanted, here in her mother's flat.

'No.' She'd made a decision, hadn't she? Determinedly, she pulled away, stiffening her defences against him. 'No, Trevor.' She spoke calmly.

'No?' His voice was confused.

She turned to face him. 'No more of that. That's finished between us.'

'Because I'm living with someone?' He was staring at her, unconvinced.

'No. Not because of that.' She thought of Gramma. 'Because it's dishonest.'

'Huh?' The blue eyes remained vacant. Well, she hadn't expected him to understand. To Trevor, it would be much simpler. To most men, probably.

117

'All the time I'm living with Robin and having a relationship with you, I'm not giving myself the chance to sort out my life.' Her words fell into silence. Perhaps there was no point in saying these things to Trevor. Perhaps she was really only saying them to herself.

'It's only a bit of fun,' he grumbled. 'Why do women have to complicate everything?'

She laughed out loud. 'Only a bit of fun.' That made everything okay for men. While women needed analysis to justify everything. Especially fun. 'And it was fun,' she agreed.

His eyes were warm as they stared into hers. 'Oh yeah. It was good all right.'

She smelled the faint aftershave mingling with his animal sweat. 'But it's over.'

At last he nodded assent. 'Okay. If that's the way you want it.'

'It is.' She was surprised, maybe even disappointed, that he'd given in so easily.

'I never really had you, did I?' Still he watched her.

She shook her head. Maybe it was impossible for her to do that kind of giving. She just didn't know.

'I envy the man who has you all to himself.' Trevor grinned, looking like a little boy again. 'Lucky sod. It won't be me, but . . . do we get to have a kiss goodbye?'

Christie hesitated. Every good intention told her, no. Every instinct told her, yes. She longed to feel the touch of his lips just one more time. And why not? She was sure – very sure – it would only be a kiss. Only a kiss goodbye.

Even before she nodded acceptance, his hands were cradling her face, tilting it gently towards his lips as he bent towards her. She felt the longing for love shooting through her veins, numbing her limbs, clearing her head of every intention, good or otherwise.

His lips pressed on to hers, his tongue exploring the cavity of her mouth. So slow . . . She gave herself up to sweet sensuality. Just a goodbye kiss. That's all it was.

The kiss seemed to go on for ever, as if it had a life of its own. But at last, reluctantly she drew them apart, opening her eyes for his smile, seeing that he would push things no further. That was good. It was settled between them now.

Over his shoulder, she glanced at a flicker of darkness in the mirror. It

118

was a momentary reality that seemed to belong to imagination – part of the story of the triangle of herself, Trevor and Robin. She looked away, and then her eyes snapped back as realisation dropped rather than dawned. A sickening thud of realisation sank deep into the pit of her stomach.

'Oh my God!' The image in the mirror was of Robin's face.

She stared, mesmerised, at the expression on that reflected face. She recognised shock as it shifted into disgust. She saw anger, and she thought she saw it smile.

Her eyes swivelled to the door. Robin stood in the doorway where Trevor had stood only minutes before. The smile had gone. Now there was only hatred.

11

Robin couldn't take his eyes off her – the girl he loved – standing in another man's arms. And what a man. Nothing but a bloody Neanderthal.

Something had told him. Some cold insinuation in Swift's voice had warned him. Made him come here.

He had often imagined her with other men, but that had belonged to fantasy. He never thought it would actually happen. Could never have let her walk out of the house if he thought it would happen.

This was his Christie. His pure, undefiled Christie. She looked the same, small and slim with spiky blonde hair. *But tousled by his fingers.* With cornflower-blue eyes that made him melt. *But touched by his desire.* With lips ready to smile or shout. *But kissed by his mouth.* Oh, God.

This wasn't his Christie, was it? This was a woman with a lover – for he could see fulfilled passion, not tension, between these two bodies. A woman with a lover – not his Christie at all.

'Robin . . .' He heard her say his name. She took a step closer and he moved inside the room.

It was as if they were playing chess, their bodies the pawns.

Trevor Swift – the bloody gardener, the bloody Neanderthal! – looked at them both and swaggered out. Bloody *swaggered*, as if he'd done something to be proud of! Bastard . . .

'Robin . . .' She tried to take his arm and he shrugged it off. He didn't want her touch. Couldn't stand the thought of her touch. It made him sick. Sick with loathing and disgust. How could she?

'It was nothing, Robin,' she said, hunching her arms round her body like a small child. 'It didn't mean a thing. You have to believe me. It was just a kiss.'

'Just a kiss,' he echoed, able to speak at last. He knew what he'd seen. How could she? And with the Neanderthal of all people. All brawn and no brain. The type that women – at least, intelligent women like Christie – were meant to despise. Had all those accusations he'd hurled at her been closer to the mark than he'd ever imagined? Was that what she wanted – some stud with brains only in his dick?

'How long has it been going on?' This seemed terribly important. 'Days? Weeks? Months?'

She looked down.

'Months, then. Jesus!' Robin tore fingers through his dark hair. His mind raced. 'No bloody wonder you've been giving every impression you've gone off sex for life.'

Christie winced.

'All you've done is find someone more satisfying to do it with, isn't it?' She shook her head.

'Oh yes, it bloody is.' He grabbed her by the elbows and violently rocked her back and forth. Wanting to shake it all out of her. The truth, the sex, the touch of the bloody Neanderthal on his wife's skin. His wife.

'It wasn't like that, Robin.' She was almost in tears, her eyes huge in her pale face.

'What *was* it like, then?' Still he shook her, governed by the madness that had taken hold of him. 'Tell me *exactly* what it was like.'

'Don't . . .' She was trembling violently.

'I want to know.' He was shouting now. He heard his own voice shouting and it seemed to be coming from somewhere else. 'I want to know exactly what it was like.'

'It was a fling.' At last she seemed to recover her strength and pull away from his grasp. 'It was just a stupid, meaningless fling. It was a fling, and now it's over.'

He stared at her. 'Over? What were you doing when I came in, Christie? Giving him the sack?' He wiped his mouth viciously with the back of his hand as if he were wiping that kiss from her lips as Christie herself had once wiped away his kiss. But it couldn't be wiped away, could it? It had happened, and it would now always be there between them.

'But, Robin . . . It was just a kiss.'

Back to where they'd begun. With just a kiss. Robin stared at her. He wanted to hit her, to hurt as he'd been hurt, and he saw that she recognised it on his face. She looked scared.

'I'm sorry, Robin.'

He couldn't listen to her any longer. He couldn't stand here talking to her. He couldn't even look at her.

'You will be.' Robin turned around and stormed out. Crashing down the stairs into the shop, ignoring the startled glances from Sarah, the young shop-assistant who had told him his wife was upstairs. But neglected to tell him who with.

His car was parked right outside. He got in, turned the key of the ignition and drove. His hands gripped the steering wheel until they seemed to become part of it, clammy with sweat and rain. His eyes stared straight ahead. The rain flooded the windscreen. He put on the wipers but he still couldn't see a thing. At last he realised – tears were blurring his vision, it was not the rain at all.

He drove wildly, careless of other road users, hardly seeing them. It was a physical pain inside him. An ache that he recognised. And he began to think about his mother. Whore or madonna – that's what she'd taught him. There were respectable ladies, and there were tramps. Christie wasn't a respectable lady. Respectable ladies didn't do it with other men. Respectable ladies didn't even much like it. That made his wife a whore.

He slammed on the brakes at the traffic lights, skidded to a halt. Part of him hated being a man. Part of him had always hated being a man.

Robin had failed his mother on the day that he gave in to base male needs and desires. It sickened her. He sickened her. She had never forgiven him.

If Robin could have been different, then he would. Oh God, he really would. But he was a man. And now it was worse. Now, he was a man betrayed.

Late afternoon that same day, Christie edged her way through the puddles that led to the front door of Fran Cassidy's house. The sky had begun darkening at four o'clock, and the rain was still pelting down from the blackness above. The woman who cleaned for them answered the door.

'They're in the front room,' she said, rolling her eyes.

Christie could hear raised voices. The door was shut. She hesitated before going further. She desperately needed to see Fran, and yet . . .

'Why can't I do things the way I want?' Fran sounded like a spoiled child. 'Why do you have to ruin everything?'

'I'm not trying to ruin anything.' Dominic's voice was calm but determined. 'I'm not against the idea of the Refuge in principle. But I'm not sure you mean it. Do you really want to go through with it, or is this your way of making a point?'

'Whatever do you mean, Dominic?' Her question was arch.

'Oh, never mind.' He sounded tired. 'Forget it. But someone has to look at the practicalities . . .'

'The practicalities . . . ?' Fran mocked. 'You always sound like a solicitor, even when you haven't got your black suit and tie on.'

Outside in the hall, Christie raised her eyebrows and took a step back towards the front door. This was a private conversation. They couldn't have heard the doorbell, it would be better to leave. She'd come here because she couldn't face going home, and neither could she face Gramma's questioning dark eyes. Gramma had warned her what would happen. She should have listened.

But she couldn't interrupt Fran and Dominic, and she certainly couldn't lurk in the hallway eavesdropping. Still, what she heard next made her stop short in horror.

'In fact, you haven't got very much on at all.' Fran's voice had changed. It was unmistakably the voice of a flirtatious woman. 'You're practically naked . . .'

'Fran . . .'

Christie couldn't even begin to define the emotion in his dark, velvet voice.

No. She put a hand to her mouth, flinching from whatever was going on between these two. Something sordid, something incestuous. It was beginning to look as though Fran hadn't been joking when she'd admired Dominic, back in the summer. And as though Christie had been right in her interpretation of their behaviour at the party. She was surprised and disappointed. So surprised at Dominic. After all, Fran was barely more than a child. '*I'm not a kid.*' Her words came back to Christie. Two years ago Fran had not been a child. She shivered with a sense of foreboding.

The two of them were talking quietly in the living-room now. They must have made it up. They could even be . . .

Appalled at her own thoughts, Christie turned away, slipping back the latch on the front door.

'Not leaving, are you?' The cleaning woman stood in the doorway of the kitchen, a knowing smile pasted on her ruddy face.

'I think I will. I . . .'

Before she could get any further, the door to the living-room opened and Fran sauntered out.

Her eyes widened. 'Christie! I thought I heard voices. What are you doing here?' She came closer to kiss her, seeming unembarrassed at being disturbed.

Christie heaved a sigh of relief. Maybe she'd got it all wrong. And as always, she was glad to see her. Fran was like a breath of fresh air.

'Hi, Fran.' She had never seen her looking so good. Her tall slim body was encased in the skimpiest of little black dresses, and her red hair was piled on top of her head. She wore a jet choker and jet ear-rings, and her make-up was immaculate. In fact she looked quite breathtaking. And certainly not a child.

Fran stared pointedly at the woman standing in the doorway, until she withdrew. 'What's up, darling?' She examined Christie at arm's length. 'You look as if you've seen a ghost.'

'It's a long story.' Christie wondered if she could tell it without releasing the hot tears that had been pent up inside her all day. 'But you're going out. You look wonderful. I'll tell you some other time.' Once again, she began to head for the door.

'Whoa!' Fran laughed. 'It's only a pre-Christmas do. Cocktails and dinner.' She peered back into the living-room. 'And Dominic isn't ready yet.' Her green eyes flashed with humour. 'You can keep me company while I'm waiting for him.'

She led the way into the living-room where a log fire was burning, and Dominic, clad only in a striped dressing-gown and flip-flops was idly towelling his hair.

'Oh, excuse me.' Christie felt her face flush with heat.

Dominic's startled hazel eyes emerged from the towel. 'You didn't tell me we had a visitor,' he said to Fran, his eyes on Christie.

Fran shrugged. 'Christie's practically family. She can cope with a man in a dressing-gown.'

Christie caught his eye, surprised to recognise the humour there. She had always considered Dominic rather serious.

'I apologise.' He seemed about to say more, then changed his mind. 'I must go and get changed.'

'Good idea,' Fran drawled.

They both watched him as he left the room. Despite her preoccupations, Christie wanted to laugh at the expression on Fran's face. Anyone would think that she was the mother and Dominic the child. She paced to the window and Fran joined her.

'He's been in the pool,' Fran whispered, as the soft slap of his footsteps disappeared up the stairs.

'In the pool?' Christie stared at her. 'In this weather?' She peered out at the wet night sky.

Fran nodded. 'I told you he was crazy. He says it's exhilarating. But I think it's totally insane.'

Christie wasn't sure what she thought. This was a strange house, with a disturbing atmosphere, and she wasn't entirely comfortable here. She remembered what Dominic had said in the yew grove – that this was Fran's house and that he disliked it. Well, he was here an awful lot for a man who didn't like the place. She twisted around to take in her surroundings.

Over the Georgian fireplace was an enlarged, framed portrait of Amy Cassidy. Like Mona Lisa, the eyes always drew Christie, seeming to follow her around the room. But now, for the first time, because of the way Fran was dressed and made up, she noticed the striking resemblance between Fran and her mother.

Amy Cassidy had been a beautiful woman – an actress, more successful on screen than on stage because the camera adored her. And it was easy to see why. Her dark hair with its reddish sheen glowed almost incandescent like flames, her green eyes were cool and yet sensual. Her lips pouted prettily in the sly beginnings of a secret smile – too thin perhaps for the rest of her face, but glossed with a tint of rust that made up for what Nature had forgotten to make entirely perfect. No wonder Dominic had been obsessed with his lovely and talented wife. No wonder he was drawn to Fran.

'*He can't say no . . .*' She remembered Fran's words. Was it the beauty of the Cassidy women that Dominic was unable to say no to?

'Tell me what's happened.' Fran patted the cream leather sofa and drew Christie down beside her.

'It's Trevor Swift . . .' she began.

'I knew it!' Fran clapped her hands. 'How could anyone work with that half-naked body next to them and not fall for him?'

'I haven't *fallen* for him.' Christie found herself laughing. Why on earth hadn't she confided in Fran before? She might have known she'd understand.

Fran's eyes gleamed. 'Tell me everything, darling.'

Christie took a deep breath and began . . .

After her initial outburst, Fran listened in silence, making no judgement, apart from the occasional rise of elegant plucked eyebrows.

'So what will you do now?' she asked when Christie had finished.

'I don't know.' And she really didn't, that was the awful thing. She knew that, whatever she'd had with Trevor, it was over, but that was about as far as she could get. Would her marriage survive? Did she even want it to?

Fran uncrossed long legs in sheer, black stockings, got to her feet and went to the drinks cabinet. 'One thing I do know. We need a drink. And I've got some Italian white chilled and waiting.'

'Only a small glass.' Christie felt better for telling her. Fran's practical streak always put everything into perspective. She hadn't killed anyone, had she? Committing adultery didn't exactly signify the end of the world. According to the news, everyone was at it.

'How will he take it, d'you think?'

'Search me.' They contemplated this in silence. Fran might be six years younger than Christie, but she was a contemporary, and there were matters she could discuss with her that she could never broach with Gramma. It struck her that Fran was behaving almost as if she approved of her affair with Trevor. But how much of that was brave pretence? Whatever Fran said or did, Christie knew she'd never be able to wipe the memory of the sad, lonely figure in Wareham Church from her mind.

'You said before that you were thinking of leaving Robin,' Fran reminded her. 'Maybe it's time to accept that your marriage hasn't worked. There's no point in flogging a dead horse.'

Christie shrank from the imagery she used. 'But there seemed so much future for us at first.' She sipped the delicious Italian wine, her fingers twirling nervously around the delicate stem of the glass. 'I thought it would be so good.'

'Maybe the promises were all in your head.' Fran watched her. 'Maybe you saw in him what you wanted to see.'

Christie considered this. Could it be true? Had her experience with Barry soured her against a certain kind of man? Had she seen in Robin a kind of antithesis to the macho chauvinism that had irritated her just once too often? Surely it wasn't as simple as that?

'I saw what was there,' she said at last. 'I saw what Robin is, and that's what I wanted.' She shrugged. 'I was on the verge of falling in love with him the first time he cooked me a Chinese meal.'

Fran giggled. 'That's not love, that's hunger.'

'It wasn't just that.' Christie grinned back at her. 'We got on so well. We used to talk about everything under the sun.' God, she remembered those discussions in the garden over endless cups of tea. Just talking to the man had turned her on to Robin Fifer and his world.

'Then maybe you saw what Robin wanted you to see.' Fran got up to re-fill her own glass. 'We all project a certain image.' She cast a resentful look towards the portrait above the fireplace. 'We all pretend.'

Christie stared at her. There was a pain in her eyes that made her want to offer comfort. What had hurt Fran so much? What was still hurting her? 'What do you pretend, Fran?' she whispered.

'Sometimes I pretend to be happy.' Christie had to lean forwards to catch the words.

She put her glass down on the table, got to her feet, and wrapped her arms around the slim figure. Fran's body was cold and trembling. 'What's wrong?' Christie looked into her eyes. 'Can't you tell me? You never know, I might even be able to help.'

For a split second Fran seemed about to speak. She hesitated, and then the moment was lost. She drew away from Christie and walked up to the portrait of her mother, facing it in a pose of angry defiance. 'Why do you think she killed herself?'

'I don't know.' Christie's arms dropped to her sides. 'Was it an accident? Or was she very unhappy?'

'Both probably.' Fran's voice held no regrets. 'She was crying out for attention and she was still in love with my father.'

Christie glanced behind her. That wasn't the kind of thing she'd care to say when Dominic Redfern was in the house. She wouldn't want to see him angry.

'Dominic knows.' Fran's voice was bleak. 'He must do. She made it obvious enough.'

'Do you miss her, Fran?' Christie wanted to steer the subject away from Dominic. Amy Cassidy had been his wife. He'd worshipped her. It wasn't fair to hurt him.

Fran didn't reply to this question. 'She went around destroying things,' she said matter-of-factly. 'And people.' She paused. 'Almost as if she couldn't help it.'

128

Christie looked up at the picture of Amy Cassidy. It seemed brutal to be criticising the dead – their right of reply had been taken from them after all. But Fran was still talking, half to herself, as if needing to release the truth.

'And sometimes I do the same,' she whispered.

'No, you don't.' Christie was quick to jump to her defence. 'You help people.'

Fran looked doubtful.

'You're always getting involved in some charity event or another.' Christie searched her memory. 'You did that sponsored marathon for the old people's home.' She paused. 'You even want to turn this place into a refuge for battered women, for goodness' sake.' How could Fran have so little self-esteem? Had it been removed at an early age? Had she always presented potential competition for her mother, rather than being a child to love and cherish? She thought of her own mother. So much bonded Fran and Christie together, in a way that others would never understand.

'Oh, that.' Fran's expression changed. 'You'd be surprised at my motives. Sometimes I do what I want the world to see.'

'How do you mean?' Christie was confused.

'Sometimes she's not sure what she means.' The voice was gentle, but teasing.

Dominic Redfern was standing in the doorway. He was wearing a sleek black dinner jacket and trousers, starched white shirt and bow tie. He looked extremely attractive, but rather forbidding until he turned towards Christie and smiled.

She smiled back uncertainly.

Dominic held some gold cuff links in his palm.

'Let me fix those.' Fran stepped quickly towards him, took the cuff links and fastened them in place. 'You look wonderful.' She gazed up at him, her hand still on his wrist.

'I have a lot to live up to.' He smiled down at her.

Christie jumped to her feet and grabbed her coat. 'I must be going.' She was beginning to feel like Cinderella, the only difference being that she had no intention of going to the ball. But she couldn't deny it: despite the difference in their ages – and, as Fran had told her, Dominic was only in his early thirties – they certainly made a handsome couple.

'Goodbye, Christie.' He held out his hand and after the briefest of hesitations she took it. Her hand felt small and cold in his. She felt cold too, and uncomfortable.

'I hope you work it out.' Fran took her to the door. 'And I hope he forgives you, if that's what you want. Call me tomorrow?'

Christie nodded, waved, and made her way back through the puddles towards the pick-up truck. She was no clearer in her own mind, and she wouldn't be until she and Robin had a chance to sit down and talk this thing through. That's what they must do. She hesitated. Would he be calmer by the time she got home? *Would* he forgive her for what she had done?

Her mind returned to her own problems, those that she had arrived here with. But still, as she started the engine and drove back towards Ulwell, she was aware of a disturbing feeling, a strange premonition that had something to do with Fran. And of words left unsaid. Words that some time would need to be spoken.

She found Robin pacing the kitchen. His shoulders were hunched and his face tightly drawn. He was smouldering – she saw that at once. Oh, God. He looked even worse than he had before.

'So you're back.' He swung round to face her, his grey eyes hooded with compressed fury. There was something very different about Robin tonight, and it wasn't just that he was bitterly angry, she realised.

'I had to look after the shop for Mum.' Christie heard the defensiveness in her own voice. 'And I called in on Fran.'

'You weren't with lover boy, then?' He swept his dark hair out of his face in a gesture of frustration.

Slowly, she shook her head. 'Robin, we should talk . . .'

His laugh exploded the tension in the brittle yellow and white kitchen. 'Talk?'

She nodded. 'I want to explain.' But how could she explain? Any explanation would sound hollow and cheap. What could she say to him? She'd betrayed his trust – that was all there was, and right now he didn't look as though he could cope with it.

'I must know you better than you know yourself.' He was looking her up and down, unpleasant and insidious. 'You don't have to explain. And besides, it's not talking you really want, is it?'

Christie tensed. This was worse than she'd feared. Much, much worse. She took a step towards him, intending to take him in her arms, hoping that the closeness of contact would remind Robin of who she was, what they had meant to each other.

But he stepped back, away from her, his lean body shaking, as Fran's body had been shaking not so long ago, every nerve and muscle raw and vulnerable. And yet she had never thought of Robin as vulnerable before. He had always seemed so self-assured and compact – so closed up in his own little world. She might have resented it before. But she wanted that Robin to come back to her now.

She reached out her hands to him, pleading, but he pretended not to see. He looked away, his body arched, as if poised for attack, and she held back. She would have been scared if this wasn't Robin. 'Of course I want to talk.' She kept her voice gentle. Something told her that she mustn't antagonise him now.

'You didn't get talking from him, did you?' He swung around to face her once more, his eyes cold and cruel. 'You didn't get talking from that bloody Neanderthal of yours, did you?'

Christie frowned. 'That's got nothing to do with us. I told you, Robin. It was a fling. It was meaningless. Stupid and meaningless.' But he wasn't even listening.

'What *did* you get from him?' He was only inches away now, his dark face flushed and heavy. 'I want to know.'

'Nothing.' She wanted to shout. 'Nothing.' If only she had never laid eyes on Trevor. If only she hadn't employed him. If only she hadn't gone with him into Wareham Forest.

'Was it this?'

Before she guessed his intention, he bent closer, pulled her roughly towards him, and forced his mouth on to hers, crushing her lips against the hardness of his mouth and teeth.

Then just as abruptly, he released her.

She stared at him. It was a long way from the gentle kisses she had shared with Robin before. She put a finger to grazed lips, and tasted blood. It had been a brutal kiss intended only to hurt, over almost before it had begun.

For a moment, she was sure he would relent, take her in his arms, console her and say he was sorry. For a moment, she thought his expression softened, but even as she waited, the fire that had almost been extinguished returned to his grey eyes. 'That's shut you up, hasn't it?' he growled.

'Robin . . .' She put a hand on his sleeve. She had to make him stop this. This wasn't the way to sort out anything between them. And it wasn't

Robin's way. He wasn't a violent man. He had never been a violent man. He was tender, loving and gentle. This wasn't Robin at all. Had she hurt him so much that this was his only release?

'Want more?' Without warning, he grabbed her again, pushing her backwards this time, tearing her hair from her face, seizing her by the shoulders, forcing a vicious mouth on to her bruised and swollen lips.

'Robin!' This time she struggled, trying to free herself. What in God's name did he think he was doing?

'Is this what you want?' He panted, hot breath into her face. Her arms were pinned to her sides. 'A bit of rough? Don't you know that anybody can give you that?' With both hands he snatched at the collar of her quilted shirt and deliberately ripped it apart, so that her bare breasts were exposed.

Christie was paralysed. All she could do was stand and stare at him, unable to comprehend that this was happening to her, that Robin was doing this. Her husband.

'Is this rough enough for you?' He shook his fists into her face, aggression bubbling to the surface, visible in the wildness of his eyes, felt in the touch of his hands as fingers that had always been sensitive and gentle dug into the flesh of her shoulders, her neck, her breasts.

She was stung into action. 'Stop it! You're hurting me. You can't punish me like this.' Her voice rose with hysteria. That was what it was – a punishment. A revenge. But she had never dreamed that it was in him, this raging monster he'd hidden away. There was no telling how far he'd go.

'But it's what you want,' he whispered. His fingertips bruised the soft flesh of her breasts. His mouth came closer . . .

'It's not what I want. Get off me! What's the matter with you?' Summoning all her strength, she pushed that face away. That dark male face that had become almost unrecognisable. Desperately, she clawed herself free.

'What's the matter with *me*?' he yelled. 'With *me*?' He laughed again, a harsh, humourless grating that slashed into her senses like his nails had cut into her skin. 'I've just found out that my wife has been having it off with some bloody cave man. And you ask what's the matter with me. My wife . . .' His eyes screwed up in pain. He took a step backwards. 'My wife . . .'

Possession. Christie leaned against the kitchen wall, her chest heaving. Everyone seemed to think they owned somebody. 'I've hurt you. I'm sorry, Robin.' Only now was the enormity of what she had done truly penetrating her mind. She had played with his emotions, lost his trust. How had she ever imagined that their marriage could survive? But this . . . Had she deserved this?

'What do you expect me to do?' He sounded calm.

For a moment she thought it was over. But as he watched her, standing two feet away from him, he slowly and deliberately began to undo the buttons of his shirt. 'Just tell you to forget it, and go on as before? Is that what you expected, Christie?'

She backed away and hit the cooker, wincing from the sharp pain in her kidneys. 'Let's sit down and talk about it,' she begged. 'You and I could always talk.'

'But talking wasn't enough for you, was it?' He loosened the belt of his trousers, his eyes not straying once from her face.

She watched, hypnotised by the black leather as it slid through the thongs of his jeans. 'You're wrong. It was enough for me.' There was fear in her voice.

'It wasn't.' He came closer, bending, his face next to hers. 'It wasn't enough for a little tramp like you.'

'Stop it, Robin.' She was really scared now. Scared of something she didn't understand, lurking in the grey waters of his eyes. Scared of his strength – male strength. Unused, rested – and ready.

'Why should I?' He jeered. 'I know what you want. Perhaps I should have sussed it a long time ago.'

Christie shook her head. 'No . . .' How could he possibly know what she wanted, when she didn't even know herself?

'And I'm going to give it to you.' He tore off the remainder of her shirt in one swift movement.

'No, Robin . . .' But she stood motionless.

'We're done with talking, you and I.' He moved in, his breath hot in her ear. His hands were on her breasts, heavy and demanding, squeezing and cruel. She couldn't move. She saw that this was all he was focused on. This had to happen. Their eyes locked together in a kind of mutual bewilderment.

And then he snapped. In seconds he was forcing back her head, tearing at the belt of her jeans, ripping down the zip, pulling the denim over her hips.

Savage hands, she thought, wondering with some detached part of herself if she would faint. Jesus, no . . .

He grabbed her thighs and shoved her hard against the cold and clammy kitchen wall. She felt condensation dripping on her neck. She felt him pushing down on to her, into her. He rammed himself into her, hot, hard and thrusting. Ripping, bruising, tearing, raping.

Christie moaned as he pounded away at her soft skin, careless of her safety, careless of her pleasure. And then she seemed to lose all feeling as wave upon wave of passion swept over her. His passion. But it engulfed her.

His orgasm shook his entire form. He collapsed inside the warmth of her, spent and fulfilled, as he had never been fulfilled before.

He dragged himself out of her and Christie sank to the floor. Tears were rolling down her cheeks. What had she done?

And then she remembered the aggression that she had sensed in him right at the beginning. Almost as if she had always known.

12

It was Christmas Day. In the sitting-room of Yew Cottage, the log fire was blazing and the big table had been pulled out for Christmas dinner, as it always was. They were all there – Christie and Robin, Faith, Isobel, and Vincent in his wheelchair. The wheelchair had become part of Vincent, attached to him like another limb. Isobel recognised that no-one thought of Vincent any more. They only thought of Vincent and his wheelchair.

'That was delicious.' Faith pushed her plate away and lit a cigarette, drawing the smoke in contemplatively.

Isobel smiled. It was good to have them all back here. 'How about a game of charades? Christie?' She was worried about her granddaughter; she seemed unusually quiet.

'Okay Gramma.' Her expression brightened. 'We always played charades, didn't we?'

'Always.' Isobel laughed. 'And when you were little you used to do a book and put your hands up to your face, like this . . .' Isobel covered her eyes.

'And say "a book!" before anyone had a chance to guess,' Vincent chimed in.

'Did I?' Christie stared at them.

'And when I came to visit, everybody but me knew it was *Janet and John* . . .' Faith's voice was wistful.

'How the hell you did *Janet and John*, I'll never know,' Vincent muttered.

'And then you realised,' Isobel reminded Faith. 'Because they were your old books that Christie had found in the attic!'

They all laughed. Everybody but Robin.

Faith remembered. Ah yes, she remembered. But how much had she missed – just visiting at Christmas and for the odd week-end, when she gave in to the urge to see Christie, unable to leave her entirely alone. She grasped her daughter's hand tightly.

'And you sang to us.' Christie turned to her, her eyes a little too bright. 'You sang all those old songs that I still can't get out of my head.' In front of her, the red candle flickered.

Folk songs from Woodstock days. Faith nodded. She had never got them out of her head either.

'And when we played charades . . .' Christie smiled.

'Charades,' Faith echoed.

'When we played charades, you always did a song. You hummed it to give us a clue. And I never knew the name of any of them . . .' There was a pause as the silence and memories filled the room. Isobel put another log on the fire and switched on the lamp.

'None of us knew the names of any of them.' Vincent snorted with laughter and Faith stared at him in surprise, feeling a smile twitch at her own lips. Imagining how foreign she must have seemed to them in her multi-coloured hippy skirts and black crocheted shawls, singing American folk songs with a sadness she'd never invited them to share in.

'Pull this one with me, Christie.' Robin Fifer's voice sliced through the family memories as he thrust a scarlet and gold cracker towards her.

Christie blinked, the expression of reminiscence fading from her face. 'What . . . ?'

'Come on. Pull it.' Faith wasn't sure that she'd heard that note of authority in Robin's voice before. She frowned.

Wordlessly Christie complied, her gaze riveted to her husband's face. She pulled, he pulled, until the crêpe was tired and twisted, but still it refused to crack.

Faith exchanged a glance with her mother. Something strange was going on here. Christie wasn't being herself at all.

'Oh, I can't do it!' Christie's shoulders sagged. 'It won't go.' She relaxed her hold and flexed her fingers.

Robin's thin smile was victorious. 'Here we are.' He edged the crêpe apart. 'A present for you, my love.'

It was a pink plastic ring.

'Revolting,' Faith remarked, grinding her half-smoked cigarette into the ashtray.

'Christie likes it, don't you, sweetheart?' Robin laughed, a cruel laugh. She shrugged, seeming afraid to look at him now.

'You like it, don't you?' he pressed. 'Try it on.'

'For heaven's sake, Robin.' Faith was exasperated. 'Leave her alone.'

Robin glared at her, his attention only diverted when Christie grabbed the ring from his palm. 'I like it,' she whispered.

'Let me.' He took it, forcing the pink plastic on to the third finger of her left hand. It sat on top of her wedding band.

Isobel found herself thinking, 'Next year I'll invest in better quality crackers.' She got to her feet to clear away, needing to diffuse the tension that was crackling and spitting between these two. She knew Faith had recognised it as well. Someone was going to get hurt, for sure.

Robin grinned. 'Christie's going to wear it for ever. It might not be the real thing. It might even be a bit tacky. But it belongs on her wedding finger, don't you think?'

What was he on about? Isobel turned to her granddaughter, waiting for the explosion or the laughter, but there was nothing. Only blank cornflower-blue eyes. She frowned.

'Christmases aren't what they were.' Faith began to stack the dishes. Her olive eyes were sad. 'So many games we used to play.'

Isobel nodded, her hand resting on the empty bottle of Bordeaux. 'So how about it . . . ?' she began, her face brightening.

'We're too old for games,' Vincent grumbled.

'Nonsense.' Isobel wondered why she was trying so hard. Why should she, when she was tired – so tired – of fighting her way through glossy paper, sentimentality and credit cards.

'Vincent's right.' Faith spoke softly and Isobel glanced at her in surprise. 'It's too late for games.'

Christie got to her feet so abruptly that they all stared at her. 'Gramma . . .' she began, a note of desperation in her voice.

'Yes, my dear? What is it? What's wrong?' Isobel reached out her hands, but already Robin was up beside her.

Christie jumped almost imperceptibly, a shudder running through the slight form, the knuckles resting on the table top, as if without it she would fall.

He clamped a hand on her shoulder.

'Nothing,' she whispered.

Isobel looked from one to the other. 'Are you sure?'

137

Christie nodded. Her face was pale, her lips dry, her eyes huge and bleak.

'Absolutely sure? You know that if you ever need . . .'

'It's time we were getting home.' It sounded like an order. Robin turned Christie around until she faced him. His grey eyes were hooded, his expression inscrutable.

'Already?' Isobel glanced at her watch. 'You haven't even finished your wine.' She picked up a glass from the table and handed it to Christie. So much for charades.

'I should be getting along too,' Faith told Isobel. 'I'm being a good neighbour. I've got a few people coming round to the flat for drinks tonight.'

And so much for family celebrations. Isobel felt disappointed in them all. 'Who?' she asked.

'Just a couple of people from Wareham with nothing better to do.' Faith laughed. 'Mrs Butler from next door. And that nice solicitor, Dominic Redfern.'

Christie's glass fell from her hand, the rich red wine staining the white skin of her knuckles and wrist, soaking into the carpet like a pool of spilled blood. The glass bounced and shattered at her feet.

'Clumsy!' Vincent clicked his tongue.

Isobel darted forward with tissues. 'Sit down for a minute, my dear.' It looked as if Christie might faint. Isobel took her arm and led her to the sofa, mopping up the trail of red liquid on her hand and sleeve.

'I'll get a cloth.' Faith ran into the kitchen.

Robin stood in the doorway. 'Don't fuss.' He spoke through clenched teeth. 'She's absolutely fine. Don't fuss, Isobel. You're fine, aren't you, Christie?'

Isobel looked up at him. Robin was so different today, so assertive – aggressive, even. Her heart skipped a beat. Surely not? She eyed them both warily, thinking of Jack and searching for signs. Had Robin found out about Christie's affair with Trevor? Had he . . . ? She caught her breath. Surely he hadn't been knocking her around?

She couldn't bear the thought. Her arm tightened around her grand-daughter's shoulders. Not Christie. They say that young generations follow old patterns. But not that. Please God, don't let that happen to Christie.

'She's perfectly all right,' Robin was insisting. Isobel glared at him. Just let him try . . .

'Yes.' Christie spoke softly. 'I'm fine.'

She rose from the chair. 'Thank you for dinner, Gramma.' She sounded like a child rehearsed in etiquette.

'It was nothing. Any time . . .' Isobel's voice tailed off. Didn't Christie know that she was always welcome here? That Yew Cottage could always be her sanctuary, that she had a place to come to. She had choices. Women had choices these days, didn't they? There were no children to keep her in Ulwell. So there was no reason for Christie to stay with him, if she were unhappy. If he was . . . No. She couldn't even think it.

Robin gripped Christie's arm. 'Let's get you home.' It sounded like a threat.

The old Christie would have shaken him off. This Christie allowed herself to be led.

And soon, Faith too was saying her goodbyes. Isobel knew that if it hadn't been for Vincent she would have stayed.

'What's wrong with Christie?' she hissed, as Isobel followed her to the door.

'Don't ask me,' Isobel hissed back.

'Can't you talk to her?'

'I tried to. What could I do, with Robin hanging over her shoulder the whole time?' Honestly, what did Faith expect?

'Will you go round there?' Faith's hand was on the doorknob, her eyes watching the hallway for signals of Vincent's approach. She knew as well as Isobel that Vincent hated them to hold private conversations. It was a symptom of his paranoia – he was convinced they were talking about him.

'Maybe you should be the one to do that.' Isobel felt perverse. 'She's your daughter.' There: it was said.

'She still doesn't trust me, not completely.' Faith opened the door as the sound of creaking wheels reached their ears. They exchanged a glance of sympathy.

'Maybe you should earn it,' Isobel whispered, angry with her for breezing back into their lives and imagining that it would be so easy. 'Maybe you should tell her about her father.'

The expression in the olive eyes that gazed back at her cut Isobel more than any words could have done.

'Oh, Mother . . .' She thought Faith might cry.

She reached out for her but at the same time the door slammed, and Vincent was there behind Isobel, the wheelchair filling the narrow hall.

'Letting in all the cold air,' he grumbled.

The embrace turned into a chaste kiss on the cheek. Faith's expression was both hurt and accusing. 'Maybe you should tell me about mine,' she whispered into Isobel's greying hair.

One last look, and then she was gone, hurrying up the path.

What more did she want to know? So often Isobel had been tempted to tell Faith what Jack had really been like. At the very least it would justify her leaving. But how could she destroy all Faith's memories? How could she do that to her?

Isobel turned. Once more she was on her own with Vincent. She followed him back into the sitting-room.

'Read to me, Isobel.' His pale eyes glinted behind the thick lenses.

Obediently, she reached for the book. He had so little to please him. But it was never a subject that interested her. It would be a war story that he could harp on about for hours and relate to his own bitterness. It seemed to be the only thing that made Vincent happy these days. Raving on.

As she read, Isobel cut herself off from the story on her lips as she always did.

There were times when she hated Vincent. Once, he had shown her how to be free. Perhaps it was the cruelest gift he had ever given her. Because now he jailed her with guilt and pity. And it was worse to give and then take away than never to have given at all.

If not for him, she would find more time – the right time – to spend with Faith and Christie. She would get to the bottom of whatever was troubling Christie, she would strive for a new closeness between the three of them. If not for Vincent . . .

Traditionally, New Year's Eve in Swanage was a riotous affair involving most of Purbeck and others besides. Thousands came to join in the fancy dress parade that thronged the village streets and pubs with colour and noise, music and laughter.

But tonight, Christie was not in the mood. Not in the mood for fun and certainly not in the mood for celebrating a new year. What would it bring? Did she care? She hardly even dared to contemplate it, after the events of the past two weeks.

The tension between her and Robin had reached breaking point. Whenever he entered a room, she jumped, unable to ignore the long, low shudder that raced from head to toe. And she flinched when he came close, goosebumps making her skin hurt, her heart pumping madly with fear and anticipation.

They hardly spoke. And yet in bed they had found a violent passion that was frightening in intensity, almost unbearable in the lack of control she had – they had – over their own bodies, their own desires.

How long could she go on like this – her energy evaporating, her identity fading, her willpower being ground down? She was being drained by him. And all in the name of possession.

But Christie had no say in tonight's celebrations either. It was both a family affair and a village affair – she could only escape it if she were bed-ridden or in a wheelchair like Vincent. And besides, Robin had decided they would go.

'We'll be Dick Whittington,' he said. 'And his cat.'

'His cat?' Christie hadn't needed to ask which part she'd be playing. She let him organise the costumes, dress her in a black body and tights, streak black and white make-up on her pale face. And she didn't dare consider the significance of her role. She was his, that was all she needed to know.

Isobel turned up at ten. Her long, charcoal coloured hair hung loosely around her shoulders, and she wore a black cloak and a pointed hat. In her hand was the birch broom she used for sweeping out the workshop. 'Vincent says it suits me,' she said. 'What do you think? Do I look like an evil old crone?'

Robin laughed. 'Of course you do, Isobel.' Christie recognised the malice. There was so much hatred in him and he hardly bothered to hide it.

'Will you do my make-up, Christie?' She saw that Gramma was trying to get her on her own. Gramma had phoned her every day in the past week and her mother had come over twice. But she couldn't talk to anyone, even these women she loved.

'I'll bring the stuff in here.' She spoke quickly, silently conspiring with Robin to avoid being alone with her. How could she begin to tell Gramma what was wrong? How could she admit to her shame?

Faith arrived in her Charlie Chaplin outfit, and the four of them made their way towards Swanage. It was so weird. Robin was chatting to people in the street, eating, drinking and laughing as if nothing had changed. Christie was bewildered. Where was the Robin she married? Could it really be so easy for him to pretend? Was all this an act, or had he never been real? She shivered. She was beginning to wonder if anyone was real.

They made their way through the square and down to the sea, the cold breeze numbing her fingers, disorientating her still further. The water was black and stormy, and for a moment she longed to be out there, away from all these people. She had a vision of herself ploughing through the waves, and then it returned. His hand on her shoulder. Her reminder.

As they turned back towards the square, the crowds surrounded them, dressed in bizarre costumes, laughing, dancing, drinking from beer cans – for the pubs were full with surreal characters spilling out of the doors, hugging and kissing, laughing and joking. A host of cavemen, nuns drinking lager, larger than life Disney characters and a shuffling pack of cards, jiggled and juggled past Christie. The image of a group of people large and small dressed in black bin liners and pinned with cereal packets and biscuit wrappers, swam in front of her. They didn't seem in the least bit real. Children with huge eyes and wide smiles clad in black plastic, clinging on to a bigger, warmer hand, 'Just a load of old rubbish' written on placards in front of them. A load of old rubbish.

It wasn't real. It couldn't be. It was all going on somewhere else. In another world that she wasn't part of. All this noise and mayhem. She was on her own now. She blinked, tried to smile. Someone thrust a can of lager into her hands, someone tried to kiss her. Robin's grip around her loosened, and suddenly she was thrust into a crowd of strangers, all laughing, leering, their faces only masks.

Christie stumbled over beer cans thrown into the street. She wanted to scream. The scream inched into her numb throat, white fire hovering in her mouth . . .

'Christie.' Gramma was beside her, familiar despite the witch's outfit, her dark eyes concerned.

The scream faded. Christie shook herself, and the masks resurfaced as people, friendly people just having a good time in Swanage.

'Where's Robin?' Her head turned but it was impossible to see more than three people away, the mass of bodies was too thick and uncompromising.

'Never mind about him.' Gramma took her hand. 'We'll find him soon enough. What about you? What's wrong with you?'

The breeze was cooling her flushed cheeks. She flung back her head. She must wake from this trance. She mustn't go under. 'Nothing.'

'Don't give me that.'

Christie shrugged. She had no energy to protest. The bodies were closer and bigger around her, and the lethargy was creeping on top of her, suffocating her until she could hardly breathe.

'Has he found out? About . . .' Isobel looked furtively around. 'About Trevor?'

Christie nodded. Useless to protest.

'He's not . . . treating you badly?' Isobel's voice became urgent.

'Badly?' What did she mean by badly? Wasn't that a question of definition, a matter of relative values? She wanted to laugh, aware that it was hysteria, and aware on yet another plane of consciousness that this should be worrying her. Good God. Was she going crazy?

Isobel took her by the shoulders, turning Christie to face her. 'He's not hitting you?'

Christie looked into the dark eyes, and suddenly understood her concern. 'No.' She shook her head. If only it were as simple as that. She reached out to touch Gramma's dark hair. 'Is that what happened to you?' she whispered, the knowledge coming from some old understanding that she'd never recognised before. For a moment she felt sane, the prospect of rescue tantalisingly close.

Isobel turned abruptly, her nod barely acknowledging the truth. 'Then what is wrong with you?' She seemed to be asking herself.

'I'm lost.' Christie was sure that she had actually spoken the words, and yet Gramma didn't seem to hear, and the next moment a surge of bodies carried her a few yards away.

Someone laughed in her face.

'I'm lost,' Christie repeated to herself.

She looked up. A cluster of monks were moving menacingly towards her. Or should it be a cloister of monks? And could monks be menacing? She wanted to giggle.

One of them bowed his head, winked and she thought she recognised him. There was something familiar about the eyes . . . Barry? Trevor?

'How about a kiss for New Year?' The words hung strangely on a monk's habit.

Just a goodbye kiss, that's all it was ever supposed to be. Her mind flitted back to the rainy morning in her mother's flat. Trevor's kiss goodbye and Robin's face in the mirror. His cruel smile.

She backed away. 'No . . .'

But he shrugged, and she saw that it wasn't Trevor at all. Trevor was probably at home with his girlfriend. Trevor was untouched by all that had gone on. It hadn't destroyed him, like it was threatening to destroy her.

'Christie! Christie!' She thought she was dreaming. She swung around.

'I thought it was you! Great costume.' Fran stood beside her. She was dressed as a charming St Trinian's school girl. A black mini-skirt revealed the full glory of her long legs clad in black, laddered stockings. Her open-necked white blouse was undone to reveal a sexy cleavage, and her red hair was tied in a loose pony tail. She was brandishing a hockey stick and giggling.

'Yours too.' Christie didn't know what to say. She felt ridiculous. She felt mad. Was she mad? Surely if she were, she'd feel free?

Beside Fran stood Dominic. Christie could hardly look at him. She felt more embarrassed with Dominic than she did with anyone else. As if he knew what was happening to her. What she was allowing to happen to her. As if he had some secret knowledge of her shame. It made her face flush even in the cold night.

'Hello, Christie.' His voice was compelling and yet kind. At last she looked up at him properly. He was dressed in the costume of a matador, his tight black trousers clinging to the curves of legs and hips, the red cape providing a dramatic contrast to his dark eyes and hair.

She nodded. 'Happy New Year.' The words croaked out of her.

'You never called me.' Fran held her arm. 'You never told me what happened.'

'Nothing happened.' She watched Dominic. She could confide in no-one this time.

'It's almost midnight.' Fran's eyes were bright. 'Listen . . .'

Around them the noise seemed to recede as the crowd waited with hushed expectancy. All the pubs had switched on their radios and everyone waited for the sound of Big Ben. It started to strike.

'Happy New Year!' At the twelfth stroke there were shouts and whoops and the sounds of champagne corks bursting from bottles and shooting into the night sky. People were kissing and dancing, joining hands and singing Auld Lang Syne.

Christie shivered. She caught Dominic's eye – he was staring at her in some sort of confusion – and the next moment, Fran had flung herself into his arms.

'Happy New Year, darling Dominic,' she murmured. She pulled him towards her into a passionate, welcoming kiss.

Christie turned to run. She didn't belong here. She had to get out. She couldn't face it. She had to escape.

'Hey . . .' She ran straight into Robin's arms. He, Faith and Isobel were standing in a small, bemused group looking for her. 'Where the hell have you been?' He grabbed her cold face tightly in his hands, and she felt the sudden rush of blood into her head. Stubbornly, she refused to answer.

He seemed about to pursue the matter, and then his dark head bent close to hers. 'Happy New Year.'

His breath was hot on her skin. It scared her. *He* scared her. Before she could protest, he was kissing her, heavy and demanding, right there in the middle of the street. And after the briefest of hesitations she was responding like a woman possessed.

'I think you two should get home.' Gramma was half-laughing, half-disapproving.

Christie's legs almost gave way under her. Meekly she let him take her arm and lead her.

When they were alone in the house in Ulwell, he took her upstairs, ripped off the body and the black tights, and threw her down naked on the bed. She stared at him with huge, uncomprehending eyes.

'What's happening to us, Robin?'

He removed his shirt, never once taking his eyes from her breasts. 'What you wanted. That's what's happening to us. That's what you're getting,'

'But I don't . . .' It became a groan as he launched himself on top of her.

'Oh, yes you do.' He taunted her as he forced himself inside her with the sudden ferocity of a rapist.

She gasped. 'But . . .'

'Quiet.' He clamped a hand over her mouth. 'I don't want you to talk. I told you. We're done with talking.'

He didn't want her to be herself. She knew that.

Christie closed her eyes. Feeling was better than feeling and seeing. She couldn't fight back. It was compulsive, this physical drive between them – as if they were being directed by forces other than themselves.

He was utterly dominant now. He arched on top of her, bending and rocking, in total control of their pleasures. Pushing, pounding, penetrating. Whilst she – she could now only see herself through him. She seemed to exist only through him. With every thrust of his body, Robin was underlining his possession of hers. What she had said to Gramma was true,

She was lost. She was losing it all, losing herself.

She couldn't even fight back. Instead, a treacherous longing rose inside her, until she was responding with violent passion, as if she wanted this desecration, for God's sake.

That was the shame of it. That was the guilt. That was what was destroying her – not Robin, but her own secret desires.

13

'Goodbye kiss? Slap-bang-in-the-middle-of-an-affair kiss? What difference does it make, Trevor? Robin isn't a fool.' Christie shifted the telephone receiver to her other hand. His very calmness irritated her. But why should Trevor be anything but calm? *He* hadn't been discovered by his girlfriend in a compromising position. *He* hadn't been going through what she had gone through over Christmas and New Year. He never would, would he? Because he was a man.

When she was apart from Robin, Christie could function – almost – as if she were still the same person underneath. Only she knew what was happening to her. Only she knew that with every day, with every sexual encounter, Robin's power over her was growing whilst her own identity was fading fast.

'Couldn't you have made up some story?'

Christie frowned. Trevor Swift was beginning to annoy her. And it was his fault. If he hadn't pushed, if he hadn't tempted, if he hadn't looked into her eyes and said *Just a goodbye kiss . . .* Those words would haunt her for ever.

'Of course I could,' she snapped. 'Silly me. You're so quick-witted, Trevor. What would you have said? Oh, Robin, I was just kissing him because I wanted to get into the Christmas spirit? Do you think he would have fallen for that, Trevor?' Half-embarrassed by her own outburst, she looked around, but it was early in the morning and Faith's Basement was deserted. Her mother was in London, and Sarah was stocktaking.

'You didn't have to tell him we were having an affair.' His voice was accusing now and that irritated her still further. 'He only saw a kiss.'

'I didn't tell him. I didn't have to tell him.' Only a kiss. Trevor was a fool. A kiss could say so much. And it had been one hell of a kiss. She shuddered, feeling the kiss soak into her once more, as it had soaked into her that day in her mother's flat. Wet and warm, peeling into her senses. She had given herself up to it gladly, as eager for his goodbye kiss as she had been eager for every one of his embraces. Wanting to feel beautiful in the way he'd made her feel beautiful. Wanting to feel wanted. Flesh on flesh. Tenderness and desire. Perhaps it had never been love, but neither was whatever she was sharing with Robin now. Trevor's touch had been closer to love. Robin's touch was closer to hatred. She shivered violently.

'You've made your bed . . .' Trevor murmured.

'Well, that's bloody helpful.' Christie felt the urge to re-dial immediately, to tell Pamela whoever-she-was what Trevor had been up to. Wouldn't it be pleasant to witness him trying to wriggle his way out of it?

But she rejected the idea immediately. Why should she hurt Pam, who had done nothing to hurt her? And what would it achieve? Trevor would only say he was sorry, take his girlfriend some flowers and then go on as before. She shook her head. That wasn't the way.

'What do you want me to do?'

'Nothing.' What she wanted – what she really wanted – was to be left alone by these people. She didn't want the bother of it. She didn't want to have to make decisions, justify, or even think. But she couldn't afford that luxury. Whatever else was wrong in her life, she had a business to run, clients to deal with. She mustn't let it slide, not now. She'd worked too hard for her independence. She must keep herself together.

'Are you okay?' His voice changed, softening into a lover's voice again. 'Did he give you a hard time?'

'That's one way of putting it.'

'Shall I speak to him? Do you need me to . . . ?'

'Drop it, Trevor.' That would only make things worse. Unfortunately, she had to handle this alone.

'Fair enough.' He sounded relieved. 'And what time do you want me there today?'

'I don't want you here at all.' She sat down. 'There's no work.'

'Are you trying to get rid of me?' A hint of aggression crept into his voice. She wondered if he could sue her for wrongful dismissal, sexual discrimination, harassment or something.

'Of course not.' Christie picked at a loose thread on her jeans. She should tell him that he was invaluable to Purbeck Garden Designs. That if she had to cope on her own right now, she would probably fold up and renounce all responsibilities. But she didn't want to give him the satisfaction of imagining he was indispensable. 'I told you. There's no work. Who wants to start re-designing their garden straight after Christmas? Most people are still working out how to get rid of the tree.'

'So have I still got a job? That husband of yours didn't issue any ultimatums, did he? He didn't tell you to give me the sack?'

'No, Trevor,' she lied.

It had been the middle of the night on Christmas Eve. Robin's hand had squeezed her breast, waking her.

'Give it up,' he muttered. His mouth moved to her nipple, closing around the dark circle. She felt his teeth, a threat not a reality.

'What?' She peered into the darkness for the green dials of the alarm clock. Please, not again. The bruises hadn't even appeared from the last time.

'Purbeck bloody Garden Designs.' His tongue darted back and forth like a knife.

'What do you mean?' She stiffened, felt his cruel fingers probing inside her, felt the white liquid heat. Oh God, Oh God. 'No . . .'

'Say please.' He took her hips in his palms, raising her up.

'No,' she shouted. Half-past three. It was half three in the bloody morning.

He entered her with a spasm of viciousness.

Christie groaned.

'Say please.' Vindictively, he ground into her.

His mouth was on hers. The liquid heat was at boiling point. 'Please . . .' It came from her throat. Came from her throat into his mouth and exploded with orgasm.

'That's better,' he laughed. 'More?'

'No.' She felt her body sail, afloat on another wave of passion.

'Give up the company.' He thrust into her, the words taking up his relentless rhythm. 'Give it up, Christie.'

'I can't,' she moaned.

'Can't or won't?' Another vengeful stroke.

'That hurt.' She shouldn't tell him that. Knowing he was hard enough to hurt her gave him all the more pleasure. That was what he wanted. She tried to pull away from him but he had her pinned under him, his hands like a vice across her arms.

'Can't or won't?' he repeated. His mouth sank to her breast, his avenging body bent over hers.

'Can't . . .' She knew the right words to say.

'Silly girl.' He sucked her nipple, draining her dry, the force of him sending new jets of hopeless desire streaking through her veins.

'Please God . . .'

'Then get rid of him.' He came inside her in violent spurts of victory. 'Get rid of that bastard.'

He sank back, away from her, on to the pillows. 'Get rid of that bloody gardener of yours or else . . .' She didn't ask him what he meant. She couldn't speak. But neither could she do as he asked. She was fighting for survival now.

Christie looked up as a man walked into the shop, setting the wind chimes singing. He was not the usual kind of customer for Faith's Basement. He was in his mid to late forties, she guessed, dressed in an immaculate and expensive suit. He had a dark Mediterranean tan that contrasted with compelling blue eyes, and his dark hair was streaked with a rather distinguishing shade of grey.

She rang the bell for Sarah in the stockroom.

'Good,' Trevor was saying. 'That's something. We've still got a business to run.'

If she wasn't so tired, she would remind him that *she* had a business to run. And if the man in the dapper suit hadn't been looking her way with a certain curiosity that made her self-conscious. Where was Sarah? She rang again.

'I know that,' she told Trevor. 'But what do you expect me to do?'

'Drum up the business. You're the boss. There must be a way.'

'We're already advertising our services, Trevor.' The stranger smiled at her, and she smiled tentatively back.

'How about leaflets through people's doors?'

She pulled a face. The man was examining the sequined waistcoats. An odd air of reminiscence touched the handsome features. 'I suppose that's one idea,' was what she actually said.

'You don't sound very enthusiastic,' he grumbled. 'Maybe I should remind you that I've got a family to support. A kid on the way. It's all very well saying there's no work, but I can't hang around not being paid until something turns up. We need the money. We can't live on fresh air.'

Christie stared at the telephone receiver as his voice droned on. A kid on the way? A family to support? What was he talking about? 'Your girlfriend's pregnant?' she whispered, oblivious of the customer's presence in the shop, of his undisguised curiosity. Pregnant? One minute she hadn't heard so much as a whisper of the girl's existence, and now she was pregnant. Trevor sounded so casual. Didn't he realise that this made everything so much worse?

'Yeah.' He was on the defensive, perhaps regretting the admission. 'What about it?'

'Why didn't you tell me before?' she croaked into the phone, knowing the answer already.

'I'm telling you now, aren't I?'

'Oh, Trevor . . .' She took a deep breath. Business. Think business. 'I can't pay you very much if there's no work available, whether Pamela is pregnant or not. I only employed you on a casual basis, remember?' Casual work, casual sex. The thought occurred to her. She could feel some of her old fire returning. She felt so indignant – with Trevor, with all men. At their wild assumptions that women's morals were as terrifyingly loose as theirs appeared to be. And yet . . . She thought of Robin. Was it true?

'Oh, I get it.' His voice changed again. 'This is some sort of revenge, isn't it?'

'Of course not.' Once more she became aware of the stranger scrutinising her, although at least Sarah had now appeared from the stockroom to deal with him.

But Trevor was on his high horse. 'I need to earn a living,' he was saying. 'You've got a husband. It's all right for you. For you it's only pin money . . .'

Christie slammed down the phone, the blood rushing to her head. How dare he?

Both Sarah and the customer turned to face her. Sarah looked surprised, but the man merely smiled.

'I was wondering . . .' He came towards her.

'Yes?' She rubbed her hands together in a manner intended to be brisk. They were clammy and cold.

'This place . . . ?' He spread his hands appealingly.

'Yes?' Christie was in no mood for guessing games.

'You don't run it yourself?' He had an American accent, blended with a smooth continental burr.

Christie shook her head. Surely Sarah could have explained all that? But Sarah was already heading back towards the stockroom.

'Faith's Basement . . .' He shook his head. 'Talk about going back in time.'

She looked around her. 'You mean the sixties and all that?' She hoped he wouldn't think her rude. But he seemed about the right age, and she couldn't be bothered to find any politeness from among the tangle of emotions churning through her mind right now.

He laughed, rich and reverberating around the shop. 'Oh, yeah, the sixties and all that. Way before your time.'

She nodded.

'But that's not all.' He came closer and she smelled the scent of expensive aftershave. He was clean-shaven but she could clearly make out the dark lines of stubble on his jaw. 'Certain things, you know?' His hand trailed over a collection of love beads. 'All this stuff . . .'

'Is there something specific you were looking for?' Christie didn't want to be saddled with some weirdo. 'Sarah would help you if you had any queries.'

His dark eyebrows rose. 'Excuse me. I'm not making any sense, right?'

Christie shook her head. 'Not really.'

'It was an impulse of mine.' The blue eyes bore into her.

'Oh?'

'I looked the name up in a phone book. Vaughan.'

Christie's interest quickened. 'Yes?'

'There was more than one. But it was the name of the shop that got me thinking. So I came to the address listed. On the off-chance.'

'Thinking?' She waited for him to explain. But he only laughed, as if at his own ridiculousness. 'It seemed kind of typical. Faith's Basement.' He lingered over the words, wandering slowly around the shop once more, with a kind of wariness as if it were somehow familiar yet dangerous territory. Or as if he were waiting for someone else to appear.

'I see.' Actually she didn't have the foggiest idea what he was on about.

'It couldn't be . . .' he murmured. He looked at her and frowned. 'So, who are you?' His question was direct, she'd say that for him.

'Christie Fifer.' She waited for him to introduce himself, but he remained silent. 'I don't have much to do with the shop,' she elaborated.

'I run a garden design business. That's why I suggested that Sarah . . .'

'And where's Faith?' He seemed full of suppressed excitement, as he leaned closer towards her.

Christie stared at him blankly. He wanted to know an awful lot, for a stranger. 'She isn't here today,' she told him. 'She's in London.'

'I see.' His face fell and Christie couldn't help feeling sorry for him. Was he a man from her mother's London past perhaps? Had he followed her here, or seen the name Faith's Basement, made the right connections, and guessed that it belonged to Faith Vaughan?

'Did you want to see my mother about anything in particular?' she asked, trying to be helpful.

'Your mother?' The expression in his eyes darkened almost imperceptibly.

She nodded. 'Only it might be better for you to come back and talk to her tomorrow.' She spoke gently. The poor man seemed confused, and for some reason she liked him. She also didn't imagine that her mother would thank her if she sent him away. He was, after all, extremely attractive.

'Maybe I should at that. Or maybe it was a dumb idea.' He was talking to himself. 'But shouldn't I find out for sure?' He glanced at Christie. 'If it's really her . . .' he murmured softly.

'Shall I tell her who called?' She reached for a pen.

'No.' He put a finger to his lips. 'Please, no.'

And before she could question him further he had turned and walked out of the shop, leaving only the wind chimes dancing and singing behind him. And leaving Christie, who shrugged, put him from her mind and turned instead to the problem of designing a leaflet for Trevor Swift to put through people's doors.

In a large warehouse somewhere in East London, Faith Vaughan was horrified to see none other than Lola Denyer dressed in tasteless stilettoes and a red silk blouse, walking past racks of clothes towards her.

'Oh, God.' She turned, but it was too late.

'What's this then?' Lola's voice held a screeching quality that Faith detested.

'Lola!' Faith tried to look both pleased and surprised and guessed that she failed dismally. 'What are you doing here?' She pulled her black overcoat closer around her.

'Shouldn't I be asking you that?' Lola's hard eyes surveyed her with a mixture of scorn and curiosity. 'I thought you were out of this business.'

Faith knew that she was treading on dangerous ground here. When she'd left The Basement boutique in Chelsea, she had told Stuart and Lola that she was returning to her family in Dorset. She hadn't mentioned that she wasn't quite ready for retirement. In fact there was a great deal that she'd omitted to mention. 'It's not the same league, Lola,' she said quickly. 'I've opened one of those touristy knickknack shops, you know? They're two a penny in Dorset.' Surely Lola wouldn't imagine that she had set herself up in competition?

'Really?' Lola adjusted the floppy silk bow of her blouse. 'Now I wonder why that doesn't ring true?'

'I thought Stuart would be taking over the buying.' Faith's voice was casual. She was only concerned with shifting the subject from her new enterprise in Dorset, and getting away from this woman as fast as possible without alerting suspicion. She had no interest in what was happening without her. That was her past. She was done with it.

'Did you now? Didn't you think I could manage it myself?'

Faith shrugged. 'I didn't say that.'

'But you thought it.'

Faith sighed. Christie had been quite mistaken when she'd suggested that the boutique in London was Faith's baby. She herself had never thought of it like that. She had desperately needed to throw herself into something heart and soul. To forget, she supposed. And the Chelsea boutique had been there – or the beginnings of it had been there – along with Stuart and Lola Denyer who seemed in need of a prod of ambition and an organised mind. Providing what they lacked had helped her forget for a while, that was all.

'And talking of Stuart . . .' Lola's voice hardened as she gripped Faith's arm.

'He's all right, isn't he?' That was all she felt guilty for – leaving Stuart. But then again, it had been unfair to him to stay so long.

A cackle of laughter erupted from Lola's red lips. 'Are you concerned? How sweet.' She moved in closer and Faith blanched at the blast of cheap perfume. How a woman in Lola Denyer's position, with a successful fashion business, always managed to look and smell so awful, never ceased to amaze her. Lola had never fitted the part.

'Of course I'm concerned.' Faith didn't want to be. She wanted to be absolutely away from it. It had been the same when she left America, and

Dorset too. A clean break – it was the only way.

Lola took a step back, pointed a vermilion-painted fingernail. 'Don't worry your pretty head about it. You've done what you set out to do.'

'Set out to do?' Faith stared at her. She stank of booze too – she had always smelled of booze since Faith had first met her back in the late sixties. It was astounding how well someone who put away a bottle of vodka a day could manage to function.

'I know you wanted to break us up.' Lola's eyes dimmed with self-pitying tears. 'I know you always wanted him to leave me.'

Faith decided she preferred her when she was being aggressive. 'Stuart would never have told you that.' She was indignant. Because it wasn't true.

'He didn't need to.' Lola came closer. 'I've got eyes. Don't think I didn't know what was going on between you two.'

Faith pulled away. 'Nothing was going on between us, Lola.' She rubbed her arm, still smarting from Lola's frenzied grip.

'Don't give me that crap.' She bit her lip and a stain of crimson crept on to one of her front teeth.

'It's true.' Faith couldn't believe it. All these years and she'd avoided a confrontation with this woman, who had seemed as oblivious to her husband's growing estrangement as she was to his growing feelings for Faith Vaughan. And now – now that she had escaped from the situation – here she was, being drawn into a row. In somebody's warehouse, for God's sake. It was unthinkable. 'Let's talk about this sensibly,' she said, trying to lead Lola towards the exit. She was a tall woman, and she bent slightly, although whether through despair or alcohol, Faith wasn't sure. 'This isn't the place . . .'

'And have you found anything you fancy for Faith's Basement?' The manager of the warehouse was approaching, beaming from ear to ear.

'*Faith's* Basement?' Lola screeched.

'I'll be back later.' Somehow Faith managed to usher her outside into the cold bleakness of East London in winter.

'You've taken our business, destroyed our marriage, pinched our name. What else is left?' Lola was hysterical.

'I adapted the name,' Faith corrected, reaching into her overcoat pocket for her cigarettes and gold lighter. 'That's entirely different. And it's not a clothing outlet.'

'Then what the hell are you doing here?'

Faith became exasperated. 'I'm not in competition with you, Lola. Either for your business or for your husband.' She lit the cigarette, drawing in the menthol and nicotine gratefully, exhaling into the cold air.

'You made him hate me.' Lola's face was flushed. She scrabbled in her bag.

'When I met you, you and Stuart were using the business as a last ditch attempt to save your marriage,' Faith snapped. 'I didn't make Stuart do anything.' Rather the opposite, she considered ruefully.

'And it would have worked. It would have worked if you hadn't come and . . .'

'I built up the business from nothing.' Faith's olive eyes flashed with barely concealed fury. 'Stuart and I did all the hard work.' She was tempted to add 'while you drank the profits,' but held back. Lola was upset enough already.

'You didn't have to take Stuart away from me.' Once more she fumbled in her bag, this time producing the small bottle of vodka that was never far from her side.

Faith watched in disgust as she put the bottle to her lips and took a deep swig. She grabbed the bottle out of Lola's claw-like hand. 'This stuff took Stuart away from you,' she told her.

Lola wiped her mouth with the back of her hand, smearing more crimson across her face. 'Stuart loves you. He's pining for you. He says the place is going to pot without you. He hasn't got the heart . . .'

'Then he's a fool.' Faith handed her back the bottle. She had always ensured that there was nothing between her and Stuart Denyer but friendship. It had been tempting – Stuart was a kind man and had always been generous with his time and advice – but Faith had known immediately that an unprofessional relationship was out of the question; there was too much at stake. And she had no wish for a man. Perhaps she had been spoiled for anything else. Spoiled by a long-ago summer in America.

She regarded the pathetic creature in front of her. She had done her bit to try and help her. In the beginning she had offered her friendship and she had always refused to let her man betray her. But Lola had rarely done more than throw it all back in her face. And so she would not let Lola hold her responsible for what she had done to herself, what she had done to her own marriage.

'If you came back . . .' Lola's voice turned to a whine. 'I wouldn't care – you know, about what the two of you did – so long as you were discreet.'

Faith stared at her, unable to believe what she was hearing. 'For God's sake . . .' She stamped out her cigarette. It was freezing out here, her fingers were blue with cold.

Lola lowered her voice confidentially. 'I've had others, you know. I'm sure you cottoned on. It was dead easy when you two went away so much and I had the house to myself.' She grinned, her mouth a red slash of cruelty on her brazen face. 'Men with a bit more balls to them than Stuart ever had.'

Faith drew back, appalled. 'I thought you'd be glad I was gone.' As she looked at Lola, she wondered why she'd stayed so long.

When she came on these visits, drawn to London to look at stock and keep up to date with what was happening in the market-place, she found herself escaping from the tall grey city with a small thrill of relief. So pleased she didn't have to live here any more. Even on the train, she'd be yearning for the peace and green of Dorset, as if she'd discovered a tranquilliser that could soothe any pain.

Lola shrugged. 'Truth is, we can't manage without you.' For a moment there was honesty in the dull eyes. And then she flipped the empty bottle into a nearby litter bin, turned around on her stilettoes and walked away, heels scraping on the pavement. 'Stuart's a bloody fool,' she called over her shoulder. As if she'd suddenly realised this. And as if she knew that Faith would never return.

Later that same day, Christie was returning from the printer's in Poole. She was sitting in the pick-up truck on the chain ferry that transported passengers and their cars from Sandbanks to Studland, when she glanced across at the car in the line next to her. Sitting in the driving seat was the man who had come to the shop today. The man so eager to meet her mother. She nodded a greeting as he smiled. The electric window on the passenger side of his car glided down.

'Hi there.' He waved.

Christie wound down her own window in response. 'Hello again.' He had a disarming smile, she decided. A smile that made him somehow more than just some stranger.

'D'you think your mother will be home by now?' He tapped his watch.

'She might be.' Christie increased the volume of her voice to compete with the rush of the water and wind against the ferry.

He eyed her appraisingly. 'Can you pull over when we get to the other side? I'd appreciate a quick word.'

Christie was doubtful. She really should be getting back to Ulwell. 'What about?' she yelled.

'I can't tell you now.' They had reached the other bank and the young lad in the yellow lifeguard's jacket was moving the barriers.

'Okay.' She switched on the ignition.

He pulled up in the parking spaces allotted for visitors to Shell Beach. There was only one other car. It was getting late, past six, and there was a bitter chill in the January wind that hit Christie's face as she jumped out of the truck. For the first time she questioned her common sense in stopping here at all.

'I don't even know your name,' she said firmly.

'Marc Dupont.' He held out his hand, which she touched briefly.

'And what did you want to ask me?' She leaned against the truck, wondering if she'd have the chance to grab a shovel from the back if he were to turn nasty.

But the stranger too seemed unsure of his ground. 'I should have mentioned it before. It seems a bit of a cheek. You see, I think I knew your mother, way back.'

'You think?' Once more Christie smelled the expensive after shave.

'The girl I knew was called Faith Vaughan, and her mother lived in Dorset.' He smiled, warily. 'But you said you were her daughter . . .'

'Yes?' Christie was growing cold out here. Why didn't he just get on with it?

He spread his hands. 'Is she married? I wouldn't want to embarrass her.'

So that was it. Christie surveyed him again with renewed interest. He was right – it was a cheek, and probably none of his business. But . . . 'She's not married.' Christie brushed back the spiky blonde hair blown into her face by the sea wind. Her voice carried the words away from them. 'Vaughan is her maiden name. And her mother does still live in Dorset. Isobel Vaughan.'

His expression cleared. 'I see.'

'And anything else you want to know you should ask her yourself.' Christie put a hand on the door of the truck. A thought occurred to her. 'Are *you* married?'

He nodded. 'Sure. Twenty years.'

So he had known Mum a long time ago, then. What did he plan to do –
re-live old times? 'Children?'

'Two teenagers.' He pulled a face. 'I was wondering . . .'

'Yes?' There was something about those blue eyes of his . . .

'Would you come along with me?'

'With you?' Her voice echoed around the bleak car park with its dunes
and clumps of coarse grass. 'To see my mother?'

He nodded. 'Would you?'

She frowned. She felt as though something or someone was trying to
pull her out of the trough of confusion and lethargy that she'd sunk into. It
wasn't him, and yet . . . She didn't understand why, but she trusted this
stranger. 'Okay.'

His face lit up. 'Shall I go on ahead?' In two steps he was back at the
BMW, his hand on the door.

She nodded. 'I'll follow you.'

The truck groaned as she heaved it into life. She knew that Robin would
be expecting her home by now. And as always, since their relationship had
lurched into its present state, she simultaneously wanted to get home and
dreaded getting home. But this time the dread – and a certain look in a
stranger's eyes – had won.

14

Christie parked the pick-up truck behind the BMW in Wareham High Street, observing that even by street-light the two vehicles made an incongruous couple.

The man so eager to meet her mother smiled – an attempt at reassurance, she guessed – as she joined him outside the shop. He took her arm, and Christie rang the bell. Was this, after all, a sensible idea? The High Street's shops were closed, the darkness of a cold January evening lay around them, and the situation seemed almost surreal.

'Just coming.' Her mother's voice. Her mother's footsteps.

Christie felt him tense beside her, sensed his apprehension, his fear. Why had she agreed to this?

Keeping the security chain in place, Faith opened the door. 'Christie!'

She caught a glimpse of her mother's smile, as Faith pushed the door to, and undid the chain. She hadn't seen him.

'This is a nice surprise . . .' Her words tailed into nothing as she realised that her daughter wasn't alone.

It took Faith only a second to absorb the sight of him. He looked different, very different. But clothes, hair-cut, signs of ageing and conservatism . . . None of that could hide what she recognised instantly.

'Mum?' Christie took a step forwards.

Faith frowned. But how could it be him? And with Christie?

'Mum, this is . . .'

'Marc,' Faith breathed. It was the first time she'd said the name aloud in a long while. And yet so many times she'd told it silently to her heart. Forget him. Forget him. Over the years it had remained a difficult name to

161

say, a hard name to get her tongue around, the pain never quite disappearing, nor the sense of what might have been.

'Hi, Faith.' His expression was warm, welcoming her back to him. 'I just knew it had to be you.' He smiled, the same old smile. The smile she wanted to reach out and touch, tuck away in her pocket for rainy days. 'It's been a long time.'

A long time indeed.

She hadn't known what she'd been letting herself in for all those years ago when she answered the ad and turned up for grape-picking in Brittany. It hadn't been easy to leave her mother and Yew Cottage, not easy at all when everything in front of her was unknown. But on the third day she had met Marc. And after that it was easy, because her life slotted into place.

During the long dusty days in the vineyard, they worked beside each other under the hot southern Brittany sun, stopping only to swig water from the bottles they'd brought with them, or to wipe sweat from their brows. But Faith hardly noticed the discomfort, almost relishing the heat, as she sneaked glances from under her wide-brimmed straw hat at the supple dark body working by her side. Marc, who moved with an easy loose rhythm and picked the most grapes by far, was the obvious leader, fluent in French and English, at home here, part of the very soil, part of Faith too before long.

'Where do we go now?' 'How much will we get?' 'What time is it?' 'Where can I get a shower?' They were always asking him questions, he was forever surrounded. Everyone drawn to him, the natural leader.

And yet he sought her out.

He walked with her one evening through the darkness to the sand dunes. It was deserted at this time of night, although they could hear the distant voices of the others back near the vineyard – laughter and the faint strumming of a guitar.

'Don't you mind?' she asked him. 'Don't you ever want to brush us all away like flies?'

'Not you . . .' He glanced across at her.

'Why not me?' She scuffed the sand with her toes, felt the tiny grains damp in the night air.

'I want to look after you, baby.' He drew her back to the high dune, down on to the sand that was still dry and untouched.

She laughed, the excitement catching in her throat. She had known they'd make love; she'd been waiting for days. 'Maybe I don't need as much looking after as you think. I'm a quick learner. You'd be surprised.' Amazed at how brave she could be.

Charmed, he slipped the straps of her skimpy cheesecloth vest over her shoulders. 'Go on. Surprise me,' he whispered.

Faith undid the tiny buttons. 'Here?'

'Why not?' He pulled off his shirt. 'It's beautiful here, wouldn't you say? And you're beautiful . . .'

Marc was her first lover, her only lover. Her life began on that late August night, lying naked on the dunes with him, sand in her hair, her mouth, sticking to her skin as the cool night breeze caressed them. Their bodies, the waves, were lit only by a narrow crescent moon, shrouded by clouds.

'Let's go in.' He pulled her to her feet, and they ran, their bare soles hardly skimming the wet sand as they plunged into the cool green-black water.

'Jesus, that feels great.' He pulled her towards him, kissing her wet salty breasts. 'You feel great. And you taste even better.'

She laughed, her head thrown back in perfect wild delight, strands of blonde hair whipping into the waves.

They swam, he ducked underneath her, grabbing her waist, his skin wet and gleaming in the darkness.

'Marc . . .' Barely a whisper.

His smile. 'We're going to be good together, we are. I just know it.'

Desperately Faith shook her head to rid herself of memories, to suspend disbelief. She needed to *breathe*. 'What are you doing here? I mean . . . Where did you come from? What on earth . . . ?'

She took in the sight of Christie's arm, still resting lightly in his, and she paled, groping for the counter. 'What do you want?' She looked from one to the other of them.

'It's all right, Mum.' Christie moved swiftly inside. 'He came here earlier today. He wanted to see you so much. I thought . . .'

'It wasn't her fault.' Marc followed her into the shop. Faith stared at him.

'What are you doing here, Marc?' Somehow, she managed to retain a semblance of control. 'What do you want?' She knew she was asking the same questions, of him, of herself, over and over.

'I'm sorry, Faith.' His voice caressed her name as if it were her body, in the way it had always done. The same voice, but with more of an American accent than before. And more experience behind it presumably. 'I should have called first.'

'Yes. Yes you should.' But if he had phoned, would she have agreed to see him? Marc – after all this time. She felt as if she could hardly stand. All the breath, all the life, had been knocked out of her.

Christie glared at him. 'You could have warned me.' She turned back to Faith. 'Do you want him to leave?'

A small part of her longed to smile at her daughter's protectiveness. But she shook her head, still unable to stop staring at him. She couldn't send him away – not yet.

'Let's go upstairs, then.' Christie led the way. 'Then you can tell me what on earth this is all about.'

Faith followed her. What was it all about? At the top of the stairs she turned. 'How did you find me?' she asked.

His eyes softened. 'It wasn't too difficult.'

She drank in the terrifying nearness of him for a moment before slipping into the flat after Christie. Why? Why had he come?

'I saw the name of the shop in the phone book.' He was only one step away.

'How did you know it was me?' Her voice sounded thin and nervous. If she'd remained in London, he would never have found her, she realised. With shaking hands she pulled a cigarette from the turquoise and gold packet.

Marc jumped forwards with a lighter. He flicked a switch and Faith bent towards the flame. He smiled once more and danger signals flashed in her head, in her heart, through every limb, every organ. Marc . . .

'Faith's Basement,' he murmured. 'It just had to be you.'

Abruptly she sat on the black leather sofa. It had to be her. She put a hand to her hair to brush it from her face, and realised. Oh, God. She'd been in London all day. She must look awful. She hadn't washed her face, repaired her make-up or even brushed her hair. And the Armani scent she'd put on this morning must surely have worn off by now.

'You look pretty good to me.' His eyes stroked her once again. 'You always did.'

Faith gazed down at the floor. The same old patter. He'd always been good at that, even in the days when he'd had to be cool. But had he ever meant it? She'd never really known for sure.

'Don't you think you two should tell me what's going on?' A white-faced Christie stepped forwards. 'Who is he?' Her voice dropped to a whisper.

'Darling, I'm sorry . . .' Faith began. She had almost forgotten Christie was still in the room. Marc had taken over, dominating her landscape in the way he always had.

'Sorry for what?' Christie stared at her. Marc Dupont stood by the doorway as if prepared to make a quick getaway, while her mother was perched on the edge of the sofa refusing even to look at him. But despite that, it was plain as anything that all they wanted to do was fall into each other's arms.

Faith looked up at last in silent appeal to Marc.

'Who is he?' Christie was rooted to the spot but her mind was racing.

'We knew each other a long time ago,' Faith began. 'Before you were born.' She stubbed out her cigarette, licked dry lips.

'Way back. More years than I care to remember.' His eyes crinkled with easy laughter. Years that had effectively been swept away, he seemed to be saying. Christie couldn't dislike him. But she disliked the effect he was having on her mother.

She turned to him. 'Before you were married?' Why had she said that? Whatever she'd expected, it was as good as a bucket of cold water.

Faith's expression changed. Shock turned to disappointment, and then to the cool mask that Christie was far more used to seeing. The mask that was very reassuring at this moment in time, because it didn't say a lot about love. 'Married?' she enquired politely. She rose to her feet.

Marc Dupont took a step closer towards her, and at the same time Faith moved back.

'Well, sure.' He spread his hands. 'Don't most of us take that road eventually? It's been almost twenty-five years, Faith. You must have been married yourself?' He glanced suggestively at Christie.

Faith shook her head. She stared beyond him, over his shoulder, as if contemplating the past.

Christie had never seen her mother looking so vulnerable, so young. It made her wonder about the efficient businesswoman who had her life so well organised. Tidy compartments. No space. No mess. This woman, here in the flat tonight, with her tangled blonde hair and big olive eyes, seemed a different person altogether. So which was real?

'Faith?' He took her face gently in his hands, compelling her to confront the urgent question in his eyes.

Seeming reluctant, she met his gaze.

He took a sharp intake of breath, searched her expression once more. Then he turned to Christie, astonishment mingling with pleasure.

'What?' She stared from one to the other. Some small fact that she may have overlooked was nudging at her subconscious, screaming to come in.

'It shouldn't be like this.' Faith looked sad, beaten and confused.

Christie wanted to protect her but she wasn't sure what from. And until she was told . . . 'Mum?' Her voice grew insistent, pressing for an answer. 'What is it? Tell me.'

Faith was silent. She gazed at Christie with smudged, pleading eyes. She bit her lip. 'I wanted to tell you. I meant to tell you . . .' She broke off.

'Do I have a daughter?' His words rang out, rich and vibrant. He was grinning all over his tanned, handsome face. 'Why the hell didn't you ever let me know about it?'

Christie stared at him, struggling to make sense of his words, trying to fight the rising panic. 'Mum?'

Faith was still gazing vacantly at the carpet, tears spilling down her cheeks.

'Are you saying that he's my . . . my . . . ?' Christie regarded the stranger, this time in a new light, with a different frame of reference. Remembered his easy confidence and barely concealed excitement when he'd walked into Faith's Basement this morning.

'Yes.' He was still waiting for an acknowledgement.

Christie looked into his blue eyes. 'Is it true?' She grabbed her mother's arm. 'Is it true?' She knew she was shouting – she could hear her own voice echoing around the small flat, around the chrome and black that said so little about her mother's personality. And what was there to say? It was beginning to seem as if her mother was a master of disguise.

The anger filled her like white light, shining into their faces. These people were toying with her parentage, devaluing it. Couldn't they see how it *mattered* to know – just to *know* – who had brought her into this world?

'It's true.' At last Faith looked up. The love had gone from her face now. She flashed a glance of resentment towards Marc.

Then she reached out to Christie. 'Darling . . .'

Christie backed away. 'Why didn't you tell me?'

'I was going to. I tried . . .' Her mother's hands were open, as if trying to pull her closer.

She faced Marc. 'I was going to tell her,' she wailed through the tears. 'Why didn't you let me tell her in my own time? She was just beginning to trust me.'

He frowned in confusion.

Trust. Christie spun around, making for the door, the stairs, the shop, the fresh air outside. Air untainted with this secret.

'Christie . . .' Her mother's voice followed her down the stairs. 'Forgive me, Christie.'

'Leave her for a moment.' His dark, velvet voice was calm. She could hear the soothing tones of it even as she struggled with the Yale lock of the front door. Desperately she yanked it open, shut them out, the mother who had never been a mother, the secret and the velvet voice of the man who was . . .

No. She couldn't think it. Not yet. She rested her back for a few minutes against the shop door, took a deep breath to gather strength, and plunged towards the pick-up truck.

As she put her key in the ignition she was dimly aware that there was only one place she could go. Only one place where she could get this information in some sort of manageable order in her mind. So she switched on her headlights and drove in the direction of Yew Cottage. A woman with some distant identity. A woman with two parents at last.

'I was going to tell her . . . Why didn't you let *me* tell her?' She couldn't stop repeating the words.

'Faith?' He seemed bewildered. 'All these years . . . ? You must have told her something.'

She stomped over to the glass table and grabbed her cigarettes, this time allowing him no time to light it for her. She didn't want him to get that close, didn't want to be able to feel him with her, to smell the scent of him. She closed her eyes. What did *he* know about anything? She was furious.

'It's incredible.' He was still grinning in astonishment. 'I can't believe it . . .'

'Marc! Please stop . . .'

He moved towards her. 'Give her a while to get used to the idea. She'll come round – you know she will.'

Faith shook her head. He knew nothing. He had no idea of the fragility between herself and Christie. She wasn't sure that Christie would come round. And it was her own fault for not telling her before. So many times she had opened her mouth to say the words. But every time, she had stopped. Saying the words would mean she'd have to elaborate – tell her daughter the whole story. And telling the story would unlock the memories, reintroduce the pain.

'So why didn't you tell her about me?' He sounded remarkably composed for a man who had just discovered he had a daughter of twenty-four. For a man confronting his old lover with the past. But then, Marc had always been able to cope with things.

She hesitated. 'Because I was ashamed.' There was some truth in that.

'Ashamed of not being married?' His brow creased.

'Of course not.' How could he think that? Did he know her so little? Faith moved to the window. Watched her daughter illuminated by the street lamp, a little flash of fury running towards the battered old pick-up truck. And she felt her heart constrict with the pain.

'Ashamed of what, then?' His voice was gentle, but Faith hardened her heart against it. When she'd opened the door this evening to see his face – the face that had hardly dimmed even in memory – the love had rushed to the surface, entirely of its own volition, like a being apart from herself. But now she could manufacture some control. She had to. She would not allow him to walk in and casually disrupt her life.

'Ashamed of depriving her of a father,' she admitted at last. She had blamed Isobel for that very same thing, because she remembered her own father loving her – that was the trouble. She remembered being her Daddy's little girl. Yes, Faith had blamed her mother for taking that away from her. What sort of a hypocrite did that make her? She hadn't only deprived Christie of a father, she had deprived her of a mother too. There were no excuses.

'Then why did you do it, Faith?' He came up behind her, something soft and animal stealing into her senses, the presence of him overshadowing everything but the here, the now and the him that was Marc. 'Why did you deprive her of a father?'

She shook her head. 'I didn't think for one moment you'd want to be one.' He had been there, in Woodstock, New York State, in 1966. He had felt it – the atmosphere of freedom that swept into everything they touched. Anti-commitment, anti-establishment, anti-convention. Babies were not on the agenda. He knew what it was like. But he hadn't known what was going on inside Faith Vaughan's head, because she'd been afraid to tell anyone about that.

Marc had been right, that evening in Brittany. It was good between them. It had always been good between them. Easy and free with the kind of loving anyone would long for. France had been a dream. Even Woodstock had been a dream, at first. But in Woodstock she hadn't been living true to herself. She'd been too good at pretending.

Faith ground the cigarette out in the ashtray.

'Why didn't you tell me you were pregnant?' he persisted, taking her by the arm and swinging her round to face him. 'I would have stuck by you. You know I would.'

Ah, but she wouldn't have wanted that, would she? She would never have known, would she, if it were free choice or duty? Her emotions were tangled, but her eyes remained perfectly calm. 'I don't have to explain anything to you, Marc.'

His eyes narrowed. 'Oh no?' His grip tightened on her arm.

'No.' She wouldn't allow herself to be bullied.

'You get yourself pregnant with my kid, don't even bother to let me know about it, write me some dumb note to make me think you've left me for some other guy . . . And you think there's nothing to explain?'

'What did it have to do with you?' Faith's voice was high-pitched, edging towards hysteria. 'It was my body. My baby. What would you have said if I'd told you? Would you have expected me to have an abortion, or would you have just run away? You would have hated me . . .'

'No.' He pulled her closer, his voice rough. 'I'd never have hated you, Faith.'

'You don't know.' She was trembling, although whether with outrage or simply the effect of his hand on her arm, she wasn't sure.

'Is that what you were afraid of?' His voice became tender.

'No!'

'What then?' His blue eyes were creeping into her soul, the way they had always crept into her soul. He had always had it – this power over her that scared the life out of her.

'I want you to leave.' She wouldn't reveal her fears to him. She wouldn't then, and she wouldn't now,

'But we've just found each other again,' he began. 'Jesus, Faith . . .'

'You're married.' She dropped the words into the chasm that was stretching wider between them.

'But . . .'

'You have a life.' She pulled herself up to her full height. 'A life apart from Christie and me.' She paused, longing to ask about it, desperate to have some snippets from that life of his to cling on to. But he was married. Nothing to cling on to there. Only potential pain. 'You have a life,' she repeated. 'You should go back to it.'

He laughed, harshly, without humour. 'And I suppose I shouldn't have got married, right? Is that what you're saying? I should have spent twenty-five years mourning you, is that it?'

Faith looked away. She had spent twenty-five years mourning him, hadn't she? Only one lover in her life. More fool her. 'Why have you come here?' Why have you come here now, she meant. Now, after all this time?

She watched him. In many ways he was unchanged. His blue eyes – those marvellous eyes the colour of cornflowers – could still hypnotise and eat away at her good intentions. Christie's eyes. She sighed. He had looked after himself; he seemed fit and hadn't put on too much weight, although he was heavier than the rake-like figure in baggy T-shirts and jeans she had first fallen in love with. His hair was greying, but it suited him. He was tanned and her experienced eye told her he was wearing expensive clothes. Marc was a success – but then she had never doubted he would be.

He turned back to her at last. 'I came because I had to see you. I was never really sure. That note you wrote . . . I believed it at the time. But it didn't fit – not really. Over the years it seemed to fit less and less. Dammit, Faith, I've never been able to get you out of my head.'

She was silent, still watching him.

'Some guy at work was talking about a vacation in England he'd just had. And I thought: I have to see that woman – just once. Because there was something so . . .'

'Unfinished between us?' She spoke without thinking.

'Exactly.' In two paces he was beside her again. Too close for comfort. Taking her hands in his. 'You always knew exactly what I was trying to say, Faith.'

She laughed, startled for a moment out of her determination to remain unmoved. It was the unfinished element of their parting that had always hurt her the most. What might have been. An utterly destructive way to think. Considering the maybes and the if onlys was negative to the core. Destroying the present, destroying the rest of her life. But it hadn't destroyed Marc's life, had it?

She removed her hands. 'You certainly took your time in getting here.'

He grabbed her shoulders. 'What did you expect, Faith? You wrote the note. Ritchie left at the same time. What was I supposed to think? Was it just some melodramatic gesture you were making? I sure thought at the time you made your feelings pretty clear.' His voice became mocking. 'Did you expect me to follow you to England? Should I have begged you to come right back?'

She shook her head. No. She had never expected him to beg. She had half-hoped he might follow her – that was true. Like some romantic fool, she had imagined him chasing after her, finding out about the baby, carrying her off or even marrying her in some quaint old Dorset church. She had never known that Ritchie had left at the same time. Ritchie. What a weird coincidence, though he'd been saying he was moving on for weeks. But how could Marc imagine that she and Ritchie . . . ?

'What did I do wrong?' he demanded. 'Why did you leave?'

His touch was pressing into her flesh, sinking further, closer into her thoughts, her heart. She closed her eyes. He had no idea, even though he now knew the truth, of why she had left Woodstock. And now? Did he know how much she wanted him? His hands pressed with growing insistence. The hot current of sexuality was tense and burning between them, charged between the skin of his hands and the curve of her shoulders. She knew she was losing herself to him, just as she had always lost herself to him. 'Nothing,' she murmured. Nothing and everything, that's what he'd done wrong.

'Jesus, Faith. I adored you.'

She let the words whisper into her mind. Marc had adored her. His lips drew closer. He was a burning flame. They were a burning flame and she longed to melt with him . . .

But Marc had a wife. Her eyes snapped open. 'I want you to leave. I can't cope with this . . .' She was blurting rubbish, she knew it. He'd know it too.

His shoulders sagged with disappointment. 'Sure.' Marc the gentleman. Even in the old days he had possessed that quality. 'Whatever you say. But we can talk again, right?'

She stared at him. Didn't he know that she was powerless against him? That a certain touch, instead of cool politeness, would have been enough? 'Yes. We must get together.' She sounded like a polite almost-stranger from an old school reunion. Yes, we simply must re-live old times,

171

exchange notes. On wives and lovers, and children we once could have shared.

'OK.' Reluctant steps took him to the staircase that his daughter had raced down less than half an hour ago. Half an hour. In half an hour Faith's world had been bruised, battered, turned upside down.

He looked back. 'I should have warned you I was coming.' His mouth twitched. 'But then you would have . . .'

'Run away. Yes.' Faith's fingers touched her hair. She felt young and helpless and hopelessly transported back to that summer of 1966.

She followed him down the stairs.

'Can I call you?' His hand rested on the Yale lock.

She nodded, unable to speak.

He opened the door. 'Take care, Faith.'

She returned to the flat, sat on the black leather armchair. Who could tell her which way to go? She had made independence her watchword. She had forced herself to need no-one. But now, who would take care of her battered heart? It had, after all, for as long as she could remember, belonged to Marc rather more than it had belonged to herself.

15

Christie sat in the truck outside Yew Cottage, hands on the steering wheel, head down, trying to take it all in. At last she opened the door, jumped down and crept like some injured animal towards the sanctuary of the yew grove.

Slightly spooky at any time of day, the trees underwent a sinister transformation at dusk. At this time of night they seemed to give off a greenish hue that put Christie in mind of witches, ritualism and black magic. Dominic Redfern had said he wouldn't come here at night, but it wasn't imagined horrors that bothered Christie. It was the real variety. And, as always, here in the yew grove, she felt as if she had come home.

Picking her way cautiously through the humus and small saplings underfoot, sniffing the sweet musty scent of damp needles and bark, she made her way by instinct to her favourite old yew. She sighed, sat gingerly on the low lateral branch that had sunk into the ground, rooted but not yet rotted and separated from the mother tree. She leaned against the knotted, rusty bark, sheltering beneath the ragged shawl of the yew's protection, marshalling her thoughts,

She had a father. Of course she'd always known that somewhere she had a father, but it had been almost easier to imagine him dead, or at least out of reach, having discarded her mother, treated her badly, or whatever a man had to do to make a woman leave him.

But no. Christie had a father who turned out to be a man she could like, even a man she could admire. She had a father who had clearly known nothing of her existence, and therefore couldn't be blamed in the manner that Christie had rather smoothly blamed him in imagination. So, she had a blameless father. But a father with his own life, his own children, his own wife.

Christie closed her eyes. Two children, he had said. Teenagers. Did she have a brother? A sister? One of each? It was mind-boggling. Only half-brothers or sisters perhaps, but still ... Would she ever meet them? Would she ever want to meet them?

And what was even more bizarre and inexplicable – and here Christie had to grip on to the branch to stop herself losing her balance – was that her mother and this stranger-father who had appeared out of the blue, seemed to be in love. The rough wood dug into her palms. In love.

Christie jumped off the branch. So why had her mother ever left him?

She tore damp, stained fingers through her hair and began pacing among the trees, dodging the fallen branches, the small saplings, the webbed roots that seemed to glow in the night like bones resting beneath the earth's surface. Heedless of her feet in trainers sinking into the sodden earth, the dank flaking bark cutting her fingers, the cold seeping through her fleece jacket. Her fingers were numb and bloodless, her eyes wet. An owl hooted somewhere. The contorted shapes of the yew trees seemed to move, making way for her, clearing a path, just as she was clearing her mind of what it had held before. Allowing her new identity to penetrate into her head, and her heart.

She had a father. That meant she had a past. It was, after all, rather wonderful. Didn't this mean that she could be a complete person at last? That this piece of identity could slot into the jigsaw of her life, so the pattern could make sense? And more then that ...

There in the yew grove, Christie came to a decision. She couldn't go on living this way. Something must change, and she was the one to make it change. It was time to explore her past, and use it to find strength for her future.

Isobel, sitting in front of the log fire in Beatrice's old oak rocking chair, opened her eyes, thinking she heard a car engine. Not a sound. She closed them again, lacking the energy to go and investigate. It had been a long and tiring day. Tiring, not so much because of her own work – although she was struggling to get Dominic's sculpture finished – but because of Vincent's silent and perpetual demands.

It wasn't so much what he asked for, she mused. It was more the way he didn't ask. With that certain look painted on those carved features that she'd once found almost noble. The look of martyrdom. Vincent's language of martyrdom could dispute any logical argument. There was no overcoming it.

I know it's too much trouble, he seemed to be saying. But look at me, I become more helpless with each day that passes, my muscles more wasted, my brain more frustrated with the messages it can no longer relay with accuracy. And do you see me complain?

Isobel shook her head. She couldn't accuse him of complaining. But he was always there, always needing, always watching her guilty movements as though her time were his, should be devoted to him alone, not to her own insignificant works and pleasures.

She heard another noise from outside, quite separate from the Vincent noise upstairs where Vincent was having a bath, alone. He had allowed her to give some assistance on the way. Into the propelled chair that got him up the stairs, into the upstairs wheelchair, into the bath ordered from London for those not fully mobile, the salesman had said – and into the water.

But now he wanted to be alone. Or was it Isobel who wanted him to be alone, and Vincent who was afraid to ask her to stay?

She shivered. 'Someone walking over my grave. I'm getting old.' But the other noise – which sounded like a car door, or maybe a gunshot – never developed into anything more. And Isobel was neither nervous nor curious. She had never been nervous in this cottage, from the day she'd moved in here with Faith in 1954.

Isobel sighed. Memories of the past were more real than her present. Would they always be that way? Had she relinquished the future so soon?

Little Faith had been only six years old when Isobel uprooted her. At first she'd been content with the excitement of the new. But after a while the child began to miss Jack.

'I want my Daddy.'

The problems with Faith started with her sense of something missing. Isobel couldn't give her all that Jack had given. She lacked the sense of fun, the physical and mental abandonment that children are always close to and that Jack, still half-child himself, had found so easy.

'When's Daddy coming?' Her small fists tight with fury, prepared to fight her mother if necessary.

'Faith . . .' Isobel leaned heavily on the broom. She was sweeping the workshop that Beatrice had never used. It was a shame simply to let it rot. Isobel had already begun pottery and sculpture classes in Poole, while Faith was at school. She had the idea that one day this might become a kind of studio. That appealed to her – the idea of creating, building from a raw material, working with her hands.

'I want Daddy.' Faith's small face was squinting with anger. A childish refusal to believe that anything was impossible if it was willed hard enough. 'Where is he?'

'He's in London.' Isobel took her hands.

'Then I want to go back to London too.' Faith's voice began as a whine and changed into aggression at the look on her mother's face. 'I hate this place,' she said.

Wait for it, Isobel thought. She knew what was coming as if it were already wrapped around her heart.

'And I hate you.'

She let Faith run from the workshop towards the trees, and after a few minutes she followed her. The child was weeping with bitterness, her face rubbing heedlessly against the rough bark of an old yew tree.

'It's just you and me now, Faith.' She stroked her daughter's blonde hair.

'Why?' Muttered into the tree trunk.

What could she tell her? Because the man you call Daddy is the man I call my persecutor? Because he beat me until I was black and silent and broken? Because he destroyed the brother or sister you could have had? Destroyed your mother, stamped on her self-esteem until she was less than even a possession?

'Sometimes things don't work out between a man and a woman who have promised to love each other, darling,' she began. How could it be said without sounding trite?

'Why?'

There were times when Isobel wished Faith would display less curiosity. 'They just don't.' That was one kind of explanation she'd vowed never to give. The *because I say so* kind of explanation.

'Was it your fault?' Faith turned to face her, her lovely green eyes smudged and accusing.

So. Already, someone had to admit blame. Already at six years old, there was fault to be attached, discussed, denied.

'It was nobody's fault,' she said firmly. 'We weren't happy. We decided to part.'

'You left.' It was clear that Faith had made some decisions. She had decided that it was a battle with two forces in conflict. And she'd decided whose side she was on. She was against the one who had walked out of the door, who'd found the strength to change things, who had needed to escape. Faith was on Jack's side, no doubt of that.

'Yes.' Isobel held her close. 'I left.' All she could do was hope that one day Faith would understand, although that was far off and of little comfort. And maybe she'd only understand by suffering the same pain herself. Isobel would do anything to prevent that, anything to protect her daughter from that particular legacy.

They settled into a wary routine. Faith made friends at school, but she wasn't the same outgoing child who had ridden on Jack's back and shouted 'Giddy-up, you horsey-horsac!' There was a new sadness in her, her first sense of loss.

'Why doesn't he come to see me?' she asked Isobel one day, six months after they'd left London. It was the day after her seventh birthday.

Isobel knew what she meant. Surely he could have sent a card? At seven, birthdays are the top of a child's world. Everything to be longed for, everyone giving, being kissed and hugged and the centre of the day. Couldn't Jack have pushed aside the bitterness for the sake of this child, on the day that must be etched into his heart, the day Faith had come into his world?

'I don't know.' Isobel only knew that she could never have given her up. But that counted for nothing.

'Doesn't he love me any more?' The innocence of childhood. Believing that love could function like a lightswitch.

Isobel couldn't bear it. 'I know he still loves you,' she said with urgency, taking Faith's hands, drawing her closer. 'I know he does.'

'Then why . . . ?'

'He must think it's better this way.' The blonde head was stiff on her shoulder. She blames me. The thought was like a dart, cutting the air and then gone.

That afternoon, Vincent turned up on the doorstep looking quite debonair and carrying a birthday card and a present in silver wrapping paper. 'For the birthday girl,' he said cheerfully.

Isobel hugged him. She hadn't seen him for six months and had pushed any thoughts of him away. Yet now she was glad he had come.

'It was yesterday.' Faith turned her back on him, the sunbeam of hope on her face at the glimpse of a male visitor bearing gifts, clouding into resentment.

'Ungrateful child.' Vincent pulled a face, and Isobel knew he was cross although he was trying to laugh it off. It was, after all, the first time he'd bothered to make an effort with Faith.

'She was hoping to see Jack.' Isobel wanted to make him understand, make him see that a few words – the right few words – from him to Faith, would make it all right between them.

But Vincent flinched, the sound of Jack's name erecting instant barriers. He barely spoke to Faith for the rest of his visit.

'Why has he come here?' Faith hissed at Isobel in the kitchen.

'He just wanted to see us, I suppose.' But Isobel understood. Faith wanted her daddy. Vincent was here and Jack was not. Even a seven-year-old child was perceptive enough to link these facts together into a new chain of bitterness. Isobel knew Vincent's visit would make Faith blame her still more.

She made tea and small talk while Faith disappeared into the garden, leaving the silver gift still wrapped and accusing in the sitting-room. But there was an awkwardness between them that had never existed when she lived with Jack. They had only ever had snatched moments before, she supposed. There had been no time for awkwardness then.

'I never thought you'd come,' she said at last.

'I didn't intend to.' Vincent had got up, and was strolling around the room, peering into every nook and cranny, perhaps trying to find clues to whatever it was that had taken her away.

'Why did you, then?' Isobel folded her arms and watched him. He wasn't happy. He had never been happy. But now there was a strung-out desperation in the way he walked, in the way he held his head, his neck craning forward like a man who's almost blind.

'I miss you.'

Isobel blinked. It was unlike Vincent to confess to need. He'd never had many friends, real friends to whom he could talk openly, and she guessed he was lonely.

'I'm lonely too, Vincent.' Her eyes darkened. 'But I need to be lonely. I need this space . . .'

'I know all that.' He waved his hand, instantly reassuring. 'I'm not going to beg you to come back, Isobel.'

She nodded, glad that he understood. She wanted to live alone with Faith. She didn't wish to be answerable to anyone, after so many years of caution and humiliation. She must recover her self-esteem alone. Vincent could be a friend, but he could never be a live-in lover.

It was with diffidence that she asked him to stay the night. 'It's a long trek to travel here and back in one day.'

And he accepted in the same spirit. 'I suppose I could . . . if you don't mind.'

They each drank a silent glass of brandy and at the top of the stairs she hesitated for only a fraction of time before she lifted her face for his cold kiss.

He followed her into her bedroom. She hadn't suggested the spare room or the settee downstairs – hadn't liked to somehow, after what they'd been through together – but she didn't feel completely comfortable with him here. Perhaps she was accustomed to solitude already.

Vincent perched on her narrow bed as she took ages brushing the long dark hair that already had a few streaks of grey. She could see him in the mirror, his bony knees pressed together, his back ram-rod straight, his proud, proud face.

'Are you going to get undressed?' She turned towards him. 'You know where the bathroom is. I haven't got a spare toothbrush but . . .'

'It doesn't matter.' He stared at her, waiting.

Slowly she took off her clothes, one thing at a time. When she was naked she gazed back at him, unflinching, until at last he looked away. 'You're a lovely woman.'

Isobel remembered Jack's words the first night they met. 'Look at you. You're a real smasher.' The note in his voice had been so sexy, that quickstep at the Palais so thrilling, that she hadn't hesitated for a moment when he bent to kiss her, although it was their first date. She had expected a quick peck. But what she got . . . Even thinking of it now made her feel faint. No-one had ever kissed her like that, before or since. It seemed to reach down and touch something deep inside her, that kiss. He had won her with his dance and his kiss.

During the kiss he took advantage of her weakened state and slipped his hand inside the buttoned bodice of her dress. Just like that! And before she could cry out, before she could shove his hand away, his fingers were caressing her breast, lacing a pathway through her cotton underclothes, stroking her nipple with such sweet expertise that she was lost to desire in a moment. Goodness, if they hadn't been standing outside her mother's house, Isobel doubted whether she would have resisted him when his lips moved to her neck and his hands inside her skirt, fleetingly brushing past the cherished nylons and up into oblivion.

The next night he'd had her though. The next night he'd taken her hand and they'd crept round the back, stifling their giggles. 'Ssh.' A finger on his lips, his eyes saying it all. 'C'mon darlin'.'

She hesitated for only a moment, a fatal fraction of time, and that was all it took. He pulled her into the neighbour's air raid shelter and took her there and then. No preamble. No foreplay. She hadn't even wanted foreplay. She'd never known anyone like Jack Vaughan, he was quite outside her experience. She may have wanted to die with shame when she heard the neighbour's radio inside their kitchen, only yards away. But she didn't say no the next night. She wanted it, wanted him. She couldn't get enough of the bold-eyed youth who turned her legs to blancmange. And she wanted more than a quickstep at the Palais, and bitter shandies at the Old Bull. She even wanted more than night-time passion in the garden.

It took her by surprise, when the call came. She couldn't bear the thought of an ending.

He laughed. 'Think I'm going to let you go . . . a little smasher like you? No chance. You're mine, you are. And I'm gonna prove it to you.'

Before she knew it, they were married, and no longer had to do it in empty air raid shelters. Before she knew it, her world had changed.

Now Isobel looked at Vincent. It had never been like that with Vincent.

She took her long nightgown out of the drawer and pulled it over her head. He kept his underclothes on. She lay awake, listening to his thin breathing, feeling his awkwardness against her. It was only in the morning, when she was wondering how soon she could leap out of bed to make tea, get Faith's breakfast, that he reached out to her, fumbling with her nightgown.

With a sigh she rolled over, allowed him to undo the buttons, to hold her breasts cradled cup-like in that child-like way he had. And when he was ready, she blocked her mind to it, ignored the alien feel of his body on hers.

It was soon over. Soon over and best forgotten. Vincent had never been a passionate man, and now the passion was dead between them. She knew it and he would know it too. Sex had occurred almost independently of the two of them – it had been a release, of sorts – but Isobel could have managed perfectly well without it.

'Can I come and visit you again?' he asked at breakfast. 'In a few months' time?'

She knew she should refuse. A clean break, she had promised herself. What point was there in continuing? And yet it was true that she missed their discussions, and there was no-one here to talk to as she had talked to Vincent. So she nodded. When all was said and done, Vincent had given her the ability to recover freedom. He had shown her that she could find her own voice. Without that, without him, where would she be? Who would she be? A nobody.

'How's the book going?' she asked as they walked down the driveway. He was waiting for a taxi to take him to the station. Isobel was surprised he hadn't driven. Vincent had always valued his old A40 and avoided the kind of public transport that threatened his sense of elitism.

'It still needs some more work.' He avoided her gaze.

'Have you sent it to a publisher?' Isobel said this out of mischief. She knew that he never would. He would use the excuses that it wasn't ready, that the publisher wasn't ready, that the world wasn't ready perhaps. But it was Vincent who wasn't ready. He would never be brave enough for rejection.

He shook his head and she felt ashamed.

The taxi arrived. Isobel watched him climb in awkwardly as if this movement was difficult for him. She frowned, but he was adjusting himself in his seat, folding his thin arms and smiling his grim smile. 'Goodbye, Isobel.'

She waved him back out of her life. An undeniable sense of relief was buzzing in her head. She almost ran back to the cottage, eager to begin her day. But underneath this, lay the certain knowledge that Vincent would come again.

Isobel had almost dropped off to sleep in the rocking chair. She was brought back to the present by a faint tapping on the front door.

She creaked to her feet, into the hall, cautiously opened the door. The wind rushed in, forcing her back. 'Christie!'

The girl looked wild. She was wet through, her hair standing proud in manic tufts of blonde daubed with earth-brown. Her eyes were smudged with tears, and there was a huge grin on her face.

'Don't just stand there. Come in.' Isobel pulled her inside. 'What's going on? Where's your key?'

'Dunno.' Christie's teeth were chattering and her jacket was soaked. Isobel realised she'd been out there for quite a while. She remembered the noises she'd heard earlier, and cursed herself for not investigating.

'Let's get you out of these wet things.' She led her into the sitting-room, tugged off the fleece jacket and scurried round looking for towels and a warm cardigan to put around her shoulders.

'Come and sit in front of the fire.' She pulled another chair up close to the blazing logs.

Christie stared into the flames. 'It's incredible. I can't believe it, Gramma.'

What couldn't she believe? The girl was obviously suffering from shock. And yet she looked . . . *alive*, that was it. More alive than she'd looked for weeks.

'Brandy.' Isobel got the bottle from a cupboard and poured a generous measure into a glass. 'Come on, my dear.' She held it to her dry lips. 'Drink this.'

She took a sip.

'More.'

Christie gulped and coughed violently.

'Now, tell me.' Isobel watched her carefully. Christie was tired and shaken but it was nothing that a good meal and a decent night's sleep wouldn't cure. 'What's happened?' She looked into the blue eyes. 'Is it Robin?'

'Robin!' At the mention of his name Christie's expression changed. 'Gramma – he'll be frantic. He'll be . . .' She bit her lip. 'Worried sick.'

Isobel snorted. 'I'll phone him.' And that wasn't all she'd do to him if she got the chance. He had some new hold over Christie and she didn't like it. 'In a minute. But first, you can tell me what happened tonight.'

Christie stared at her. She took a deep breath and launched into some story of a man called Marc Dupont who had visited the shop. She began with his strange behaviour and ended with a confrontation between him and Faith. 'He says he's my father.' She hunched herself closer into the cardigan.

Isobel's eyebrows arched high. So that's what all this was about. He'd turned up, after all this time. 'What does your mother say?'

Christie blinked. 'She says it's true.'

'And how do you feel?' Isobel leaned closer. Poor child.

'Good.' Christie grinned again. 'And cold.'

Well, at least she was taking it positively. Isobel was relieved. But that was now. What about later, when she'd had time to digest all this? 'You need a hot bath. A hot bath and a cup of tea, something to eat . . .' Isobel ran into the kitchen to fill the kettle, her mind reeling. Faith shouldn't have kept so much from her. It wasn't right.

She returned to the sitting-room. 'I'll run the bath.'

The bath! Suddenly she remembered – and her stomach dipped with panic. Vincent. What with reminiscences and then Christie turning up out of the night, it had gone right out of her mind. She'd left Vincent up there alone in the bath. 'Vincent!' Isobel pelted up the stairs. '*Vincent!*'

16

Robin Fifer was pacing the length of the terraced house in Ulwell as if it were too small to contain him and his temper.

He had thought she wouldn't dare to be late, wouldn't dare to defy him, that the power he now held over her would be more than enough for control. But now it was . . . what? He glanced at his watch. Past nine o'clock and Christie still hadn't come home.

Robin slammed his fist against the top of the PC monitor as he passed by. Glaring bright, grinning at him. Even the world of computers – which had been his life blood, his salvation for as long as he could remember – couldn't console him or occupy his treacherous mind. Because all he could think of was Christie, and what he must do to her when she returned.

And she would return. He couldn't harbour the thought that she was gone for good, that he'd driven her from him.

Not surprising, my lad, when you look at how you've been behaving. His mother's voice.

Robin clamped his hands to his ears. No. He wouldn't listen to her. He didn't want that voice in his head. He had listened to her for too long. He had other voices now. Listening to her was too strong a reminder of the cheated years.

His mother had denied every part of him that was normal, natural, masculine. She had drawn him into her celibate feminine world. She had made the rest of his life dirty and unmentionable.

'Mother . . .' he groaned. Head on her lap. Head on her breast. Voices. She had taught him what was good, not tolerated what was bad. Good was virtuous and upstanding and might live for ever. And bad? Bad was destruction, bad was obliteration of every right to live. And he was bad.

'Christie . . .' Her name echoed around the empty house.

He stared out of the patio doors, into the darkness of the winter garden she'd created for him. What had gone wrong? It could have been good, it should have been right between them. There had been problems, yes, but they would have worked them out somehow.

He twisted away from the mocking black garden and stomped into the hall. Why had she done it? Why?

He grabbed his coat. Why had she become the whore that part of him needed to conquer? Why had she brought it out, this base, unsatisfied, twisted part of him that was taking him over, casting a film over his eyes. He rubbed and he rubbed, but he couldn't find Robin Fifer, the Mr Nice Guy she'd married. He was lost, trodden underfoot, like all the other ants in a non-militant army.

Christie might protest. She might scream and plead, but wasn't that what they all did? Robin knew better. He saw in her eyes that she enjoyed being the whore. She enjoyed sex. She wasn't special, she had never been special. She was a tart like all the rest of them, and he had to punish her. He had to punish her with some more of what she liked best.

One last look at the phone. Should he call Yew Cottage? Robin shrank from the idea of speaking to Vincent or Isobel. Of the pretence of polite conversation.

Christie was bound to be there, snivelling away to her grandmother. Robin knew that Isobel Vaughan despised him. Faith Vaughan did too, although she had no right, and she didn't mind showing it either. He remembered that day she'd turned up from London, the day of Fran Cassidy's party when he'd been waiting for Christie to get back. Waiting and drinking and pacing the room.

'For heaven's sake.' Not just disapproval in Faith Vaughan's eyes. Not just pity, but something that went much deeper.

'She should be with me. She should be at home. I'm her husband.' He had wanted to cry in her arms, the arms of this mother-in-law he hardly knew. That's how desperate he'd become.

'Don't be ridiculous.' She had made a pot of black coffee. 'Drink some.'

'Why should I?' He was sullen. Little boy sullen.

'What's she going to think if she sees you like this?' Her eyes flashed. 'Pull yourself together, man.'

'I don't care.'

'Drink it.' She plonked the cup in front of him. 'If you want to keep her.'

But she'd been wrong. He'd sobered up, but he'd still lost her. And what did Faith Vaughan care? She and Isobel both wanted something different for Christie.

He straightened his back and flexed the muscles of his chest. And why should they assume he didn't have it? This something special that was required? Why should they imagine he wasn't capable of it? That he was doomed to be meek and mild, or to get drunk when his wife went out without him?

'No.' Robin spoke aloud. He wouldn't phone because that was a sign of weakness. He would go out.

He opened the door. He knew a place in Swanage. At the end of the High Street, near the square, was a place where there would be dim lights, loud music and a willing body or two. That was what he needed to sustain his strength and nourish his potency. Christie had taken another man. He would take another woman or two. That would be part of the punishment.

Robin paused. There were more voices in his head that he must listen to, voices that spoke of betrayal and denial. Voices that resisted heart, head and morals. He must listen to them to feed his hatred. They shouted louder than his mother. They knew it was all her fault.

He jumped into his car, turned the key of the ignition and smiled. For a moment he thought he heard the phone ringing back in the house, but he ignored it. He would find that willing body or two. And he would fuck all his hatred for womankind into those willing bodies, just like he did into Christie.

And when she returned, she would pay for it. Over and over she would pay.

'Vincent!'

His frail puny body, long, lank and dripping, was half lying on the floor.

He glared at her. 'I can manage.'

Isobel had to smile. The stubbornness of the man. Was there no end to it?

'Vincent, I'm so sorry.' She grabbed a huge white towel and draped it over him as if she must conceal his nakedness. And it was true that, naked, he was humiliated. 'Let me help you.'

'Get off, woman!'

But she heaved. At last he gave her his weight and soon he was wrapped in the towel and seated in the wheelchair. Frail he might be, but there was still a lot of him. And Isobel was getting too old and tired for all this lifting.

'Nothing but a bloody vegetable,' he muttered.

'You should have called me.' Now she felt anger mixing with the relief. He could have hurt himself with his stubborn independence. 'Why didn't you?'

'Don't need you to do everything, do I?' He stared at her, his pale eyes without their spectacles unblinking and defenceless.

Ah, but he did. And how he hated it. 'I'll get your glasses.' Gently she put them on.

'What a fuss,' he moaned. 'Just leave me be.'

'I fell asleep . . .'

He waved her excuses away. 'I'll get dressed in the bedroom. Everyone needs a bit of privacy.'

Isobel repressed a smile. 'I'll help you.'

'No, you bloody won't.' She stood, he sat, the two of them locked in battle.

'Oh, all right.' She couldn't force him to accept her help, though she knew him to be paying her back for neglect. Vincent might be a pacifist, but there was a streak of cruelty in him that had increased in proportion to the sacrifices Isobel had made. Dishonest sacrifices, she told herself. Was he angry with himself for allowing her to make such sacrifices? Was he angry with her?

'Christie's here,' she said. 'She's wet through and I'm going to run her a hot bath.'

He grunted. 'May as well open to the bloody public. Charge for admission.'

'Christie isn't the public. She's family.' She ran down the stairs. All right. Let him have it his own way. She'd leave him to it. That would teach him to say he didn't need her help.

An hour later she was making hot chocolate for Christie who was tucked up with a hot water bottle under the faded blue candlewick bedspread of her childhood. She hadn't protested too much, as if content to be a child again.

'Did you get hold of Robin?' she asked, as her grandmother sat down on the bed.

'Still no answer.' Isobel passed her the cup. 'Do you think he's gone out looking for you?'

Christie shook her head. She had washed her hair, and it was thick and shining blonde once more. 'I doubt it.'

Isobel repressed the urge to ask why. Time enough to worry about her granddaughter's marriage. There were other things on Christie's mind, and right now it was more important for the girl to get a good night's sleep.

'I'll keep trying,' Isobel promised.

'And Mum?' It was more of a whisper. 'Have you rung Mum?'

Isobel nodded. 'She didn't say much. She was relieved you were here. And she said she'd come over tomorrow.' There was a lot more that Isobel had wanted to ask Faith – would have asked, if it hadn't been for the thought of Christie upstairs waiting for her hot drink. But perhaps it was best to leave it. Faith had sounded emotionally spent. It would all come out in time.

Christie nodded. 'Is he still with her?'

'He left.' Isobel got to her feet. That had been the first thing she'd asked Faith. 'I rather think they had a row.' She smoothed Christie's hair from her forehead. 'But don't fret. She'll tell you everything tomorrow.'

'Everything?' Christie sounded wistful, and Isobel felt a wave of guilt. Wasn't it about time that she and Faith were honest with each other, with Christie, and with themselves too?

Isobel hesitated. 'It hasn't been easy for your mother,' she told her. 'She's well aware that she's made some mistakes . . .'

'Did you know?' Christie interrupted.

'Know?'

'About my father, who he was, who he is?'

Isobel shook her head. 'She never said a word about him.' She had asked. Of course she had often asked, but Faith had hugged her life and everything in it into a tight secret ball that excluded her. Had always excluded her since the day they'd moved to Dorset. Since the day Isobel had taken her away from Jack, Isobel was probably the last person Faith would have confided in.

Where had she gone wrong? Slowly Isobel walked down the stairs and sank into her old rocker. The fire had died down to ashes and the room was growing cold. Had it been so selfish of her to leave a vicious man? Had it been so selfish of her to claim a voice, to refuse to be sucked into obscurity?

But in her heart she knew that, in time, Faith might have forgiven her for that. What Faith would not forgive her for, was allowing Vincent Pascoe back into their lives when Jack had been denied admittance.

Isobel shook her head. It had never been intentional.

After that first occasion, Vincent had come to Yew Cottage once every few months, and she had to admit that she started looking forward to his visits. She and Faith got on well enough alone in the cottage, but it was pleasant to have adult company. To have dinner by candlelight with a man who understood the workings of her mind, to give free rein to the solo debates that had been stored in her head since the last time they'd spoken. Yes, even to hold his thin body close in the small hours of the night. Not for passion, but for warmth. It was a companionship she valued.

'You don't *love* Vincent, do you?' Faith was ten years old when she asked that question. Always mature for her age, she had already adopted a kind of jeering adolescent rebelliousness when things didn't go her way.

'Maybe I do.' Isobel refused to elaborate. But in her heart she wondered more closely. She loved him as a friend – but it was wound up with being grateful for the old days, for the fact that he'd always listened, and she'd never had to shout. But as a lover? No, she didn't love him as a man who made her move inside, as a man she needed to see at the beginning of every day. Perhaps Isobel cared for her solitude too much for love.

She hardly noticed when the visits from Vincent became more frequent – although her daughter pointed it out to her.

'He won't leave you alone these days. And there's something wrong with him.' The wide mouth sneered so beautifully. At thirteen, Faith had become a teenage dream.

'Something wrong with him?' Isobel frowned. And yet she knew that Faith was right. There *was* something in the back of her mind, some nagging doubt. She pushed this worry aside to work on her wood sculpture. It had become an important part of her life, this outlet for creative energy, and was taking up more and more of her time and passion, as Faith's independence drew her from Yew Cottage more often. Isobel pushed the worry aside, not wanting to listen, until at last she could push it aside no longer. It was there in front of her face. It was true. There was something wrong with Vincent.

He had become more clumsy and awkward with each visit. Some days he hardly seemed able to manage the passage of teacup to mouth. His

190

hands often shook uncontrollably. He had stopped going for long walks with Isobel in the Dorset countryside – she couldn't even remember when this had last happened – although once they had both loved walking and talking the miles away. They had even stopped sleeping together out of a mutual and silent consent. And Vincent had become unaccountably depressed.

One day, in the early spring of 1962, she tackled him about it.

'There's something wrong with you,' she said. 'I know there is. You look ill.'

'What are you talking about?' he snapped. 'I'm fine.'

'Have you seen a doctor?' Isobel's voice might be gentle but she was persistent.

'There's no need.'

'Vincent . . .'

'Stop it, Isobel.' He looked her square in the face. 'Don't interfere.'

Reluctantly Isobel gave in. It was his life. She wasn't his judge, his automatic confidante. He could make his own decisions: there was nothing whatever wrong with his mental faculties, that was for sure.

Vincent didn't visit again until the autumn. Isobel wrote him occasional chatty letters, but she received little in the way of a reply. She wondered if he'd grown tired of their times together. They had begun out of friendship and even love, but maybe passing years and circumstances had drained all the life out of this relationship, leaving too little to hold them together.

In the autumn he was pale and tired. For most of the time he sat, watching Isobel in her workshop. He seemed to have become an old man, yet he was still only in his forties. But his head had drooped and his shoulders were rounded. He was certainly not the man she'd once known.

'You have to tell me what's wrong with you,' she demanded on the Saturday, when he picked up a piece of wood sculpture from the table in the workshop and inadvertently let it fall to the floor.

He stared at the wooden carving, not at her. 'I've got multiple sclerosis.'

His voice echoed in Isobel's head. She was beside him in seconds. 'What? Vincent, why didn't you tell me?'

Over that week-end she pestered him for every detail he knew about the hardening patches of sclerosis on his spinal cord which scrambled nerve messages and prevented some signals from getting through to the right parts of the body.

'I ignored it at first.' He took her hand, and Isobel felt that at last she was seeing the real Vincent, the raw Vincent with all the tetchiness and fastidiousness wiped away. And she could understand why he'd wanted to ignore it. It would be hard for anyone to accept that their future was in jeopardy. And besides, poor Vincent had no-one to share it with.

'What's the prognosis?' She tried to be sensible. But inside she was crying. Crying for him, and for herself too.

'The symptoms change all the time. Hour to hour. Day to day. There's possibilities of remission.' He laughed harshly. 'A bit like cancer.'

'Don't, Vincent.' She stroked his hand. It twitched awkwardly in response. Oh, God. Already, it was happening already.

'Then again, some of us can only hope for a slow decline.' His eyes became curiously glazed. 'Which is worse, do you think?'

'Is there a cure?' Isobel watched him carefully. Somewhere, in certain respects, he was the same Vincent she'd always known, but it was true that he was thinner, less confident. There was less *of* him somehow, as if the most significant bits were dimming into distance. There was a vein throbbing in his temple, but otherwise he remained still.

After a moment he shook his head. 'No cure.'

'But there must be treatment, some kind of therapy available?' She could feel herself shaking with anger. Why Vincent?

'Yes. Perhaps.' He pulled his hand from her grasp. 'But that's my concern.'

'Mine too.' She stood, impotent watching him drag himself away from her. Don't reject me now, Vincent, she was thinking. Don't reject me now.

'I only told you, Isobel . . .' He paused. 'To explain why I can't always answer your letters. And why I might have to stop visiting you soon.' His mouth worked. 'In this lovely little hideaway cottage of yours.'

She fell on her knees, her mind racing. 'Please don't talk like that, Vincent.'

His hand seemed to rest absent-mindedly on her dark hair, caught up into the long plait she invariably wore these days. 'It's the uncertainty that's the worst,' he murmured. 'Not knowing what will happen next, not knowing how far it will let you go before . . . Bang.' His fist hit his palm. 'It stops you.' His voice lowered. 'Never knowing what you can do today or what you'll be able to do tomorrow. Can you imagine that, Isobel?'

She shook her head. And with no-one to talk to, no-one to turn to. That was Vincent's fate.

'You're not in charge of your life,' he went on, in a slow monotone that tore at her. 'You're trapped, you can't plan ahead. You don't even know when you can control your muscles and when they'll decide to do their own thing.'

'Vincent. You must let me help you.' Isobel too had experienced that lack of control over her own life, although for very different reasons. And Vincent had helped set her free.

'How can you?' He turned away. 'It's my problem.'

She heard his bitterness, his inner rage. And she knew that she must help Vincent come to terms with this, however hard it proved to be. She must offer herself to him.

'You could come and live here,' she said softly.

He stared at her. 'Here?'

'Why not?' She got to her feet. Now she had his full attention. 'We could keep each other company. And I could help you if you'd let me,' she added humbly. Vincent was a proud man.

'I couldn't allow you to do that.' He began to walk away, out of the workshop, towards the yew grove.

'Why not?' She followed him, grabbing on to his arm. 'Why not, when that's what I want to do?'

'I thought you wanted your own space.' His expression was cruel as he glanced over her and beyond her. 'You said that once – when I was a healthy man.'

'I did want that space.' She couldn't tell him quite how important it still remained. 'But I know you won't encroach on my life. I know that you'll respect my boundaries.' She watched him. 'You're the only man I could say that to.'

Something in her tone or in the words she spoke seemed to get through his pain, his stubborn pride. He stopped dead, turned and took her face roughly in his hands. For once those hands were warm. 'I can't let you be a sacrifice,' he said.

From somewhere came a memory of a feminine wile. She wouldn't allow Vincent to cope with this alone. 'I want you here with me,' she said. 'I love you. I've always loved you.'

Vincent Pascoe moved to Dorset at the beginning of the following year on a cold February day. Isobel prayed that Faith – who was now fifteen and would soon have her own life to live – would understand.

But it hadn't worked out that way. Right from the start Faith had hated him. And she had hated him with a venom that Isobel could neither condone nor understand.

In the morning Christie woke early. For a moment she savoured the warm cosiness of her childhood bed, and the sight of the yellow ducks painted on the wallpaper that she'd never quite grown out of. She wondered what she was doing here.

Then it came to her, in fits and starts. Marc, the dark and handsome stranger from another world who had turned out to be her father. Her mother, crying, love in her eyes. The yew grove sheltering the new sense of self that she hadn't quite come to grips with. Gramma, taking her in and looking after her, as she always had.

She stretched, lazily like a cat. Could it really be true?

And then she thought of Robin and her heart somersaulted with dread. She curled up once more. She hadn't gone home last night. Supposing Gramma hadn't managed to get through to him on the phone? He would be raging, furious, animal-angry.

With a shudder, Christie crept back under the covers. How could she return to the house in Ulwell? What would be waiting for her there? She needed to think. Her mother would come here today – she knew it. But first Christie needed to think. So where could she go?

She crawled out of bed, got dressed and washed her face, marvelling at how normal she felt. And yet she was an altered person now, wasn't she? With a new identity and a real past. Shouldn't she feel different?

Outside, the sky was a crisp winter blue, the trees and hedgerows were laced with frost, and Christie made up her mind. She would go for a walk. A walk along the cliffs, across Ballard Down and up to Old Harry Rock perhaps, a well-trodden path that would be deserted at this time on a winter's day. It was just what she needed.

She crept downstairs, unwilling to wake her grandmother, scribbled a quick note of explanation, grabbed some crusty bread and cheese, and slipped out of the door. There was a chill in the early morning breeze that made her catch her breath. She strode out, the wind quickly clearing her head, the freshness of the day teasing a smile from the set mouth. She felt good. For the first time in ages she felt good about herself, about the world.

At the end of the drive the sight of a tall figure made her stop in her tracks. Not Robin? Surely not Robin? The thought made her freeze. But the figure moved closer towards her and she saw at once that he was too well built, too dark, too distinguished, too old.

'You . . .' She stared cautiously at Marc, wanting to let the huge grin resting inside her erupt to the surface. Wanting to laugh out loud. Just how did you greet a father you had never even known?

17

Marc Dupont – her father – smiled slowly, lifting his arm in a friendly greeting. No debonair suit this morning. He was dressed casually in jeans and thick woolly sweater and he seemed relaxed, as if to be discovered lurking outside her grandmother's cottage at this hour of the day was quite normal. What's more, he didn't seem surprised to see her.

He walked up the track, his breath a cloud of steam in the cold morning air. 'Hi, Christie. How are you this morning?'

'Better.' Impulsively, she smiled back.

'So this is your grandmother's house?' It was only a half-question. He nodded towards the gabled cottage of Purbeck stone, whose pale fawn chimneys glinted in the distance.

'Yew Cottage. Yes.' Christie shifted her weight on to her other foot. This was bizarre. They could be any two strangers engaged in an impersonal discussion, at seven-thirty on a winter's morning. 'I stayed here last night,' she explained unnecessarily. But why was he here? Was he hoping to see her grandmother, or was he merely continuing his exploration of Faith Vaughan's past?

He nodded, his eyes concerned. 'You were upset. I'm sorry. It was dumb of me to blurt it out like that.'

'It doesn't matter.' Christie shivered as the cold wind cut into her. This wasn't a day for standing still.

'I hadn't even figured it out for myself.' He took her arm and they continued walking in step. 'It was one hell of a shock. I didn't come here expecting a daughter.'

Christie briefly scanned him from under her eyelashes. 'What were you expecting?'

'Do you know, Christie . . .' He glanced towards her. 'I don't have a clue what I was expecting.'

'Then why *did* you come?' It might be abrupt, but she sensed she could find out more from this man in five minutes than she'd been able to glean from her mother in twenty years.

'I guess I was curious,' he said. 'Things happened – between me and your mother, I mean – and I kind of accepted them. But I never knew the half of it. And I got to thinking: find out, man. If you never try to find out you'll never be free of it. This doubt, you know? It kind of wears you down over the years.'

Christie nodded. She thought she understood. But was the news of her existence good news or bad for the man walking beside her?

He squeezed her arm lightly as if answering her silent question. 'And where are you off to this morning?' He eyed the bread and cheese inquisitively. 'Gonna have a secret feast some place?'

'Breakfast,' Christie told him. 'I'm going for a walk.' She waited for the dread that he might suggest coming with her, but it didn't materialise. As a matter of fact it felt rather pleasant to be walking with the attractive man who was her father.

'And how about you? What are you doing here?' She laughed. 'At this unearthly hour?'

He looked shamefaced, like a young boy caught crying, and she felt a sudden and unexpected burst of affection. 'Me, I'm still on the wrong time scale,' he said. 'My body doesn't believe it's an unearthly time. Probably doesn't even believe it's morning.'

'But why here?' she persisted.

'Looking for clues, maybe.' He shrugged. 'Some more of that curiosity I was telling you about. Your mother grew up here. She often used to talk about it. I felt as if I'd actually sat in that wood with her.'

'The wood?' Christie's steps faltered. He must mean the yew grove. Had it been important to her mother too? And yet, she'd left it more than once. She had left Yew Cottage, and she had left Christie. She shivered.

'And how usual is it for you to go off hiking at this "unearthly hour"?' he teased.

They reached the gate with the stile. One way led across Ballard Down and the ridge of Purbeck Hills, rising green and dark into the early morning. One way led to the road and civilisation. She paused. 'I always walk when I need to work something out.'

'Me too. Although England's the place for hiking, if you ask me.' He leaned on the gate, waiting. 'A green and pleasant land, don't they call it?'

Christie turned to scrutinise him. 'Will you walk with me?' she asked, almost shyly.

A wide grin spread across the tanned face. 'Sure thing. It would be my pleasure.' He jumped over the stile. 'And where are you gonna take me?'

'To Old Harry Rock at Handfast Point.' She smiled. 'And beyond.'

They walked for some time in companionable silence, Christie absorbing the presence of him, the confidence of his long easy stride and the occasional elusive scent of sandalwood and musk aftershave in the breeze. She wanted to find out about the life he had shared with her mother. There were so many questions she longed to ask. But she was nervous about beginning.

'Tourists flock here in the summer,' she said instead, as they cut across to the track that led to Old Harry Rock. 'It's the perfect walk for non-walkers. No steep climbs, a decent track to follow, and brilliant views.' Small talk, babbling, inconsequential. Not what she wanted at all.

He followed her into a tiny clearing by the cliff where there was a wooden bench and a breathtaking view of Poole Harbour – almost deserted at this time of day. The sea was calm, the only sound the water caressing the cliffs and the occasional screech of a sea bird.

'And where do the real hikers go?' he asked her, his eyes gleaming with humour.

'They carry on beyond Old Harry. The cliff path leads on, and eventually down into Swanage.'

He laughed. 'I should have brought my boots, right?'

'Yes, you should.' She passed him a hunk of bread and cheese, plucking up courage, eager to launch into the history that wasn't safe, that would never be safe. But she was encouraged by the open honesty of his face. 'Where did the two of you meet?' she asked after an eternity. 'You and my mother?'

He glanced at her as they walked on towards the headland. Perhaps he was surprised that she knew nothing of all this. 'In France. Faith left home at eighteen. She came over on the Channel ferry, lost, lonely and looking for work grape-picking. I guess she was unhappy. She always had this sad look in her eyes, I know that much.' His expression softened.

But Christie frowned. How could anyone be unhappy at Yew Cottage? How could anyone be unhappy with Gramma? 'You were living in

France?' she asked. It would explain the continental burr behind the American accent, and the tanned brown skin. There was a self-assurance about him too that she associated with the European male. Almost an arrogance, although it wasn't threatening, only appealing.

He nodded. 'I'm half-French. My mother was American. She met my father in Paris.' He rolled his eyes. 'Romance of the century apparently. She couldn't resist all that French charm.'

'And . . .' She hesitated. 'What was she like, my mother – when you first knew her?'

'Beautiful.' His eyes misted with the memory. 'She sure was beautiful. Like a lost and forlorn Marianne Faithfull. Have you heard of her?'

Christie nodded.

'Huge green eyes, pouting lips, fragile, innocent. You know the sort?' He sighed. 'Anyone who saw her would want to seduce her and protect her at the same time. I know I did.' Christie stared at him and his voice tailed off. 'Sorry, didn't mean to offend you.'

'You didn't.' She paused. 'What did the two of you do next?'

'We saved up some money. Took off to Woodstock.' He laughed. 'It was very much *the* place to be.'

'Flower power and all that sixties stuff?' Christie narrowed her eyes as she stared into the distance, trying to picture this debonair man as a hippy. He didn't seem the type somehow. But types change, she reminded herself.

He nodded. 'It's easy to mock it now. Even I do that. But at the time . . .' He shrugged. 'It was exciting. Tuning into a new world. Dropping out. Doing your own thing.' He laughed. 'We lived for the day and to hell with the past and the future.'

'And what happened in Woodstock?' she pressed.

He turned to her in contemplation as the wide track narrowed into a path that led out on to the open headland. 'It felt like life happened in Woodstock. We lived in a rambling apartment, with people who thought the same way as we did. You know the kind of stuff – searching for your self, making love not war. It all seems a bit dumb now.'

'Optimistic, anyway.' Christie laughed.

'Oh, yeah, we were optimists all right. Not a worry in the world.' His voice softened. 'We got into the whole scene – the music, the bars, the art, even the theatre when we had enough cash.'

'That was before the Festival though, right?' Christie was trying to place them there – in the home of the musical culture of the young – in the late 1960s. Everyone had heard of Woodstock Festival, even her generation.

He nodded. 'But it already had one hell of a reputation as a music town. A performance town. Bob Dylan lived there, you know.' He laughed. 'And Dylan was our hero.' His voice went on, soft and hypnotic, weaving a kind of magic around the words, painting a landscape for Christie of the town where her parents had lived and loved. And where she herself had been conceived, presumably.

'There were music performances almost every week-end – informal, you know? Not arranged. Not seats in a concert hall, but in the open air, like a festival.' He hummed softly, some gentle folk tune from his past.

Christie tensed, recognising immediately the melody that she'd heard her mother sing so often.

'There was theatre at the playhouse, lectures at the artists' association. Exhibitions of local talent. Man, it was a whole new world for us, all right. We never doubted that.'

'I would have liked to have seen it. Been part of it.' Christie led the way towards Old Harry Rock. Why did her generation seem to exist in a kind of void? Gramma had been involved in the fighting spirit of the Second World War, whilst her mother and this man had fought for freedom from convention and hypocrisy. A freedom of lifestyle that encompassed marriage, sexuality, even reality sometimes. But Christie had no cause to call her own, nothing to link her with others of her generation.

She wiped the thought from her mind. 'Old Harry is an erosion from the main spit,' she explained to Marc as they both surveyed the squat and chalky stack of rock.

Some seagulls perched on the worn rug of grass topping the jagged white contours of Old Harry. The sky and the sea were a huge expanse of winter grey. Light moving into dark, merging into horizon. 'You can just make out the Needles on the Isle of Wight.' She pointed.

He squinted into the distance. 'Can you get across to Old Harry?'

She showed him the narrow and treacherous path. 'There was a wife but she submerged over a hundred years ago now. Poor Old Harry is a widower.'

'You make them sound like people.' He was staring at her. Staring and smiling as if she were an apparition from his past. 'And those other rocks, what are they called?'

'That's St Lucas Leap.' She pointed at the clump of rock separated from Old Harry. 'For obvious reasons. And this cliff . . .' She gestured to where they were standing, their bodies listing from the force of the wind. 'Is known as Old Nick's Ground.'

'Sounds ominous.' He pulled a face.

'It's because Old Harry has another name. He's called the devil in disguise.' Christie smiled. She wouldn't think about that now. About pretences and disguises and people not being what they were supposed to be, what they'd always been. Robin . . . She wouldn't think about Robin.

He was still watching her curiously. 'You sure are knowledgeable about this place.'

'I grew up here. Gramma and I . . .' She was about to say more, about to explain to him that she and Gramma had come walking here ever since she could remember. But something stopped her. He would wonder – wouldn't he? – where her mother had been while all this was going on? Christie wasn't sure that she should tell him too much about her childhood; it seemed akin to betrayal.

Instead she twisted around and marched purposefully along the cliff edge.

'Don't get too close,' he shouted, running to catch up with her.

She turned, walking backwards, her hair funnelling towards her face. 'Tell me more about Woodstock,' she insisted.

He laughed. 'There were great music studios. All kinds of bands came to record there. And it was an arty place. There was a craft centre, before craft shows sprang up all over the world. People made jewellery, wove rugs. Took them down to the flea market to sell. And your mother . . .'

'Yes?' She encouraged him.

'Faith did wonderful things with fabric. She should have been a designer, you know?' His blue eyes dimmed. 'Batik and tie-dye, that's what everyone wanted back then. But her designs were special.'

'Mum did all that?' Christie struggled to equate the efficient businesswoman she knew with a young girl painting wax on fabric and tying string around T-shirts to produce weird and wonderful patterns.

'Oh, yeah.' His head drooped forwards into what looked like despair.

'And you loved her.' Christie didn't need to ask that. It was stamped on his handsome features, drawn into the lines of his mouth when he talked of her, reflected in his eyes when he remembered their past. Of course he had loved her. Perhaps he loved her still.

'I loved her.' His mouth tightened. 'And I thought she loved me. I thought we had it all sussed. But maybe . . .'

'Maybe?'

'Maybe it was just that we loved everyone, you know? That's how it was. Freedom, love, peace. All experience was good experience.' His voice was surprisingly bitter.

Christie frowned. 'I see.' She was beginning to, but it was still only a glimmer. 'What happened?' she asked.

'Faith took off.' His stride lengthened and Christie almost had to run to keep up. 'She just disappeared one day. She left a note saying she was coming back to England.' He raked his fingers through his dark, greying hair. 'She left at the same time as . . .' He surveyed her. 'Well, it doesn't matter now what I thought. Maybe I got it all wrong. Maybe I let myself listen to the others. I guess I jumped to all the wrong conclusions.'

Christie frowned. 'It was a shock, then, when she left?'

He groaned. 'You're not kidding. I couldn't believe it. I thought we were living in paradise. Why would she want to throw that away?' He looked at Christie as though she could tell him what he needed to know, at least provide some clue.

'She never told me anything,' she reminded him. 'I didn't even know about you. I knew she'd spent a while in America, because Gramma told me. But that was about it.' All this was revelation to Christie. She felt as if she were discovering a lost part of her mother into which her own identity could be fitted, something that had helped to make her what she was. The Christie of today.

'It's hard to come to terms with that. It's weird, if you ask me.' He shook his head in bewilderment. 'But you must have asked her about her life? What did she say?'

Christie nodded. 'I tried. But it seemed . . . too painful for her.' How could she explain her mother's wistful air of vulnerability whenever the past was spoken of? Or the wariness in her eyes that made you want to protect her, even if it meant remaining in ignorance?

'It was bloody painful for the one she left behind.' He stomped on, his words hanging fractionally in the wind as she paused for breath.

Christie realised that her mother had run away from this man. Was that how she solved all her problems? By running away?

'What did you do after she left?' The path was narrowing, and Christie went first, pushing away the winter brambles and bare branches scratching her numb face. The mud was sticking to her walking boots, making the going tough. She was cold, but exhilarated by all the walking and the talking, learning of the past.

'I hung around for a bit. But it wasn't the same without Faith.' He sighed. 'In the end I took off. I went to stay with relatives in Boston, got a job, became respectable.' He laughed at himself. 'Well, almost respectable.'

Christie turned around. 'Got married,' she supplied, completing his list. 'Had children.'

He frowned. 'I'm not gonna apologise for that, Christie. Your mother left me. What was I supposed to do?'

What indeed? 'Nothing.' Christie hunched her shoulders. 'And you still live in Boston?' The thought was like a rain cloud. She had discovered her father, talked to the man, even – and she knew this was a little hasty – become fond of him. And yet he lived on the other side of the world. Chances were she'd never even see him again.

'On the outskirts of Old Boston.' He knocked some mud from his trainers and she waited for him. They were descending the path into Swanage now. The bay was laid out beneath them in the morning sunshine, the waves rippling grey, drawing back their life blood from the beach below. On a ledge quite close by, she could make out the hermit's shack. An uncertain spiral of smoke drifted from the makeshift chimney. Christie stood and watched for a moment. Everyone round here thought the hermit was crazy. But sometimes she understood how he felt – wanting to escape the pressures and pretences of the world they lived in. Seeking only solitude and a decent view of the sea.

'I'd like to show you Boston.'

She jumped, his words taking her by surprise.

'Not only where I live,' he elaborated. 'I'd like you to meet my family.'

'Oh, I don't know . . .' It was nice of him to offer, it proved that he wanted her at least on the borderlines of his life, but Christie wasn't sure that she was ready for it.

'It's kind of your family too. You've got two half-brothers,' he told her.

Brothers. Christie was glad they were brothers. Strangely glad that she was his only daughter. 'But Mum . . .'

'Your mother's got no right to deny me access.' His voice was harsh, slicing through the cold air. 'Jesus, she's denied me knowledge of your existence for twenty-four years. It's not so easy to forgive her that, I can tell you.'

Christie heard his bitterness, and it joined with her own. Her mother had denied her too, denied her a father for twenty-four years. Wasn't that even worse? Could *she* forgive her?

And yet they had become close in the months since Faith Vaughan had returned to Dorset. It was something that Christie had clung to while her marriage slid from under her. Her relationship with her mother seemed to grow stronger with every day that went by – marred only by Faith's reluctance to talk of the past. And now that past had caught up with them.

'I'm an adult in my own right,' she said softly. An independent woman. If it weren't for Robin . . . 'I can make my own decisions. But if it were to upset Mum . . . you see, she and I . . .' How could she tell him that they too were only just beginning? He didn't know that her mother had left her with Gramma at Yew Cottage. Faith might have relinquished her right to a say in Christie's affairs, but neither did Christie want to lose sight of the mother she'd only just found.

'Please come.' He grabbed her hands as they reached the bottom of the path and they were able to walk two abreast once more. 'Won't you give me a chance to get to know you after all this time?'

Christie hesitated. She had such an urge to say, yes. Such an urge to fling caution and responsibilities to the wind, and shout, YES from the skyline. Yes, she'd love to go to the States, yes she yearned for the chance to get to know this man, and to meet her half-brothers – she wanted to meet them desperately, with all the hunger of an only child. 'I would love to, really, but it isn't just Mum . . .'

'It's your husband, right?' His voice held understanding. 'I'd like to meet him. How about if he came too?'

'No!' She pulled her hands from his grasp,

'Christie . . . ?' He eyed her searchingly. 'What is it? Is something wrong?'

'No.' No, no, no. Why did it all have to come back to Robin? The truth was, she was desperate to get away from Robin too. A separation would give them both some much needed breathing space. And it would release her from this fear – a fear that was already hammering inside her once more at the very thought of him. At the very mention of his name. Some time she had to go home. She had to face him. And how would he respond to this latest bombshell?

She took a deep breath. 'I just don't see how I could come at the moment . . .' She wanted to say the word – the word that was hiding behind other words. Dad. Or Father? At the moment it was next to impossible to say either.

'But why not?'

They reached the pavement. Back to civilisation. And where could they go now? There were buses, of course. She could easily go back to Yew Cottage or even to Wareham. They were within walking distance of Christie's house in Ulwell, but she wasn't ready to go back there – and especially not with her father in tow.

'Because of the business,' she told him. 'I run Purbeck Garden Designs, remember? I can't just take off and leave.' She knew the regret was in her voice.

'It's winter.' He was being very persuasive. 'There can't be much to do in winter, surely? Don't you deserve a break? You look like you could use one. Haven't you got anyone who could stand in for you for a month or two?'

A month or two? It was tempting. 'Well, there's Trevor . . .' She faltered. Trevor would relish the idea. But could she trust him?

'If it's just a question of money . . .' His voice purred. Already he was reaching into his inside pocket.

'No.' She held up her hand. 'I can manage. Thank you.'

'But you must let me pay your fare. You must be my guest.' His eyes bored into hers. She knew if she went home and looked in the mirror, she would see his cornflower-blue eyes staring back at her.

'Well . . .' The fare would be a problem. But she didn't want to feel beholden to him, father or no father.

'It would make me feel a whole lot better. It might even make up some of what I should have given you before,' he said. 'In a material sense at least.'

She smiled. He was a kind, thoughtful man. 'Okay.' The word lifted her into a wonderful release. 'I will come. Although I don't know how Mum will take it.' Or Robin.

He took her arm and linked it through his. 'Don't you worry about a thing, Christie. You just leave your mother to me.'

18

'Anybody at home?' There was no response to the front doorbell, so Christie walked round to the side of the house. Fran was usually in at this time of day and her white sports car was in the drive. So where was she?

She heard movement on the other side of the gate, the sound of a padlock being released. 'Fran?'

Christie jumped back as the door was opened by Dominic Redfern.

'Oh . . .' She'd come on a weekday afternoon to avoid him – or to avoid Fran and Dominic together, to be more accurate. That New Year's Eve kiss might have meant nothing. But not from where she'd been standing. She felt a faint flush stealing on to her cheeks.

'Hello, Christie.' He smiled, his slightly hawklike features relaxing. He looked tired, and there was a faint bead of sweat on his brow. 'Come through.'

'Is Fran around?' She followed him down the path and into the back garden. He was wearing mud-stained jeans, a huge ribbed fisherman's jumper and green gumboots. Christie had seen the immaculate solicitor, the dinner guest in full regalia, the casual attire of the country man. But she hadn't seen this side of Dominic before. How many sides were there?

'She went out for five minutes half an hour ago.' He smiled grimly.

'Oh. Only I saw the car . . .' she began.

'She took mine.' He turned to face her, looking none too pleased about it.

'Do you think she'll be long?'

His laugh was humourless. 'You know Fran as well as I do.'

Christie stared at him. Hardly. The sophisticated Fran who whizzed around in a white sports car and was infatuated with her own step-father was a long way from the distressed teenager she'd found in the church more than two years ago. Fran had grown up, and Christie was beginning to wonder if they had all that much in common any more. And yet, hadn't she forged a bond with Fran that was special? There was so much more below the surface that Fran had got too used to hiding. Fran needed a friend. And come to think of it, so did Christie. She needed Fran's cool voice of common sense, Fran's easy laughter, her instinctive perspective on her problems. But she didn't need the disturbing company of Dominic Redfern.

'Then I'd better get back. I don't want to hold you up. Perhaps you could tell Fran I called?' She knew that her voice was ridiculously stiff and formal. She turned, heading for the side gate, but realised he'd already padlocked it behind them.

'Don't rush off.' His voice softened. 'Sorry if I sound bad-tempered. It's Fran . . . We had words.'

Christie hesitated.

'Stay and have some coffee. Please?'

She nodded warily. 'Okay.' Why was she so drawn to him? How could she suspect that Dominic and Fran . . . and still even like the man?

She thought of Barry. He had made her laugh but his chauvinism had driven her crazy, and every time he got her on her own his wandering hands moved as fast as his motor bike. And Trevor. Sex with Trevor had been a liberating experience, free, easy and wonderful. But Trevor had deceived her. And sex, alone, had never been enough. Then, despite herself, she thought of Robin. He had seemed so different. She had held out such hope for Robin. And yet, he too was behaving in a way she couldn't hope to understand. Yes, she'd made love with another man; yes, she expected him to be hurt. But this – this violent passion, this sexual punishment, this determined treatment of her as a sex object and nothing else – it was threatening to destroy her. Certainly it was destroying their marriage.

She glanced at Dominic. Was she so bad, then, at assessing character in her men? Her men. She flushed heavily. For heaven's sake, what was wrong with her? Dominic wasn't her man, far from it.

She watched him brush some loose dirt from his jeans and noticed that his hands were earthy and damp. Scanning the sloping garden, she spotted a trowel and wheelbarrow. 'You've been gardening.'

'That sounds like an accusation.' Dominic led the way inside through the conservatory, casually pulling off his boots by the kitchen door. 'Isn't it the right time of year, or do you reckon I'm just not fit for it?'

He turned, looking down at her, his hazel eyes glinting with humour. He was laughing at her. Dominic Redfern often seemed to be half-laughing at her. And he was always around at the most emotionally difficult times of her life. Now why should that be?

'No . . .' She paused. 'I'm just surprised.'

'Surprised that I get my hands dirty?' He walked into the immaculate kitchen, and Christie followed. 'Or surprised that I don't pay someone else to get their hands dirty?' He laughed again as he turned on the tap. 'Someone like you, perhaps?' He shot her a glance over his shoulder.

'I assumed you'd be at work in the middle of a Tuesday afternoon, that's all,' she replied primly. His remarks were more than a little accurate, and she found his perception irritating.

'I've taken the afternoon off.' He dried his hands on the towel, still surveying her thoughtfully. 'Is that why you came round to see Fran today? Because you were trying to avoid me?'

'Why on earth should I want to do that?' Too late, Christie realised that she should have left when she had the chance. He was getting too close for comfort. He always got too close to comfort.

She paced to the window, looked out at the pines of Wareham Forest – a tall proud fringe lining this landscaped garden – and found herself thinking of the summer party Fran had thrown. The heat, her loose blue sundress, the bodies in the pool. She recalled the conversation with Robin on the phone, her frustration, and the sight of Dominic Redfern walking down the stairs. The compassion in his eyes. There had been a moment, then, when she might have confided in this man. Until Trevor appeared with wine and come-to-bed eyes. Until Trevor took her into Wareham Forest and told her she was beautiful. Until Trevor took off the blue sundress and gave her a simple pleasure that now returned sometimes in the heat of night, to mock her.

'You tell me.' Dominic was watching her.

It was true that seeing Fran and Dominic together embarrassed her. Even thinking about the two of them together embarrassed her. And the last thing she intended doing was talking to this man about it. 'I think I'd better go.' She headed determinedly for the kitchen door.

'Hang on a minute, will you?' He grabbed her wrist lightly, pulling her round to face him. 'I'm sorry, Christie. I didn't mean to play games.'

She stared at him. Games? What games?

Abruptly, Dominic dropped her wrist and she rubbed at the skin absent-mindedly, as one might ease a nettle sting. He hadn't hurt her, but the touch of him was there nevertheless.

'Stay and have some coffee. Please. Come and talk gardening with me.' His expression was penitent.

She hesitated.

'As a matter of fact, I could do with some advice.' He had his back to her now, as he filled the coffee machine, spooning fresh coffee into the filter paper.

'What about?' She remained wary.

'Oh, you know. Which plants to put where. That sort of thing.'

Christie wasn't sure whether to be relieved or disappointed. 'Of course. About the garden.'

'We'll have this in the conservatory.'

They walked through in silence. Dominic placed the tray of fragrant, steaming coffee on to the bamboo table, they settled themselves in cane chairs with plump green and gold cushions, and gradually Christie began to relax. She loved this conservatory, the sensation that even on a winter's day with the sun shining through copper-tinted glass, it could almost be summer, would soon be summer. And she loved the exotic palms and figs that flourished here, the rush matting, hessian blinds, and bamboo, cane and wicker furnishings. It was a beautiful room. A small oasis of paradise in a winter's desert. If this was her house, Christie vowed, she would live in this room.

'Christie . . .' His voice broke smoothly in on her thoughts, dark satin on her senses.

She jumped. 'What was it you wanted to ask me about the garden?'

For a moment, Dominic regarded her in silence. 'I'm thinking of putting up some trellises,' he said at last.

'Where?'

'I'll show you.' In seconds he was out of his chair, tugging on his boots, pulling her to her feet.

She followed him outside.

'Here.' He pointed to the spot. 'Now. What would you recommend?'

At last Christie was back on familiar ground. 'It depends what you want. Big, glorious blooms, or old-fashioned scented. There are hundreds of climbers. Does it matter when it flowers? Is the foliage important? How high do you want it to grow?'

'Whoa!' He grinned, shoved his hands in the pockets of his jeans. 'Is this the kind of Spanish Inquisition you inflict on your clients?'

She became mock-indignant. 'We chat – yes. I have to get a good idea of the kind of person they are, their lifestyle, what they want out of their garden. I wouldn't inflict my own taste on a client. Their needs might be quite different.'

'And what kind of a person am I?' He moved closer. Tall, lean, hungry and brooding.

She flinched. 'I'm not sure.' Was he laughing at her again? She decided not. 'I would have said you were quite solitary.' But if so, why had he invited her for coffee? 'Intelligent.' That couldn't be disputed, and seemed relatively safe. She wanted to say enigmatic, but it didn't seem appropriate.

'And my lifestyle?' He brushed his fingers through his dark hair. 'How would you define that?'

Christie thought of the night-time swimming, the strange Oriental dancing, his relationship with his step-daughter. 'Unusual interests?' she ventured.

He laughed. 'You don't know the half of it.'

She wasn't sure she'd dare to. But she was just getting into her stride. 'I suppose you wouldn't be living here all the time,' she added as an afterthought. 'Isn't this just your part-time home?' Hadn't he told her he disliked the place? If that was so, then how come he wanted to re-design the garden? Fran. The answer came in a flash.

'Part-time home,' he echoed, as if he hadn't considered this before.

'Or do you spend less time in your Wareham flat these days?' Christie could see that the thrust had hit home.

'Is that relevant?' His voice had grown cold. So she had gone too far. Why should she mind?

'Everything's relevant.' Christie wandered over to the potential site for the trellises, knelt down to examine the soil. 'Quite chalky, inclined to get waterlogged . . .'

'And what's your taste, Christie?' He had moved quickly and was now standing beside her. She looked down at his boots, conscious only of very long denim-clad legs.

She stumbled to her feet, and he caught her arm, held it for a moment longer than necessary.

'My taste?'

211

'Yes.' He folded his arms. 'What about your lifestyle? What needs do you have?'

She blushed furiously. Dominic had seen her with Trevor on the day of the party. Had he seen them walk into Wareham Forest? Had he imagined them to be having an affair, even before it had actually happened? Did he know that she'd been unfaithful to her husband? Had Fran told him about the problems in her marriage? Oh God, please no. Not Dominic. 'I don't know what you're talking about.' Her voice was cool. This was a dangerous man. She'd always known it and yet never been sure from where the danger came.

'Tell me which flowers you'd choose, Christie.' He spoke softly, his words forming a strange tune in her head.

She glanced over towards the tall conifers that hid the pool from the house. 'I'm a cottage garden enthusiast. I'd have sweet peas and honeysuckle growing up your trellises. Blue delphiniums at the base here.' She pointed. 'And maybe a white rambling rose.' She looked away, not wanting to imagine it, not wanting to think of the garden she'd made for herself and Robin. The white fragrant rose that was already climbing high.

'An old-fashioned girl at heart?' He raised dark eyebrows.

'Perhaps.' She flashed him a defiant glance.

But Dominic only smiled and beckoned her back into the conservatory. He poured the coffee. 'Did you want to see Fran about anything special?' The question seemed casual, and yet Christie suspected him of an ulterior motive.

'Not really.' She hesitated, taking the mug he offered her, wanting to tell him more, although not sure why. 'I'm thinking of going to the States,' she supplied after a moment.

'For good?' He stared at her.

'Oh, no.' She laughed awkwardly. 'For a holiday.'

'Lucky you.' His tone was dry. 'The gardening business must be more lucrative than I thought.'

'Not really.' Christie stirred in some cream. She might as well tell him the whole story – he'd find out soon enough. 'You see, my father lives over there.'

'Does he indeed?' Dominic settled back into the cane chair he'd vacated earlier, and Christie followed his example.

Without having intended to, she told him about her father visiting Purbeck. About her shock, and her desire to get to know him properly.

Dominic was a good listener, saying little, his eyes showing his interest, his gaze hardly leaving her face.

'I think it's a great idea,' he said when she'd finished.

Christie smiled.

'And what does your husband say about all this?' Dominic poured them more coffee, apparently oblivious of the kind of question he was asking. The enormity of it.

Christie looked down at her hands, holding the mug of coffee, eking out its warmth. Surprisingly, they weren't trembling.

She had spoken to Robin on the phone from Yew Cottage yesterday. Told him about meeting her father. It hadn't been easy – far from it. But didn't Robin have the right to know what was going on? Shouldn't she try and explain why she hadn't been home? She couldn't put it off for ever.

When the familiar voice had answered, her throat constricted as if paralysing her vocal cords.

'Christie? Is that you?'

Silence. And then, 'Robin?' It came out as a hoarse croak.

'What's going on?' He sounded tired. Tired of her? Tired of whatever was happening between them?

Haltingly she told him about her father, although not about his offer to visit Boston.

'Why haven't you been home?'

Didn't he know? Wasn't it obvious?

'How can I come home?' she hissed, looking around to ensure no-one was listening. Vincent had perfected the art of making his wheelchair silent when he so desired.

'What do you mean, Christie?' He sounded so innocent. Had she imagined it all, then?

'The way you've been, what you've done to me . . . I can't stand any more of it. I have to stay away.'

'Silly girl,' he mocked. What was Robin thinking? How would she ever know if she didn't go back there?

'We can't pretend it never happened.' She spoke aloud, although really she was telling herself. They couldn't pretend. It was there between them, part of their relationship now, one of the bricks they were using to build whatever future lay in store. Even if their relationship should change, it wouldn't be forgotten, the potential for a repeat would remain.

'Come home, Christie.' His voice was compelling. She remembered the love she had always hoped for, and she remembered – against her will – those nights of dark passion locked into her innermost soul, that she was quite unable to forget.

'I'm scared, Robin.' A deep shudder ran though her.

'Come home.' Dark secrets. He was pulling her again, drawing her back, bewitching her with his promises . . . Abruptly she put down the phone.

'What's wrong?' Dominic removed the mug from her quivering hands. He took them in his, gently, as a friend might, his touch tender on her fingers. 'I thought you were looking a bit shaky. What is it?'

'It's Robin . . .' She looked down at her hands, safe in his. How could she tell him? Why was she telling him? He was little more than a stranger, and a disturbing stranger at that. 'Things have been difficult between us.' Her eyes pleaded with his for compassion. He squeezed her hand.

'You need some time away.' He nodded. 'This break will be a good thing.'

Good for whom? Herself, Robin or their marriage? Somehow it seemed that the three weren't synonymous any more. That there were entirely different interests at stake. 'I must go.' She stumbled to her feet. She knew where she must go.

'If you're sure you're all right.' His dense hazel eyes remained kind and concerned. 'If you ever want to talk, I'd be glad. I mean . . .' He seemed about to say more. For a fleeting moment she wanted to hug him.

'Thank you. But I'm fine.' And she was feeling stronger. Was it being away from Robin that gave her strength? Or was it the knowledge that she would soon be far away from them all?

'Tell Fran, will you?' she asked as he opened the front door. 'Tell her I'll write if I don't get the chance to see her before I go.'

He nodded solemnly. 'She'll miss you.'

His hand was on the door.

'She's got you.' Christie spoke without thinking. But Dominic's brow creased, and the shutters of politeness came down in his eyes.

'Yes, of course.' She got the impression he was brushing her away. That he'd had enough.

'Goodbye, Dominic.'

But all she got in reply was a curt nod as Dominic Redfern closed the door.

214

* * *

Christie drove away with a sense of purpose, as if talking to Dominic had cleared her head of all the clutter.

She must go back to Ulwell. Apart from the purely practical – she needed clothes and some of her things – it was her home. Her home as much as it was Robin's, although he had always owned it, always regarded it as more his, despite her contributions to their financial outgoings.

She drove the pick-up truck towards Corfe. All roads in Purbeck led to Corfe. It was the centre of Purbeck's existence – the great, proud ruins of the old castle perched high on a tufted mound of earth affording a view for miles around.

She couldn't continue running away. Gramma had hinted as much last night. 'Face up to things, Christie,' she'd said, with a certain look in her dark eyes that made Christie shiver.

And she was right. It was no answer – running back to Yew Cottage when things went wrong. What would she have done if there were no Yew Cottage? No handy second home to run to?

She slowed as she took the bend. But it had never taken its place as a second home. She had never left Yew Cottage, not really. It was still her home. She had never committed herself to Robin, not completely, in the way that a wife or a husband should commit.

Marriage should be binding, body and soul; theirs had never been. Perhaps she had married for all the wrong reasons. For a supportive background, while she lived her own life, achieved her own ambitions, dreamed her own dreams. She had married him because he was different. She had married him for the promise of a love that still lay in the future and had never come to fruition. Married him half-heartedly, but never given. Never given him it all. Never given them a chance.

Was that what this was all about? She drew up outside the small terraced house in Ulwell. Was she seeing it clearly for the first time? Was that why Robin had been behaving as he had? Was it nothing more than frustration and anger because Christie had held back some essential part of herself?

She sighed, slow and deep. Was that why he was forcing her to bend under his will – in the only way he knew? Making her bend with pure masculine aggression? An aggression that was so close to passion that she could no longer separate them in her mind, no longer perceive differences in their physical touch.

She could see his car parked further down the road. But she stayed in

215

the driving seat, watching the windows of the house, her fingers still on the ignition key as if she might need a quick getaway.

'Robin . . .' she murmured. She wanted nothing more than a new start. That was what she would tell him. A holiday in Boston with her father, a bit of space from the scary creature that their marriage had become. It was not her and it was not him. It was what the two of them had somehow created between them.

She would take time away from it. And then there would be a new start with Robin.

In a burst of energy she opened the door, jumped down from the truck and self-consciously patted her hair. Robin would see that it could be different between them. He had to see. She'd make him see.

She took the path at a run, fumbled for her front door key, put it in the lock and eased the door open.

There was silence in the house. It smelled different, unlived in.

'Robin! I'm home,' she called.

19

'Robin?' Christie crept into the hall.

No answer.

'Robin?' Her voice became louder, she was getting braver now.

But the house remained silent – cold, silent and very definitely empty.

Quelling the growing sensation that she had no right to wake this house up, no right to be here, skulking around, Christie poked her head round the kitchen door. The yellow and white room was sterile and bare but there was a faint sour smell clinging to the cold walls. Not one solitary cup in the sink, no sign of human habitation. Could this be her house? The house she'd shared with Robin, the house they'd laughed in and lived in, almost even loved in? It didn't seem possible.

The sitting-room was equally tidy, the cushions plumped and neat, no magazines or books strewn over the coffee table, no crumbs on the floor, or piles of ironing balanced precariously on the backs of chairs. But then, she was the one responsible for all that, wasn't she? It was she herself who left debris carelessly in her wake in a manner that had always infuriated Robin.

In how many other ways had she driven him crazy? Christie shivered. The house was freezing, inhumanly cold. It felt as if the heating hadn't been on for days. Where could he be?

Reluctantly she approached the stairs, climbing slowly, unwilling to visit the scene of her latest degradation and excitement. But the bedroom too was empty.

Christie sat down uncertainly on the smooth blue quilt of the bed they'd shared. What now?

Slowly she opened drawers, began to collect some clothes together in a

217

black hold-all. She hadn't wanted it to be like this. This kind of clandestine packing made it look as if she'd sneaked back here when she knew Robin to be out, as if she'd wanted to avoid a confrontation, when in fact she'd decided on confrontation as the only action open to her.

She went downstairs, slung the hold-all by the front door, and was just about to return to the kitchen when the phone rang, stridently breaking the silence of the house, making her jump.

'Don't be silly,' she told herself sternly. But nevertheless her hand rested on the receiver for at least twenty seconds before she picked it up, while her heart thumped painfully against her ribcage and the goosebumps crawled slowly up her skin.

'Hello?'

'Christie?'

Relief swamped her as she recognised Fran's voice. She sank down on the stair.

'Sorry I missed you, darling.' Sounding wonderfully cool and normal, Fran babbled on in meaningless chatter and Christie listened gratefully.

'Did Dominic – you know – say anything while you were here?' she said at last, as if this were her main reason for calling after all.

Christie stared at the telephone receiver. 'About what?' Now was the time to find out, wasn't it? It would be so easy. Are you having an affair with him? That's all she had to say. The words were simple enough. And Fran, being Fran, would give her an honest reply. But those words wouldn't shape themselves on her lips. She couldn't just ask her outright – it was impossible.

'About me. I had a row with him,' Fran admitted, her voice changing, allowing the vulnerability in. 'He's always on at me. He wants me to get a proper job. He says that Mummy's money won't last for ever.' She gulped loudly. 'Christie, he's been saying some hateful things.'

'And you don't want to get a job?' What sort of hateful things? Christie had to admit to mixed loyalties. Not that she considered Fran to be a spoilt little rich kid – hadn't she always been involved in some voluntary charity work or other? And wasn't she still doing training for counselling – on and off? Those things said a lot about good intentions. But were intentions always enough? She could see Dominic's point – everyone had to live, and unless Amy had left her a fortune, then Fran was no different from the rest of them.

'I'd rather go to college. I'm thinking of studying psychology.'

'Really?' Christie was unable to hide her surprise. Fran and psychology seemed as unlikely a combination as Christie and glamour modelling. And what about the counselling? What about the Refuge?

'Well, why not?' The edge returned to Fran's voice. 'Don't you think I could do it?'

'It's not that. I'm sure you could. It's just that . . .'

'He doesn't think I can do it.' The venom was undisguised.

'Dominic?'

'He doesn't think I'm capable. Because I never tried hard enough at school, because I was hopeless at everything, and Mummy said I'd never be an academic, and . . .'

'Of course you could do it,' Christie cut in. 'If you want to do it enough.' She hesitated. 'Do you? Want to do it enough, I mean?'

There was silence.

'Dominic thinks I'm too stupid,' she said at last. A whisper that seemed to contain all Fran's hurt and lost affections. And how much else did it contain, that Fran wasn't saying?

Christie's heart went out to her. 'You know you're not stupid. I know you're not stupid.' She paused, an unwelcome thought occurring to her. 'Dominic doesn't have some sort of control over you, does he?' She wasn't sure why she had said it.

Silence once more. Christie shivered. Control. It was a word that was beginning to scare her. 'Does he?'

'Of course not.' She didn't sound very convincing. 'I have to go now.'

'Fran . . .' She must tell her about Robin, about going away.

'Yes?'

The words dried in her mouth. 'Nothing.' This wasn't the time. Fran had her own problems to worry about. Dominic would tell her about the States and Christie would write to her about the rest. She felt a pang of guilt, a certainty that Fran needed her friendship now, needed her to be close at hand. But she had needs too, didn't she? Fran was getting to be a big girl; she must learn to stand on her own two feet.

After she'd put down the phone, Christie went back to the kitchen. In the fridge she found half a bottle of sour milk. Grimacing with distaste, she chucked it down the sink and let the tap run. It wasn't like Robin to let food go off like that. But what was like Robin? Did she have the slightest idea?

The fridge was now almost empty but for a lump of hard yellow cheese

219

and a bottle of white wine. Christie poured herself a generous glass and returned to the sitting-room. She would wait for him. She switched on the gas fire, considered the television, but axed the idea immediately. She didn't want tinny laughter or even melodrama. She just wanted a bit of peace.

So she curled up on the sofa, and before she knew it, she was fast asleep.

In the meantime, Robin was sitting on a high bar-stool in a rather disreputable pub in Swanage, getting drunk on pints of bitter with whisky chasers. The decor wasn't up to much – the carpet was worn and stained with a cocktail of alcoholic beverages and cigarette burns, but all this was half-hidden by the dingy lighting. At least the place was warm, even if the air was soaked with stale tobacco, the barman was friendly, and it would do him nicely until he got to the club at ten.

On his first visit, Robin had been pleasantly surprised at how easy it was to pick up girls in this club. He'd never tried it before. When his mother had been alive he'd never dared to ask a girl for a date. And since she'd died . . . Well, after the guilt there had been a solitary existence. Until he'd met Christie.

But of course he knew how it worked – he'd even dreamed of it sometimes. Women changed when they walked into a nightclub. Something happened to their common sense and precaution when their ears were pounded by the throbbing bass line of the disco music, when their eyes were blinded by the strobes and lasers. It got them in the mood. Or maybe they'd been in the mood all along, and just not shown it. Perhaps his mother had been right – most girls were asking for it.

They swanned around in low-cut dresses slashed to the thigh, or tight T-shirts and figure-hugging jeans, drinking Bacardi or Babycham, their lipstick making its mark, their warm breath steaming the cool glasses they held in nervous sweaty palms. They danced in pairs or groups around handbags and purses, until perspiration stood proud like tiny pearls on thick foundation, until mascara streaked and eyeshadow creased.

They became grotesque, clown-like, thinking themselves more desirable, more beautiful, the more they disguised themselves. What was the matter with these girls? They were so undiscriminating, so easy. Didn't they even care what bastards men could be?

All Robin had to do was pick the one he most liked the look of – who maybe had the fullest, reddest lips or the most promising cleavage. He'd buy her a couple of drinks – not cheap in this place but cheaper than a prostitute would be – and have a smoochy dance or two. A smooch was a male convenience. It replaced the chat-up line and all the other lovey dovey stuff that some girls wanted to hear and few men could be bothered to provide. Sometimes Robin gave them a bit of a sob story to get their emotional juices flowing. And Bob's your uncle.

You could achieve more in half an hour at a nightclub than you could in six months of going to the flicks. And as long as Robin hadn't picked one that was too young, he'd have a place to stay the night. A place to stay the night with a warm obliging body and soft breasts to squeeze his way into. Even breakfast if he was lucky.

They fed his ego, and he gave them a good time – there was no disputing that. He had no emotions regarding these girls. So he could give it his best. He was as good a performer as any stud Christie used to hang around with. No worries there. He hadn't had any complaints so far. And he liked to see them panting, with their breasts heaving, their big eyes begging for more, liking it more the harder he pushed into them. He could do it to them – it meant nothing.

Like the men who had done it to his Christie. The men she had allowed to come inside her. Oh yes. He'd seen that Barry with the macho bike that he thought every woman would want between her legs. He'd gone through Christie's photo album and his imagination had soon provided what wasn't there. How could she? He could have cried. He thought it would be different once he'd saved her from herself. But it never had been, had it? Because she had wanted the sort of sex from him that he couldn't provide. And then she had gone to *him* – that bloody Neanderthal – and let him do it to her. Let him spurt his filth into her again and again, God knows how many times.

He should have listened to his mother. His mother had told him, although not in so many words. Once a tart, always a tart.

Robin downed his beer and got groggily to his feet. He knew that all this was a kind of madness. He knew that he couldn't possibly go on this way, but right now there seemed no other way open to him.

He didn't want a relationship with any of these girls – of course he didn't. That wasn't what he went to the club for. He doubted if any of the men lurking around the sidelines of the dance floor, eyeing up tight bums and swaying hips, wanted lasting relationships. It was hardly the sort of place you'd go to look, was it?

And neither did he go for drugs. Robin wasn't into that at all, although he knew they were readily available at the club. No. Robin wanted sex from these girls – that was what he needed. Because sex gave him the right kind of revenge.

And he wouldn't be able to do it stone cold sober. Some men found that they drooped in direct correlation with the amount of beer they'd poured down their throats. With Robin it was different. Getting half-pissed enabled him to shut out the voice of a distant conscience. A conscience that had perhaps belonged to the Robin Fifer who'd married Christie, who had offered her love and support till death parted them. Getting half-pissed enabled him to find a different side of Robin Fifer. The side of him – the *inside* of him – that his mother had turned into a monster of manhood.

It was two-thirty am when Christie woke with a start, for a moment not knowing where she was, not recognising her own sitting-room, the orange glare of her own gas fire, tickling her throat and scorching her tired eyes. 'Robin?' She glanced at her watch. 'Robin . . .'

She pulled herself out of the chair, wondering if he'd returned without her knowing. But a quick exploration of the house persuaded her otherwise. So where was he?

Frowning, she found paper and a pen and scribbled a quick note of explanation. She didn't mention that she had waited here for him, that she knew he'd been out all night. She propped it up on the mantelpiece above the fire, switched the gas off, carefully washed and wiped her wine glass to remove all traces that might betray the length of her visit, and let herself out of the house.

As she drove to Yew Cottage in the early hours of the morning along dark deserted roads, she tried not to think about it. Where was he? What was he doing? And most of all, after what had happened between them, knowing she had no right, Christie tried very hard not to mind.

'He's taking her back to Boston!' Faith paced the floor, drawing in on her cigarette. 'First he just turns up out of the blue. Then he carts Christie away with him!'

'It's only for a holiday, my dear.' Isobel smiled. 'God knows the poor girl could do with one.'

'I know that, Mother.' They exchanged a glance of concern, both aware that Christie's marriage had reached a crisis point. Was it also a crashing point? In their different ways, perhaps, both women were worried that there was more to it than they understood.

'What are you scared of, Faith?' Isobel watched her, knowing her so well. There was a certain turbulence in Faith tonight.

'I was just getting close to her. I don't want to lose her.' Barely a whisper.

'Oh, Faith . . .' Isobel reached out and drew her daughter's half-protesting body into her arms as she had not done for so many years. It felt good, this lack of space between them, this warmth. And she understood Faith's irrational fear of losing the daughter she was just getting close to. Or was it more than that? Was there another fear – something to do with the man who had turned up to remind her of the past, to disrupt her life?

She held her close, breathing in the fragrance of her daughter's hair. Motherhood was far more fragile than most people assumed. Motherhood had to be worked at from the birth on, and just got harder as the years went by. Mothers were the perfect people to hate. They'd given up their lives for their sons and daughters, hadn't they? And in return they expected at least a little finger on the steering wheel of control.

It was different for Faith, of course. But it must seem so very cruel of Marc Dupont to arrive now, providing both a threat and bitter reminders.

'I know I'm being silly.' Faith's smile as she drew away from Isobel was a rueful one. 'It's just that . . .'

'Christie will be all right.' Isobel stroked the soft hair. 'She only wants the chance to get to know her father a little. It's a good opportunity for her to get away from Purbeck. To see something of the world. She'll be back.'

The door to the sitting-room swung open and Vincent appeared. They were framed in the doorway – man and wheelchair.

Isobel felt Faith's tension radiating through her, spoiling the rare moment of intimacy. She shook her head at Vincent, needing this time alone with her daughter.

'Bloody hell,' Vincent moaned. He reversed out, the wheels groaning in protest.

Faith drew back from her mother's embrace, her eyes wet with tears. 'Why do you have him here, Mother?' she asked. 'Just what do you owe him?'

Isobel stared at her. Was that what it came to in the end? Was that why she had taken him in, pulled him into her life, sacrificed what she had with her daughter?

* * *

'Why do you want him here? Why? Why?' The voice belonged to the past. Faith at sixteen. Faith on the day she'd told her daughter that Vincent Pascoe would be moving in with them.

'He's ill. He needs my help. Our help.' Isobel tried to calm her, but Faith had always possessed this streak of hysteria just under the surface, that was quite beyond calming.

'He won't get any bloody help from me!' Faith clenched angry fists, bigger perhaps than the fists she had clenched at the age of six when they'd first moved to Dorset, but no less stubborn.

'Faith!'

'I mean it, Mother.' In the last year Faith had begun to call her that, dropped the more casual 'Mum' from their lives. Isobel felt that her very role had been eradicated, Faith's love eroding with every 'Mother' she uttered.

'You won't have a choice. You're my daughter. I make the decisions.' Isobel always hated it afterwards, when she'd been high-handed with her, but Faith ripped this anger out of Isobel with her sulky resentments, her stubborn refusal to see any position but her own.

'I'll leave home.' The green eyes flashed.

'You will not, my girl!' Isobel grabbed her by the shoulders. 'You're only sixteen years old. I'd drag you back.'

'Why bother?' Her mood changed in the abrupt way that Faith's moods always changed. Too much love, too many tears all crammed into too few moments. Much too much for most people to cope with.

Faith crumpled in front of her mother's fury. Her face took on the expression of the persecuted. 'You don't want me here. You only want *him*!'

Isobel's voice softened. 'Don't be silly. Of course I want you here.' She tried to hug her but Faith resisted, standing stiff and straight and very distant. 'I love you.'

'Then why are you letting *him* come here?' Tears were rolling down Faith's cheeks.

'He's ill, I told you.'

Faith pulled one of her faces. A childhood face that resented any illness that might interrupt her life. 'I don't see what it's got to do with us,' she grumbled. 'What has *he* got to do with us?'

'It's called friendship,' Isobel snapped, uncomfortably aware that she was letting her daughter down. She had promised herself that Faith's interests would always come first, and yet now, confronted by this decision, she had been unable to keep to that promise. Other loyalties . . . 'He needs my help. And I don't see why we can't all live here together. There's plenty of room. It won't affect you and me.'

Faith looked disbelieving. It might as well be the end of the world according to the expression on her lovely face.

Isobel became irritated. 'Come on, Faith. Half the time you're not even here. You've got your own life to lead, that's plain enough.'

'Oh, I see.' Faith nodded, tossed back her head in that infuriating teenage way she had. 'Back to that record again, are we? Why can't I be home by ten o'clock, and why do I have to keep going *out*.' She sneered.

Isobel turned away. It was useless to explain that she worried, that parents always worried. How could they help it when they were no longer in charge? It wasn't so long since Faith had needed to hold her hand whenever they walked down the street. Isobel had spent so many years watching for every imagined accident in the book, that it was hard to relinquish the responsibility. Too hard not to worry. 'Before I know it you'll be leaving home,' Isobel said instead, although it was a prospect she dreaded.

'So that's what you want!' Faith stormed up the stairs, long hair flying like an angry mane behind her. 'I knew it.'

'No, I don't want that,' Isobel called uselessly after her. What was wrong with the girl?

Faith leaned over the banister. 'Well, that's what you'll have if he moves in here. I'm telling you, Mother. I'll be leaving first chance I get!'

Isobel sighed. She had never understood just what it was that Faith hated so much about Vincent. He had never been cruel to her, rarely even unkind. But despite all her efforts there had never been closeness between them, at best stiff politeness. And it made her sadder than she could say. But how could she change her mind now? How could she turn away a man with multiple sclerosis who had given her the strength to find her own freedom, given her in fact everything she now held dear? Yes, she did owe him.

So Vincent moved in, and Faith suffered his presence in sulky silence. She went out more and more, stopped even the pretence of bothering with school work and rebuffed every one of Isobel's attempts to keep the lines of communication open at all costs.

Slowly, Isobel came to realise that she had made perhaps the biggest mistake of her life.

The day after her eighteenth birthday Faith packed a rucksack and told them she was going to France. Isobel was horrified. She had never believed Faith would actually do it, still recalling her too clearly as the shy vulnerable child who needed security even more than she needed attention.

Worried for her safety, Isobel tried to stop her, but Faith seemed deaf to her concern, blind to the pitfalls that lay ahead. So Isobel gave her money – the only thing her daughter would accept – that might at least afford her some protection and release her from the fate of sleeping rough on the streets.

Faith walked down the drive of Yew Cottage with a determined swing in her step. She had not even kissed her mother goodbye.

'I owe Vincent a lot more than you know,' she told Faith now. 'For goodness' sake, Faith. Can't you let bygones be bygones after all these years? We've got Christie to think of, haven't we?' Isobel longed, so much she longed, for Faith to bury her old resentments. But as time went by it seemed more and more unlikely.

Faith looked away. As if in a dream, she reached for her pack of cigarettes. 'What if Marc persuades her to stay there for good?' she suggested darkly, lighting one, the flame illuminating her face. She was still a lovely woman, but sometimes she still looked like a child.

'Surely he wouldn't do that?' Isobel rocked gently in her chair. 'He's got his own family now . . .'

Faith's eyes filled with tears once more.

So. She still loved him.

'You don't know Marc.' She sniffed.

Isobel leaned closer towards her. 'Why don't I? Why have you never told me about him?'

'There never seemed much point.' Faith's voice was so low that Isobel had to strain to hear the words.

'But you loved him.' Isobel watched her.

Faith nodded. 'Yes, I loved him.' She raised her head, her eyes defiant once more.

Isobel smiled. That was her daughter. She'd never really changed, although she might pretend in front of the rest of the world. 'And was it so very terrible to want to stay with the father of your child?'

Abruptly, Faith got to her feet, moved towards the window. 'I don't know.' She pulled the curtain aside, gazing out into the cold January blackness, her body tight and drawn into herself. 'You tell *me*. Was it so very terrible?'

Isobel put a hand to her head. Would Faith make this guilt go on for ever? What do you owe Vincent, Faith had asked her. Come to that, what did she owe Jack's memory? Much, much less. Yet still she kept it intact for her daughter. More fool her.

But Faith wasn't thinking of Jack or Vincent. She was thinking of Marc.

From the moment she'd seen them on her doorstep – Marc and Christie – her emotions had been in turmoil. Was it just morbid curiosity that had brought him here? Had he just woken up one day to wonder: now what could have happened to Faith Vaughan? Maybe I should look her up, see if she's ended up with someone as successful as I am. Faith's lip curled.

He kept phoning, asking to see her. She longed to give in to the temptation – ah, it would be so easy. But, like Mother said, he had a wife and family of his own. So she wouldn't see him. What was the point? It would only hurt her. And it would hurt her for nothing now that his future was sewn up and so removed from her grasp.

Christie had said she should have told her everything before. Christie had said she was trying to forgive her, and trying to understand.

And what could Faith say to Christie in her defence? Yes, I loved him, but I was scared? Yes, I loved him, but it was different then. We had free love then. Everybody loved everybody else. So the girl from Purbeck, who knew so little of life, worried that love was meaningless, that this was nothing special for Marc. Everybody adored Marc. He was the leader of the group, the most intelligent, the funniest, the one who made all the parties swing and always got hold of the best dope. Everyone looked up to Marc.

Marc had chosen her back in France, when their paths first crossed. She had been feeling unloved, and Marc had changed all that. She was his woman, and she loved him with a passion that bordered dangerously on obsession.

Almost against her will, Faith found herself remembering that love. Those days back in Brittany, and the day they'd moved on.

'I wanna take you to the States,' he had breathed, hot in her ear.

'America?' To Faith it seemed like a million miles away. Certainly much further from Dorset than she'd ever intended – or dreamed of – travelling.

'Why not?' His eyes were the bluest she'd ever seen. 'We make a good partnership, don't we? And it's time to move on.'

Time to move on. Faith felt as if someone were wafting a dark curtain in front of her eyes, a premonition of discontent, blurring her vision, promising fear. 'Do we have to leave?'

She loved it here in France. Everything was so perfect, and she was scared of change. What would happen to Marc and Faith if they uprooted themselves from this, their ideal background? Might they not reach a crossroads in their road together?

'Nothing stays the same for ever, baby.' The restlessness was in his eyes. She recognised it and she shivered. 'The picking'll be finished, we'll have no bread, nowhere to crash.'

'I guess so.' Faith shrank from practicalities. She supposed that she'd envisaged returning to Dorset after France, as if her departure had been only a temporary stand, an attempt at telling her mother who she was – that she had a life, rights of her own. That she didn't want Vincent Pascoe in their house. But now there was Marc.

'A guy I know ended up in Woodstock,' Marc told her. 'He sent me a card, says it's a groove.'

'Woodstock,' she echoed. It meant little to her. Idly she traced a pattern in the sand.

'So will you come along?' He sounded casual.

She concentrated on the fine grains of sand sifting back into the hollows she'd made. Did he care as much as she believed him to?

'Sure.' She grinned, pretending everything was fine. 'Why not?'

The journey to Woodstock had taken much longer than she'd anticipated – a weird mixture of hiking, hitching, trains, buses and an aeroplane flight. They were bound into a close, knotted twosome. Faith and Marc against the rest of the world.

And then they arrived in Woodstock and it was different. The English language pulled them apart instead of uniting them. In Woodstock there were mostly Americans who talked like Marc did, who shared similar backgrounds, the same culture. There were people everywhere, people like them, hippies and travellers with no place special to go. People who wanted to wind away an hour or three, smoking pot and strumming guitars. People who had dropped out, tuned in to a different world. Faith had imagined it to be hers and Marc's world, but there were many interlopers, even in their apartment. These days they were rarely alone.

And then there were the drugs. The occasional smoke in the evening crept into the rest of the day; there were uppers and downers, pills of all colours and sizes, lines of coke to sniff when there was money around. Faith was out of her depth. Out of her depth and sinking fast. Clinging on, barely clinging on to the something special she imagined them to share.

There was still passion, but somehow passion wasn't enough in the end. And the end began one day as Faith stood at the stove, wearing headband, love beads and a loose paisley dress, stirring the gigantic vegetable hotpot she'd made for as many people as might turn up – you never knew for sure. It didn't seem to bother the rest of them, but it drove Faith wild with frustration when it was her turn to cook, not knowing how many mouths she was cooking for. A hotpot using vegetables that could be bought cheaply from the open-air market, was about the only half-satisfactory answer.

Marc and Lindy – a girl who had been living in their apartment for a few months – were lounging on beanbags on the floor of the living-room, smoking and chatting desultorily. Lindy was like Marc – very cool, very casual, very hip – and Faith didn't understand her at all.

Every now and then something they said made Faith tense, the hand that held the wooden spoon stiffening involuntarily, or crushing a defenceless vegetable. She wished – how she wished that she could be like them.

'I'm gonna go back to Europe for a while,' Lindy said. 'Do some more travelling. I'm getting that restless feeling again, you know?'

'Cool,' Marc agreed.

Faith frowned. Was Marc getting that restless feeling again? Did he want to go travelling with Faith, or would he have preferred to choose the free and easy Lindy as his travelling companion? Lindy knew where it was at, all right. She was almost as expert as Marc at procuring the best dope, and she rolled joints which were proclaimed as mindblowing by the rest of them. Faith wouldn't know. She had no desire to smoke dope. That made her square, didn't it? That meant she couldn't relate to them as they sat around getting high. It meant that she didn't belong. The spoon ground into the lentils resting at the bottom of the pan.

'I'll come back here, though.' Lindy stretched out long legs. 'I really dig this place. But man, I wanna feel free to come and go, not get stuck in time, stuck in geography, you know?'

Once more Marc agreed.

From her position in the kitchen, Faith peered through the open kitchen door at him. His eyes were half-closed. Marc didn't like conversation when he was getting stoned. But what did he think about being free to come and go? Wasn't liberty his lifeline? For Faith, it was a heavy burden to bear. The easy-going atmosphere of their life here was sometimes almost a torture for one who needed reassurance the way she did. But she had to be here. Marc was here. She was his woman and so she could never tell him how she felt.

Later that night they made love as they often made love, slow and gentle. It was wonderful – but then it always was. She wanted to say *I love you* but she couldn't bring herself to be thought crass. Neither could she admit need. Her vulnerability was bottled up inside her, forever close to exploding point. And she was still tense, unable to contemplate sleep.

'You like Lindy, don't you?' she asked at last.

'Sure. She's a great lady.' Marc rolled over.

'She sleeps with lots of men. But she never gets involved with them.' Faith was talking half to herself, trying to work out why she too couldn't be more like Lindy. Maybe then she might feel secure.

'She's into freedom,' Marc said. 'Lindy is a true Bohemian.'

He said it as though that was all there was. Faith hoisted herself up on to her elbow. 'But is freedom *always* such a good thing?'

He half-turned, opened one eye. 'How d'you mean?'

They could have these conversations, these kind of half-hypothetical discussions about the issues that most bothered her, as long as they didn't get too personal. It was the abstract world that mattered.

Lindy had once said that if she sensed she could dig a guy then she asked him what he thought of William Blake, Dante or Vietnam. If he gave the right answer then they'd screw.

Faith had been horrified, every instinct shrinking from such cool casual appraisals. But Marc had laughed and agreed. It was a decadent hedonism, a hedonism that both scared and suffocated Faith. It didn't seem real to her – it seemed an illusion, and behind the illusion lurked a gradual decay she couldn't quite come to grips with, or even rationalise to herself.

But to them – the people who now made up her world – it was everything important: it was what they were in relation to the rest of the population, what they were saying to it, summed up in a two-fingered salute.

She said some of this to Marc, but he disagreed.

'Isn't there any room for trust?' she murmured.

He closed his eyes again. 'A guy could trust Lindy,' he said. 'She'd never try and trap a man.'

'How d'you mean?' Her stomach dropped into panic.

He rolled over once more. 'Oh, you know, baby. The way some chicks do.' His breathing became heavy. He had crucified her and then gone to sleep. She watched him for a long time before finally switching out the light.

The next day Faith went to the doctor at last – she'd put it off for too long. She already knew that she was pregnant.

She'd never try and trap a man. The way some chicks do. Faith couldn't forget that.

The following day she packed her bag while Marc was out at a concert. This lifestyle wasn't for her. It had never been for her. She had been driven to France by the presence of Vincent Pascoe at home in Dorset, and then pulled to Woodstock by Marc. She had never really come here out of choice.

Whereas Marc belonged here. He was wedded to this lifestyle. She knew that now.

Of course Faith had left. She was his woman. How could she disillusion him? What else could she do?

'Have you told Christie all this?' Isobel asked her.

Faith turned from her contemplation of the full moon outside. Her cigarette had burned down to the filter, and was scorching her fingers. She put it on the ashtray. She would give up soon. 'I tried.' There was a bitterness in her voice. 'But it sounded as if I was making excuses.'

'What did she say?' Isobel heaved herself out of the rocking chair and came to stand beside her daughter, taking her hand, squeezing gently.

Faith met her searching gaze. 'She asked me why I hadn't told her before. She said she'd try to understand. And she said that whatever I think about it, she's still going to Boston.'

20

As the taxi took Christie and her father along the wide carriageway that stretched from the airport towards the city of Boston, she relaxed back in her seat. It was time to contemplate this meeting with her father's wife, her father's sons. She knew he had phoned to warn them – but what did they really think about some long-lost daughter appearing from England, laying some claim perhaps to the father, or to the husband they doubtless considered exclusively theirs?

Fathers, husbands . . . Why were families so complicated? What was it Dominic Redfern had said about how hard they were to like, how difficult to satisfy when they laid so many claims on you?

Husbands . . . Unwillingly, she thought back to the showdown with Robin. Not a row – perhaps they were beyond rows, she certainly hoped so – but their final stilted conversation before she left for the States, in the doorway of the house in Ulwell.

Christie had stood awkwardly on the red step and reached for the doorbell, reluctant to use her key. Since her long vigil a few nights before, she'd forced herself to appreciate that this was a separation, one that she herself had instigated. She couldn't barge in as if she still lived here, as if she had some claim on the house or on his time.

She was taken aback to hear heavy footsteps coming down the stairs, and the bolt being shot. Nervous, too.

Robin's face appeared first – a surprised, undecided face that could go either way. Depending . . .

'Christie.' He leaned heavily on the open door, inching it open, not inviting her in.

'Robin . . . I've been trying to contact you.' No, stop. That sounded accusing. 'I wanted to talk to you.' She began again. Wanted and dreaded, was nearer the truth.

'What about?' His jaw was unshaven, his grey eyes bleary.

'About us, of course.' She dropped her voice, folded her arms, glanced around at neighbouring houses to see if curtains were twitching. Why didn't he ask her in? Could he – surely he couldn't have someone there? She shivered.

'I thought you were scared to come in.' He seemed to see right through her. 'You said you were frightened to come home.'

Christie looked down. Everything couldn't be entirely hopeless between them if he could so easily read her mind. 'I was. I am.'

For a moment she was transported back to their last night together. His touch burning her flesh, singeing her very soul, it seemed. His anger in the mouth that clamped heavily on to hers. His fury, his passion. Her wild, undiluted response. Her horror. Her fear.

'It isn't as simple as that.' She was telling herself as well as him. 'We've got a lot of thinking to do, haven't we?'

He stared at her, unsmiling, unresponsive, not helping in the least. As if she alone had thinking to do.

'I can't come back to be as we *were*,' she stressed. 'You must see that.'

His eyes narrowed. 'Then how do you think we should be?'

'I don't know.' It was more like a wail. This wasn't going at all as she'd planned. How could she launch into the rehearsed speech that hadn't sounded at all bad in the bath? Her hope that their marriage wasn't over, her desire to begin again with him, the small bud of promise still resting in her heart, despite everything, that they could love each other in the way they'd always meant to? How could she do all that when she was standing on the blasted doorstep, for heaven's sake?

'I'm sorry.' Christie shifted her feet, poking at the cracks in the red step with the toe of one black, laced ankle boot. 'You'll never know how sorry I am for what I did.'

No reply.

At last she looked up at him, but it was impossible to tell what he was thinking, he had all the barriers down by now. 'Robin?'

'Isn't it a bit late for apologies?'

She shook her head. 'I don't think so.'

He shrugged, apparently not caring, his hand shifting on the doorknob as if he wanted her out of here.

'I'm going away for a while,' she blurted. 'With my father.'

'Oh?' Could she be mistaken? Was she absolutely mad, or was there relief in his eyes?

'To Boston.' The words came out in a rush. 'That's where he lives. In the States. I want to get to know him. I want to meet his family. I want a break.' From all this, she added silently. From you. From what we've become.

He smiled, a thin crease dividing his sallow face. 'Christie wants . . .' he said softly.

She sighed, brushing her hair from her face in a gesture of irritation. 'Well, Robin . . . If you ever – for once – told me what *you* want, if you talked to me like you used to in the beginning . . .'

'Things aren't what they used to be. In the beginning.' His voice was rough and mocking, refusing her the access anger might bring. But Christie sensed a glimmer of salvation. She stepped forward.

'Can't they be better?' she whispered. 'When I come back? Can't we try again?'

There was a long pause. Eventually he said, 'I suppose . . .' but his eyes remained wary. 'If you think it's possible.'

'Of course it is.' Christie sounded sure. She reached up to kiss his cheek, just missing his mouth.

Robin half-flinched away from her as though her lips were a flame. Was he scared too? Was he scared of what he was doing to her, what they were doing to themselves, to each other?

'Robin?' He smelled stale and unwashed. There were so many questions crowding her brain, confusing her. She was unable to make them queue for attention. They picked and nagged at her. Was she crucifying him, or was he trying to destroy himself? Was he struggling simply to get himself together?

'What?' His stare was cold, unloving.

Christie sighed. Maybe he needed this separation even more than she did. 'I'll miss you.' She let the words hover in the air between them, not even sure if they were true. Robin nodded, but she sensed he didn't fully believe them either.

She half-turned from him. The pick-up truck was parked outside. There was work to plan for Purbeck Garden Designs in the coming month or two, work that she must discuss with Trevor. She had to leave the company, her baby, in the arms of a man she wasn't even sure she trusted. But she couldn't ask Robin to get involved with the business, and her mother was much too busy. Had she made a mistake? Christie's slim shoulders sagged slightly. Was she crazy to leave like this? 'Shall I write to you?'

He shrugged. 'If you like.' Did it mean so little to him?

She unlatched the gate, turned to wave goodbye to her husband. But all that confronted her was the closed wooden door. She stared at it for a moment. How could this ever be her home? It was as unwelcoming as a grave, and she wasn't ready for any kind of burial.

Almost at a run she reached the pick-up truck, unlocked the door and jumped in. The engine rumbled into life, she glanced behind and pulled away. As she passed the house, she looked towards the front upstairs window. She thought she saw a shadowy figure watching her departure. But she couldn't be sure. Robin had travelled farther away than the mere distance of miles that Christie had now put between them. She really couldn't be sure.

Her husband had seemed to want her to come here; her mother had begged her not to consider it. And as for Christie – she felt pulled by a thread of something that was more than curiosity. It was part of the very roots of her, part of what made her real.

'Don't worry.' Marc squeezed her hand. 'They're not so bad. They'll probably welcome you with open arms, and have the red carpet stretching halfway down the road.' He laughed. But Christie heard the laugh catch in his throat, and she glanced at him in surprise.

The smile was fixed on his handsome tanned face, his expression was calm and confident, but she saw something else in the blue eyes so like her own. He wasn't sure of her reception in the least. He was, after all, as apprehensive as she was herself. Her father was a worried man.

Christie had been staying at the house in Old Boston for two weeks before she overheard a raised adult voice. The family seemed too good to be true.

Glenda Dupont was tall, elegant and immaculate. The platinum blonde hair coiled on her head never had a strand out of place, her make-up was discreet and effective, highlighting the faintly haughty lines of her sharp features, accentuating the cool blue-greyness of her eyes and the perfectly formed narrow mouth. She was icy, serene, and perfectly terrifying.

The two boys on the other hand were a cliché of American youth. They were typical teenagers, she supposed, but of a variety quite different from the ones she'd ever come across in Dorset, and a long way from her memories of her own teenage anxieties about exams, self-consciousness and the right hemlines. Tyler and Brad played baseball, hung out in the downtown mall, drank Coke and milk straight from the fridge, and slouched around the house in baggy football shirts and jeans. They talked – loudly and often, and usually in strident competition – about the latest baseball game or the value of American cars.

When Christie had arrived, prepared to fall into the arms of her new family, they had avoided looking at her, listened dutifully to their father's introductions, said, 'hi', and disappeared.

Her father laughed it off. 'Boys . . .' he said, shaking his head. But Christie detected a glint of anger in his blue eyes, and she wondered – could these two American teenagers possibly be her father's children?

'How lovely she is.' Glenda Dupont bent her stem of a body, allowing her scarlet lips to brush within a centimetre of each side of Christie's face in an air kiss. 'How on earth did you find her, darling?' One perfectly manicured white hand rested on the arm of her husband.

'I was looking up some old ties.' Her father's eyes briefly met those of Christie, before he stooped only slightly to kiss his wife's delicately rouged cheek. 'It's a long story.'

A glint of something very close to malice briefly crossed the elegant features. 'And one best saved for later, darling, surely?' Without waiting for a reply, Glenda Dupont glided up the stairs, beckoning to Christie to follow.

'This is your room.' The smile was there, on her face, but strangely distant, as if not meant for Christie at all.

'We're very glad to welcome you, my dear,' she said. So why did Christie not quite believe it? Was she just being churlish?

Glenda spoke rapidly – of outings that had been arranged, people that would visit, of Boston's attractions and the routines of the household. So helpful. So polite.

She glanced at the gold watch on her slender wrist. 'Dinner will be in an hour, so you'll have time to wash and change. Let me take your coat.' She paused, as Christie struggled to free her arms from the overcoat Robin had bought her last year.

'Thanks.'

'Or would you prefer to rest?' Glenda's cool appraising gaze travelled the length of Christie's woollen turquoise dress – her best dress, almost her only dress – as if calculating how much she'd paid for it.

'I'm fine,' Christie lied. The dress was creased and clung to her after the long journey. She would have to shower and change. But what on earth would she wear? Apart from this dress she only had jeans and leggings. She'd had no idea that Glenda Dupont would look like she did. So cool and elegant. She might not object to her sons' scruffy appearance, but Christie sensed she would expect something smarter from her guest. And if Christie failed to deliver, wouldn't she in some strange way be failing her own mother too? But – what the hell. She held her head higher. The Duponts – all of them – would have to take her as she was. Why should she pretend to be someone else?

Since then, Glenda Dupont's manners had remained as impeccable as her fingernails. And since Christie was quite happy either to explore Boston on her own, when her father was tied up with work, or be taken around by him when he was free, she wasn't in the least worried by the lack of warmth shown to her by her father's wife. And why should she be warm? Wasn't she – Christie Fifer, the English stranger – a threat to this American family with the careful French overtones, living in discreet luxury among the old cobbled streets and four-storeyed shuttered houses of Old Boston?

And it wasn't just Christie, was it? Glenda Dupont must be aware of the past – a past that her husband shared with Christie's mother. It wouldn't surprise Christie – although she was sure she'd never know for certain, because Glenda wouldn't allow so much as a flicker of emotion to threaten the smooth inscrutability of her face – if her father's wife didn't actually hate her.

The evening she first heard raised voices, Christie had come back early from a solitary walk down to the waterfront, where she'd been wandering through the multi-levelled New England Aquarium on Central Wharf. It fascinated her – this gigantic seawater fish tank, displaying sharks, butterfly fish, and salmon, cruising and darting, each existing at its specific depth in the ocean. If she ran up the staircases in between, she could see them all, bit by bit, while the layers of sea, fathoms upon fathoms, wrapped themselves around her as if there were no glass separating her from this hypnotic, moving, underwater world.

Christie was still half in dream-land as she slipped back into the house unnoticed. She was about to go into the front room to announce her arrival, when her father's voice stopped her.

'I'm not taking them with me, Glenda, and that's final.' Christie froze. She had no wish to interrupt an argument or intrude on their privacy. Slowly she crept towards the stairs.

'They're your kids.' Glenda's voice was hard and accusing.

'So is Christie.'

'Oh, *Christie* . . .' Words couldn't describe the venom injected into that single word.

Christie shivered, but meanwhile Glenda was still speaking. 'Your precious Christie. For God's sake, Marc, you spend every spare minute with that girl. Don't you see how you're neglecting your family?'

'She is my family.'

'And what about us?' Christie imagined Glenda pulling at his arm, tugging him round to her own point of view. 'Aren't we your family? Aren't the boys your family?'

'Sure you are.' His voice was muffled. 'You know damn well you are.' Marc let out a deep sigh, and for the first time it struck Christie how brave he'd been to bring her back here. How easy it would have been for him to acknowledge her existence in other ways, even for him to visit her without his family knowing. But this – this confrontation – showed her for the first time how much she meant to him, how much her mother had meant to him too.

'You'd never know it.'

'Jesus, Glenda.' She imagined him tearing his hands through his dark hair, drumming his fingers impatiently on the table in that way he had. 'She's my daughter and I never even knew of her existence. My flesh and blood. She's twenty-four years old. She's married. I know damn all about her. And I want to get to know her, I want her to know she has a father as well as a . . .'

'And what makes you so sure you are her father?' The cold cruel voice cut through his emotion.

'Oh, Glenda . . .' He sounded weary, as if they'd had this conversation many times before. And he sounded hurt, too.

Christie crept to the top stair and sat down, her knees huddled against her chest. This wasn't just an argument about her presence here, she realised. This concerned some deep-seated resentment, some flaw in their relationship that she knew nothing about. Unexpectedly, she felt a longing for home. For the yew grove and Yew Cottage. For her mother's sudden grin and Gramma's comforting arms.

'Don't tell me,' Glenda was saying. 'You only have to look at her to know she's your daughter. You've already told me all that.' She paused for breath. 'I suppose you think I should be grateful that she doesn't look like her mother. Is that it?'

Christie closed her eyes. Jealousy – obsessive and destructive.

'It's not just that. Of course she's mine. I know. And anyway, her mother wouldn't have . . .'

'I don't want to hear about her mother, Marc,' Glenda spat at him. 'I have the daughter in my house. Spare me her mother at least.'

There was silence. Christie stared dry-eyed at the front door at the bottom of the stairs. The stained glass in aquamarine, the polished banisters, the soft whispering carpeted floor. It was a house for the beautiful people. Its shop-window surface gloss might be appealing enough to beckon you inside, but once there, what did you find? The same jealousies and pain you'd find anywhere else. She wasn't wanted here. She shouldn't have come.

'I still haven't figured out why you can't take the boys.' Glenda opened the door and although she was well hidden, Christie shrank back against the Edwardian-style striped wallpaper. To be caught eavesdropping on this conversation would be too dreadful. It wasn't even as if she'd wanted to hear it.

'Because this is a time for me and Christie.' Her father's voice was firm. 'I've made up my mind. The boys should be at school. Tyler's only just been away with Bobby and his folks. I'll take them fishing later in the year. They wouldn't want to hang around doing what I'm gonna be doing.'

'You want to re-live all those precious memories,' she sneered. 'That's what you want to do. You want to tell her what it was like for you and her mother. You'll go to Woodstock and you'll moon around the place, holding hands, the two of you, wallowing in nostalgia.' Her voice trembled. 'You make me sick. You both make me sick.'

'Stop it, Glenda.' Christie recognised the controlled anger in his voice. 'That's enough. I've had enough, d'you hear?'

He strode past her, out of the room and up the stairs, two at a time before Christie had a chance to move.

When he got to the top he stared at her. 'How long have you been there?'

240

'Long enough.' She got slowly to her feet. 'I had no idea. I should leave. I should go home.'

But her father had his hands on her shoulders, pressing and insistent. 'I promised you the Catskills and that's what you'll get,' he said. 'We need some time alone, you and I. I'm sorry you had to hear all that. But you mustn't let Glenda get to you.'

'She matters. She's your wife.' Christie stared at him.

His eyes barely flickered. 'I know what she is. But there are times when even Glenda can't have exactly what she wants.'

'She was a model,' he told her the following day, as the sleek car ate up the miles on the highway going through New York State. 'An international model,' he added, as if no further explanation was needed. 'Used to being number one.'

'She's still very beautiful.' Christie tore herself from her immersion in the glorious evergreen scenery of the Catskills. 'Did you meet her in Boston?'

He nodded. 'I was doing some designs for a show. She was one of the models. She hardly seemed real to me at the time. She was so damn professional that one minute we could be arguing about which pizza to buy, next thing she'd be swanning down the catwalk like a creation of Coco Chanel.'

Christie smiled. 'Very different from Mum.'

He glanced at her briefly, his hands tightening around the steering wheel. 'She sure was different,' he agreed. 'But I was different too.'

'How?' Christie watched him. He was such a relaxed, confident driver. In fact everything about her father oozed confidence, and Christie loved listening to him reminisce, loved imagining what he'd been like as a young man.

He laughed. 'I landed a sweet little job when I got to Boston. You know what they say . . . it's not what you know, but who.'

'And who did you know?' she teased.

'An uncle right at the top who'd made it in Boston.' He smiled. 'I was swamped with opportunities all right, even an aimless hippy like me. And what a transformation I made. Jet-setting businessman in less than six months.'

Christie thought she detected some resentment in his tone against what he had become. About what he had lost in the process, perhaps. 'And

Glenda was the right kind of woman to have on your arm?' She said it without thinking, not intending to be cruel.

'Maybe she was at that.' His expression changed.

Christie knew it wasn't that simple. She felt a wave of sympathy for him.

'These are the Catskills,' he informed her. 'Over a hundred thousand acres of the best hiking, fishing and hunting you could hope to find.'

Christie didn't object to the change of subject. However much she wanted to find out about the past, the intensity woven into what she was discovering often scared her. Her eyes widened as she looked around them. 'Everything's so big . . .'

He laughed. 'You bet your life. And we think big too.'

'Where are we going to stay?' She stretched out like a cat. American travel wasn't like the English variety. Americans thought nothing of travelling hundreds of miles a day along their wide freeways in their air-conditioned automobiles with push-button control for almost everything you could think of.

'That's up to you. Round here we'll be spoilt for choice – it can be as uncivilised or luxurious as you want.' He glanced her way. 'You took me hiking in Purbeck. Now it's my turn; I'll show you my favourite trail.'

'What's it called?' Christie was really beginning to enjoy herself. This was more like it – seeing, truly seeing the country, and knowing it was just her and her father. No icy looks of disdain to fend off at the dinner table, no blow-by-blow account of the latest baseball game or the technicalities lurking under a car bonnet.

'Slide Mountain.' He pulled a face. 'There's a ranch resort not far away, and it'll be close to deserted at this time of year. You, my dear, will see the Catskills at their best.' He grinned. 'And when you've had enough of climbing mountains . . . we'll go to Woodstock.'

In the event, they stayed for almost a week at the ranch resort situated in a small hamlet that seemed carved into the very mountain slopes. Christie was enchanted with the Catskill mountains.

Every morning they got up late, ate a huge breakfast of eggs, waffles, pancakes and maple syrup, and then lingered over fresh coffee, planning their route for the day.

They would pack a few provisions in a back-pack, along with the compass and Marc's binoculars, don hiking boots, and set off on yet another trail. Every trail brought Christie a sense of adventure, every day a new wonder at the pure, panoramic size of this place, and the kind of winter-crisp views that stretched for ever into the distance, and quite took her breath away.

They were lucky. According to Marc, it was more usual to find snow at this time of year, and although they saw plenty on the peaks, one bright spring day of bitter sunshine followed another – perfect conditions for walking on the hard, frosty earth, their breath steaming around them, their faces freezing to the touch.

Each afternoon they returned in time for Christie to have a long soak in the bath and maybe write a letter to England, while Marc showered and read the paper, sometimes making a few phone calls to Boston. Then it was time for dinner – and dinners here had to be eaten to be believed. There were huge bowls of home-made soup with loaves of crusty malted bread and great slabs of butter. There were giant baked potatoes, massive pieces of steak or fresh tuna, salmon or lobster. All this was accompanied by an abundance of salad, every variety imaginable, and washed down by Chablis or Beaujolais followed by mocha coffee, gateaux and fresh fruit.

'I must be putting on pounds.' Christie rubbed her stomach and groaned. But she didn't care. Truly she didn't care.

'You look kind of wonderful to me.' His gaze held a fatherly pride that made her shy. But she knew what he meant. She caught glimpses of herself as she got ready for bed, about to sink into the wonderfully comfortable four poster bed in her room, and she was astonished at the vivid eyed girl she saw there. Yes, she had filled out, but as Gramma had often told her, she had been getting too skinny. Her hair seemed to have grown and become bleached almost white by the harsh winter sun, her skin was glowing as a result of so much fresh air and exercise, and her blue eyes were simply alive.

That was my trouble, she thought as she crept between the covers. I wasn't living. Not properly. I was half dead back in Dorset. But this – this is living.

Several times she felt a stab of guilt at their hedonistic lifestyle, at what she was taking from Marc.

'Shouldn't you be back in Boston?' she worried. 'What about the business? The family?'

His dark brow furrowed for only a second. 'They can all manage just fine without me,' he informed her. 'I've organised it all down to the last detail. And I've got one heck of a good second-in-command.' His expression changed. 'So good that sometimes I reckon I should just chuck it in and let him take over.'

Then before Christie could reply, he said, 'Now where shall we go today . . . ?'

But the best part of it – by far the best bit for Christie – was talking to her father. Talking as she'd never talked with her mother. Talking about everything under the sun in a way she'd only ever before talked to Robin. Robin . . . The thought of him brought the only clouds that dimmed the days as they stretched into a week. Her failed marriage was a blot on her horizon that she yearned to wipe away. Sooner or later she must return to Purbeck. Return to Robin and whatever was left of their relationship. She shuddered at the thought. She couldn't run away for ever – or could she?

Her father was quieter when they reached the village of Woodstock. 'Not really a village any more,' he said ruefully, as they tried to find a place to park.

She knew he'd been trying to put it off. 'Have you never been back before?' she asked him gently.

Marc shook his head. 'And I'm beginning to think I was right not to.'

'Because?'

'Because it's so different.' He gestured towards the restaurants and the shops filled with a profusion of tourist dreams, from teddy bears to Woodstock T-shirts and key rings. The celebration of the famous festival would go on until the end of time, it seemed.

'It always is different, going back.' And Christie almost felt the older of the two as she watched him trying to accept the place that Woodstock had become – not a tourist trap exactly, but a place with a hard commercial edge that he insisted hadn't been there before. An innocent place, it had been, he said, this centre of art and music that he and her mother had lived in, loved in, that her mother had left just as she'd left him.

They 'did' Woodstock in just two days. He showed her where they used to live, where the concerts had been held, the site of the old playhouse. They visited the Artists' Cemetery, the monument to Johnny Appleseed. They wandered the streets, past shops selling the mystical, the spiritual, rock music regalia, discovering the head shop, which specialised in pipes and other equipment for drug use. He laughed.

'Want to go in?' she challenged him. Respectable now, was he?

'Don't tempt me.' But she saw his expression when they were passed by one of the old VW campers covered with graphic psychedelia, belonging to some travellers. For her father, it was all – like Faith – a long way away.

It wasn't long before they decided to head out of the town. Christie was glad that she'd seen it, doubly glad that she'd seen it with her father. But, as he said, nothing was the same second time around.

On the way to New Hampshire and the White Mountains, he asked her about Robin.

'You're not happy with him.' It was a statement rather than a question. 'Have you decided what to do?'

'I'm going to give it another try.' Christie straightened her shoulders. They had never tried quite hard enough. It would have been different if they had ever shared the kind of closeness and blossoming passion she'd always thought possible, before growing apart. Then they would have had it; maybe then she would have been free to move on. But this way there was such a sense of not knowing, such a conviction of the unfinished, like a chain still binding them together. 'I owe it another try,' she murmured softly.

'You be careful now, Christie.' He glanced at her and she wondered how much he could possibly know. But that part of her marriage was over, wasn't it? That sexual madness that threatened to destroy them both. It would have to be if she were to return. Time would do the trick, she was convinced of it. That madness had only been Robin's reaction to her infidelity, that was all. It was a punishment and it was over. It wasn't part of him, part of their life together, or in any way part of their future.

'I need to give us a decent chance,' she told him, speaking her thoughts aloud.

'But how long does it take to give a relationship a decent chance?' He braked too suddenly and she risked a covert glance at him. 'How hard do you have to try?'

'Is that how you feel too?' she dared to ask.

'Marriage is a trap.' She wasn't sure if he was answering her question, or if she should even have asked it. 'Marriage sucks you in and under.'

'Not always,' she insisted. She knew it didn't have to be like that. There was so much that could be positive in a marriage. Long-term partnership. Long-term commitment. The kind of love and sharing that wasn't desperate or frantic, but was based on trust and understanding. That was the kind of marriage she wanted.

But his eyes were fixed on the road. They had discussed so much, but she knew he found this hard. Emotions were so often hard for men.

'Mum still cares, you know . . .' she began.

'She wouldn't even see me after that first time!' He slammed a tight fist against the dashboard. 'Why the hell not?'

Christie flinched. 'I've never really understood Mum,' she confessed. 'But I think she's always been scared.'

'Scared?' His laughter was cruel. 'She might give that impression. She always did give that impression. But I've come to the conclusion that your mother is hard as nails.'

'No . . .' Christie knew he was wrong. She knew that her mother's apparent strength was an armour she'd cultivated over the years. She knew that there was a good deal about her life that her mother had been unable to tell her, and she knew that Faith was vulnerable rather than in control. She had simply built more effective bridges and barriers than most people managed – that was all.

'Glenda's eaten up with jealousy of Faith,' her father admitted, as if forgetting who he was talking to. 'I told her too many things about the past one night. I guess I was drunk. Drunk and bitter and expecting far too much of her.'

Christie nodded. 'That's why she hates me.'

'She doesn't hate you.' He said it automatically, his gaze swivelling to meet her more honest one. 'Okay, she thinks she does. But she doesn't know you. She only hates you because you're part of Faith.'

'Part of what you and Mum had,' Christie corrected.

He stared at her. 'That's right. That's exactly it. Because you've come from our love. And Glenda couldn't bear knowing that. She always wanted to be the only one.'

A love child. Christie closed her eyes. She'd never thought of herself like that before. And yet that's what she was, quite clearly. She smiled.

Marc put his foot on the accelerator. 'I've been patching up holes in my marriage since I can remember,' he said.

'And now?' She waited, sensing for the first time, that this was a period of crisis for her father too. Perhaps that was what had sent him to England. He too had to think about new directions, take stock of what had been lost, what was left and what might lie ahead.

'The patchwork is of my own making,' he said obliquely. 'What else do I have?'

'Don't forget what Mum told you. She never married.' Christie wasn't sure why she said this.

Marc raised dark cynical eyebrows. 'Maybe she's too good at running away.'

'I don't think that's it.' Christie smiled back at him. But if it was, then she herself must have inherited that tendency. She too kept running away. Was that why she was so determined to try again with Robin? Was she just fed up with being on the run?

Tucked away that evening in the paisley bedroom of their hotel in the White Mountains, a hotel full of Laura Ashley prints – so much more English than English hotels, American only with regard to its vast menu – Christie wrote once more to Fran. She'd heard nothing from her in reply, although her father had received mail forwarded to the Catskills from Boston. So why wasn't Fran replying to her letters? Robin hadn't written back either, but she hadn't really expected him to. Hoped, maybe, but that was all.

Still, she expected more from Fran. She wanted to reach beyond Fran's careless bravery and find out what really made her tick. Friends must have those kinds of honesty, mustn't they? They must know what lies underneath the social veneer.

'My father is being the perfect host,' she wrote. 'He's taken me to all the tourist places. Today it was the Polar caves and yesterday Lost River, two legacies from glaciers, mazes of caves, passageways and sculptured granite. The trails are incredible – well-marked but you hardly see a soul this time of year. One minute you're walking through some trees or crossing a stream then before you know it you come to a ridge looking down into the rapids of some gorge or other. Amazing! We're doing so much walking that I'd be stick thin if it weren't for all this wonderful food.' She hesitated, biting her pen.

'How's everything back home? I'm a bit worried about Robin – you know how things have been. I've written to him, but I don't want him to go under while I'm away.' That sounded presumptuous, but Fran would understand. Christie shifted in her chair. 'Would you go and see him, Fran?' This was asking a lot, she knew, since they'd never got on. But who else could she ask? She didn't want either Gramma or her mother to get any more involved in worrying over her marriage than they were already. And Fran was so good at providing a cool objective viewpoint.

Christie remembered their last conversation. 'I hope you haven't changed your mind about the psychology. I know you can do it. As for me, I'm having a great time, honestly. Dad . . .' Here she paused to stare at the word she'd written – a word she hadn't yet managed to say. 'Well, he's such a nice man. He's spoiling me – I hadn't even been here two days before he was taking me round the Faneuil Hall shopping centre in Boston, buying me all these fantastic clothes.'

Absent-mindedly, Christie touched the silk robe she was wearing, a shade of deep burgundy. It had been impossible to object in the face of her father's determination, knowing it made him feel good, as if buying her these material things made up for the past and a neglect that couldn't by any stretch of the imagination be called his fault. Anyway . . . She smiled. Glenda Dupont would have been absolutely impossible if she'd had to face her day after day dressed in old jeans and jumpers. There was something about the sleek lines of a well-fitting dress or jacket that gave a girl . . . well, confidence for starters.

She returned to her letter. 'We've done the Freedom Trail (a tour of the historical sites of the revolution, darling, nothing remotely to do with feminism), the Boston Tea Party, Paul Revere's house . . .' Christie hesitated – she was beginning to sound like a guide book. 'But I can't stay here for much longer. I can't get rid of the feeling that I'm copping out of real life all the time I'm here.' She sighed. 'And Dad's wife can't stand the sight of me,' she added as an afterthought.

'Write to the Boston address, Fran. I'll be back there by the time you get this. Please write soon.' Surely Fran would realise how much she needed to hear from her? Surely she must respond, however involved she was with her own life and with Dominic. Dominic . . .

Christie had a sudden flash of memory, an image of Dominic Redfern, tall, dark and dressed in black, his lean frame poised, his arms easing gracefully out and away from his body in a natural, effortless harmony of movement. Lost in the dance, lost in his own mental world. Why was it that no matter how many times she saw him, this remained the picture of him held in her mind?

Christie sighed. Here she was, having the time of her life, and yet the memories of Purbeck – of Robin and her marriage, of her mother's rejection, of Trevor and the business she herself had nurtured like a baby, of Fran and Dominic – continued to jostle and cavort for attention.

Why did she feel that she must get back to Purbeck, and quickly? That she risked losing everything from the old world? Why couldn't she let those she'd left behind simply get on with their own lives?

Somehow, it seemed impossible. It was as if she were joined to them, irrevocably joined. Purbeck, and the people who lived there, were apparently impossible to disregard.

21

Back in Purbeck, Isobel Vaughan was writing to her granddaughter, whom she missed much more than she'd bargained for.

'Don't worry,' she wrote, 'Trevor is doing a grand job of looking after the business.' Isobel smiled to herself. She'd been right – Trevor Swift had nothing to offer Christie in some departments, but a bit of responsibility had done him the world of good as far as his career was concerned.

'He's invested a fair bit in advertising,' she wrote. 'Not that a penny's been wasted as far as I can see. I think you'll find plenty of work waiting for Purbeck Garden Designs when you come home.'

If you come home . . . Isobel pushed the thought quickly from her mind. Of course she would come home. She had lost Faith too early, much too early, just at the time when mother and daughter were supposed to come close again after the trauma of adolescent conflict. Just when two women should re-emerge as two adults, each appreciating the other's independence and adulthood. That had never really happened between Faith and Isobel . . .

Isobel shook her head in reminiscence. Perhaps she should have been more honest with her. Why did parents always see their children as incapable of understanding anything but the simplest rules?

But if she lost Christie now, it would be much too soon. Christie was a married woman, she no longer lived at Yew Cottage. But it didn't *feel* as if she'd quite flown the nest. And Isobel didn't want her to fly, at least not for a while.

'What makes you think she doesn't want to come home?' Vincent had asked yesterday when Isobel had confided her fears. They talked more intimately now, although the subject of her family – those he saw as

Jack's family – still touched a raw nerve.

'It was something in her letter.' She waved the blue airmail sheet towards him. 'A distance. As if being in the States isn't just a holiday.'

'She has a husband to come home to, doesn't she?' Vincent growled, his thin fingers plucking at a loose thread on the faded cardigan he wore.

'But does she?' Isobel was thoughtful. There was a certain errand she had to do for Vincent – a duty she hated but performed once a month – which took her into Swanage, to the village square. She had been there last night, and she had seen . . . Well, she had seen Robin, his arm slung around some woman. A tart, no mistaking that. Isobel sighed. Skirt up to the top of her thighs, black stockings, high heels, thick make-up, too much cheap fashion jewellery. A type. A tart all right, and Robin certainly looked as though he was getting some of what was on offer. She sighed. Added to that, Dominic Redfern had dropped rather a bombshell earlier. What on earth was Robin Fifer up to?

'Christie should make up her mind where she's going and what she wants,' Vincent commented. 'She can't keep running back here every time they have a quarrel.'

'Oh, you're a fine one to talk.' Isobel couldn't help laughing. Had he forgotten the past they shared? Isobel's marriage to Jack and those clenched ready fists that had more than once sent her running to Vincent for consolation. He hadn't had a good word to say about marriage in those days.

But Vincent wouldn't be drawn back into memory. That particular light in his pale eyes had long since gone out. 'Roll me another, Isobel.' He leaned back his head.

Isobel groaned. The room was already thick with marijuana smoke. 'Haven't you had enough?' If he carried on like this she'd be back in Swanage before the week was out.

'You know it helps me relax.' His voice changed.

Isobel watched him. Where was Vincent going? She could feel him inching away from her these days. But where was there for Vincent to go?

Here perhaps? She painstakingly rolled him another joint of tobacco laced with the weed, as she called it. She'd been forced to learn how, Vincent couldn't possibly do it himself. It was true that the drug helped him relax, it was another MS patient whom they'd met at the hospital who had recommended it in the first place. But the amount Vincent was consuming these days made him practically comatose. She knew the stuff wasn't addictive – it was probably less harmful than alcohol – so why not? Vincent was looking for an escape route. Maybe it was part of her job to help him find one.

Isobel signed and sealed her letter to Christie, put another log on the fire, lit the low lamp and a scented candle, and settled back into her rocking chair. She had worked hard today, struggling to finish Dominic's sculpture. He had picked it up two hours ago.

Had he been pleased? She wasn't sure. The piece, meant to represent a kind of eternal woman – the kind that always stayed in your heart and mind – had emerged quite separate from her intention. It was a memorial to Amy all right, but did it represent the kind of memory Dominic wanted of his ex-wife? There was a hardness to the features, a kind of brittle quality of untruth, that echoed Amy's acting talents perhaps. Talents she'd used throughout her life, in Isobel's opinion.

A thought occurred to her. Was that why Dominic had asked her to do the sculpture, rather than some accommodating stranger? Because she knew her so well, and because she would refuse to pretend?

A smile had seemed to twitch at Dominic's lips as she unveiled the piece. 'Amy . . .' he said softly.

His hand stretched – apparently involuntarily – towards the wood. He touched the burnished cheek of the statuette. It wasn't perfect. In some ways the natural defects of yew wood had affected the design and the image itself. Dominic let out a sigh that might have been of regret as he let his hand fall to his side.

'Where will you put her?' Isobel was compelled to fill the silence. Of course, she wanted to know if he liked the sculpture, but she was wary of asking outright. What if he hated it? What if it hadn't been what he'd intended at all? What if this Amy – who really seemed to have a life of her own – would only hurt him rather than allow him to grieve in peace?

'In her house.' He glanced out the window of the studio where two men were waiting to help him move the statuette to its resting place. 'That's where she always belonged.'

Isobel nodded. He must still love her then, if he wanted to transform his own home into some sort of mausoleum for his dead wife. 'I think I'm going to miss her,' she said out loud.

His glance was sharp. 'You liked having her here, Isobel?' He sounded surprised. 'I would have thought she'd make you feel uncomfortable.'

'Well, I did have to cover her up a few times.' They both laughed.

It was true that the sculpture had seemed oddly capable of silent criticism. Isobel had often found herself talking to it, as if talking to a refreshingly quiet Amy, even asking its opinion. Sometimes it was something she needed to hear, although she might resent it at the time. Sometimes she went away, thought about it, and realised that Amy or the statue or her alter ego – whatever it was – was quite right. It was extremely irritating. And sometimes she just threw the black drape back over the figure because sometimes just looking at Amy's knowing face drove Isobel wild.

He took her hands. 'Thanks, Isobel.'

'Is it . . . ? I mean, is she . . . ?' How exactly could she put this?

'How else could she be?' His dark eyes were tinted with sadness.

Isobel felt the urge to put her arms around him, the urge to offer comfort.

But in a moment Dominic had reverted to his usual self, friendly, polite, but always formal, always holding back. And so Isobel only nodded and smiled. One day perhaps they might talk about it. But not today . . .

It was in the morning that Isobel found him.

She slipped in with his early morning tea, and pulled the curtains as she always did, her mind still on Christie and Faith. Her dreams last night had been strange fragments of the past. Fractured moments – when she'd discovered that she was pregnant with Faith, the day she had moved into Yew Cottage, the time when Christie had been left in her arms. And images, half-forgotten images, drifting past her eyelids – Jack's handsome face, his big hands moving towards her, Faith storming up the stairs before she left for France, Vincent's expression as he told her of his illness, Christie's confusion last New Year's Eve in Swanage. Voices too, humming through from the old days, Vincent reciting the poetry of Wilfred Owen. Smells – Jack's aftershave splashed carelessly on to his dark face, Vincent's tweed, the sweet scent from the marijuana he smoked to ease his pain . . . A kaleidoscope of restlessness, last night had been.

'How are you feeling today?' She opened the window. It was a beautiful spring morning. He might feel brighter today, more hopeful, ready with the old repartee. Yesterday he had seemed – well, different somehow,

'Cat got your tongue, has it?'

No reply.

'Vincent?' She spun around, knowing something was wrong. He was always awake at this time, always he would complain of the cold, the heat, or the sun being too bright.

The figure on the bed was still . . . lifeless. 'Vincent?' He was already cold to her touch.

Isobel stared at the man who had given her so much, taken so much, been such a part of her life.

'Vincent,' she murmured. Bending, she kissed his brow. 'Dear Vincent.'

He had been granted escape. He was different this morning too. He was at peace at last.

Isobel asked Faith to come round an hour before they were due to leave for the funeral service. They must talk. She knew they must talk.

Faith was quiet and subdued, her eyes empty. 'I'm sorry, Mum.'

Her daughter hadn't called her that for almost thirty years. 'I want to tell you about your father,' she said softly. Time for honesty at last. 'Come inside.'

Warily Faith complied. 'Now?'

'Now.' Isobel settled herself in the rocker. This was long overdue. She took a deep breath. 'You always wanted to know why I left Jack.' She searched her daughter's face. 'You always blamed me for taking you away from him.'

Faith turned from her, as if unwilling to listen.

'But you see, my dear, it was impossible for me to stay.'

Faith heard the tale of Jack's violence in absolute silence. When Isobel had finished, she lit a cigarette, seeming unaffected, although her face was white, as if she'd been drained of feeling.

She had always half-known – that was the worst of it – always been aware that there was something, some knowledge that her mother was protecting her from.

'Why did he do it?' she asked. Why had her mother told her this? What did she expect her to say?

'I don't know.' Isobel's eyes were closed. Her face was lined in weariness. The exhaustion from looking after Vincent Pascoe . . .

'Maybe he couldn't bear to see you with another man.' Faith was perversely pleased to see her mother's eyes snap open.

'It wasn't that. He knew nothing about Vincent. And Vincent came later.' Isobel seemed angry. She was right to be angry, of course – nothing could excuse a man beating up his wife. Faith couldn't think about it, couldn't bear to imagine her adored father doing that – and to the mother she loved. She felt tears stinging her eyes.

'I married him knowing next to nothing about him,' Isobel continued. 'He went away to fight in the war, and I tell you, I ached for him to come back to me.'

Faith blinked. 'You loved him then?' She thought she recalled a one-sided relationship – her father pouring out affection in that way he'd had, and her mother . . . Her mother preferring a wet fish like Vincent Pascoe.

'Of course I loved him.' Isobel stared at her, and Faith caught a flash of what her mother had been like when she'd met Jack Vaughan. Of how bowled over she must have been by the good-looking young man with the broad shoulders and rich laughter.

'What went wrong?' she began. 'I still don't understand why he . . . ?'

'Maybe he got a taste for it in the war,' Isobel said. 'Some did. Some of their women put up with it.'

'But not you.' Faith stubbed out her cigarette.

'I put up with it for seven years.'

Seven years . . . Faith wandered over to the window. Seven years was a long time. 'But why didn't he ever come and see me?' she whispered. That was what hurt the most. 'Why did it have to be so . . . so *final*?'

'He must have thought it was best that way.' Isobel spoke slowly. Faith could see how much this was costing her – even talking of the past.

But she had to know it all. Still she worried at it. 'Other fathers see their daughters, don't they? Even if their wives have married again?' She folded her arms tightly, hugging them in to her chest as if she could stop the emotions spilling out of her. 'I know he hit you, Mum. But I can't help loving him . . .'

Faith could feel the tears, damn it. She had to go on. 'He was like the bright light of my childhood.' How could she explain about the darkness that had come when the lights went out? How the rest of her life – what was left – had remained in sad shadow?

'He may have been violent at times. But it wasn't all bad, my dear,' Isobel said softly. 'Don't think that. You don't have to stop loving him.' She paused. 'He loved you.'

'I loved a child too,' Faith murmured. 'And I let her go . . .'

'That was different.' Her mother looked up.

256

'Not so different.' Faith stared out into the darkness. 'We both had a choice. I had a choice as much as Dad ever did.'

'You were only a child yourself.' Isobel spoke gently.

'No.' Faith shook her head. 'I wasn't a child – I was a mother.' And it wasn't possible to be both. She had been confused when she'd run away from America and the man she loved. But she hadn't been a child. Childhood had been swept away by Marc and the independence she'd experienced but never claimed as her own.

Isobel was silent.

'I had my reasons . . .' Faith hesitated. 'I thought that I'd never be able to bring Christie up in the way she deserved. I thought she'd be better off with you.' She lit another cigarette. And she hadn't changed her mind so very much. At least Christie was well-balanced and cheerful. Could she possibly have turned out that way with Faith – along with her inevitable emotional baggage – as a mother?

'You did your best,' Isobel told her. 'That's all any of us can do – what we think is best.' She rose wearily to her feet. 'But there comes a time when we realise we've made a mistake. When we have to come clean . . .'

Faith hardly seemed to be listening to her.

'He beat you,' she was saying, as if it had just sunk in. 'He beat you and yet you stayed with him for seven years. My own father . . .'

'He's not,' Isobel blurted.

'What?' Faith stared at her. 'What are you telling me?'

'He's not your father.' Isobel said it again, firmer this time.

'But . . . ?' Faith looked wildly around. 'Then who?' Her brain was racing. 'Who is my father?' All these years of missing him, all those years of loving him. All those years of hating. Hating her mother, hating Vincent Pascoe . . .

'Vincent!' She hardly dared speak his name. She looked up, saw the truth written in her mother's eyes. 'Not Vincent?'

Who was she then? Who was she really? Someone must have picked her up, plonked her down in some imaginary landscape and said: this is who you are, where you belong; the rest was a joke. A sick joke. 'No.' Faith laid her warm cheek against the window-glass. Not Vincent . . .

'I'm so sorry, my dear.'

Faith heard the words from afar. Was she sorry? Was she really sorry?

'How do you know?' she asked at last. The way she understood it, she could have been either man's daughter.

'Jack and I went a while without making love,' Isobel told her. 'It was after one of his . . .' she hesitated, ' . . . more vicious beatings. He felt guilty. He was always sorry afterwards.' She closed her eyes as if the pain could still reach her. 'So I knew. I always knew you were Vincent's child. Most of the time we were pretty careful. But once . . .' Her voice tailed off. Her lips formed a half-smile as if recalling the good times.

'But he was your lover.' Faith stared at her. 'He must have suspected.'

Isobel got heavily to her feet. This was a problem she had often grappled with. Surely any man would have wondered? Faith was right. 'When I found out I was pregnant I decided not to see Vincent for a while,' she said. 'I thought I should try to make a go of it with Jack. He was my husband. I had to give it another chance.' And Vincent obviously wasn't too good at mathematics, she added silently. He had, she was sure, never made the connection.

'So you pretended I was your husband's baby?' Faith's voice was dense with sarcasm. Isobel remembered it so well, this terrible sarcasm of Faith's that she used to blanket all her hurts, to hide her vulnerability.

'Yes,' she admitted. 'I pretended you were Jack's baby. When all the time I knew. I thought it was for the best.' She turned to face her, glad now that the truth was out in the open, no longer an unspoken wall between them. Whatever Faith felt, whatever she said, at least there was honesty now between them.

'For the best,' Faith murmured. For a moment her expression softened as if she were recalling her own dilemma. 'But why?'

'I didn't want to be labelled. I was scared to be labelled.' Isobel unclenched her tight fists, stretched her arthritic fingers. Soon her sculpting days would be over.

Faith remained silent. Silent and listening, her eyes hurting, her hair tangled around the heart-shaped frame of her face. Isobel could hardly bear to look at her.

'And I didn't want *you* to be labelled.' Isobel's voice became more urgent. 'People weren't as blasé about illegitimacy as they pretend to be now. I didn't want you to carry the stigma and the shame of it all your life.'

'But you were prepared to let me think the man who beat you up was my father,' Faith pointed out.

'It wasn't an easy decision.' If Faith only knew how many nights she had lain worrying while the baby was slowly growing inside her. If Vincent had been a different kind of person, then maybe . . . But, no. It was wrong to blame Vincent. She had never given him the opportunity for an opinion.

'Would Vincent have wanted me?' Sometimes, Faith was too perceptive for her own good.

Isobel blinked. 'I don't know.'

'He wouldn't, would he?' Faith laughed. 'He never really liked children, did he?'

Isobel stared at her. The truth, now. She was committed to that. 'No, I didn't think he would want a baby.' Although . . . Who knows, when it's your own? Or when you think it's your own? She hadn't even been sure that Vincent had wanted her. After all, he had never asked her to be with him, had he? He had never invited her to move in, or to marry him, or to share his life in any way. In any way that meant something – other than snatched visits including sex and typing in a mix that was sometimes heady, more often faintly degrading.

'And he didn't find it rather odd that you went back to him after six months with a baby in tow?' Faith shook her head in disbelief. 'Surely he must have guessed.'

No, he hadn't seemed to wonder. He had merely taken her words at face value. Yes, she had tried again with Jack, and yes it had failed as Vincent had predicted. There was a baby to show for it. So what? How did a baby in her Jack-world affect what she had with him?

She got up, went to her daughter and took her in her arms. 'I'm sorry, Faith.'

Their eyes met. She could see Faith struggling with it, as she too had struggled. 'I was wrong. I should never have tried to live a lie, forced you to live a lie.'

'We should be going.' Faith took her arm and Isobel knew that she had done the right thing at last. Some kind of forgiveness was there in her daughter's touch.

'Yes, of course.' Isobel opened the front door of Yew Cottage as Faith turned to her, eyes wet with tears.

'It's time to lay Vincent to rest,' Faith said.

259

22

Christie spent her last day in Boston whale watching.

'You have to,' her father told her. 'Everyone does. If you have a good trip, you'll remember it when everything else has gone plain out of your mind.'

Christie doubted it. What she would remember most about this country was the panoramic beauty of the National Parks and the winter wilderness of the trails. Chatting to her father in front of a blazing log fire, making her discovery of him into the memory she'd cherish. Those were the things that had made it a trip of a lifetime.

In the event, however, he had a point. It was a cold day, and there weren't many prepared to face the stormy, unpredictable Atlantic at this time of year. But there was something special about being out on a lonely vessel, a speck in an ocean stretching into an interminable distance of grey sea and grey sky, scouring the freezing water for glimpses of those dark companions arching through the rolling waves and spume. The marvellous sensation of nearness, as a whale or a dolphin reared from the waves almost near enough to touch, wasn't one she could have envisaged. And she was close enough to look them in the eye, an eye sunken in great glistening curves of flesh and blubber, close enough to be soaked with spray from the heaving and splashing of the great creatures, and from the massive waves that crashed into the boat making it reel precariously. She hung on to the rails until her fingers were wet and numb, balancing, feet apart, with some difficulty, to take pictures. She'd used two reels of film, but Christie still wasn't sure that she'd captured them in the least, not convinced that these creatures in their natural habitat could be observed in any but the most fleeting manner, any more than they could be controlled.

'Thanks, Dad,' she said as the car drew up beside the house in Old Boston.

'For what?' He tried to hide it, but she sensed his pleasure.

'For that.' She pointed back towards the sea. 'And for taking the time to be with me, for showing me where you live. For the past seven weeks. About the best weeks of my life.' Her face was still flushed with the exhilaration of the whale watching expedition. His too, she realised.

Marc smiled. 'I loved every minute of it.' His words were studied and slow. 'It felt good, like seeing it all through new eyes,' he added half to himself, as he glanced in the mirror, making no move to get out of the car.

'Aren't you coming into the house?' She surveyed his damp dark hair, the soaked collar of the sweatshirt that hadn't been protected by his wet weather gear. It had certainly been wild out there today.

'I have a couple of errands to do.' He indicated the briefcase slung in the back of the car. 'Tell Glenda I'll be tied up for about an hour. She's not expecting us until dinner time at any rate.' He wagged his finger. 'And get yourself out of those wet things. Okay?'

Christie was grinning as she ran up the path. She put the key he'd given her in the lock of the front door. It might not be quite such fun back in Boston with the rest of her father's family breaking up their intimacy, but she'd had more than her fair share of him and she was grateful. It would have to last her for quite some time.

The living-room door was shut, but she could hear the sound of Vivaldi's Four Seasons rising to a crescendo. Glenda was most particular about music and moods. She preferred neither classical, rock, jazz nor rhythm and blues. But what she did play was a careful selection from each, depending on circumstance. Christie waited for a pause between movements before opening the door. 'Dad says . . .' she began.

She blinked, frozen to the spot. Her wet hair was dripping down her neck, and her damp leggings were beginning to cling unpleasantly.

Glenda was half-lying on the Chesterfield, her legs – clad in black stockings – elegantly draped over the tapestry cushions, her skirt half way up her thighs. Her blouse was undone, slipping over her white shoulders, her bra was unclasped, and one of her perfectly formed breasts was being sucked with childish passion. They were too perfectly formed, Christie found herself observing with unexpected objectivity. Definitely not the untampered-with breasts of a woman of Glenda's age . . .

'You!' Glenda pushed the blond head of her son's friend Bobby, away from her breast. 'Get out.' Her eyes were slits of fury. 'Get out of here.'

'I'm sorry . . .' Christie took a step backwards. She knew she must look a fool. But she couldn't stop staring at the two of them, woman and boy, staged in this bizarre scenario. Her step-mother – although she could hardly think of her that way – the elegant, immaculate and classy Glenda Dupont, half-undressed like a character from some porn movie, allowing some kid to do *that* . . . It was mind-boggling.

'Out!' Glenda rose from the sofa, re-buttoning her blouse with remarkable poise. Christie was unable to take her eyes off her. Still not a hair out of place, but her eyes were flashing warning signals. Vivaldi moved smoothly into Autumn.

Glenda turned to Bobby. 'And you. Out.'

His face was crimson with embarrassment, poor lad. Christie felt strangely sorry for him as he left the room, head hung low, burly shoulders unfitting on someone who was just a kid. He was unable to even glance her way. And Christie couldn't look at her step-mother. She turned to make for the stairs. Raced up them two at a time.

'Where's Marc?' Glenda was following her. 'Christie! I said where's your father?' In seconds she had caught her up, trapped her against the wall of the landing. She was out of breath, the beginnings of panic flaring in her angry eyes, the heaving of her breasts. She pushed her face closer. 'Jesus. He's not here, is he?' She gazed wildly around. 'He didn't come back with you?' Her hands trembled, her thin mouth squeezed into a tight red dash of fear on her face.

'He said he'd be home in an hour.' Christie drew back as far as she could. The disgust she felt for her father's wife would show in her eyes, she knew it would. And she didn't give a damn.

Glenda leaned still closer. Waves of rich perfume rose into nausea. Opium. Yves St Laurent, she registered blindly.

'You haven't seen a thing,' Glenda intoned. 'Do you understand me? Not a goddamn thing.'

Christie turned her face away. The woman had hated her even before she'd set foot in this house, and now she expected her to defend her sordid little secrets. Why the hell should she? 'You mean, don't tell my father?'

'That's exactly what I mean and you know it, you little . . .' Glenda tailed off, as if recalling Christie's new influence on her life. She breathed deeply. 'That's exactly what I mean. Do I have your word?'

Christie stared at her. 'I won't tell him because he would be hurt and humiliated,' she said softly. 'Not because of your threats. And not because of any promises – I don't intend to make any.'

'Oh, very high and mighty, aren't we?' Glenda's harsh laughter rang throughout the hall. 'Very sanctimonious, holier than thou.'

Christie waited. She knew there'd be more. A woman like her step-mother would have much more to say than that.

'Let me tell you something, you little bitch . . .' Glenda's voice was slurred, and Christie realised that she'd been drinking, probably heavily. It had not escaped her notice that Glenda's brittle and social veneer sometimes looked a little flawed and fragile. Neither could she ignore the fast-depleting bottle of tequila in the drinks cabinet that was unobtrusively replaced most days. But however unhappy she was – and it didn't take a genius to work out that their marriage had its problems – that didn't excuse her. Infidelity was one thing – Christie was hardly the person to judge that – but to choose her own son's best friend . . . That was another thing entirely. It was sordid and humiliating. And if her father were to ever find out . . .

But Glenda was still raving. 'You don't know what that man has done to me. You don't have to look at me like I'm a piece of shit. If you knew the half of it . . .'

Christie wasn't sure she wanted to know any of it. She was being berated by a woman whom she'd just discovered in the throes of fulfilling some kind of adolescent fantasy. Here she was, dripping on the exquisite pile carpet, only wanting to peel off her wet clothes and climb under the shower. She didn't want to hear this. She didn't want justification or abuse or to be involved in any capacity whatever. But she knew that Glenda would never allow her to leave before she'd said her piece.

'He's my father,' she said at last, when she paused for breath. 'I love him. But your problems are your own affair.' Affair . . . She bit her lip as, too late, she considered her unfortunate choice of words.

'You love him,' Glenda jeered. 'And he loves you. He loves your mother too. Did you know that? Jesus – talk about happy families. But where does that leave me and the boys, I'd like to know?'

'Glenda, I . . .' She got no further.

'He's never wanted me. He's always hankered after your mother, and I know it. Second best, that's me.'

'I'm sure you're wrong.' Christie didn't like the way this conversation was developing. Why didn't her father come home? Why couldn't she be on a plane going back to England? Why couldn't she be anywhere rather than here, listening to this woman, her father's wife, who was turning out to be quite different from the image she'd presented up till now.

'It's true.' Glenda swayed closer. 'He's never wanted me. But there sure have been plenty that have.'

Christie tried to edge past. 'I really must get out of these wet clothes.'

With a moan, Glenda Dupont leaned heavily against the wall, and Christie slipped past her, into the relative sanctuary of her room.

'I want you out of here,' she heard Glenda shrieking after her. 'I want you out of this house, d'you hear?'

She needn't have worried. Christie had no intention of staying.

In the taxi from the airport, she fingered the last letter she'd had from her mother, less than a week ago. It was a hopeful letter. She wrote that she was looking forward to seeing Christie again, and that she wanted it to be a new start between them. An honest start. At the end, she'd written some words that haunted Christie and made her realise how much she longed to see her again.

'I know you feel I've cheated you out of a father . . . but at the time it felt like I was protecting you. Don't ask me from what. I couldn't cope, Christie, I have to admit that now. I couldn't cope with that world I was existing in, and I couldn't cope with the responsibility of another life. I failed you, I suppose. You don't have to tell me that.'

No, her mother hadn't failed her, Christie thought as the taxi pulled up at last outside Yew Cottage, the end of an interminable journey. Her mother had given her life where someone else might not have had the courage. She had done what she considered best. Despite her own feelings, she had given Christie to Gramma to look after. She had cared and she had returned. After all, what might Christie herself have done in the same set of circumstances? What right did she – or anyone else – have to judge or blame?

When she arrived at the familiar building of Purbeck stone, Christie was disappointed to find Yew Cottage deserted. It was strange to be back on English soil. Even after such a short time she felt Americanised in some indefinable way. And the cottage itself seemed different, a blank face replacing its habitual warm welcome.

She phoned her mother's flat but there was no answer. Where on earth was everybody? She considered phoning Robin, and found herself dialling

Fran's number instead. That was safer. And she was more than a little curious. Fran had not replied to her letters and she wanted to find out why.

'Christie?' Fran sounded weird. 'Does . . . does anyone know you're back?'

'You're the first.' Christie laughed, but there was no response. 'I tried to phone from the airport. I got an earlier flight.' The scene with Glenda had shaken her more than she cared to admit. Her father had seemed surprised, but he hadn't tried to stop her, or – thank God – cross-question her about it.

'You never wrote to me,' she accused, half-teasing.

'No, I didn't.' There was an awkward silence.

'Is anything wrong?' Christie wished she could see her face. Fran was hiding something from her – she was convinced of it.

'Of course not.' Fran tried to laugh and failed. 'I've been terribly busy. You know how it is . . .' Christie was sure she heard her voice catch with some indefinable emotion.

'A job?'

'No . . .'

'Studying?'

'Heavens, no.' For a moment she sounded like the old Fran.

Christie hesitated. 'A new man?' She thought of Dominic. Hardly a new man. A man who had been in Fran's life for such a long time.

'You could say that.' Fran laughed, but Christie didn't like the sound of it. There was an artful quality in Fran's voice that reminded her of something. Or someone . . .

She gripped the receiver more tightly. 'When shall we meet?' Her words dropped into the strained silence, standing on the borderlines, threatening this stilted conversation. What was happening here? Could she and Fran have drifted so far apart in just two months?

'I'm a bit rushed this week,' Fran told her. 'I'll try and ring you sometime.'

A bit rushed? Ring you some time? Christie stared at the phone in her hand. Fran was the closest friend she had. Perhaps it was true that they had less in common than they used to, perhaps Fran no longer needed her in the way she had seemed to need her before. But they hadn't met for two months. How could she be too busy to see her? She groaned silently. It must be Dominic. There could be no other reason. Dominic wanted to destroy their friendship. He wanted his step-daughter to himself.

She took a deep breath. 'I must see you, Fran. I need to see you.' If she could just talk to her . . .

'I can't.' Fran's voice became brittle, almost unrecognisable. 'Not right now. I'm sorry.'

'I see.' Christie hardened her heart. 'Then I may as well say goodbye.' She slammed the phone down, instantly regretted it and waited for Fran to phone her right back. She didn't.

Disconsolately Christie wandered outside, picking her way down the path to the yew grove. America had given her a new positive outlook, almost made her forget the problems with Robin. Her life had been decidedly threadbare around the edges. But all that was changing, wasn't it? A new beginning . . .

There was a dim and sombre atmosphere in the yew wood today. It was dark as death, a damp afternoon, the kind of early spring afternoon that made it seem unlikely that winter would ever end. The dampness was clinging to the old red bark, the dingy green needles and the rotting humus at her feet.

Heedless of the soft wet sponginess that would soon soak through her jeans, Christie perched on the low mossy branch where she sat so often, and took stock.

She would start her life from this point, looking firmly to the future. She would make Trevor a partner in the business, so that she could slide more responsibility his way and spend more time with Gramma and her mother. And Robin.

Christie jumped down from the branch, almost tripping on the jutting roots. She bent close to the hollow of the tree, its coronet of fungi laced by cobweb-wheels. She breathed deeply, sniffing the damp and the rotting wood, the sharp scent of the needles. She dropped to her knees and allowed her body to slowly sink down to the damp earth. Was she mad? She stared up. Above her, a small spiral of sky was just visible through the branches of the yews. The outside world seemed a long distance away. She closed her eyes and slept.

When at last she awoke, Christie realised she must have been there for a long time. Her limbs were stiff, her skin chilled. The sky had become almost dark and edgeless, merging into the blackness of the trees. Only a faint shaft of light signalled the presence of a bald moon. The wood was silent.

Reluctantly Christie brushed her damp clothes down and made her way back to the cottage, turning for one last long look at the yew trees whose tentacled branches spiked the night.

Outside the cottage they stood, waiting for her. Gramma, her mother, and a few other half-strangers. They were dressed in black. Christie wondered if she were still dreaming, still asleep in the yew grove, still drenched in its dark secrets. But it all seemed very real. She stared at them. 'What . . . ?'

Faith sensed her mother about to move forwards to Christie, and she stayed her with a hand on her arm. 'Let me.'

She stepped hesitantly, unwilling to break the trance-like state that Christie seemed to be in. Her cornflower-blue eyes were wide and unblinking, her limbs moving as if she were under someone else's control.

As she reached her, Christie looked into her eyes. 'Mum . . . ?' And Faith saw that whatever she'd dreaded, whatever she'd done, her daughter had forgiven her. Thank God.

'Darling.' She folded her in her arms. She had been in the yew grove, this precious daughter of hers. Faith smelled the fragrance of the yews themselves in her daughter's hair, and for a moment she allowed herself to drift back to childhood traumas, teenage rebellions. There was only one place she ever used to run to, since they'd come to Dorset. The yew grove had been her sanctuary, her peace. And when Christie was born . . .

'I brought you here when you were a baby,' she whispered. 'We sat in the yew grove, you and I. It was the only place where we could be alone together, you and I.'

She saw Christie absorbing her words. At last she nodded. 'What's happened?' She was shivering uncontrollably.

'It's Vincent, darling,' Faith told her. She could hardly find the words to tell her. 'We tried to get in touch with you before. But when we heard you were coming home . . .'

Christie had hardly recovered from the shock of Vincent's death by the following day when she went to Ulwell to see Robin. Gramma was acting strangely. She'd said there was something Christie should know, but then refused actually to spit it out.

'You've heard about Vincent?' she said as he opened the door.

He nodded. 'I'm sorry.'

She stared at him. Was he sorry? She didn't like the look of Robin at all – he seemed older, more weary than when she'd seen him last. And there was a kind of hopelessness about him that didn't bode well for the new beginning she had in mind. His hair was tangled and uncombed, his clothes crumpled on his spare frame, and he didn't look as if he'd washed for a week. As for being sorry about Vincent – well, they were all sorry. But there had also been a kind of relief in the faces that had huddled around the fire at Yew Cottage last night, talking it out, sharing their different kinds of grief. Vincent had been immersed in more than one kind of pain. For Vincent, Gramma insisted, it was release.

Gramma said he'd been tired of that pain, weary of the frustrations that had made him cruel at times. He never intended to be cruel, she said. Gramma said lots of things, talking quickly in that bird-like way she had, as if those things needed to be said for someone's protection.

Whilst Faith had cried. Yes, her mother had cried, on and on in a way that Christie had never seen her cry before, as though Vincent had meant so much to her, as though she'd never hated him at all.

She watched Robin cautiously. 'Can I come in?'

He stepped back, hands thrust deep in the pockets of his jeans. 'How was America?'

She shrugged. 'It was good.' She wondered whether or not to kiss him. Surely it was appropriate, and yet she shrank from it somehow.

Robin nodded. 'Bad news to come home to.' He held himself slightly hunched as always, but away from her as if she were a threat. It made Christie sad. Was she deluding herself – to think they could begin again?

'How have you been?' To avoid looking at him, she went into the sitting-room, moved towards the patio doors, pushed them open and walked into their garden. The garden that she had created for them both – a spring garden now, with a meandering path, curving beds, crocuses and snowdrops scattered under the maple by the pond, and a bank of blowsy daffodils lining the far fence. Almost as she'd envisaged it. Soon the white roses with the sweet heady perfume would be clambering the back wall. Would she see them clamber any higher? Would she sniff their fragrance on the breeze?

'I've been busy.'

Christie looked at him. 'Too busy to think about what I said?' She wouldn't allow him to evade the issue. It must be settled, and the sooner the better.

'A new start?'

Christie nodded. Robin still wouldn't look at her. 'A new start,' she murmured. But it felt all wrong. This seemed so wrong. Suddenly she wasn't sure if she even felt anything for this man any more. Why was she so determined to make it work between them? Was it just that she couldn't bear to fail?

He took a step towards her – she'd swear he knew what she was thinking. He said, 'But it'll be different this time.' Softly.

'I certainly hope so.' She said it without thinking, referring to the aggressive brand of sexuality he'd forced on her, the sexuality that had made her doubt herself, like nothing else ever had. And then she became conscious of a new light in the hooded grey eyes as he took a step towards her.

'Oh yes, Christie.' He was close, very close. He took her chin between his finger and thumb, forcing it upwards until she was looking into those eyes. 'Very different.'

'A partnership.' She broke away, feeling her heart thumping against her ribcage. This was a mistake. That's all she could think. This was a mistake and she was being sucked into it again.

Robin laughed. 'Oh, no.'

'No?' She stared at him, mesmerised.

'You forget. I learnt a lot from my mother.' Turning from her, he stooped to pick a tiny white crocus.

'Your mother?' She was confused. Or were they getting to the truth at last?

'My mother.' He began to shred the delicate white petals between his fingers. The last of the late crocuses, she thought.

'She understood so much about being the boss,' he said vaguely.

'The boss . . .' Christie didn't trust this conversation. She didn't trust Robin.

'She was always the boss, just like you were always the boss, Christie.' He strolled towards the fence. 'Someone has to be, don't they? One's the boss and the other is the one who gets bossed around. Stands to reason.'

'It doesn't have to be like that.' She followed him.

'Oh, but it does.' He smiled, a narrow, evil kind of smile that she hated. 'My mother was the boss because she was pure and good. But you don't deserve it, Christie. Because you're nothing but a dirty little slut.'

'Oh, for heaven's sake.' She turned, beginning to move away, but, like lightning, he grabbed her wrist, pulling, twisting, his fingernails digging an ugly welt into her skin.

'You're a slut, Christie,' he repeated. 'So if we get together again it's on my terms. Do you understand? I'll be the boss – in every way.'

She stared at him, shocked into silence. He was no longer hurting her wrist, or maybe she had lost all feeling. But his skin was still touching hers, and there was an air of repressed violence in the atmosphere between them. She glanced over his shoulder. In the distance an ominous regiment of dark clouds were gathering greyness, gathering force, and she shivered. It wasn't summer yet. She had to stand up to him now or she'd be lost for ever. He was waiting, a half-smile on his face. Waiting for capitulation.

'Oh, yeah?' She glared at him. 'Forget it, then. That's not how it'll be. No way.'

His eyes glazed over as if he'd hardly heard her. 'I failed her, you know.' Abruptly, Robin let go of her wrist and she staggered, almost fell. His thin shoulders were shaking. Christie knew she should leave, get out while she could, but she felt compelled to stay, needing to discover the truth.

'How did you fail her?' Christie knew he was talking about his mother. Somehow, that woman had warped Robin's entire judgement as far as women were concerned.

'I was never what she wanted. I'd have had to be bloody sexless to be what she wanted.' He sighed. 'And when she died I wasn't even around.'

'Where were you?' Never before had he talked of this. Never before. If he had . . . well, maybe it could have been different.

'On holiday,' he groaned. 'The first one I'd ever had without her. I went with some mates. She didn't want me to go. But I was stifled. I had to get away from her. She said that she needed me . . .' His voice tailed off.

'It wasn't your fault.' Christie spoke automatically. 'Please, Robin, try to understand . . .' Her arms reached out to offer comfort. But he pushed her away.

'I hated her,' he said.

And all women. All women who turned out to be human, rather than the ideal of purity his mother had forced him to expect. The idea was irrefutable. Robin hated all women. Why hadn't she seen it before? Everything fell into place for Christie. There was no future for her and Robin. How could there be? There would only be hatred and violence, never love.

'I thought I could make you happy.' He stepped closer. She realised that the aggression was unquelled in his eyes.

Christie looked around at the new-born garden, now in its third year. The garden she'd had so much hope for. 'You need to make yourself happy first,' she said softly. She turned to go.

Her heart was hammering ferociously with every step as she walked with a carefully measured pace back through the patio, crossed the sitting-room into the hall and out of the front door. But Robin didn't try and stop her.

When she reached the safety of the truck, she let out the breath she'd been holding. Where now? Gramma had said that Yew Cottage was her home for as long as she wanted it, perhaps for ever. And why not? There was no future for her in Ulwell. She couldn't stay and fight with Robin all her life.

'Why does it have to be a fight?' She spoke aloud as she started the truck's engine. She was fighting for her sexuality, for her right to possess her own identity, her own independence.

She remembered what Gramma had said about being lucky. Yes, she had more choices than women ever had before. But did that make her more fortunate? More possibilities made for harder decisions. And which decisions were worth fighting for?

'But I'm fighting to be me,' she whispered. 'That's all I want.' Damn conventions. Damn what everyone else wanted her to be. She was fighting for herself. How could it be too much to ask?

Early the next morning Christie drove to Wareham, to her mother's flat. Despite everything, it was good to be back in Purbeck once more, to see the proud ruins of Corfe Castle rear up from the morning mist against the backdrop of the Purbeck Hills, like some weird modernistic sculpture that no-one could hope to understand.

'Christie.' They embraced, and Faith led the way up to the flat.

'There's something I have to tell you,' Faith said sadly. 'About Vincent.'

'I already know.' Their eyes met. 'Gramma told me yesterday.' Gramma had told her the whole story as she sat in Beatrice's old rocking chair, with Christie at her feet, knees hunched to her chest. The whole story of Isobel, Jack, Vincent and Faith. They hadn't talked about it afterwards. It had been enough that the story was told. Gramma had seemed glad to release the truth, as if a burden had been shed. But Christie had still sensed there was more . . .

'How do you feel about it?' Faith asked her gently.

Christie shrugged. 'I never knew him, did I? The man you thought was your father. He was only ever a name to me.'

Faith shook her head, looked away, into the distance of the past perhaps.

'And Vincent was always good to me.' Christie watched her. 'I suppose I thought of him more as my grandfather than I did this person you called Grandad Jack.'

'You did?' Her mother's eyes were confused. 'I wish I . . .' She hung her head. 'I suppose I never gave him a chance.' She looked up. 'You must be upset – about his death, I mean.'

Christie frowned. 'Not exactly.' She and Vincent had never been close. She had witnessed his health deteriorate and she had watched his frustration and pain divide him from the world he lived in – herself included. Was she upset by his death? Like Gramma had said, it seemed more of a release somehow. Vincent never seemed destined for dependence on other human beings. Gramma might have offered, but he plainly detested the idea.

'I guess he won't be suffering any more,' Christie said. 'I can't object to that.'

'You sound so American.' Faith smiled.

'And you? Are you upset?' How did her mother now feel about the man she'd hated?

Faith looked away. 'It's too late for me to feel very much at all. That's what makes me sad.'

'But not too late for you and me.' Christie reached out, touched her mother's hand.

'No.' Faith drummed her fingers lightly on the table. 'Thank God.' She scrutinised Christie thoughtfully, and her expression changed. 'And how about Robin? Is it too late for you two?'

Haltingly, Christie told her what had happened.

'Hmm.' Faith put a cool hand on Christie's face. 'He was wrong for you. Some marriages simply don't work out. That's life. We don't have to stay trapped in them for ever.'

'Just like that?' Christie frowned.

Faith shook her head. 'Of course not. Never just like that. You should know.'

Christie eyed her thoughtfully. 'About Dad . . . ?'

'Yes?'

'You haven't asked about him, about his life.' This had been bothering her, especially since there was a new kind of peacefulness in her mother's demeanour – as if she'd come to terms with her life at last. Didn't she care about Marc Dupont any longer? Had Christie been mistaken?

She looked around the flat – it seemed different. A couple of bright tapestries had been hung on the walls, and over the mantelpiece was an Impressionist print – one of Renoir's café scenes, sensual, rich in colour and mood. An indigo throw obscured the black sofa, and a multi-coloured rag rug from Faith's Basement peeped out of the door that led to her mother's bedroom.

Faith got up to put some toast in the rack. 'No, I haven't asked about him.'

'Don't you want to know?' Christie stared at her. Come to think of it, she was behaving rather oddly too. Her hair was brushed into a different style, she was wearing a discreet amount of attractive make-up and Christie was sure she could detect a hint of the Armani perfume that her mother would never normally wear at this time in the morning . . . Unless she was expecting someone.

'Where are your cigarettes?' she asked.

'I've given up.' Faith smiled.

'Since when?'

'Since yesterday morning.'

Christie folded her arms and narrowed her eyes. 'Aren't you curious about Dad?'

Faith shrugged. 'Why should I be?'

'His marriage . . .' Christie began.

'I know.' She smiled once more.

What did she know? Why did she keep smiling? Christie spread butter and marmalade. And as she did so, she noticed an air mail letter at the far end of the table. She stopped, mid-bite, bending closer. It was her father's long, looping and untidy scrawl. 'Mum?'

'Yes?'

'What's this all about?' Christie pointed.

'What?' Infuriatingly her mother disappeared into the kitchen. When she came back, she was wearing a different smile – the enigmatic half-smile that told Christie nothing of what she was thinking. And she was humming softly. It was that old melody that Christie remembered from the visits of the beautiful stranger-mother of her childhood. The folk song that her father seemed to have equally etched on his memory.

So . . . She leaned back and watched her mother as she cleared the table. Secrets clinging to every part of her. She'd never change. Christie shook her head in mock despair. And she didn't want her to change. Inside, Christie was grinning so wide that she thought she'd burst. Could this be a signal for another beginning after all?

23

As the days passed, Christie felt more and more compelled to see Fran, determined to sort things out between them, to find out what had changed.

She went to the house on an April day when it didn't know whether to laugh or cry – scorching sun signalled an imminent downpour.

There was no car in the drive, but when she rang the bell it was answered by Dominic Redfern. The story of her life . . .

She took a step back, confused by the conflicting emotions that shot through her. It was the middle of Thursday afternoon, and she'd left Trevor in charge so that she could see Fran alone. Didn't this man ever work?

His face broke into a smile of welcome. 'Christie . . .'

Her nod was cool. She suspected that Dominic had helped to create the new tensions existing between herself and Fran. 'Is she here?' she demanded.

His expression changed to what looked like embarrassment. And with good reason perhaps. 'Fran? No, she's not.' With some effort his level gaze met hers.

'Are you sure?' Christie peered over his shoulder doubtfully, only to see his smile return. She looked away. What was it about this man that made her feel such a child?

'Why don't you come in and wait?' Almost as if he were daring her.

Christie hesitated. She didn't feel comfortable alone with Dominic, she never had. It wasn't just a matter of not trusting him. No. It was something else, some disturbing quality of self-possession he had.

'I don't bite.' Laughing, he opened the door wider. Leaving her no choice.

Christie walked into the hall. If she had an ounce of self-containment then she could have invented some place she had to be, glanced at her watch, said no with regret in her eyes. But by the time she thought of it, it was much too late. So she looked at Dominic's retreating figure instead, straight and lean, clothed in a checked red and brown shirt and jeans.

'Did you have a good time in the States?' he asked her.

'Wonderful. Absolutely wonderful.' She wondered idly if he was going away somewhere, if he was taking Fran. Where would a man like Dominic Redfern travel – the Far East perhaps? She could imagine him in Thailand or Singapore, perfectly confident with chopsticks and Oriental ways, practising his strange Chinese exercises with perfect balance and control. Dominic seemed to be the kind of man who could control whatever he touched. Was that what had happened with Fran? She shuddered involuntarily.

'Christie?'

'What?' She blinked. He was watching her with amusement once more. 'What did you say?'

'I was asking you what you thought of my latest acquisition.' He pointed to the stained glassed recess by the inner door.

'Oh.' Christie stared. It was a wooden statuette of Amy Redfern – or at least she thought it was Amy, although when she looked again, she wasn't so sure. And there was something else very familiar about it. She remembered the rough that she'd picked up in Gramma's studio. It was more of a universal then than an individual. It was a type of woman. So – she recalled her conversation with Gramma – it was Dominic who had loved Amy so very much. Was that why he had fallen in love with her daughter?

'Well?' He folded his arms.

'My grandmother's handiwork?' Tentatively, she reached out to touch the burnished shoulder. It was warm from where the wood had absorbed the sun, and yet there was something slightly forbidding about the piece. She shivered.

'It gets me a bit like that too,' he admitted. 'Don't you think Isobel's excelled herself?'

'It's certainly different.' Christie was curious. Why should this man want a statue of his ex-wife in the entrance hall of the house he now shared with her daughter? Didn't he feel in the least bit guilty?

'She seemed to belong here.' Dominic beckoned Christie into the kitchen, and she remembered the last time she'd been with him in this house, when she'd found him outside digging in the garden. It seemed like years rather than months ago.

'Does it comfort you – her presence here?' Christie couldn't imagine it somehow.

He shook his dark head. 'Hardly. But then she never comforted me when she was alive.'

She stared at him. Wasn't that rather – well, disrespectful? 'In that case, why bother?'

'It's more a case of laying her to rest.' He grinned. 'I thought Fran might appreciate the gesture.'

'And does she?' Christie's voice became cold once more.

His gaze barely flickered. 'Apparently not.'

'But if *you* like it . . .' She had the sensation that she was missing something here. What was he hiding from her? What was he trying to say?

'Me? I'm not here very much these days. I only came round today to pack some of my stuff.' His voice changed once more, and he looked away. Sadness? Regret? She couldn't be sure.

'I see.' She watched him, not seeing in the slightest. She couldn't work out what made Dominic Redfern tick. He didn't seem the sort of man to be doing what he was doing, and yet he was a mystery, wasn't he? And determined to remain that way it seemed.

He filled the kettle, his eyes staring sightlessly out of the window into the distance, towards the barrier of trees that made up Wareham Forest. 'Do you see?' He turned to face her, and she was shocked to recognise pain drawn into the hawk-like features, the creased brow, the wariness in his hazel eyes. 'Under the circumstances . . .' He seemed about to say more, hesitated, then apparently changed his mind.

Christie frowned. What circumstances? He was talking in riddles. And come to that, why wasn't he here in this house all the time, if he was in love with the daughter who was the image of her mother?

'I'll make some tea.' Dominic began to clatter mugs on to a tray. 'It's not my place to interfere. And I wouldn't want to hurt anyone.'

Christie gazed at him. 'I'm not thirsty.'

'Then I'll show you the garden.' Abruptly he took her hand, leading her into the conservatory and on outside. 'It's so beautiful at this time of year.'

She stared in surprise at the hand holding hers, the dark skin touching her skin, the black hair so close to her fingertips. She felt . . . What did she feel? She tried to feel nothing, but there was an undercurrent of heat that startled her, made her snatch her hand back as if he'd assaulted her.

Dominic flung open the doors.

He was quite right, the garden was certainly beautiful at this time of year. The magnolias were out – globes of white and pale pink drooping like wistful pearl tears. Banks of purple and white tulips edged the patio, the lawn was sprinkled with late crocuses and narcissus, and the forsythia on the side walls was a brilliant primary yellow, like a child's version of sunshine. In the distance, apple blossom swathed the trees of the small orchard. Christie remembered when she'd been here before in the spring, having lunch with Fran. The day they'd spied on Dominic by the pool. A year ago.

'It is beautiful. Really beautiful.' She leaned against the white wall. 'You must love it here. In the summer . . .'

He stepped in front of her, blocking the sun. 'There are different sorts of love,' he said.

She was aware of the magnetism of his dark eyes. 'Dominic, I . . .'

'I was infatuated with Amy when I first met her.' His arm stretched upwards, his hand resting on the wall above her, his body leaning slightly towards her.

It made Christie feel strangely vulnerable. And yet she was fascinated. She wanted to hear this, she realised.

'I couldn't believe that a woman like her could possibly be interested in a young bloke like me. What did I have to offer?'

Christie said nothing. Gramma had given her a good idea of what Dominic Redfern might have had to offer. And she herself could enlarge on the reasons. He was doing himself an injustice it seemed.

'She was exciting.' He smiled. 'Electrifying. Proud, crazy, stunning to look at. That was what Amy was all about – she stunned a man into doing irrational things. She made me illogical, she made me mad for her.'

'I can see the attraction.' Christie smiled wryly. Why was he telling her all this? Was it leading into some sort of personal confession about Fran – because if so, she didn't want to hear it.

'But she was playing a part.' His fist thumped against the wall. 'Doing a bloody good job of it as well. Once an actress, always an actress.'

'And?' Christie watched him.

'None of it was real, don't you see? It didn't take me long to realise that it would be disastrous between us. We had nothing at all in common.

Nothing.' He bent his head in despair. 'Once she'd got tired of my body, what would have been left?'

Christie looked down at the ground. The less she thought about Dominic Redfern's body the better.

'I even wished her dead.'

She glanced up at him in astonishment. Not love then, it hadn't been love – far from it.

He drew his fingers through his unruly dark hair. 'Are you shocked?'

Wordlessly, she shook her head. Shocked at his honesty perhaps. But she could understand that kind of desperation. Still, why was he telling her all this? And, 'Why the statuette in the hall?' she asked him. People didn't have memorials created for those they hated.

'She begged me to have it made.' He shook his head. 'Can you believe that? There were two things she asked me to do if she were to die, and that was one of them. She was the vainest woman I've ever met.'

'And the other thing?' Christie had the strangest feeling – a kind of premonition that she wouldn't want to hear this.

'She asked me to look after Fran,' he said.

Christie was silent. But surely even Dominic couldn't justify a love affair with Fran on the grounds that her mother had asked him to look after her? That was hardly the kind of looking after that Amy would have had in mind. It would have made her turn in her grave.

Christie paled as a thought occurred to her. Had Dominic done it on purpose? He said that he'd come to hate his wife. So was the enigmatic quality that intrigued Christie, merely a mask for revenge?

'Why did she kill herself?' she whispered.

Dominic's face was dark with an emotion she couldn't immediately catalogue. 'She was crying out to be heard. The little plan that I was an unknowing part of, hadn't worked. Her ex-husband still didn't want to know. Even when he saw her with me.' He sighed. 'But the cry misfired. I didn't find Amy when she expected me to. I was somewhere else, trying to work out how to get free of my marriage.' He stared over Christie's shoulder. 'And when I got back, it was too late, as they say. Too late for Amy, anyway.'

Christie stared at him, feeling herself sinking deeper and deeper into his life, the experiences that had made the man. She had thought she didn't want to be involved. And yet . . .

In the distance, from the pool beyond the hedge of conifers she distinctly heard voices, and at the same time the sky darkened and the first huge drops of rain fell from the grey, pregnant sky.

'Let's go inside.' Dominic grabbed her arm.

'I heard someone.' She resisted the pressure of his hand.

'Christie, please.' His face was shadowed concern. Goblets of rain were falling on to his dark hair, resting on the thick curls.

'Is Fran here?' She shook him off. 'Is that it?'

He didn't reply.

'Why are you trying to stop me seeing her?' Her eyes blazed. The rain was pelting now, drenching them, sticking her hair to her forehead.

'I'm not.' They stared at each other like protagonists in battle. He blinked the rain out of his eyelashes. 'I didn't know she was here.'

Should she believe him? Christie hesitated.

'Come inside,' he urged. 'I'll go and get her.'

'No!'

She waited. The voices were getting closer to the hedge. Any moment they would be visible – Fran and whoever she was with. Who was she with? Christie frowned. Was it a woman? She had only heard Fran's voice and Fran's laughter, but it sounded like lovers' laughter. Lovers' laughter? She turned to Dominic. He was her lover, wasn't he? 'But I thought . . . ?'

'I'm begging you, Christie.' His voice was more urgent than ever. 'Come inside. You'll get soaked out here.'

'I don't care.' She glared at him through the rain that was dripping down her face, clinging to her hair, stinging her eyes. Suddenly she had to know. 'I thought you and Fran . . . ?' She hesitated to say it, now, it seemed next to impossible to say it.

He frowned. 'What?'

She saw understanding edge bit by bit into the confusion on his face, and she knew. She had been mistaken. Fran and Dominic were not lovers. Had never been lovers.

He grabbed her by the shoulders. 'What the hell gave you that idea?' He was angry, almost the first time the self-assurance had slipped. She remembered his embarrassment earlier. But why?

Their eyes met, his grip loosened, and in one movement, they turned together to stare at the hedge of conifers that separated the pool from the rest of the garden and the house. They turned and watched two naked figures scampering round the hedge like demons. Each had a towel slung around their neck, each was screaming with delight as the rain drenched their naked glistening bodies. One was Fran, her red hair clinging in tendrils that framed her narrow face. And the other was Robin.

'Robin . . .' Christie stared. She felt her knees buckle, and then Dominic's arms were around her, or perhaps they had always been round her, half lifting her through the french windows and into the cream and burgundy leather luxury of the sitting-room.

'I didn't want you to find out like that,' he was muttering.

'You knew. Why didn't you tell me?' Christie felt numb. She didn't know what else she felt – not yet. She struggled to sit up. It explained everything – certainly explained Fran's coldness on the phone, and why she hadn't replied to Christie's letters. She had been too busy stealing her husband.

'I didn't know how to tell you.' He was smoothing her wet hair from her face and she found she couldn't object to this touch as she had objected to his touch just now. In her present state it was strangely comforting. 'I wasn't even sure if you already knew, when you came here on the warpath.'

She hadn't been on that kind of jealous wife warpath. It had been a very different mission. 'She wouldn't see me.' Christie was beginning to feel self-righteous anger, not – thankfully not – the crushing sadness of loss. 'I wanted to know why.'

And now she knew. Christie staggered to her feet and watched the two naked figures running across the lawn hand in hand. Unbelievable. A giggle, hysteria perhaps, rose in her throat. Wouldn't they be surprised when they saw who had come visiting?

'You thought that Fran and I . . . ?' He moved behind her. 'How could you think that?' She could sense his presence, feel his breath. 'With Amy's daughter, for God's sake?'

'I don't know. I . . .' Christie's voice tailed off. She was watching them, and it seemed quite crazy that she could just watch her husband and her best friend in this detached manner, as if they were people she hardly knew.

Fran and Robin half fell through the french windows.

'What the hell?' Fran wrapped her soaking towel around her body. For a moment, she blinked in astonishment at the sight of Christie, and then her expression changed to a cool, shocking arrogance. She turned to Dominic, her slender body arching like a cat's. 'What are *you* doing here?' she spat. 'Did you bring her?'

Robin gazed at Christie, saying nothing. She had no idea what he was thinking, no idea at all.

'It's my house,' Dominic replied in his even tones. 'And I believe Christie came to visit *you*.'

'You don't live here.' The green eyes were alive with hatred. It was scary. Christie wondered how she had got it so wrong. Fran clearly loathed her step-father. And as for their friendship – it had, apparently been little more than a farce.

'It's still my house.' He stared back at Fran, apparently unconcerned. 'And I'm selling it.'

'You can't do that.' Her voice rose into a squeal.

He stepped forwards. 'Watch me.'

Christie's disbelieving gaze swept to Robin. He'd always said that he hated Fran. He'd always said she was a slut . . .

Robin seemed unconcerned at their discovery. As he saw Christie staring at him, he let the towel drop slightly from his waist. She saw his half-smile and the unmistakable rise of his erection.

'For God's sake . . .' She rushed from the room, from the house.

Dominic was right behind her as she struggled with the door of the pick-up. 'You can't drive in this state.'

'I'm not in a state, and I've got to get out of here,' she muttered.

'Let me.'

'No.' Calming herself for a moment, she paused, touched his arm. 'I'm all right.'

His eyes remained both questioning and concerned.

'I don't mind,' she insisted. What she and Robin had was dead if not buried. Why should she mind? 'I'm more upset about Fran. I trusted her.' It was true, she realised with a slight shock. She thought of the evening before Christmas when Fran had stood defiant in front of Amy's portrait. Would things have worked out differently if Fran had confided in her then? If their friendship had reached the deeper levels of honesty that had remained elusive for them?

'Friendship . . .' he murmured. 'She's her mother's daughter. There's a good side to Fran. But the bad side's a force to be reckoned with.'

'So is Robin.' Christie heard her own voice shaking. 'Robin's out for destruction and I pity anyone who gets in his way.' Her eyes narrowed. 'Even Fran.'

She jumped into the truck, her glance straying to the front door of the house as Fran emerged. She had pulled on a robe which she clutched around her, and her red hair was hanging in tails around her shoulders. She looked, once more, terribly young.

'Why did you do it, Fran?' Christie watched as she came closer.

'I never meant to.' Fran's eyes were huge, she seemed to have shed the arrogance that had sat so easily on her five minutes ago. 'He still loves you, you know, Christie.'

'It's over.' She knew that as surely as she knew anything. Whatever Robin said or did, they were finished.

'He thought he was using me.' Fran stared at her. 'To get at you.'

'And why did you let him?' Christie wanted to understand. Did Fran crave affection so desperately? Was she – underneath the bravado – the same lonely child Christie had first come across in the church at Wareham?

Fran shrugged. Her gaze switched to Dominic. 'Maybe I was using him in the same way.'

Christie frowned, suddenly irritated with her. 'What happened to the counselling? What happened to the Refuge? The studying? The psychology?'

'I thought I might do some travelling instead,' she said vaguely. 'Around Europe. Then I can decide.'

'Oh yeah ... ' Christie put the key in the ignition. 'Sure.' She wanted to get out of here. She was beginning to realise that Fran had never intended to carry any of her ideas through to fruition. She had been a spoilt kid all the time; that was all she ever would be.

'I wanted to do those things, Christie.' She stood next to Dominic, her hands on the open window of the truck as if she could force Christie to stay and listen. 'I really did.'

'Maybe you did.' Christie wasn't sure what to believe. Gramma and Dominic had both tried to warn her about Fran. Perhaps they were right and she'd been deluding herself. Or perhaps she herself had only wanted to be needed. 'I'll phone you some time,' she heard herself saying.

Fran turned and walked back into the house. For a moment, Christie thought she was crying, and then she saw her brace her shoulders, sweep inside with the casual arrogance that came so easily. As Dominic had said, she was her mother's daughter all right.

'And what will you do now?' His hand was insistent, resting on the truck door.

She closed her eyes. 'I want to walk. I want to think.'

'Alone?'

A hundred thoughts screamed through Christie's brain. Normally she would have said: yes, alone – no hesitation. How could you hope to think if you weren't alone? People made you talk.

She looked at Dominic. He was very different from the average person. She might even want to talk to him. She indicated the passenger seat. If Dominic thought she was going to slide over and let him drive her truck he was mistaken. 'Shell Beach okay with you?' she asked, a half smile on her lips. All this and she could still smile. She realised she was even pleased. That it wasn't Dominic and Fran . . .

The sun blazed out from behind the clouds.

In no time he was sitting beside her. 'Sounds perfectly okay to me.'

Isobel had been doing some errands in Corfe, and was just climbing back into her Landrover, when she saw the familiar sight of Christie's white pick-up truck, heading towards Studland village. She waved, but they didn't see her. They were engrossed in conversation. Christie and Dominic Redfern.

Isobel stared after them. Dominic had told her that something was going on between his step-daughter and Christie's husband. He had explained that he'd tried to stop it but they'd only laughed at him, dared him to tell Christie. Had it been more than fatherly concern? Dominic had asked Isobel's advice. Should they interfere? Who could say for sure?

It was finished for Christie and Robin – she'd known that for a long time. And as for the rest – well, maybe she'd see it, and maybe she wouldn't. Her time wasn't over yet, but it wouldn't be long, she felt it in her bones. Something inside her had died when Vincent passed on. Isobel had expected only relief. But she was lonely. And she wanted to make her peace.

They left the pick-up in the same car park by Shell Beach where Christie and Marc had parked after leaving the chain ferry on the evening she first took him to see her mother. The evening she'd discovered that Marc Dupont was her father. Christie shook her head at the memory. She hadn't been here since, although this had always been one of her favourite haunts – at least outside the tourist season. And now? Could it possibly be true that her father was coming over to England? That he and her mother might get together again after all these years?

They trudged in silence towards the wooden bridge that led to the dunes, the hot afternoon sun burning her shoulders as they crossed the boardwalk edged with grass head-height on either side. There were a few people around – two children unsuccessfully trying to fly a kite, a couple sitting on the coarse clumps of grass in front of the long shelf of sand that stretched into the distance.

Of one mind, Dominic and Christie avoided the openness of the sea and sand, heading instead for the maze of narrow and haphazard pathways that wound between the wilderness of the dunes. They walked in single file, their breath laboured in the still air. The sand was thick and grainy, heavy to plough through, and soon they stopped to take off their shoes, letting the sand shift between their bare toes.

At last they came to a halt. They had walked a long way up the beach, and here the dunes and sands seemed deserted. Christie flopped on to a flat rock sprinkled with sand and edged by gorse. A plateau for the weary traveller. She was emotionally exhausted, she realised. But she felt good. It had taken her a long time to accept that her marriage wouldn't be for ever. And now she was liberated, she could begin to be herself again.

She stared at Dominic. He had slung his sweatshirt around his shoulders. Underneath he wore a black T-shirt. His bare arms were brown and brushed with dark hair. Abruptly, she looked away, her thoughts returning to Robin and Fran.

'I wouldn't worry too much about Fran.' He spoke softly.

'But *you* do, don't you?' Christie turned over on her stomach. 'You promised Amy you'd look out for her.'

His expression changed. 'I don't owe Amy a thing. She taught me about being made a fool of, but that's about all she ever did apart from make me feel guilty. As for her daughter . . . I've done all I can. She's a big girl now.' He watched Christie thoughtfully. 'And you were right in a way. Fran wanted something that . . .' he hesitated. 'That I couldn't give her.'

'Because she's too like her mother?' Christie hazarded a guess.

'For all sorts of reasons.' His voice was firm. 'Not least that however bright and beautiful she might be, she's my step-daughter. I could never think of her that way.'

Christie was relieved to hear it. 'When I saw you on New Year's Eve . . .' Her voice tailed off.

'She took me by surprise that night,' he admitted. 'I gave her a good talking to, but I ended up having to fight her off when we got home.'

Christie laughed at the picture he painted, surprised at herself for being able to.

'It wasn't funny at the time.' But Dominic grinned, as he paced over to a nearby dune, threw down his sweatshirt and shoes and sat cross-legged, facing the distant sea.

She followed the direction of his gaze. The tide was coming in, tiny waves curling on to the shimmering sand, smooth as skin, drawing the tiny shells that covered this beach and gave it its name, back into the water.

'She didn't take it too well?' Christie asked.

'She did a passable imitation of a woman scorned, told me that I would live to regret it, and flounced off to her room.' He stretched out long legs. 'That's when I decided enough was enough. I moved out most of my stuff and gave up trying to tell her what to do.'

Christie leaned up on one elbow, squinting into the sun towards him. 'Why did she bother with all those schemes – the Refuge for starters?'

'The Refuge!' He snorted. 'Truth is, she overheard a row between Amy and me.' Dominic sounded reluctant to go on. 'We had dreadful rows, real melodramatic stuff. I think it was in Amy's blood – she didn't feel she'd had a good day until she'd shouted at a few people and shed a bucket of tears.'

Christie smiled.

'And in the middle of the row she slapped me hard around the face.' He touched his cheek ruefully. 'That was one of her favourite moves, knowing I wouldn't hit her back. Because if I did, she could start on the victimised woman routine.'

'And?' Christie watched him carefully.

'I said, how would you like it if I slapped you back, or something like that, I don't know, I can't even remember.' His expression grew solemn. 'I didn't hit her. But she went wild. She started ranting on about battered women and having to go to a refuge and all sorts of stuff like that. Crazy woman.' He shook his head confusedly. 'She flung open the door and there was Fran listening outside. Gathering ammunition apparently.'

'So Fran only said it to wind you up?' Christie was astonished.

'It looks that way.' Dominic's mouth tightened imperceptibly.

'Maybe she just wanted to be needed.' Fran couldn't be all bad. Christie wouldn't have that. She couldn't have imagined the bond between them. Perhaps Fran was simply a confused woman grown from a confused teenager who'd had to compete with her mother for every iota of attention when Amy was alive, and was now unable to stop.

Christie laid back and closed her eyes. Whatever it was, it wasn't her problem. Robin wasn't her problem and neither was Fran. The sun was beating hard on her eyelids. She felt free. All she could see were dazzling strobes forming images in the darkness. It was hard to believe this was only April, hard to believe that an hour ago rain had been tipping from the sky, hard to believe that she and Robin . . . Well, it was over. And she knew that she was glad.

She heard the sounds of Dominic moving closer. And the faint murmuring of a breeze picking up from the sea.

'When I'm here on this beach,' he said softly. 'That's when I'm really aware of how separate Purbeck is from the rest of Dorset. It seems more of an island here than it does anywhere else.'

'It's a special place,' she agreed sleepily. She had long known that the whole of Purbeck was special – to her at least – and her visit to America had only confirmed her sense of belonging here.

'Purbeck was completely cut off once upon a time,' he told her. 'It was a real island. It was wild and remote. Secretive.'

Like Dominic, she thought. He belonged here too.

'The banks of the River Frome were like a boggy kind of heathland,' he went on. 'And Purbeck was a royal forest in Norman times.'

'Really?' She wondered how he knew all this.

'And no-one from the island could marry an outsider without a royal decree.' His voice was slow and hypnotic. It was as if he were reading her a bedtime story. A fairy story, with dragons and witches, princesses and kings. She could feel herself slowly relaxing, body and mind, under the caressing warmth of the sun and in the tenderness of his voice.

'No wonder Purbeck was a separate community.' He paused. 'But it's different now. There are roads. And outsiders.'

Outsiders. Christie was aware of her thoughts drifting. It was deserted here and so so warm. She could be naked and she'd still be warm. They were surrounded by sand dunes and they weren't overlooked. It was their own small world in a world. They could make love here and no-one would see . . .

Her eyes snapped open in shock at the direction her thoughts had taken. 'I think we should be getting back.' She jumped to her feet.

With only a slight glance of regret, Dominic picked up his stuff and they walked down to the sea, letting the cool waves trickle over their feet.

'I saw you once,' she blurted. 'By the pool at the house. I felt dreadful, it seemed like spying.'

'I know.' He was looking out towards the Needles on the Isle of Wight.

'You know?' She stopped walking. How could he have known?

He turned to face her. 'I sensed something. A presence. Maybe I heard voices. I knew it was you and Fran.'

'And you didn't mind?' She turned to stare at their footsteps in the sand, some already swept away by the sea. Gone so soon. It seemed very sad for them to be gone so soon. She continued walking. Dominic was a very unusual man.

He shook his head. 'It didn't affect the form.'

She was baffled. 'The form?'

'I was doing T'ai Chi.' He smiled.

'What does it teach you?' Christie felt strangely shy.

Dominic's gaze drifted towards the ridge of the Purbeck Hills. 'It builds inner strength without force. It's about balance – you know, yang and yin, dual divisions like hard with soft. It's all about harmony rather than opposition.'

Harmony. That's what she needed in her life after all this conflict. She didn't want to fight any more. 'When did you start learning?' she asked him.

'After Amy died.' He shot her a look that she couldn't interpret. 'I needed to find a way of relaxing, a way of accepting, easing my guilt.'

'And did it work?' Christie thought she already knew the answer to that one.

He nodded. 'You have to learn not to deal with troublesome situations when they are at their worst. You must wait for strength.'

Christie thought of Robin. The philosophy Dominic was describing appealed to her so strongly. 'Will you teach me some time?'

His eyes clouded over. 'Maybe.'

Christie looked back at the spine of Ballard Down in the distance. Was that all he was offering? A maybe?

When they reached the end of the beach, she paused instead of following him back over the bridge, looking out to sea, silently considering what had happened to her, assessing her position. Don't try and fight during the worst moments, he had said. Wait for strength.

Her marriage was over, and she wanted it finished, sorted. She didn't want to bicker over possessions: Robin could have the lot as far as she was concerned. Christie folded her arms tightly around her body, shielding herself from the sudden breeze that was blowing up, whipping her hair from her face, gusting the fine sand on to her bare legs.

She would not be trapped like the female generations before her. Gramma had been pulled into a relationship by passion, dominated first by violence and then by guilt and pity. And her mother had been trapped by the liberation of the sixties that pretended to make women free but sometimes offered only a different sort of imprisonment.

Christie looked out to sea. It was getting choppy out there. And what of the woman of the nineties? A woman with her own business, her own life? She had choices, didn't she? And she saw that Gramma had been right. She was lucky to have choices. it might make the decisions harder; it might present much more of a challenge. But choice offered freedom. It was the only way forward.

She watched Dominic trudging back over the bridge, his tall dark figure cut into the background of the Purbeck where she belonged. The Purbeck she loved. At this moment, she wasn't sure what her choices would be. But the important thing was that she had them. She had created them for herself, forged her own independence.

Maybe . . . An echo of his voice returned as she followed his progress into the distance. Christie smiled. *Maybe* was enough. Maybe was absolutely right. She had herself. She was herself. She didn't have to fight any more. And her strength was beginning to flow.

Resolutely she turned to follow him, striding across the sand, her bare feet hardly sinking into the thick dry grains. She didn't have to fight any more. She didn't even have to pretend. But the living? The living had only just begun.